ISBN -13 978-1719253864

PERFECT DAY

BY

PJ SHANN

1

'I'm thinking about it a lot just lately, and I don't know why. It isn't as if I dream about it anymore, and I don't get those flashbacks when I'm walking down the street, either. No sweating, or heavy breathing. No serious panic-attacks, they're pretty much gone. But still…something keeps taking my mind back there, and the memory has never been as clear as it is now. I don't know, maybe I'm just embellishing it myself, with my imagination. The details seem richer than they were. Sharper. And the textures are real. They have depth, if you know what I mean?'

A small grunt of encouragement from the man at the other side of the room, a minute nod of the head, and she goes on.

'Okay, so this is early January - just five days into the New Year - and I'm on the pedestrian crossing. It's cold enough for me to see my breath in front of my face, but I'm really warm because I'm wearing Olivia's thick wool coat, the brown one, the one with the hat. No, actually it's my coat, Olivia only borrowed it. I'd just been to get it back... I think. That's one of the things that still won't come clear. I know it's just a small, insignificant detail, but it's just so damn stubborn... Anyway, I'm crossing the road quickly, almost jogging, and for some reason I'm crying really badly — that's something else I don't

understand yet — and then I hear it, the engine, racing like mad. I stop moving, and I turn, and I see it. There it is...'

After a long pause, another prompting grunt.

'Yeah, so... I see it. A big black 4x4 jeepy thing, huge wheels, black tinted windscreen, the whole middle-class school-run tank-job, and it's coming straight at me. I know immediately that it's going to hit me, and I mean immediately. I just know it. It isn't going to stop at the crossing, and it won't do me any good to run because the jeep's going too fast. The damn thing wants to kill me, that's the thing. It wants to, and it's just using the fact that I'm crossing the road as an excuse. This is what I feel at the time, you understand, what I think I know. It's actually accelerating as it comes toward me, and it's getting bigger and bigger, like something out of a stupid cartoon...'

Another long pause, another grunt.

'Then I realise there's someone else on the crossing, too, following me. This really beautiful black woman I'm noticing for the first time, very heavily pregnant, and she's looking down at her coat stretched over her lovely full belly, or down at the road, or maybe at the way the toes of her shoes flick out from underneath the curve of her stomach as she walks. All I really know is that she doesn't seem to see or hear the jeep at all, and I can't warn her. I try to, but I just can't. My throat's closed up so tight and I can hardly breathe, let alone...

'When I look back at the jeep again, it's almost on top of me, and it's enormous, it's gigantic. We're looking at each other, the car and me, like it's alive,

2

and we both know that I'm going to die. But then something amazing happens. It seems to change its mind. Suddenly it doesn't want to kill me anymore, and it tries to stop. The tyres screech, there's smoke coming off them, like they're on fire almost. The whole front of the jeep goes down all the way to the road-surface and there are sparks flying from somewhere. But it's too late now for the brakes to stop it. It's still going to hit me, and when it does…

'All of this is like slow motion now, like a film. At this stage I can almost hear the jeep thinking, and it's thinking that it's got a choice to make here; it can just come on and kill me, or it can try to turn away. To its right there's a lamppost, a parked car, things like that. To its left is a pregnant woman. That's its choice. Me, the other woman, or the things that don't matter, the things that won't die if it hits them. Then I think I can hear its thoughts again, and I know that it's going to turn away from the people and toward the lamppost and the parked car. Of course it is. That's what I would do. That's what anyone would do, isn't it? But the jeep isn't human, you see, and it doesn't think the same as us…

'At the last moment, at absolutely the very last moment, it swerves to my left and I start to scream at it to stop. It pays no attention, just plows on through, accelerating again. If nobody else had been on the crossing it would have missed me by four or five feet at least, and I wouldn't have been hurt at all. But someone was there, of course. And she was so pregnant. She was so hugely, obviously pregnant…

'I saw it hit her. I saw her… just before she hit me…'

3

2

As she sat in the familiar worn leather armchair, Joan Crosby was quite aware that her lips were flapping with the even regularity of a metronome, and equally aware that apparently coherent phrases were passing through them on a zephyr of minty breath, partially deodorising her part of the consulting room. But Joan wasn't paying too much attention to herself this afternoon, and didn't really hear the specifics of her own monologue. She was quite sure, though, that it wasn't anything she hadn't said before.

Blah blah *this*, blah blah *that*.

In fact, it was far more likely that she'd told the same story a dozen times over and her doctor was as bored as Joan was herself, now that she had become desensitised to the genuine horror of her recent history. Those polite and vaguely encouraging grunts of his were probably discreet snores. Oddly enough, she found that this potentially unsettling idea made her feel a little like chuckling.

Joan was pleasantly adrift from herself. For the first time in what seemed a very long while, there were other things to consider besides the terrible events that had landed her here. Other things she found more interesting than her own over-familiar problems.

For instance… she had suddenly decided that the décor of the consulting room, which she had visited once every week for the last four months, was truly gruesome. It was as though she were seeing it for the first time - or for the first time with clear eyes, at any rate. The walls had been painted a uniform pale green, an Art Deco shade called *Eau De Nil*, which she recognised from her former life as an interior designer. It was a calm colour, a restful colour it was presumably hoped would suggest peace and tranquillity to the mentally vulnerable. But today the colour's psychologically well-intentioned effect, if any, was indeed *nil*, and instead Joan speculated that this was what it must be like to be imprisoned within a vast block of mouldering cheese.

A deep, long-dormant, long-denied part of her longed to repaint the walls in a more empathetic shade, to restore the ceiling mouldings to their original elegance, to breathe warmth into the room and help bring it back to life.

For instance… the tropical fish in the aquarium that had appeared after her second or third visit here seemed to have undergone a quite dramatic reduction in their numbers. This may or may not have had something to do with the brooding presence of a squat black fish with long fleshy whiskers she could see lurking ominously at the bottom of the tank. This microcosmic predator now seemed a little too large for its environment, and she thought that the remaining fish - guppies and yellow- and black-striped angelfish, mostly - looked as though they were living on their nerves.

Running vertically down the centre of the aquarium's front-plate was a long hairline crack for which Joan was responsible. It had been casually repaired with a strip of all-weather greenhouse tape.

For instance… she had finally noticed, quite obviously some months after it had begun, that her doctor, the great and good Robert Stratton, Dr Bob, appeared to be in the midst of a fairly obvious mid-life crisis. He sat opposite but not facing her in a matching armchair, his chin almost on his chest. The first three fingertips of his left hand were lightly pressed to his broad forehead, and his eyes were closed. It was the same carefully considered listening pose he had adopted on her very first appointment, and maintained thereafter, but almost everything else about him had changed.

At some point over the months, his mop of salt and pepper hair had been mown down and gelled to something approaching trendy neatness, most likely at the same time the unkempt matching beard had been made to disappear. Mild, gentle brown eyes, previously corralled by severe horn-rims, had been liberated by either contact lenses or laser surgery. The musty tweed suits that had been far too old for him had been replaced by designer label casuals which, like his hairstyle, Joan considered to be just a little too young for him. Most tellingly, one of the fingers pressed to his forehead had once sported a slim gold wedding band and now did not. Even the tan line around the finger was no longer visible.

When exactly had all this happened? Where had Joan been while it happened?

But with hindsight, these questions were easy enough to answer. She'd been lost, swallowed up by the Dragon - by Life itself - and so far she had spent a whole year trying to crawl back out of its gullet.

And she was getting there, she really believed she was; for just as she was beginning to notice the world around her once more, Joan was also beginning to remember aspects of the past that were not just memories of terror and revulsion, pain and guilt. From somewhere deep within herself she was rediscovering memories of what life had been for her before the Dragon had taken her - and if those memories were true memories, then her life had been, in part, wonderfully, uneventfully normal. Average, boring, in the best possible way.

She sometimes saw these random moments as fiery bright still images, static but full of light and life, and they came at her out of the blue, often at times when she least expected them. But whenever they came, however they came, they warmed her whole being, body and soul.

Here are some of them:

She is sitting cross-legged on the floorboards in a stripped, unoccupied house that is like a three-dimensional canvas, a blank canvas, just waiting for her to begin work; the floor around her is covered by the colour swatches and fabric patterns she has sourced for her unknown, invisible clients, and her face is radiant with gleeful, concentrated delight. It is the joy of beginning.

She is out shopping with her friends, having a frivolous, girly afternoon in town; they are trying on clothes that they are never going to buy, shoes they can't even walk in, make-up they wouldn't be seen dead in, and laughing at things men would never understand if they lived to be a million years old.

She is getting ready to go out somewhere, to dinner in a favourite restaurant, perhaps, and is wrapped in a towel sitting at her dressing table applying her make-up; her husband stands behind her gazing into the mirror, supposedly tying his tie, but in reality he is just watching her, admiring her, and has been unable to resist laying a warm, possessive hand on her heated, naked shoulder.

She is standing at the kitchen sink, washing the Waterford crystal glasses she doesn't trust to the dishwasher. She is forking canned tuna fish onto a saucer for a stray cat. She is lying on a foreign beach, half-asleep, having sun-cream stroked over her back by her husband's large hands while the sun dries out the soles of her feet. She is watching a young mother hoist a crying toddler back to his feet after a fall, and wishing that the arms about to enfold the child, the voice about to sooth his tears, could have been hers.

Moments, that was all, nothing special. Just brief moments.

But now they had begun to feel like things that might actually have happened to her, and not just images culled from a movie of her former life, with an actress playing Joan's part, and playing it badly. Dr Stratton had told her that these pictures would soon begin to move, to shimmer into a facsimile of life, and then grow into self-contained scenes, which would then splice together to become a complete film. He had assured her that she, and not some look-alike actress, would be the star of this movie.

It was quite impossible for her to doubt Dr Bob. Joan knew this for a fact - she had tried.

3

The final moment of temporary madness that had sent Joan reeling into the gentle clutches of her psychiatrist's armchair had been classified as an incidence of road rage. At least, that was what her husband had called it, even though technically she had been a pedestrian at the time. ROAD RAGE! Joan remembered that the words had flown out of Stephen's mouth already fully capitalised, as though she had been transformed into a living tabloid headline. When she later saw the actual headline over a report of the incident in the local newspaper, she had felt an immediate sense of déjà vu that was suffocatingly complete.

According to Stephen, her rage and her inability to control it was just one more inadequacy to add to an already daunting collection. It was, as he'd put it, in tones of shock and embarrassment worthy of their own banner headline, The Straw That Broke The Camel's Back. It was almost funny, in retrospect. Back in January, immediately after the hit-and-run that had put Joan into hospital - an event which Stephen persisted in calling her "little accident" - she had been his Princess, his Queen, and even, in their most mawkish moments, his Brave Little Girl. But by Easter she was a Disgrace, and a Public Spectacle. She had Taken Leave Of Her Senses, and was Out Of Her Mind. It was a long way to travel in three short months.

This is how the final stage of the journey was achieved.

It was Easter Monday, the 16th, and Stephen had taken a rare day off from his office to stay home with Joan, but had contrived to spend the whole morning and most of the afternoon working in his study on the top floor of their Georgian townhouse. About three-fifteen, he'd slunk guiltily downstairs to find Joan sitting in the kitchen, staring at the blank wall over a cup of coffee that had gone cold to the touch. He'd suggested a slow stroll around the block just to get her out of the house for a while, an activity that had been enthusiastically recommended by their GP. Joan, who had been far away in a different place and time, had agreed in the lacklustre manner that had become the norm ever since her "little accident".

Ten minutes later they stepped out on to the street and began to wander beneath the boughs of trees that overhung the garden walls of million pound Hampstead properties much like their own. At the bedroom window of the house directly opposite theirs on the other side of the road, Joan noticed the pale ovoid of Gordon Unwill's face unapologetically tracking their slow progress. Unwill was a widower aged around seventy. He was a former stockbroker who acted like a retired Brigadier, and seemed to spend the majority of his time at his window minding other people's business. Stephen liked to call him M, after the spymaster in the older James Bond films, and used to claim to friends that Unwill was the head of the Neighbourhood Watch's Secret Service.

Once upon a time, Joan had found this conceit amusing, and had even used the joke once or twice herself.

Despite the unseasonably warm weather there had been a heavy rain shower that morning, and the roof and half the windscreen of a white MG parked at the curb had been plastered with early blossom, making the car look as though someone had thrown a bucket of blood over it. Joan averted her eyes until they had passed it by. She was still walking with crutches, but as Stephen had often remarked over the previous three or four weeks, she didn't really need them anymore; or if she did, the support they offered was no longer physical.

In this assumption, if in no other, her husband was perfectly correct. This was amply demonstrated a few moments later, when Joan carelessly dropped one of the steel crutches and used the other to smash the windscreen, batter the door-panels, and terrorise the occupants of a Suzuki four-wheel drive jeep.

It wasn't the driver's fault. The Suzuki had screeched to a stop beside them to avoid running over a stray dog that had run out into the road between two illegally parked cars. No damage had been done. The dog hadn't been hit, and in truth had never even come close to being hit. But the dog didn't matter. It was the sound of the screeching tyres that did it for Joan. It was the sight of the front of the vehicle dipping toward the road-surface as the car ground to a halt. It was the fraction-of-a-second visceral flashback to the MG that looked as though it were covered in blood.

That was what set her off.

Later, whenever she accidentally overheard him describing this singular moment to friends, Joan noticed that Stephen had turned her reaction, the whole situation, into a bizarre joke, as though that was the only way he could cope with it. Well, that way and by throwing her to the psychiatric wolves, of course. Perhaps unconsciously, he did the same thing when discussing her therapy, too, and their friends smiled, accepting that Joan's treatment was no more serious than a discreet little tweak to tighten a few loose screws. But she had noticed that their smiles never quite reached their eyes, which were full of sadness and a sympathy that she felt she did not deserve.

The woman driving the Suzuki had a young child in the back seat, and with her vehicle stalled in the middle of the road, she had turned about to check on its safety harness, which seemed to be secure. The child - Joan could not tell whether it was male or female - was unharmed and untroubled by the abrupt halt in their journey. He or She appeared to be more interested in catching one last sight of the stray mongrel, which was streaking off down the pavement at the other side of the road. His or Her chubby hand followed the dog's progress like a compass pointer following magnetic north. His or Her mother did not see or hear Joan drop one of her crutches like a piece of litter as she stepped out into the road to approach the vehicle.

The mother thought she heard a distant male voice calling a woman's name, but that was all the warning she got before the windscreen in front of her face exploded into a frosted caul.

The impact was so loud that the mother curled up into a ball on her seat and screamed, thinking that they had been hit by another car. Then she heard the man's voice again, this time not calling but shouting, and she dared to look up. Through the front passenger window, she found herself suddenly staring into the red-rimmed, weeping eyes of a madwoman, who was pointing a long piece of metal directly at her face. Like the kind of surrealistic detail encountered in a bad dream, the mother recognized the weapon as a steel crutch. She could even see the label featuring the medical supply company's logo.

The madwoman's face was working furiously, shifting between anger and fear, both expressions so extreme that they were almost disfiguring. The small child began to cry, to wail, really. The madwoman's mouth opened and shut like a mechanical device, but the mother couldn't make out any of her words. Then a man about a head taller than the madwoman, with a handsome middle-aged face and a pair of eyes that were simultaneously frantic and yet infinitely saner, came up from behind and tried to restrain her. The madwoman instantly shrugged his hands away from her shoulders and began to hammer at the passenger doors with her crutch.

Impacts that sounded like gunshots rocked the entire car. The child's cries escalated into outright screams, highly pitched, penetrating, like the sound of a dentist's drill, and the mother scrabbled in the glove compartment for her mobile phone.

Joan managed to strike the car a dozen more times before Stephen was finally able to restrain her, and once he had, she simply went into zombie-mode. She missed out on the Public Spectacle she had made of herself, the arrival of a blue-light flashing, siren-wailing police patrol car, and even the tawdry drama of her subsequent arrest. The next time she was really aware of anything at all, she found she was in an interview room, listening to her husband trying to explain her behaviour to two rather sceptical uniformed police officers.

She remembered watching Stephen's face out of the corner of her eye while he tried to excuse her actions by sketching out for the policemen a timetable of her recent history. He had not yet managed to turn her plight into a joke.

She remembered watching some indefinable quality in the policemen's faces changing as Stephen asked to speak to Phil Richardson. Detective Chief Inspector Phil Richardson, whom she had met on many different occasions over the years. All but two of the occasions had been social.

The first of these non-social meetings had also taken place in a police interview room, approximately six months earlier. Dr Stratton had traced it all back and was now convinced that this was where everything had begun to spin out of control for her.

4

It had been October 29th, a Tuesday, two days before Halloween, a week after the second anniversary of her mother's death, when Joan had finally worked up the courage to walk into the police station. Half an hour alone in the blandly anonymous interview room had eroded some of that courage, but she was still determined to express her concerns to the one person she knew who might be able to address them. She wasn't going to back out.

When Richardson eventually put his head around the door and looked at her, Joan held her breath. After a second or two his facial expression abruptly altered itself, swiftly moving from a rigidly composed mask she would have found difficult to recognize if she had passed it in the street to the pleasant-looking, amiable man she had met through her husband's circle of friends. She started to breathe again.

'Joan!' He came forward quickly to shake her hand and offer a small peck on her cheek. 'When they told me a Mrs Crosby wanted to see me, I didn't make the connection — some detective I am!' He laughed at his own lame joke and pulled out the chair at the other side of the grey steel table. 'Sorry I kept you waiting so long. How's Stephen?'

Joan said that Stephen was fine.

'Louise has been asking after you. We'll all have to get together soon, make a night of it.'

Joan said that she'd like that.

Still smiling, Richardson spread his palms wide. 'So, what can I do for you?'

Joan told him about the disappearance of Kath Meadows over two months earlier, in the middle of August.

Kath was Joan's best friend. Their husbands were old friends from way back, with Stephen occasionally acting in his professional capacity as a solicitor on behalf of Lee Meadow's import/export company, and they lived just a couple of streets from each other in their exclusive neighbourhood. Over the years the two women had discovered that they shared a lot of common interests, art and design chief among them, but what they mainly liked about each other were their differences, not their similarities.

Kath appreciated the fact that Joan had started own interior design company and, from a client base originally limited to friends and friends of friends, had steadily built it up into a real going concern. It seemed to tickle her that Joan, who had such a gentle, accepting nature, also had the kind of tenacious energy that she herself lacked, and had refused to sit back and let her husband's career become the dominating factor in her life.

In turn, Joan liked everything about Kath. Her charming indolence, her poor watercolours, her worse pottery, and her waspish sense of humour, which so often, to Joan's secret delight, was directed either at their husbands or at men just like them. Fat Cats, she sometimes called them, or Fat Rats, or The Suits. Joan especially liked the impression Kath gave of being as free as air. She had a Bohemian attitude of being able to go anywhere and do anything she pleased, which Joan would have loved to have shared, but simply didn't. It was an attitude you had to be born with, she believed, otherwise it was just pretence. That it was entirely natural in Kath's case gave her a certain moral licence, like that traditionally allowed to artists and poets. Even when Kath had confided to her that she occasionally took lovers, Joan had found herself pleasantly scandalized instead of genuinely shocked.

And they had been there for each other at the difficult times, of course. Kath had taken Joan in hand when her mother had been engaged in the long, messy process of dying, and had been her sister when Joan's real sister, Olivia, had proved incapable of offering the support Joan both needed and longed to give in return. Kath was the person to whom she was able to confide the depth of her misery, as well as the disgust and hatred she felt for the disease that was stealing her mother even as she nursed her, the disease that had stolen her father, too, years before.

For her part, Joan had helped Kath through the black depressions that sometimes engulfed her for days or even weeks at a time, guiding her back to the light with her optimism, good humour, and cheerful bossiness. She had also commiserated with Kath whenever her younger brother, Joe, known as the black toad of the family, had got himself into trouble which he expected her to dig him out of. This trouble was usually, though not exclusively, financial, and he had broken Kath's heart on a regular basis. It had been relatively easy for Joan to empathise, bearing in mind the on-going difficulties with her own sibling.

The real point to remember, she told the policeman, was that she and Kath were firm friends, best friends, tight, and it was a friendship that Joan had assumed would endure for as long as they lived. But now Kath had gone. She had disappeared off the face of the earth, and no one else really seemed concerned about it, least of all Kath's own husband.

Richardson listened patiently to her story, and then smiled again.

'I always liked Kath,' he said. 'She's great, and it's nice that you care for her. But I don't think you should worry yourself.'

Joan reminded him that at this stage, Kath had been gone for two and a half months. Ten whole weeks, without a phone call, a text, nothing...

'I know that,' Richardson said. 'In fact, Lee spoke to me about this situation some time ago. He also mentioned that you'd been asking him some pretty tough questions...' He took in Joan's expression of surprise and shrugged. 'I check every week or so to see if any of her credit, debit, or store cards have been used. Other than that, there's nothing much I can really do to try and find her. Not through official channels. She hasn't done anything illegal by leaving.'

He explained that as soon as Lee Meadows had discovered that his wife had taken two large suitcases full of clothes and personal possessions from their home, as well as a few thousand pounds from one of their shared savings accounts, he had contacted Richardson and asked him to keep an eye out for any sign of her. But this was not a police matter, it was merely a personal favour. Lee didn't want Kath tracked down and returned like some errant teenage runaway. He just wanted a rough idea of where she might be, and most of all to be sure that she was safe.

Joan expressed amazement at Richardson's calm. How did he know that Kath's husband had told him the truth? How did Richardson know that Lee hadn't... harmed her?

'Why would he? What reason could he have?' Richardson asked calmly, and then grinned. 'Unless you're thinking that Lee found out she was seeing someone else and went crazy with jealousy.'

Joan blushed. This kind of scenario was exactly what she had been thinking of. Well, it was one of them.

Richardson nodded, as though acknowledging Joan's blush, and she knew that he was also aware of the accusation her badgering of Lee had veiled. 'Now let me ask you a question, Joan,' he said. 'How long have you known the Meadows?'

Joan had known them for three and a half years.

'I've known them for nearly eight years,' he said. 'They're a great couple, great people, but they've always done their own thing. Always. As far as I'm aware, they've both had any number of affairs. And I should think, of the two, that Lee's probably had the lion's share.'

Joan was taken aback. Kath had never mentioned Lee's affairs to her, not once. She wondered if Kath had actually known about her husband's infidelities, or if the knowledge of them had been the trigger for her own. Kath *had* been quite seriously concerned about Lee shortly before she disappeared, but Joan had got the impression that it was nothing to do with their relationship. As far as she'd known it was to do with his business, some kind of risk he had taken or was considering taking, but Kath hadn't wanted to fully explain and Joan hadn't pushed. That wasn't the way their friendship worked.

Richardson explained that it was fairly common knowledge among their older friends that the Meadows had something of an open marriage. That's just the way they were, and it suited them both.

'As far as I can see,' Richardson went on, 'the only difference between the two of them is that Lee seems to prefer one-night stands, while Kath has always been one for little adventures. She likes to go out on a limb from time to time, pretend that she's changing her life, starting over. It's happened before, and Lee's asked me to keep an eye out for her before.'

Shocked now, Joan asked when this had been.

'The first time must have been about, oh, a year or so after we became friendly,' Richardson said. 'Kath took off to Dorset with a dustbin man, if you can believe that. They rented a cottage together for the summer, somewhere near Christchurch. About a year and a half later she ran off to Brighton with a taxi driver. She was away for three months that time, too.' He shrugged again, and smiled. 'What can I say, the lady obviously likes adventures by the sea.'

He looked at Joan carefully, to see how she was taking it.

'Once Kath even asked for my help directly,' he said. 'She'd taken a lover, some client of Lee's, who turned out to be a really nasty piece of work when she decided it was time to end it. He'd knocked her about a bit, made some very ugly threats, and scared her badly. I warned him off for her, unofficially, but she made me promise not to tell anyone, and especially not Lee, in case he reacted badly and it affected his business, which at the time was in a bit of a slump. So, you see, Kath did have secrets, even from those closest to her. What's happening now isn't at all unusual or unexpected.'

It was true that Kath had admitted she was having another affair perhaps a month before she disappeared, but she wouldn't tell Joan anything specific about her new lover. Just someone you don't know, was all she would ever say; just another walking builders' bum with rough but clever hands. Kath had seemed happy enough with the situation at the time, and Joan knew that Richardson could well be right. She could easily imagine Bohemian Kath and her bit of rough living in a spartan bathing hut somewhere on the Sussex coastline, waking up at dawn and running naked down the shingle beach to plunge into the freezing surf.

The trouble from Joan's point of view was that although this theory was eminently plausible, perfectly in character, she didn't believe that it was true. She told Richardson that this time it might be something different, because of Kath's brother.

Richardson sighed. Once again, it seemed that he was ahead of her. 'Black toad of the family, right?' he said.

Right.

A few weeks before she had disappeared, Kath had got into a terrible argument with Joe, an argument that had once again begun over money, but this time it had almost become a stand-up fight. A lifetime of repressed grievances had erupted through the thin crust of their adult relationship, shattering it completely. Just days after this argument, in what later seemed to Joan to be an eerie foreshadowing of her own future "little accident", Joe had been hit and killed by a speeding car in the early hours of the morning near his Ealing flat as he staggered home drunk from a pub lock-in. The car hadn't stopped and the driver had never been brought to justice.

Kath hadn't managed to speak to Joe since their argument, and she'd been destroyed by his death. Her misery and her sense of guilt were so immense that most of the time Joan had been unable to even reach her, much less offer consolation. The only thing that gave Kath the strength to go on, she'd admitted to Joan a few days after the funeral, was that she still had the comfort of her lover.

The man, previously just another trivial dalliance among the many, had revealed hidden depths. His support was becoming more and more important to her with every day that passed. She said that this was the first time she'd ever grown emotionally dependent on a man other than her husband.

This was not just an affair, she'd said. This was love.

And after Kath had disappeared, Joan had thought: what if at this moment in her life, this time of unaccustomed vulnerability, this blackest and deepest of her depressions, her lover had abandoned her? What then? How would she have coped? What might she have done?

Joan explained to Richardson she feared that her friend was not away on an adventure. She was afraid that Kath might have done something to herself, out of grief.

'Suicide, you mean?' Richardson shook his head instantly. 'Joan, no one packs suitcases for that kind of journey,' he said. 'Plus, she took about three grand along for company - and as we all know, you can't take it with you.'

Joan said she couldn't believe that Kath wouldn't have contacted her by now, if she were able to.

'I can understand you feeling that way,' Richardson said. 'It's a completely natural reaction. And despite the sporting way he takes it all, I'm sure that's just how Lee feels, too. Imagine how hard this is for him, the poor devil.'

He reached across the table to take Joan's hand, which she allowed.

'Look, granted there may be more to this latest adventure than the usual bit of fun, maybe because of her brother - more emotions, more intensity. But you shouldn't worry, Joan. One day she'll turn up, and it'll be as though she was never away. You'll see.'

He smiled again, forcing Joan to smile in return.

'Besides, bad things don't happen to people like Kath. I've seen them before. They're immune."

He let go of her hand suddenly and glanced at his watch.

'Joan, I hate to say it, but I have to go.' He stood up. 'So if there's nothing else I can do for you…?'

No, there wasn't. Not until two months later.

5

Even though he had followed in his father's footsteps and joined the family firm, Stephen hadn't become wealthy purely by an accident of birth. He was a very good, very ambitious solicitor, and he was absolutely determined that the Road Rage case would never go to court. Joan sometimes suspected that he was far more worried for his own reputation and image than he was for hers, but whatever his motivation may have been she remained grateful for his efforts. If he was successful it was one less hardship she would have to endure.

Using the full force of his eloquence, he pleaded her case to the police, among whom he had a good many friends and acquaintances besides DCI Richardson, and also with the poor woman whose car Joan had so comprehensively trashed. He personally paid to have the vehicle repaired, and negotiated with the woman's husband a one-off compensation payment for a sum that he would only refer to obliquely as 'substantial'. In this way he bargained for his wife's liberty and good name, but only on the plain understanding that she in turn would immediately agree to consult a psychiatrist, and would cooperate fully with any treatment he deemed necessary.

This condition was something that Joan was not at all grateful for, but which circumstances forced her to reluctantly accept. It happened quickly, too. Her preliminary appointment was set up for April the 23rd, exactly seven days after her attack on the four-wheel drive. It was St. George's Day; an auspicious day, she later thought in hindsight, upon which to begin reclaiming herself from the Dragon.

At that stage, Stephen was still concerned enough that he actually made the effort to accompany Joan to her consultation with the psychiatrist she imagined either he or his secretary had chosen at random out of the phone book. Dr Stratton's office was in Devonshire Place, a stone's throw from Harley Street, which ensured that both his rent and his hourly rates were high enough to command Stephen's automatic respect.

For all that Joan cared, Stratton could have been a quack working out of a grotty bedsit above a Kilburn chip-shop, and it turned out to be a good thing that Stephen was there. Ever since her attack on the car, Joan had grown ever more introverted and self-contained, and without her husband's presence the entire fifty-minute hour may have passed in complete silence.

In the calm green room with the worn leather chairs, Stephen explained the circumstances that had brought him and his wife to the psychiatrist's office, not stinting on either the extent of the damage Joan had caused or his own sense of shock. At the time, Joan had felt sure that he was exaggerating both.

Prompted by Dr Stratton's gentle questioning, Stephen went on to give an account of the hit and run that could so easily have killed her three months earlier. Once again, Joan began to feel that the details her husband was conjuring up were, if not outright works of fiction, then at least excessively lurid, just the sort of images that would be gathered and gloated over by uninvolved spectators to an atrocity. Gradually, she came to understand that this was how Stephen had actually learned the story, at second-hand, from other people. She had certainly never spoken to him of it, not in this or in any other way, and yet his conviction was absolute, as though he had been there and Joan had not.

He described how the car had instantly killed the pregnant woman on the pedestrian crossing, causing massive trauma, and how her shattered body had careened into Joan, swatting her to the ground. He described the injuries Joan had sustained, the broken ribs, the body-length bruises, the broken tibia, and the skull she fractured as her head bounced off the road surface. He described how Joan had regained consciousness just before the ambulance arrived, and how she had at first believed that all the blood and body tissue she was covered with was her own. That was before she had been told that most of it had come from the pregnant woman, and realised that the torn and twisted lump of meat on the road beside her, still steaming in the chill afternoon air, was all that was left of the woman and her unborn child.

Throughout all this, Joan sat in her chair staring down at her lap, and at her clasped hands, which were shaking. Although her face betrayed no emotion, at one point a large single tear escaped from her right eye and slipped unacknowledged down her cheek. She was fighting hard to maintain even this level of control, being aware that while Dr Stratton may have been listening intently to what her husband was saying, he never once took his eyes off her. She knew that he saw her shaking hands, and her single bitter tear. She knew he saw the beads of perspiration that gathered along the hairline on her forehead as Stephen described the car accelerating, then breaking, then beginning to turn...

Suddenly, Joan became infuriated, incensed. It was maddening to have Stephen reducing her experience to this shallow, black and white sketch that was totally incapable of communicating the terror she had felt. Which she still felt, even now. It was maddening to have been placed in this situation by her own husband. In the past she had always had a low opinion of the type of people willing to subject themselves to the attentions of a psychiatrist - recreational victims, she had always thought of these sad creatures - and this enforced visit had done absolutely nothing to change her mind.

She wanted to jump up out of the leather chair and storm from the room, leaving the two men behind. When she had gone they could talk about investments, or pension plans, or their golf handicaps, or anything they bloody well pleased. They could talk about her all they wanted, because she wouldn't be here. She didn't want to even think about this...this...event.

In her head, and only in her head, Joan was screaming. She was screaming into their faces, 'I

26

won't be a victim! I will *not* be a victim!' It would be some weeks before she could admit that she already was.

When Stephen had finished his account, Dr Stratton sat back in his chair and thought for a while. Once again, his eyes never left the mask of Joan's face. She could feel his mind like nimble fingers tracing the edges of her mask and gauging its thickness and strength. She was trembling violently, as though in the grip of a fever. Then Stratton asked Stephen to listen to a list of symptoms and to tell him if they sounded at all familiar. Joan knew that he was really talking to her.

Intrusive symptoms of the disorder he had in mind, the doctor said, included unwanted memories of the traumatic event itself, disturbing dreams that interfered with sleep, and flashbacks so vivid it was as though the person were actually experiencing the event all over again. Symptoms of avoidance included a rejection of intimacy with family and friends, and numbing, a condition where the affected person simply seems not to care about anything, has no sense of the future, and displays a general lack of interest and lack of feelings. Hyper-arousal symptoms included an emotional, sometimes violent reaction to anything related to the original traumatic event, irritability, jumpiness, and a constant fear that danger was close at hand.

Stephen nodded his head sagely throughout this long list, empathy and compassion evident in every line on his face, just as though the dismissive expression "little accident" had never tripped so glibly off his tongue. At the same time, Joan's attention had become riveted to the doctor. He was actually describing her now. This was Joan Crosby, this was the person she had become. This was her life.

It sounded, Dr Stratton said at length, very much like PTSD, or Post-Traumatic Stress Disorder.

Stephen frowned. Wasn't that the thing that soldiers got? Vietnam, the Falklands, Desert Storm, Iraq...

Stratton explained that while combat veterans were particularly prone to PTSD, many civilians suffered from it too. Rape victims, for example, and victims of violence or domestic abuse, and survivors of natural disasters like earthquakes, or fires, or - as in Joan's case - automobile accidents. Practically any event, in other words, which involved real or threatened physical harm.

In civilians, Dr Stratton said, there were usually factors other than the trauma itself that related to the development of symptoms. Home life could be a factor, for instance if there was a personal history of anxiety or stress. Another factor might be the presence of other mental disorders.

Stephen made a sound that caused Stratton to look at him directly for almost the first time since they had introduced themselves. Was there something?

Oh yes. Oh yes, there certainly was.

So then Joan had to sit and listen as Stephen told, in his typically monochromatic yet sensationalised fashion, the story of Kath Meadow's disappearance, and the stress and anguish it had caused his wife. He played heavily on the severe paranoia that followed, especially on that pivotal moment when Joan had gone from thinking that something terrible had happened to her friend Kath to imagining that something equally terrible was going to happen to her.

To Joan's acute embarrassment, he even went so far as to tell the doctor about her second non-social meeting with Detective Chief Inspector Phil Richardson, and it amazed her that hidden underneath the surface concern and the confessional tone she could still sense the irritation in her husband's voice.

6

Joan had chosen Café Bleu on Hampstead High Street as the venue for her meeting with Richardson, mainly because it was an establishment she and Kath had been in the habit of frequenting, and she felt badly in need of the familiar, the safe, the known. They had chosen the venue because not only was the café within walking distance of their homes, the staff were mostly attractive young men and the management didn't get upset if two female friends dawdled for an hour or more over a single cafetiere of French Roast. Perhaps this was because of the many times when that mid-morning coffee break had lengthened and escalated into lunch, with one or possibly two bottles of good wine. Ladies who lunched were good for business.

Back in those days, Kath and Joan had usually taken the window seat, if it was available, so that they could people-watch as they chatted - and also, or so Kath always claimed, so that any passing tradesmen would be able to check out her legs. Usually Kath had very obligingly shown off those legs by wearing a very short skirt. Let me be ogled by a white-van-man and I'm in Heaven, she would say. Given Kath's taste in men, they had both known that it was at best only half a joke, but it still made them laugh. It was also the past.

That afternoon, Joan had chosen the booth at the very back of the café, next to the door to the toilets, where she was blessed by the occasional gust of corrupted disinfectant whenever someone came in or out. It was December the 21st, four days before Christmas, and people seemed festive even in the face of the steady drizzle that had blanketed London for most of the last week. A fake snowdrift had been sprayed on the café's windows and the watercolours of Mediterranean scenes on the walls had been trimmed with tinsel.

Although the café was well heated, Joan had not removed her overcoat. Her fingers were tightly laced around her coffee cup, but her hands still trembled. She was pale and on edge as she waited for DCI Richardson to join her. He was already fifteen minutes late.

Joan had taken a risk in arranging this meeting. Stephen was at the end of his tether with her, and had absolutely forbidden her to speak to Richardson about her fears, which he claimed were completely imaginary, the paranoid fantasies of a selfish, self-obsessed woman. She jumped in her seat whenever the café's outer door opened, and her coffee had gone cold by the time Richardson eventually arrived.

The policeman spotted her over the top of the booth from ten feet away, and she watched his already apprehensive face fall with dismay. She realised that she must look even worse than she had thought. After a short internal debate that Joan found entirely visible and which set her stomach churning, Richardson joined her in the booth. He sat opposite her. This time he did not try to shake her hand or kiss her cheek.

He said her name, but she didn't give him the chance to say another word, jumping in with both feet.

'I'm being stalked,' she told him.

He glanced down at the table and blew out his cheeks. His disbelief was immediate.

'Somebody's watching me,' she persisted. 'Spying on me. Wherever I go, I'm followed. Whatever I do, I'm watched. I have to keep all the curtains shut during the day, and I'm scared to go outside anymore. Just coming here was a nightmare. I feel so exposed.'

Reluctantly, Richardson asked if she was being watched at that moment.

'Of course I am, I told you, it never stops!' Joan was alarmed to find herself close to tears.

Richardson stood up and looked around the café, attracting the attentions of a waiter who he immediately waved away, a subtle message to Joan that he wasn't planning to stay long. He stared out through the café's floor to ceiling windows, over the layer of fake snow, scanning the street beyond for several long moments before retaking his seat. He told Joan that he didn't see anyone watching them.

'No, he's too clever. He knows exactly what he's doing.' She faked a laugh. 'I'm turning into a nervous wreck, and Stephen thinks I'm going crazy.'

So the stalker was a he?

'Of course it's a he,' she said. 'Aren't they always?

Not always, no, Richardson replied shortly.

He asked her if she had seen the stalker clearly enough to give him a physical description, and then Joan had to admit that she had never actually seen the man at all. As she'd already said, he was too clever. But she didn't have to see the stalker to know he was there. She could feel his eyes on her, could feel his attention every moment of every day.

She even knew who he was.

Richardson, remembering Stephen's anecdotes about his nosy neighbour, tried to lighten the moment by asking if it might be M, spymaster of the Neighbourhood Watch. The look Joan gave him in response killed his already poor attempt at a smile.

Okay. So who was he?

'It's him,' Joan whispered. 'Him. The man who murdered Kath.'

This time when Richardson lowered his face to the table, he closed his eyes and audibly groaned.

'You don't believe me,' Joan said.

Richardson gently told her that it wasn't a question of believing or not believing. It was obvious to him that her fear, at least, was very real, but she had not one shred of evidence to back up her claim that anyone was stalking her. These people followed a well-defined pattern, he said. They sent letters, they made phone-calls. They wanted the object of their adoration to notice them, they wanted to be seen. Above all, they wanted contact.

He told her, reluctantly, that he was sorry but mere 'feelings' weren't enough to attract the attention of the police.

'Please, *please* listen to me,' Joan said. She didn't care now that she was crying, or that her shaking voice had risen to an almost hysterical pitch. 'He abducted Kath, and then he murdered her. Now he's going to do the same to me, and nobody cares. Nobody cares!'

Richardson gently shushed her as people glanced curiously over at their booth. He said that he had something to tell Joan. Something important that might help her.

Kath Meadows, he said, was alive.

For a moment Joan could not react. Then she grabbed Richardson's hands. 'She's been seen? Where? Where is she? Is she back?'

In her excitement, Joan had half-risen from her seat. Richardson held onto her hands and guided her back down, but then quickly let go, as if whatever mania she had might be catching.

No, Kath wasn't back, he told her, and she hadn't really been 'seen' as such. But her debit card had been used a total of eleven times over the last week or so to withdraw sums ranging from £10 to £50 from a number of ATMs in the Leicester area.

Joan stared at Richardson, and could hardly believe what she was hearing. It was so flimsy. 'That proves nothing,' she said. 'All it means is that he's using her cards. He took her life and now he's helping himself to her money!'

Richardson had checked with the bank, though, and had learned that the cash withdrawals amounted in total to only slightly more than three hundred pounds, which was not at all consistent with the type of fraud that Joan was suggesting. Kath's husband Lee, he explained, was convinced that this was the beginning of Kath's preparations to return home, a process that might take many weeks, but also a process he was happy to endure. After all, he'd already done the same thing at least twice before. To further facilitate Kath's return he had also deposited extra cash in her account, as a message to her that he was still there, still waiting, and all was well at home.

Joan was not convinced. She shook her head. 'No, that's not good enough. It's a smokescreen, why can't you see that?'

Richardson shook his head and told her that the truth was inescapable; Kath Meadows was alive and well and living in or near Leicester, still, for the time being, enjoying the fantasy of her latest adventure. The only real surprise, as far as the policeman was concerned, was that this time she hadn't chosen a coastal location for the love-nest.

'You don't understand!' she shouted. 'You don't even want to understand! If she was okay, she'd call me! She never went more than two days without calling, ever, whatever she was doing or whoever she was with! If she couldn't speak, she'd text!'

Richardson looked aghast at the scene she was making, and she tried to get herself back under control.

'Listen to me, Phil, please,' Joan said, desperately fighting to keep her voice low and the tears at bay. 'Kath had a phrase she used, that we both used like a code, if she was having one of her little flings. Just to let me know that she was okay, that she was happy and safe. When she called I'd ask her how she was, and she'd tell me that she was having a *perfect day* – that was the code. Having an absolutely Perfect Day, darling, don't worry about me. Just got out of bed bow-legged, Joanie, it's the start of another Perfect Day...'

Almost gasping for breath, Joan relapsed into a hopeless silence, quite aware that everyone in the cafe was staring at her. She didn't care. Richardson didn't believe her, and he wasn't going to help her. No one was going to help her. She was alone. Her mind began to close down. She could feel it happening. Her field of vision narrowed down to a small cone of light centred on the cup of cold coffee between her shaking hands. She was so far inside herself, so cloaked by fear, that when the café door opened a moment later and closed with a crash, she hardly jumped at all. Richardson glanced around the booth seat to see who had come in, and when he turned back she looked up and saw that he was almost smiling with relief.

She heard him say her husband's name.

Then Stephen was there, standing at the side of their table, his face flushed as though he had been running. He should have been at his office now. He never came home before seven at the earliest. He never used this café either, claiming that it was a women-only club, a hairdressing salon without the pansies. Why was he here?

Joan heard Stephen thank Richardson for calling him and apologising for his waste of time and his discomfort. She saw Richardson pat Stephen on the back as he walked away. Consolation - for Stephen, not for her. The policeman didn't look back.

Stephen sat down heavily opposite her, his dark hair glistening with raindrops, and she saw that the flush in his face had not been caused by exertion, but by anger. His eyes were hot little lights that burned into her own, until a film of tears blinded her.

In the blurred darkness, she heard him speak.

'How dare you embarrass me like this,' he said. 'How dare you...'

7

Following Dr Stratton's diagnosis, Joan's treatment began with the immediate prescription of a course of medication - specifically, a selective serotonin reuptake inhibitor. When Stratton announced this amazing title, Joan saw Stephen nodding as though he actually understood what the doctor was talking about, and his gall astounded her. A moment later, she almost laughed at her husband's somewhat crestfallen expression when Stratton went on to add that in this case the drug was in fact plain, ordinary Prozac.

She didn't know what Stephen had been expecting - some kind of heavy-duty experimental junk about the size of a horse-tablet which would knock her out for days at a time, probably - but it certainly wasn't Prozac, which it seemed doctors dished out like aspirins these days. Everyone knew someone who was on it. Joan had even heard that veterinarians were prescribing it for their four-legged patients.

But Dr Stratton went on to explain that Prozac had many advantages over the other drugs that had been used in the treatment of PTSD. In tests, it had performed better than any other medication in targeting all of the symptoms associated with the disorder rather than just one or two, and there were no real side-effects to worry about as long as the dosage was prescribed correctly.

What, me worry? Joan had thought to herself.

During her first real consultation the following Friday morning, at which Stephen was not present, Stratton encouraged her to talk about both her hit-and-run experience and the Road Rage episode, which she found herself unable to do without displaying all the warning signs of an imminent panic attack. Identifying these signs quickly and accurately, the doctor immediately stopped her and let her calm down again. Crying once more, this time openly, Joan admitted that she felt she had failed him, and failed herself, but Stratton very earnestly assured her that she had done nothing of the sort. It was a very good beginning, he said. They had to prepare the ground a little more, that was all.

Preparing the ground involved embarking on what Dr Stratton called 'a process of desensitisation'. Once again, Joan was almost forced into laughter by the commonplace reality that the high-blown technical jargon masked. On a small occasional table, Stratton had used long strips of masking tape to construct a gridiron of roads, and, instructing her to watch, he began to move toy cars along them. Like a child, he also made little *brum-brum* noises to accompany his actions.

For five or so minutes Joan watched with no apparent sense of discomfort - but with an acute sense of absurdity - while the man who had asked her to call him Dr Bob drove a Mercedes convertible, a police car, an ambulance, and a funky jeep over the table's surface, overtaking, passing, stopping at junctions, and carefully reversing around corners. But the very instant that he placed a small plastic figure on a section of tape zebra-striped with a felt tip to represent a crossing, Joan felt her anxiety level abruptly ramp up.

Suddenly hyperventilating and perspiring heavily, she watched the jeep negotiate the roads leading up to the crossing, circling, circling, and to her it was no longer a toy car, just as the tiny plastic figure on the crossing was no longer a toy person. It was real, all of it. All the memories and emotions she had tried to push so far away from her began to surge back, and although she was unaware of it at the time, she had begun to moan warnings to herself.

She could actually feel the impact closing in on her, a vibration beneath her feet, an agitation in the air, and the terror inside herself building, and building...

She blinked in complete disorientation when Dr Stratton abruptly removed the plastic figure and all the vehicles from the table, announcing that he thought that was enough for one day. Joan, her heart racing, felt as though a tragedy had only just been averted.

Over the following weeks, as the medication began to kick in, Joan found it easier to talk. Stratton would sometimes sit her in front of the aquarium he'd

38

installed in his office and ask her to speak about the details of her trauma while he quietly directed her attention from fish to fish. This was, he explained, a kind of therapy called eye-movement desensitisation and reprocessing, which was not at all well understood - and was of questionable value, he admitted, since the research findings had been inconclusive and no one was sure if it really worked.

It certainly hadn't work for Joan. During one memorable session, glancing from fish to fish while describing the emotions she had experienced as the jeep hurtled toward her, Joan's hyper-arousal symptoms got out of hand and she had exploded out of her chair in a violent rage. The heavy chair went over backwards, scraping a deep line down one of the sickly green walls, and she had grabbed something off a shelf - she still hadn't the slightest idea what it had been - and hurled it at the aquarium. The following week, as a precaution, they were back on toy cars. This was one of the rare backward steps.

As the weeks passed they gradually moved on to watching videos, which at first were amateur recordings of normal traffic movement Dr Stratton had made himself from the vantage point of his office window. Then they moved on to professionally produced sell-through DVDs with titles like 'Dancing Cars', where sports cars driven by stunt drivers performed choreographed routines like ice-skaters in a large arena for the entertainment of enthusiastic audiences. The cars pirouetted gracefully in tandem, or moved sideways in controlled skids and slides, passing each other by inches without ever touching. Progressing in easy stages, they watched Formula

One races, and rally cars hurtling around dirt tracks, and eventually American stock car racing and something called 'The Universe's Worst Drivers', which Dr Stratton had recorded at home off his Sky box.

After this, the excursions began, little outings designed to counteract the paralysing fear of traffic and roads that forced Joan to travel to and from her consultations in pre-booked taxis door to door - these journeys conducted at first with her eyes clamped tightly shut. To begin with these excursions were just short walks along the streets adjacent to Stratton's offices, but they slowly increased in length until one day she and Stratton made it all the way up Portland Place, across the cluttered and frantic nightmare of Marylebone Road, and into Regent's Park.

This was a real turning point in Joan's treatment. From then on their excursions grew longer and more varied.

They strolled through the West End together, usually arm-in-arm; Oxford Street, Soho, Piccadilly, and tourist traps like Trafalgar Square and Covent Garden. One day they took a bus ride to a car showroom that specialised in top of the range jeeps and 4x4s, and spent a half-hour admiring gleaming bodywork and lush interiors, and huge tyres with treads like the skin of dinosaurs. It was all part of the same desensitisation process, a way of putting a positive spin on Joan's experiences; window-shopping as cars flew by only feet away, negotiating a minefield of crossings to achieve the peace and safety of a public park, examining beautiful new vehicles that could be admired instead of feared.

And finally - finally - Joan was able to make the excursion that Dr Bob had intended her to take all along.

Together they took a tube to Kentish Town, and came up out of the earth to face the road where Joan had almost lost her life. Stratton called this aspect of the desensitisation process 'flooding', which Joan thought strangely appropriate, because for the first few minutes she had felt as though she were drowning. Drowning in memory, in the gaps in her memory, and drowning in the inevitable, terrible, and unfounded guilt of the survivor.

She had stood with her back to the facade of a HSBC bank that faced the pedestrian crossing itself, and she remembered approaching it from the direction of her sister's flat. She had been crying - who knew why? - and blindly heading for the Underground station.

Then she was on the crossing, and the black and white stripes beneath her feet had suddenly become electrically charged, and her sensory radar had sounded the strident alarm that made her turn and see the car.

At that point almost six months had passed since the incident, and yet Joan could still make out the place where she had lain and where the pregnant woman's remains had lain. Even though the blood had been washed away long ago, she found that she could still see it, trace its violent trajectories with her eyes.

It was like a huge maroon shadow indelibly printed on the tarmac and in her mind, there for evermore.

8

'Huh?'

Joan looked up abruptly, somehow disturbed, and felt the consulting room swiftly reassembling itself around her, the walls sliding into place and the ceiling smoothly descending like a lift. Everything slotted together with a neat click that brought her back to the moment. Street sounds from the half-open first-floor window reasserted themselves, and she noticed that the block of August sunlight entering the room from the same source had advanced another couple of inches across the plain carpet and was almost touching her sandaled feet. Time had passed.

Across the room, she saw that Dr Bob had uncoiled from his habitual listening pose and was looking back at her expectantly, his lips curved in an amused half-smile she had seen more than a few times before over the course of her treatment. It was the expression he used to administer a gentle rebuke.

Obviously, Joan had missed something of significance. Again.

'I'm sorry, I must have drifted,' she apologised. 'What was it you said?'

Stratton shrugged gently, his little smile remaining in place throughout the gesture. 'I didn't say anything, Joan.'

'Oh… so, what did I say?'

'It's more what you didn't say.'

Her puzzled expression made his smile grow until it had taken over his whole face.

'You're not going to make me guess, are you?'

The doctor shook his head and then glanced at his watch. 'According to my calculations, you stopped talking about seven minutes ago. Even for you, Joan, that's something of a record.'

'I'm sorry.' Joan was truly penitent, a good if not properly attentive patient. 'I was just thinking.'

'About?'

'Well.' Joan smiled ruefully. 'To be honest, it was about a dream I had last night.'

'Was it about the accident?'

'No, I told you, I don't do that anymore. This was different.'

Stratton gestured for her to continue, and Joan shrugged.

'It isn't important, honestly. It's just this dream where I'm in a dark place and I can hear the sea roaring. Just before I wake up, I hear a faint voice calling for help. That's it, that's all. I don't think it has any deep psychological meaning. Do you?'

'I shouldn't think so. But you *were* thinking about it.'

'Yes, but…' Joan sighed. 'It isn't the first time I've had this dream, that's all, and I was wondering why. It sort of… preoccupied me.'

'It "preoccupied" you,' her doctor echoed as his smile slowly faded. 'Preoccupied is a good word, Joan. So is "drifted", as in "I must have". I wonder what else you've been thinking about this afternoon. Why do you think you're drifting, Joan? Saying one thing while thinking about something else?'

She ran her fingers through her auburn hair - shorter now than at any time of her life other than during her rebellious teens, when she had been a sort

43

of weekend punk - and prepared to make a further apology. But Stratton didn't allow her to begin.

'Another good word, and probably a better word to describe your present condition, Joan, would be "bored".' Dr Stratton nodded as he held her eyes with his own. 'You wanted to be honest, so let's be honest — you are bored, aren't you? There's no point denying it.'

Joan *had* been about to deny it, despite its rather obvious truth. For an instant, she felt as though Stratton had read her mind with supernatural ease, and that she was completely naked before him, bereft of the smallest secret. Embarrassed, she blustered.

'Look, I'm sorry, okay? It won't happen again. I'll try harder, I'll—'

Solemnly, Stratton straightened up in his chair and took a very deep breath. 'Joan, I'll be sorry to see you go,' he said.

'What?'

Joan could hardly speak, and felt as though she'd been plunged into an icy pool. Her arms and legs instantly became leaden weights, her face was numb, and she felt stupid. She remembered this feeling uncomfortably well. This was what rejection felt like. Surely she wasn't being dumped by her own doctor?

'What are you…?'

'Joan, I believe you're on the verge of coming to the same conclusion that I have already reached.' Stratton calmly held up a hand to silence her pre-emptive objections. 'The fact is I don't see any therapeutic value in you being here today - or any day soon, for that matter. Of course, on a sub-conscious level, you've known this yourself for some time. Hence the "drifting", hence the "preoccupation".'

'But I…'

'Are you aware that for most of our appointments over the last four weeks you've mainly been repeating yourself? It becomes tedious after a while, you know. And I must say, I think it's unfair of you to expect me to carry on listening to your stories even though you've stopped.'

He was being mock-serious now. The humour was only visible as a low gleam in his eyes, but Joan could see it, like a guiding light.

'The truth is,' he added, 'you're talking for my benefit now, not your own, and I usually regard that as the end of the line.'

It took Joan a moment or two to understand what he seemed to be saying, but when she had, euphoria struck her like a fist and left her breathless.

'Then it's over?' she asked, completely stunned. 'I'm cured?'

'Cured? Now that's a word psychiatrists never like to use,' Stratton scowled, still acting. 'Bad for the bank balance, all that "cured" business. Goodness me, the trouble it causes. But…' The smile returned, warming Joan with a pulse of heat that started at her heart. 'Yes, I think we might go that far on this occasion.'

'And you think I'm ready? It isn't too soon?'

'It's been four months, Joan,' he shrugged. 'Four long months of hard work. That seems about right to me.'

Joan bit her lip. 'I don't know if I'm ready.'

'You're just nervous, that's all. Remember, you can always call me if you get desperate - but I know that you won't need to. Like it says in all the TV shows,' he added, 'trust me, I'm a doctor.'

Joan suddenly shot to her feet, excited, elated, released. As soon as Stratton stood up to join her, she threw her arms around him and thanked him so passionately that soon he was laughing and so was she. It surprised neither of them when her laughter turned into tears. He held her as she leaned against him, her face pressed into his shoulder.

'I suppose I could have said this a couple of weeks ago,' he said, 'but I wanted to be absolutely sure. And besides, I couldn't quite bring myself to discharge you.'

'What do you mean?' she asked, trying hard not to snot on Stratton's shirt.

'You've become one of my favourite patients, Joan. Probably the favourite. It's been a joy to see you each week.' He paused for a second or two, and she could feel that he was holding his breath. 'Genuinely, I will miss you.'

'I'll miss you too.'

He gently laughed again. 'Perhaps not in quite the same way.'

Abruptly, Joan became very still, holding her breath just as her doctor had. She was suddenly conscious that Stratton had returned her embrace in full measure. Through her thin summer dress, she could feel his warm hands pressed against her back, and the greater heat of their bodies pressed so close together.

Very slowly, she lifted her head from his shoulder and dropped her arms to her side, and as soon as he released her she stepped back, trying to hide the sudden and unwelcome wariness she felt.

'Of course,' Stratton said, 'I'll want to see you for a follow up examination, just to check your progress.'

'When?' Joan asked, her voice sharper than she had intended.

Against her will, unpleasant thoughts were suddenly scampering around in Joan's head. In a roundabout way, Stratton had just admitted to extending her treatment unnecessarily because he liked seeing her. Was that normal? She began to wonder about his midlife crisis, too, and the grooming and the new wardrobe that she had believed were the outward signs of his new freedom. But maybe that wasn't the whole story. Maybe the changes had been made specifically with her in mind.

She tried to recall how many times Stratton had touched her over the months, and how he had touched her. She thought of his mannered listening pose, and calculated where his eyes might have lingered if he had been watching her through his eyelashes. She wondered what might have happened if he had been successful on the couple of occasions he had tried to hypnotise her into total recall of the hit and run and the events preceding it.

In fact, with just the two of them alone in this room, who was there to say that he hadn't succeeded in hypnotising her? What might have happened while she was in the trance?

Joan took a sequence of very long slow breaths. Stratton had put his hands in his trouser pockets and seemed to be completely at ease. His smile was inoffensive and, as far as she could tell, genuine, and his brown eyes were as mild as ever. Clearly, as far as he was concerned nothing strange had just happened between them.

She tried some more deep breaths, and felt a little more stable.

'Oh, not for about six months,' Stratton said.

Joan had found a crumpled tissue in her sleeve and was blowing her nose and wiping her eyes. 'What's that?'

'The check up,' Stratton said patiently. 'In about six months or so. Nothing to worry about - it's standard practise, just to see how you're coping. Relapses do occur, but to be honest I wouldn't be discharging you if I really believed that would happen. You're as strong as you'll ever need to be, Joan. Remember that and you'll be just fine.'

'I've got to go,' Joan said.

Stratton consulted his watch. 'There are about fifteen minutes of our session left. We could chat for a while, purely as friends.' He grinned. 'Who knows, perhaps we could discuss *my* problems for a change…'

'No, I've got to go,' Joan insisted. As soon as the words were out she realised how offensive they and her tone of voice both were. She shrugged helplessly, unsure how to explain herself. 'I'm sorry, but I just feel like I have to leave, now that I know I *can*.' She stared into his eyes, willing him to understand.

Stratton nodded immediately. 'That's fine, Joan. Whatever you want to do. It's your life.'

'I'm sorry.'

She turned away and quickly gathered up her shoulder bag and cardigan from the floor beside her chair, aware that she would be presenting Stratton with a grandstand view of her bottom. But she knew that he wouldn't be looking. Both hoped and knew at the same time. This was Dr Bob, after all. She headed for the door. 'Joan.'

She slowly turned about. 'Yes?'

'I want you to do one last thing for me.'

Joan defensively held her bag between them. 'What's that?'

Stratton smiled. 'Please, stop apologising for everything.'

9

Joan quickly stepped out of Dr Stratton's consulting room and into his waiting room, closing the door firmly behind her. Despite the fact that her mind was in freefall and her feet wanted to fly, she noticed that the man was there yet again. The man with the paper. *Financial Times* Man.

He was one of the first details she had picked up on as she had begun the long process of coming back to herself. Each week when she arrived for her appointment, the waiting room was always empty. But when she left, *Financial Times* Man was always there, sitting with his back to the opposite wall, hiding behind his large pink paper. At first Joan had believed, rather typically, that he was hiding from her specifically, but had eventually come to understand that the man - like so many other things in life - was nothing to do with her. The poor man was hiding from the whole world.

Once or twice, if she'd happened to walk through the waiting room mid-page turn, she had caught a brief glimpse of the man himself, who seemed familiar in a very vague way. He also seemed to be losing weight week on week. Always smartly, if not exquisitely, dressed, his expensive suits were looking progressively large on his diminishing body. She wondered whether his weight loss was the problem itself, or merely a symptom of the problem. Of course, she couldn't ask.

Right now she felt guilty that she was leaving the psychiatrist behind, while she had the feeling that the unfortunate *Financial Times* Man was destined to be here forever. She had the sudden urge to say something, even if it was just hello, goodbye, and good luck, but then she heard soft footsteps from inside the consulting room approaching the door and she got moving again. She didn't want to be caught spying on Dr Bob's next patient when he opened the door, and so she fled.

Running along the corridor and down the winding staircase from Stratton's offices to the building's lobby, Joan uncomfortably reminded herself of a rat trying to find its way out of a maze, but she was unable to make herself slow down. The hard soles of her sandals slapped and scraped across the lobby's marble floor and she all but leapt through the front door and down the three shallow steps to the pavement outside. Briefly dazzled by the strong sunlight, she immediately collided with a businessman who didn't even glance at her as he disentangled his briefcase from her shoulder bag and wheeled away again. She called out an apology as he veered back into his purposeful, somehow desperate stride, but he didn't respond at all.

Stop apologising for everything, Stratton had told her just a moment or two ago. Might as well, she now thought. Nobody seems to be listening, anyway.

For a short while, Joan simply stood there in the street with her eyes closed as the sunlight bathed her face, allowing the fresh air to surround her and the breeze, slight as it was, to blow through her. Unlike panic, which pounced with the suddenness of an ambush, calm arrived in gradual stages, like the incoming tide. Sometimes it was maddeningly slow, but it did come. She had found that if she waited long enough it always came.

Now that she was out of the building, out of that hideous green room, she could hardly believe that she had even for one second entertained such awful suspicions about Dr Stratton, someone who she knew with absolute certainty could be trusted implicitly. Her misreading of the situation and her over-reaction to it reminded her of the person she used to be. It felt a lot like backsliding, which was the very last thing that Joan needed in her life right now.

Angry and impatient with herself, she rooted around in her bag and eventually found her sunglasses. She slipped them on and saw through the tinted lenses the world that Stratton had given back to her. The world, and the freedom to move through it all. In other words, Life. He had helped her slay the Dragon. How ungrateful could she be?

51

Of course, she had known for some time that paranoia was still very much a part of her psychological make-up. She still had the occasional moment when she felt that she was being followed or watched. The difference now was that she no longer trusted her senses to the same degree. In such situations, she generally found it useful to employ the breathing techniques Stratton had taught her to counter panic-attacks, as they seemed to clarify her perception too.

Although Joan's paranoia easily outdated the hit-and-run, the two had somehow become linked in her mind, and Stratton had once told her that she had forged the link herself. Because her paranoia was an almost supernatural dread, it had attached itself quite naturally to the car that had nearly killed her, which her imagination had gradually transformed into some kind of haunted car out of a horror movie.

Even today, going through the story once again, completely untroubled, hardly even listening to herself speak, she'd done the very same thing:

It wants *to kill me, that's the thing.*

The car - not the maniac inside it.

Joan began to stroll along the pavement, keeping half an eye out for a taxi. She shook her head at the absurdity. A haunted car, patiently stalking her along the city streets until it found the right opportunity to attack. Yeah, right - hello, Stephen King! Truth may well be stranger than fiction, but in this case the truth was merely depressingly mundane, as the details supplied by her husband's friends in the police force a couple of days after the hit-and-run clearly showed.

It turned out that the offending 4x4 had belonged to a local Camden Town villain, who, it was suspected, used the vehicle as a storefront to sell drugs - hence the heavily tinted windows that had prevented Joan from seeing the driver that day. Privacy for shady deals, and all that. It had been reported stolen before six that morning by the villain himself, and had been discovered burnt out in a Kennington side street sometime after nine in the evening. The police conclusion - joyriding.

Joyriding; at the best of times it was a dubious term for the activity it described. In this context it was an obscenity.

Sometimes, when Joan really thought about it, she could get past the image of the horror movie car and see him in her imagination as she never had in reality. *Him*. The joyrider. It was a mental mug-shot of vapid youth. He was a sixteen-year-old nothing and nobody, with bad skin and a pocketful of pills, the ego of an immortal and the morality of a cornered rat. It helped a little, to have a face to focus on, even if it was imaginary.

She always wondered what, if anything, had been going through his mind as he accelerated toward the pedestrian crossing. Did he actually see her, Joan Crosby the person? Or was he, high as a kite, playing some kind of 18 certificate XBOX game in his head in which she was merely another expendable sprite? Was it a real accident, or had he intended to kill someone all along? Someone, anyone? Why did he change direction at the last moment, choosing to spare Joan and kill the pregnant woman and her unborn child? Was the decision racially motivated?

Or had he, for the mere thrill of it, simply chosen the greater evil?

There were too many questions, too few answers. For a time, she had been completely obsessed by them, until Dr Bob had suggested that she could try writing a letter to this unknown, imaginary boy, believing that the therapy could help clear Joan's largely inarticulate blockage of rage and fear. This letter became one of a whole sequence of similar letters she composed during those early days; one to the so-called joyrider, one to the dead woman and her baby expressing Joan's sorrow, and one to herself, absolving herself of guilt for surviving.

She also wrote one other letter, entirely off her own back.

Originally, it was intended for Lee Meadows, apologising for ever suspecting him of harming Kath, and telling him she now accepted that her friend had simply left him. Left them all. She had glimpsed Lee a few times over the months following the accident, always from the distance he seemed determined to maintain, but each time he'd looked a little worse, a little more ragged, a little thinner, his face a little more lined. She didn't blame him for trying to avoid her, and meant to tell him so in her letter.

An apology to Lee was what she meant to write. In the end, though, it became a letter to Kath herself, expressing Joan's dismay at the way Kath had deserted from the lives of the people who had loved her best, without a care, without a single word of explanation.

All the rage and bitterness that had poisoned Joan's life had spilled out of her pen in way that might have been destructive, but was instead cathartic. When he'd read the letter, Dr Bob had looked up at her, raised his eyebrows, and said, 'Wow!' and Joan had laughed till she cried.

She reached the intersection of Devonshire Place and Harley Street, and paused. Then she turned back to look at Stratton's building. As she had known she would, she saw Dr Bob himself standing framed in his consulting room window, offering her a small wave. Seeing his latest triumph off into the world, she supposed. She guessed that if he had known what had been going through her mind as they said their goodbyes, he might well have changed his mind about the wisdom of that decision.

But on the other hand, here she was. Walking down the street, unmindful of the cars that rushed by in a blur only a few feet from where she stood. She was not running away from them. She was not hiding behind a newspaper.

She waved back at him for longer than was necessary. Her way of saying sorry, yet again. Then she turned the corner and walked away, no longer conscious of Stratton's eyes on her back, in precisely the same place his hands had been five minutes ago. She spotted a vacant taxi about to cruise past her and stepped toward the kerb to hail it. The toes of her sandals overhung the gutter as the taxi swooped toward her, but she didn't falter and she didn't step back. She was not afraid.

She was free, and all her fears were behind her.

And a hundred yards away, a pair of cold eyes flickered with concentration and slid from the profile of her face to the contours of the breasts beneath her summer dress.

10

Joan asked the taxi driver to take her to Kentish Town and then settled back in her seat for the journey to her sister's flat, already anticipating the sights and hold-ups that were now as familiar to her as Dr Bob's worn leather chairs and ghastly green walls. Encouraged by Stratton, she had been visiting Olivia every Friday afternoon immediately after her appointment for the last couple of months, staying until the early evening before heading home to wait for Stephen to get back from his office.

Her doctor believed that these frequent visits to the general location of her trauma were a useful way of continuing the desensitisation process, and although Joan knew that he was probably right, this was not the real purpose of her weekly visits. As far as she was concerned, they were a different kind of therapy altogether.

If there was one single positive to have come out of the last twelve months, then it had to be the establishment of a fledgling but genuine friendship between the former Joan Weir and her only sibling. This was a development for which Joan had often wished over the years, but just as often despaired of. For as long as she could remember their relationship had been soured by a rivalry and jealousy on her younger sister's part that had increasingly bordered on the obsessional. Joan now found it slightly amusing that she was the one who had ended up in the care of a psychiatrist when for years it was Olivia who had appeared to be the girl-most-likely.

Two years younger than Joan, from early adolescence Olivia had always seemed to view her elder sister as both role model and competition. When she wasn't copying Joan's clothes-sense, her interests, and even her modes of expression, she was trying to steal the parts of her life that could be stolen, which could be anything from personal possessions, to friendships, to early boyfriends.

Joan's mother, all too aware of the situation, had always assured Joan that one day Olivia would grow up to be her own person, but as the years passed she had not shown even the slightest desire to change. Their late teens, twenties and early thirties had been a virtual wasteland, but the two years following their mother's death were the lowest ever point in their relationship.

At that moment in time, Olivia's flat had resembled a miniature reproduction of the home Joan had made for herself and Stephen, employing just the same colours, furniture, fabrics, and accents. Her wardrobe was almost identical to Joan's, and she had had her naturally blonde hair dyed to match Joan's auburn shade and cut to exactly the same style. Having dogged Joan's educational and career choices, Olivia also made her living as an interior designer and had been finalising plans to start her own business, just as Joan had. Over the years she had succeeded in infiltrating Joan's social circle and had dated a number of solicitor friends of Stephen's, but had thankfully baulked at an actual copy-cat marriage.

There had been many times during this period when Joan felt as though she were being haunted by an evil clone, a malevolent twin, who wanted nothing more or less than to shunt her from her own life and take her place. The hit-and-run, however, performed a minor miracle. Perhaps more than a minor miracle.

In fact, it changed everything.

As soon as Joan's therapy had reached the stage where she had been able to see anything besides herself and that dark, looming vehicle, she had found, to her considerable surprise, Olivia waiting for her. This was a new Olivia, not the Joan-clone. It was Joan's sister, all right, but she was almost a stranger. The auburn dye had already faded from her blonde hair, which had grown long enough to brush her shoulders, and her clothes were those she wished to wear rather than clothes she imagined Joan would choose.

This person, all but unrecognisable and alarmingly kind, had an interest in her that was sympathetic and caring, and not envy and bitterness in masquerade.

By the time of Joan's first dubiously accepted invitation to lunch, Olivia's flat had changed too, and looked nothing like her own home. Soon, Joan's initial suspicions simply began to melt away. As the weeks passed they spent their afternoons together doing nothing more meaningful that eating lunch, drinking tea, and chatting. They talked about everything, anything, nothing was too trivial. Sometimes, the more inconsequential their conversations the better they were. But no matter what they did or said, every day they spent together they were forming bonds, discovering each other in ways that had never before been possible.

Joan often wished that their mother could have lived long enough to see it. It would have made her life complete to see the daughters she had named after a couple of old-time Hollywood movie stars, also sisters, reconciled in this way.

There was only one subject they were never able to properly discuss. Joan's sole memory of the day of the hit-and-run began just as she approached the pedestrian crossing. Everything of the day before that moment was a complete blank. She still had no idea why she had gone to her sister's, or even how she had got there, much less why she had been crying. But she suspected that she and Olivia had had some kind of argument, some parting of the ways so acrimonious that it had driven her to complete despair. What could have caused such an argument, Joan couldn't guess, and Olivia wouldn't say.

According to Stephen, as far as he knew Joan had gone around to reclaim the winter coat that Olivia had taken from her bedroom wardrobe without asking, but surely it couldn't have been just that. An argument over a coat with a matching hat? After years of losing her possessions to her younger sister, some of them highly treasured, she didn't understand how one more petty theft could have provoked such an intense reaction.

The one and only time she had asked about that morning outright, Olivia had simply shrugged and claimed ignorance, and despite her curiosity Joan knew that she would never force the issue again. Olivia had consigned it to the past, and Joan had resolved that she would do the same. The present was all that mattered now. And the present was proving to be a joy.

Joan thought that it was a curiously symmetrical change of circumstances. Her friend Kath Meadows had once filled the place in her life that should naturally have been her sister's, and now Olivia had begun to fill the void that Kath's elopement had left behind. It was like a dance, with Joan at its centre.

A frying-bacon crackle of static from the taxi's two-way radio made Joan glance up and realise that they were currently stuck in a traffic jam. No big surprise. In this part of the city, half the roads were up and the other half were crammed with vehicles standing nose-to-tail like an extended elephant family. Congestion Charge, be damned. Once in this very spot she had been stuck for thirty minutes or more. Sighing, she glanced around the cab's interior, looking for some kind of diversion. She noticed the prominent no-smoking signs, and another vivid memory flooded up from the recesses of her mind.

Joan had taken up smoking once, when she was about seventeen years old and under the influence of an unsuitable boyfriend her mother despised and her sister coveted. She had smoked like someone with a death wish for two months, but when the boyfriend went, so did the cigarettes. Oddly, although she could remember the brand of cigarettes they had shared - they were Rothmans - she had entirely forgotten the name of the boy himself. Her husband disliked cigarettes, regarding them as common. Stephen only smoked the large cigars he bought in bulk from Lee Meadow's import/export business.

She read the taxi's hackney carriage licence number, and examined the back of the driver's head, his ears waggling fractionally as he chewed a wad of gum. A clean line of demarcation ran square across his nape, separating his short sandy hair from his shaved neck. She remembered that if Stephen was working hard and went too long without a haircut, two undignified clumps of black fuzz grew on the back of his neck above his shirt collar like misplaced pubic hair, and for days he would frown uncomprehendingly at his reflection in mirrors until he realised what the problem was. These performances had always made her laugh.

When the taxi driver went home at night, Joan suddenly wondered, did his wife run her fingers up through the short, freshly trimmed bristles and make him shiver, the way she used to with Stephen? She wondered if the taxi driver had anyone to go home to at all, a wife, a girlfriend, or lover. Or was he alone?

Without warning the jam began to break up. The two lines of traffic reduced to one started to flow through the bottleneck and expand again at the other side.

Out through her window, Joan watched the faces of the pedestrians begin to whip by as the taxi picked up speed. Man, woman, man, woman. Couples, groups, singles, couples. She looked at her watch, realising that even if there were other hold-ups along the way she would probably still get to Olivia's earlier than usual. Joan could have called ahead to let her sister know, but when she checked she found that her mobile phone was dead; uncharged, as usual. She put that on her mental to-do list - keep the damn mobile charged - along with all the other small aspects of managing a life that her new sense of freedom had suddenly made seem possible once more.

For a while, several ideas bounced around inside her head, making shapes and following patterns that seemed at the same time both strange and completely familiar. Possibilities; she heard this word so clearly that she thought that she may have spoken it aloud.

But what did it mean?

She glanced back at the driver's head, somehow drawn. Once again she studied the line of his hair and the smooth skin below, and she was suddenly overcome by an intense olfactory hallucination. She imagined that she could smell Stephen's aftershave, that the entire taxi was suffused with her husband's scent. Every idea in her head abruptly jelled, and the shape of her thoughts made sense. Belatedly, she realised that she was taking her good news in entirely the wrong direction.

Joan leant toward the inch-wide gap in the driver's plexi-glass partition. 'I'm sorry, I've changed my mind,' she said. 'Can you take me to Hampstead?'

The driver nodded without speaking, quickly checked his mirrors, and then performed the kind of opportunistic manoeuvre that only a London taxi could truly get away with. Amidst the fanfare of aggravated horn-blowing which greeted their illegal u-turn, neither the driver nor Joan noticed that the taxi was not, in fact, the real subject of the other motorists' ire.

The primary focus of everyone's anger was the vehicle that had been shadowing the taxi ever since it left Devonshire Place, and had recklessly followed its abrupt change of direction.

11

Joan had paid off the taxi at Hampstead High Street, dashed in and out of a supermarket, an off-licence, and a delicatessen, and was now walking the short distance home carrying a number of heavily-laden shopping bags, the weight of which she hardly noticed in her excitement. Inside the bags were a selection of cold meats, cheeses, fruits, pates, olives, dips, breads, biscuits, and wines, all of which she intended to set up and present on a blanket before the living room fire while Stephen was upstairs in the shower.

Being August, it would be far too warm for a fire, of course, but the scene in her head seemed to demand firelight. Firelight, and the intimacy of curtains closed against the fading summer evening.

It was another snapshot of normality, of real life. Just as Dr Stratton had promised, it was coming alive for her, now more motion picture than still photograph. She still had a slight sense that the person playing her was only an actress. But now Joan accepted that she didn't have to be.

By the time her husband came home, Joan decided, she would have taken a long soak in the bath, and transformed the living room itself into a fragrant bower with incense and a few of the altar candles she used to light whenever they had dinner parties in the past. When Stephen had finished his shower and came down from the bathroom in his robe, thinking, no doubt, of ordering a takeaway meal, she would be waiting for him, perhaps wearing some of the beautiful silk lingerie he had once bought for her on a trip to Brussels but which she had never worn.

Surprise, surprise!

Her head felt light and there was a pleasant knot of anticipation at the core of her body. She felt refreshed, cleansed and energised, as though the sequence of events she had planned for this evening had already been played out, everything happening just as she had imagined, every word and gesture, every caress delivered perfectly on time. This was the sort of evening she and Stephen had shared in the early years of their relationship, when they had been wrapped up in each other so completely that no one and nothing else mattered. Suddenly, this was what Joan wanted again.

Every aspect of her fantasy was suffused with nostalgia, and with a sense of not only revisiting the past but actually improving upon it, because now she recognised how important certain moments could be, and how vital it was to experience and appreciate them fully. It had come to her in the taxi as she had thought about the reconciliation between herself and Olivia, at how far they had come in so short a space of time and after so many years of miserable battle.

She had realised that nothing was impossible, that broken things could be mended. If she made just half the effort for her husband that Olivia had made for her, who knew what might happen?

Joan's marriage had been in decline for a long time, and her gradual recovery through therapy had done nothing to slow the process. Most of the time, she and Stephen were like distant acquaintances who just happened to share the same bed and no more. And sometimes not even that. To say that they had drifted apart would be a terrible cliché, but that is exactly what had happened. It was hard to remember where the decay had started, but she knew that it had begun long before her own troubles.

Part of it, she knew, was Stephen's over-riding ambition, the twelve and fourteen hour days and the interminable business trips. But she was also prepared to accept her share of the blame. At some stage she had unintentionally stopped being the woman Stephen had fallen in love with, grown colder somehow, and a large part of his coldness, she believed, was merely a reciprocal reaction to hers.

She turned into Haversham Row, the street where she and Stephen lived, and with her thoughts turned entirely inward blindly passed a seven-year-old Ford Escort van parked on the corner, its engine still ticking away as it cooled. The van was white, but grimy with exhaust dust. The long side panels each sported a sharply delineated square patch only slightly less filthy than the rest of the car, where sign-written placards had recently been removed. The hubcaps and most of the lower quarter of the van were streaked with dry, flaking mud, and the licence plates were practically unreadable as a result.

Joan knew that she was probably hoping for too much from this evening. Presented with the scenario she had planned, a part of her could see Stephen's face contorting into the severely cynical frown he had developed over the last couple of years. She could see him turning his back on her, dismissing her efforts as too little, too late, and, in a way, she wouldn't blame him if he did. But she didn't think that this would happen - or she hoped not, at any rate.

Either way, she believed it would be worth the risk of humiliation to find out if they still had a real future together.

With her expectations bounding well ahead of reality, Joan dodged between parked cars and skipped across the road, and was almost trotting as she approached their garden gate.

All Stephen had to do was meet her half way, that was all, and then she really would have her life back. Together they could erase the past. With their marriage back on track, everything else would fall into place, and new challenges could be faced. Her interior design company could be revived, perhaps in partnership with Olivia. And in a couple of years, if everything else went well, Stephen could even change his mind and there might be a chance of that holiest of holies, that most unmentionable of her secret wishes, a baby.

They were both still young enough if they really wanted it. Time was still on their side, and not yet their enemy.

Joan threw open the gate and ran up the short path to the front door and fumbled her keys into the lock. She bundled all her bags into the hallway and pushed the door closed behind her with the heel of her sandal. She dropped her shoulder bag at the bottom of the staircase and hurried through the house, taking her carrier bags into the kitchen.

In her excitement, Joan did not notice that the alarm system she had set that morning as she left for her appointment with Dr Bob did not beep to warn her that she needed to punch in its six-figure deactivating code.

It had already been deactivated.

12

Dumping the shopping bags on the kitchen table, Joan immediately started to unload them onto the work-surface beside the refrigerator, stacking the items in neatly ordered rows. She began to check each item off against the menu scrolling in her head, and soon realised that she had forgotten to buy fresh figs, which were one of Stephen's old favourites, an erotic little fruit that stirred the imagination. She wondered if she had time to go out and find some with everything else that needed to be done, and then she wondered if she had forgotten anything else.

Stephen's Valpolicella – check; the imported Normandy brie they had first sampled on their honeymoon – check; the ciabatta – check; the special…and then she realised that the only other thing she had forgotten wasn't on the menu at all. She had forgotten Olivia. Engrossed in the preparations for her fantasy, Joan hadn't let her sister know that she wouldn't be paying her usual visit today, and bearing in mind Joan's history, Olivia was bound to be worried. Fortunately, this was an oversight that was easily rectified.

Joan abandoned the groceries and crossed the kitchen to the window looking out over the back garden, which had once been her pride and joy, her project whenever Stephen was away on business and her work had temporarily dried up. Beyond the small patio she had designed and helped build was a long smooth expanse of well-manicured lawn and a series of immaculate flowerbeds which Joan would have liked to say were all her own work, but were in fact achieved by the efforts of the garden services company Stephen had hired when Joan had become incapable of taking care of them. Maybe one day soon she would go back out there herself and get her hands dirty again. It would be as good a way of reintroducing herself to the real world as any other, she thought.

Suddenly, a linked snapshot jumped into her mind, incredibly vivid. Herself and Olivia, when they were just little girls, before the jealousy really kicked in; they were in the greenhouse with their mother, giggling together as they were taught how to transplant tomato seedlings to larger staked pots. Joan could actually smell the rich compost that had crumbled in their small hands like cake, and the randy scent of the tomato plants, and she could feel the heat of the sun coming through the glass roof and blazing in her hair like fire. Then the vision jumped forward a few weeks, and she saw the girls eating the tiny tomatoes straight from the vine, the fruit all but exploding in their little mouths, like a concentrated taste of the sun.

Maybe that's what she'd do, she thought. Forget flowers, forget the merely pretty, and try to grow something - nurture something - edible and nourishing instead.

Mounted on the narrow strip of wall between the window and the door to the garden was the telephone extension. Joan lifted the receiver from its cradle and began to dial Olivia's number. Five digits in, a pigeon drifted down from the roof outside and awkwardly settled on the low wall at the edge of the patio, fluttering its wings wildly before finding its balance. The movement caught Joan's eye, and when she glanced up at the bird she saw in the kitchen window the reflected image of the doorway behind her, a translucent rectangular block of sun-filled hallway.

She also saw that a large dark shape was moving through it toward her.

Joan's heart began to hammer in her chest, and her whole body felt both hot and cold at the same time. The telephone receiver slipped out of her suddenly strengthless grip, bounced off the tile counter, then spun down and hit the floor-tiles with a loud crack. Joan twisted around, her arms rising defensively of their own accord.

'It's okay,' Stephen said. 'Calm down, it's just me.'

He had frozen a few steps into the kitchen, and seeing in her face the shock he had given Joan, quickly retreated to the doorway. He had both arms held out at chest level with his hands palm down, and he was making a calming gesture with them that made him look like he was bouncing a large invisible beach ball.

'I'm sorry I startled you, I didn't mean to creep up like that.'

Joan let out a long shuddering breath. 'Jesus Christ!' Then she started to laugh. 'Jesus Christ, you really scared me!' She could see that Stephen was puzzled, maybe even a little worried, by her laughter, but that only made her laugh more. 'Sorry, sorry.' Which made her think of Dr Bob telling her to stop apologising for everything, and caused her to laugh even louder. 'Sorry, sorry, sorry…'

Stephen had straightened up and dropped his arms, waiting for her laughing fit to subside, and though he still looked puzzled and concerned, there was the hint of a smile at the corners of his lips that Joan liked. There was something else she liked, too. Stephen had recently showered and wore only his bathrobe, conforming perfectly to the entrance he had made in her fantasy.

The only differences were that it was the wrong room and he was about six hours too early.

'What are you doing back so soon?' he asked.

'I was just going to ask you the same thing,' Joan replied, gulping in a large breath of air.

Stephen closed the kitchen door and leant back against it with his bare legs crossed and his arms folded. 'I needed to get out of the office for a while. Just an hour or so, away from all the pressure.' He shrugged. 'So I came home, had a shower, and relaxed.'

'Well, that's good,' Joan said. 'I always said you should take some time out, just for yourself.'

'I know. You were right.' After an awkward pause, Stephen said, 'I thought you always went to Olivia's after your therapy?'

'I do usually.'

'Nothing's gone wrong, has it? I mean, you haven't fallen out again or anything like that?'

'No, no, not at all.' She reached down and hoisted the telephone up by its curling flex. 'I was just about to call her to let her know I'd be coming straight home today.' She put the cracked receiver to her ear, listened, and then shook her head. 'Broken. I'll have to use the one in the living room now.'

'Nothing's happened to upset you?' Stephen asked. 'With the doctor, or on the way over there?'

'No, everything's fine. Better than fine, in fact.' Joan managed to get the receiver back into its cradle. Her fingers had gone stupid on her, and she was having trouble meeting her husband's eyes. 'I... I won't be seeing Dr Stratton again. I mean, I'll have to see him once more, in about six months, but otherwise... that's it. I'm done.'

Stephen angled his head. 'Meaning... You mean you're okay?'

'Yes.'

'Okay okay?'

'As good as I ever was, anyway. Actually, I feel great.' She smiled broadly, unable to stop herself. 'You know, it's funny, but a doctor tells you you're well again, and suddenly you feel well. The power of suggestion, I suppose. Like a kind of benign voodoo, or a...'

Shut up, she thought, you're babbling.

She risked a quick glance and saw that Stephen was nodding and cautiously smiling. 'You spoiled my surprise, you know,' she said. 'I had the whole evening planned. Sort of a celebration.'

'We could go out for dinner, if you'd like.'

'I was thinking of something a little more intimate.' She waved a hand at the foods she had bought. 'I thought we could try to have one of our special evenings. Like we used to. Remember? In front of the fire. Just you, me. Us.'

This time when she glanced at Stephen, she saw him looking at the groceries and really seeing them, understanding what they represented, and she was thrilled. Just the thought that they meant exactly the same thing to him as they did to her filled her with hope.

When Stephen turned back to her, his face now a study in astonishment, Joan looked down at her feet. Prepared herself.

'Stephen, I know we've had our problems the last couple of years,' she began. 'Aside from the accident, I mean, and, you know, the stuff before, about Kath. I also accept that the vast majority of the problems have been mine - well, probably ninety-nine-point-nine percent of them have been mine - and I know that one good day can't put them all right. Nor can one good fuck, for that matter. But I want to try. I really want to try.'

She raised her head, forced herself to hold his eyes.

'Do you think that's still possible?'

Stephen's face was now unreadable. When he eventually opened his mouth to reply, Joan closed her eyes, as though that might protect her if he should say the unthinkable. His voice, when it came, was hoarse.

'Yes, of course it's possible,' he said. 'That's what I want. That's what I've wanted all the time.'

Joan opened her eyes and saw him coming toward her. She stepped forward into his embrace and locked her arms tight around his waist, burrowing her head into the folds of his robe, inhaling the scent of soap from his warm body. He kissed her hair, spoke her name. It was the first part of her fantasy fulfilled. She began to cry.

'Oh thank you. Thank you for putting up with me. Thank you for waiting for me. Thank you for being my husband.'

And in that moment, from behind the closed kitchen door, Joan heard the front door snick closed. She drew back her head from Stephen's chest.

'What was that?'

'What was what? It was nothing.'

'It was the door. Somebody closed the front door.'

'I didn't hear it. It was the wind, or a car, or something. It's not important.'

Joan looked up at Stephen's face, and drew back her head when he tried to kiss her lips. She started to pull away from him. 'I've got to look. It was definitely the door. Someone could have walked in off the street. Either that or someone was going…'

Maybe she saw it in his face, or in his eyes. Maybe it was the increasing pressure of his embrace.

'…or someone was going out.'

Joan tried to pull away and step around him, but Stephen caught her arms in his hands and held on tight.

'Joan, leave it. Please. Just let it go. This is more important. We're more important.'

But in his eyes, she could see the guilt behind the sincerity, and it gave her the strength to wrench herself free and stumble toward the kitchen door. She pulled it open, ran past the staircase and yanked the front door wide open. As she stepped outside the door hit the interior wall and the doorknob punched a hole in the plaster. Behind her she could hear Stephen calling her name, but his voice seemed very far away and unimportant.

At the other side of the road, standing beside the driver's door of a red two-seater sports car, a dark-haired young woman was frantically pulling all the paraphernalia out of her handbag, tossing a jumble of tissues and envelopes and gum-wrappers and pens onto the car's soft-top. Her short hair was still wet from the shower and gleamed shiny-black in the sunlight, and her clothes had obviously been dragged on over damp, resisting skin. Her blouse was open to her sternum, revealing a lacy black half-cup bra. Visible on the top of her left breast was a large suck-mark that was an identical shade of red to her flushed face.

As Joan watched in disbelief, a small make-up case tumbled out of the woman's handbag, hit the road surface, and burst open. A shower of cosmetics bounced on the tarmac and rolled under the car and into the gutter. The woman swore loudly, and then finally found the keys for which she had been desperately searching. She rammed them into the door lock and jumped into the car.

A second later the engine roared into life and she pulled out into the road without checking her mirrors. A driver who had to brake drastically to avoid tail-ending her laid his fist on the horn and left it there. The woman put her foot down and tore away, and all the items she had piled on top of her car flew off into the road, the envelopes and receipts fluttering down like pieces of confetti. The sports car slewed out of Haversham Row and was gone. The woman hadn't looked back at the house once.

Half a dozen pedestrians had stopped in their tracks to gawk at the woman's appearance and performance, and for a few moments, before they began to go their separate ways again, they turned their curious and speculating eyes on Joan.

She could hear their thoughts. They were thinking, *the wife is always the last to know*.

One of the spectators was her nosy neighbour, Gordon Unwill, the head of the Neighbourhood Watch's Secret Service, who looked disgusted beyond all expression. After staring at her for a few seconds longer than anyone else, he turned on his heel and marched briskly away.

13

'Can I just explain this? Will you listen? Will you do me the courtesy of listening?'
Stephen was leaning against the architrave of the kitchen doorway as though afraid to come all the way into the room, just as he had seemed afraid as Joan had walked past him in an almost drunken gait on her way back into the house. Joan didn't know why he was afraid. She didn't have the strength to attack him, even if she wanted to. She didn't have *any* strength. She was wounded, perhaps fatally so.

What was he talking about now - courtesy?

Mentally and physically numb, Joan had taken a seat at the kitchen table and was staring at the half-emptied carrier bags she had so carefully filled. Certain so far unpacked items peered out from folds of plastic to mock her; a pate she hated but had bought because Stephen loved it, the label of the Champagne with which they had celebrated their first wedding anniversary. She remembered the toast she had planned to make as they touched flutes, naked in the firelight. Oh, everything seemed like a black joke now, everything. Her shopping spree, her fantasy, her false optimism, the stumbling, emotional proposal she'd made to Stephen, and the choked acceptance he had given in return.

Courtesy? Really?

Floating on top of reality, Joan could see the humour of it, she really could. Actually, forget black comedy - this was pure slapstick. She was the woman with her head held high and lofty ideas of her station in life, the poor cow who always seemed to catch a custard pie in the face or ended up on her backside in the mud. Yes, that was her.

'Will you at least try to understand?'

'I'm listening,' she said. Her voice was a flat monotone, the voice of the damned speaking from the abyss, from the Dragon's gullet. Here she was again. One step forward, two steps back.

'Her name is Elaine. She's a legal secretary. We met at a conference four months ago, at the Connaught, but nothing happened then. I didn't want anything to happen. But then we bumped into each other again a few weeks ago, arranged to meet for a drink, and it started there.'

Stephen was almost hugging himself as he spoke. The temperature in the kitchen was in the low seventies, but the land of Found Out, he had discovered, was a cold, unhappy place. He looked smaller, diminished.

'It isn't… there's no emotional involvement on either part. I'm not in love with her, or her with me. It's just physical. It's just sex.'

'Is that all,' Joan's voice echoed from the gullet.

'Yes, I promise you.'

'Well, that's all right, then.'

Stephen was silent for a few moments. 'I'm sorry, Joan. I hate myself afterwards, when we're done, when it's over.'

'Thanks, that makes everything better. Thank you for your courtesy.'

He sighed heavily, and when he spoke again, his voice was louder, more confident. 'Joan, you know, this attitude of yours isn't helping. I feel bad enough as it is, and it hasn't *all* been my fault, has it?'

Joan nearly smiled. An emotional gypsy, Stephen had emigrated from the land of Found Out to the republic of Wronged Husband in double-quick time, finding the climate much more to his liking. Joan knew it had been coming. It had only been a matter of time before he began laying the blame squarely on her shoulders.

'Do you know how lonely I've been this last year?' Stephen asked. 'Do you know how long I've been waiting for just a little bit of warmth from you? I'm not only talking about sex here, I'm talking about everything. Elaine is…she *talks* to me, and she looks at me as if she can see me - she doesn't look *through* me like I'm a bloody ghost. She's interested in me, in what I have to say, like you used to be.'

He stared at her as he tried to work out if he was getting through.

'You've got to understand, as far as I knew, you were never going to change back. That was it. Our relationship, such as it was, was going to be the same for the rest of our lives. And I needed more than that, I needed… contact. That's all I wanted, that connection. To be wanted, desired…I don't think that's too much to ask.'

'All I ever wanted was loyalty,' Joan said. 'I didn't think that was too much to ask, either.'

'It has to go both ways to work, Joan. You abandoned me a long time ago, you went someplace where I wasn't wanted.'

'That's not an excuse.'

'No, it isn't. It isn't meant to be. There are no excuses, it's just an explanation. It's the way I feel.'

Joan made herself look up at him, forced herself to keep looking even as she felt the Dragon begin to digest her feet.

'I know that there's some truth in what you're saying. I did turn off toward you, but I don't know why, I honestly don't.' She shook her head slowly. 'Sometimes I feel that I almost know, I *almost* understand…It was like I didn't…' Her gaze suddenly intensified on him. 'It was like I didn't trust you, Stephen. Why would I feel that way? Do you know?'

Stephen looked away from her, and his face went red, reminding her of the woman with the sports car, Elaine.

'Stephen?'

'No, I don't. I wish I did.' His voice was gruff, unyielding.

She was into the gullet up to her knees now. The pain was terrible, unrelenting, and yet it seemed to clear her mind, honing her perception to a razor's edge. She knew that he was lying to her.

'How many times?' she whispered. 'How many have there been before this one?'

Stephen shook his lowered head. 'You're getting paranoid again, Joan. I thought Stratton had cured you of all that. Maybe you should go back and let him have another crack.'

'Don't you dare try to do that to me!' Joan shouted. 'Tell me the truth! How many more were there before Elaine?'

'This is ridiculous,' Stephen mumbled angrily. He glanced at his wrist, looking for a watch that wasn't there. 'I'm going to get dressed. I have to be back at the office soon.'

Joan watched him turn away and head for the stairs, felt her thighs and hips slip into the gullet and the biting chill envelop her belly. The thud of his footsteps ascending the stairs became her heartbeat. She heard him walk into their bedroom, and hangers clattering as he pulled clothes out of his wardrobe. Her eyes were stinging, and she closed them tightly, fighting back tears, refusing to let them come. Not now, not yet.

She stood up, and felt an instant wave of dizziness and nausea wash over her. After a moment, when it seemed that her legs would refuse to move at all, she walked around the table, then out of the kitchen, and followed Stephen upstairs.

Her husband was in the bathroom, having taken his clothes in there to get dressed in certain privacy, like a visiting stranger. In their bedroom, Joan saw that he had left all the doors of his wardrobes wide open. At the bottom of one of them was the small overnight case Stephen used on his shorter business trips. After a moment's thought, Joan pulled it out, put it on the bed, and opened it.

By the time she heard the toilet flush and the bathroom door open, Joan had most of the things she'd need in the short-term already packed, and was in the process of raiding her underwear drawer when Stephen appeared in a fresh suit and tie, armoured against the world in his solicitor's uniform. She could see him in her dressing table mirror, much as she had remembered seeing him in one of her little memory snapshots of happiness, as he watched her apply her make-up, mesmerised by her beauty and by the fact that she was his, and entirely unable to prevent himself touching her. But that was before. Now she was on the other side of the mirror again, and everything was reversed.

Happy was unhappy, trust was suspicion, and joy was misery.

As he had downstairs, Stephen remained in the doorway, watching her every movement, his head following her hands from drawers to case and back again like a tennis spectator following the ball. She ignored him.

'Where will you go?' he asked.

He seemed to have immediately accepted her departure without even a token attempt at persuading her to stay. For a moment, she wished that she had begun to pack his clothes instead of her own.

'It doesn't matter, does it?'

'Of course it matters.' He pondered. 'You need somewhere quiet and anonymous, where you can think this through.'

Joan nodded to herself. Yes, she thought. Quiet and anonymous, that would suit Stephen.

'I know a nice hotel not far from here…'

'I just bet you do,' Joan sneered.

Stephen hung his head again. 'I mean it's comfortable, and no one bothers you.'

'Must have been very handy for you during all that time when I didn't want to leave the house. Still, at least you're saving money on room rental now.'

'Joan, please think about this.'

'I don't want to think about you screwing another woman in my bed, thank you.'

'We didn't use this bed, we were in the guest room,' he said, as if it mattered.

Joan slipped a couple of pairs of shoes down the sides of the case, bitterly recalling the erotic plans she herself had made. The atmosphere she had intended, hoped, to create. 'Did you light candles?' she asked, looking up at him.

'What for?' he frowned.

Joan laughed, and the jagged, brittle sound of it frightened her.

'While you're away,' Stephen persisted, 'think about us. Think about me. Have I ever left you? Have I ever asked for a divorce? No, I haven't. Why do you think that is, Joan? Why? It's because you're my wife, and I love you.'

Joan zipped up the bag and set it upright on the bed. 'I know, it's just you've got a funny way of showing it.'

'Everything I did was out of need. Pure physical need. Emotionally, you are all I've ever wanted.'

'How unfortunate for you.'

Joan picked up the overnight bag and approached the door. For a couple of seconds before stepping back, Stephen held his ground.

'Just think about it,' he said quietly. 'Promise me you'll think about it.'

Joan walked past him without promising anything.

14

Another taxi ride, back along an almost identical route to the first, but Joan's emotions could not have been any more different to how they had been during the journey to Hampstead. Less than an hour ago she had been riding high on a vast wave, a virtual tsunami, of hope and expectation. Now she was deep under the water, caught in a riptide and drowning in despair, disorientated and desperately trying to remember the direction of the shore.

Her driver this time was an older, more garrulous man, an old school taxi driver who obviously believed that his role of conveyor included the additional service of a free running commentary. His theme was something along the lines of What Is This Country Coming To? His topics were depressingly familiar; asylum seekers, political correctness gone mad, youth crime, drug culture, taxes, modern architecture, corporal punishment, road planning. All the usual suspects.

Joan felt his spiel hammering away at the fragile shell of self-control it was taking all her energy to maintain. The monotonous rhythm of his voice and the unrelenting certainty of his biased opinions were slowly wearing her down. She felt that at any moment her shell might break, and then she knew that she would succumb to emotional collapse.

The back of a taxi, she realised, was not the place to let herself go, because when she did it was going to be loud and messy. She had held it together for this long, and she hoped that she would be able to wait a little longer until she reached a place of safety. At her lowest moment, she did not want to be comforted by an unconsciously bigoted taxi driver, because she thought that might drive her completely insane.

Close to the end of the journey, as they entered Kentish Town, the taxi driver finally exhausted his one-sided conversation and belatedly tried to bring Joan into the frame, asking if she was going anywhere nice with her little overnight bag. Foolishly she told him she was going to stay with her sister for a few days, and then the driver was off and running again, this time on the subject of his own family. Brothers and sister. Father and mother. Children and wife.

This was more than Joan could bear. She asked him to stop, paid her fare, and escaped on to the streets.

Ten minutes later, she had reached the row of Victorian terrace houses where Olivia lived alone in her two-bedroom first-floor flat, and she walked along the row of neat hedges and gates, so weary that she hardly noticed she was weaving from side to side. By this time her legs seemed to have developed an odd dual composition, being simultaneously both stiff and rubbery. The small case, light though it should have been, now seemed to weigh much more than it feasibly could, and her head, aching unbearably, felt ready to burst at any moment. Beams of the late afternoon sunlight were like knives in her eyes, and she approached the door of her sister's house feeling jetlagged, as though she had crossed continents and time zones. Dimensions, even.

Oh God, Olivia, she thought, please be in. Don't have gone out. I need you.

She rang the bell, and to her relief the door was immediately buzzed open. She went inside the common hallway, the soles of her sandals slipping on a scuffed parquet floor littered with uncollected post, reams of junk-mail, and multiple week-old editions of the local free paper. She had hardly begun to climb the stairs before she heard footsteps hurrying down from the floor above.

She looked up as Olivia rounded the corner, almost swinging herself around as she held on to the newel post, and at the sight of her face, Joan's composure finally dissolved. Rushing down, Olivia caught her in her arms just as she collapsed on to the steps, and held on as Joan's whole body attempted to contract, to curl up into a protective ball. The wordless cries that forced themselves through her lips sounded like steam escaping under enormous pressure.

On the larger of Olivia's two facing sofas, swaddled up in a colourful African throw like one of her taxi driver's stereotyped scrounging refugees, Joan lay back in a state closer to sleep than to consciousness. The excesses of her emotions had taken their toll, and she watched heavy-lidded as Olivia came in through the alcove from the kitchen carrying a crowded tea tray. She carefully made her way over to Joan, placed the tray on the cedar-wood ottoman that served as her coffee table, and knelt down beside it.

The tags of herbal tea-bags hung over the rims of two steaming mugs, and into each Olivia spooned a small section of honeycomb and added a liberal amount of Napoleon brandy. 'This'll help,' she said, and Joan nodded apathetically.

It had taken Olivia all of ten minutes to coax Joan upstairs into her flat, supporting her all the way, and then it had been twenty more before she was able to leave her and go to the kitchen to turn on the kettle. In between, she had cradled Joan and stroked her hair as she cried and battled to turn broken fragments of the new tragedy that had befallen her into recognisable words. While the kettle boiled, Olivia had wrapped her sister up in the throw, given her a box of tissues, and assured her that she could stay as long as she liked. Forever, if she wanted. She collected Joan's case and shoulder bag from where they had fallen at the very bottom of the staircase and left them by the coat-rack when she closed her flat door.

Watching Olivia as she prepared their drinks, Joan could now see that her sister was recognisably upset on her behalf, although the poker-face had fooled her for a time. The anguish was there, but it was all in the eyes. Olivia was hurting just as much as she was, and Joan took some comfort from that evidence of empathy. But there was something else there, too, she thought, another layer, and as Olivia passed over one of the mugs, Joan realised just how easily she seemed to have adjusted to this new, unexpected development.

She had answered the ringing of her bell instantly, without using the security intercom as she usually would. She had run down the stairs as if she had known that Joan would need her support, and she hadn't immediately asked where Joan had been all this time, or what had happened to put her into this terrible state. Nor had she expressed any kind of surprise when Joan had finally managed to tell her what had Stephen had done to her.

Looking back, Joan would have said that Olivia's reaction to her arrival seemed abnormal. Unless…

Unless she had already been prepared for it.

Joan tried to speak, but only managed to croak. She cleared her throat noisily, and then said, 'He guessed I would come here, didn't he? He called and told you I was on my way?'

Olivia nodded. 'But don't go thinking that it means he knows you better than you do yourself, or any kind of rubbish like that. It only means that he's aware of your options.' She shrugged. 'After all, where else could you go?'

A good question. Apart from a few far-flung cousins, Olivia was her only living blood relative now. As if in recompense, Joan had had a lot of friends. Once. Lots of good friends besides Kath

86

Meadows who she might have taken refuge with, if things had been different. If she hadn't managed to drive even the hardiest of them away.

'He suggested a hotel,' Joan said. She sipped her tea, wincing a little at the alcohol's bite. 'Somewhere quiet, where I wouldn't be noticed.'

'Sounds about right,' Olivia replied with a sour, humourless smile.

'That's what I said.'

Olivia shook her head. 'How's that tea going down?'

Joan took another careful sip. 'It's almost all booze now, I think.'

'Let's put that right, shall we,' Olivia said, and added another large dollop of alcohol to both mugs. 'Now it's definitely *all* booze. What the hell, it can't hurt, can it?'

'What the hell,' Joan echoed.

They sat in silence for a while, sipping their drinks. Joan's mind drifted, and she wondered if Olivia was relishing this moment of silent calm, the way a new mother relishes the quiet when her squalling baby finally falls asleep.

'What was she like?' Olivia asked abruptly. 'Stephen's bit on the side.'

Joan sighed. 'Everything you'd expect, I suppose. Young. Pretty. Independent. Slim, dark-haired, and probably rich. Racy. Fun to be with. Entirely unlike me.' She began to cry again and put her mug back on the tray so that she could hold a tissue over her eyes. She felt Olivia's comforting hand arrive in her lap, and gripped it tightly. 'The

87

worst thing is, I can see it from Stephen's point of view.'

Olivia shook her hand gently. 'Don't say that, Joan. Don't even think it. It wasn't your fault.'

'Yes, a part of it was. Yesterday I probably wouldn't have been able to think this way, but today I can. It's awful, but I *can* see his point of view. I can understand why he would need more than I've been able to give him for the last year. Probably the year before, too. Maybe I'd feel the same way in his place.'

'There's a big difference. You might feel the same way, but you'd never do what he has.'

'I'm not so sure.' Joan wiped her eyes with the tissue and then blew her nose. 'I believe he was telling the truth when he said he still loved me. When I told him that I'd finished with Dr Stratton, when I told him I wanted us to start over, he seemed genuinely pleased.' She looked up at Olivia. 'Should I forgive him?'

'Do you think you could?'

Joan thought for a long time. 'I think so. I think so. If…'

'If what?'

'If she really was the only one.'

Olivia peered at her intently. 'What do you mean?'

'As long as this Elaine person really was his only mistake, as he claims, and not just the latest.' Joan used her free hand to roughly finger-comb her hair, as though she was scourging herself. 'I have some suspicions, you see,' she said at length.

'Suspicions?'

'That she *wasn't* the first. I can't really explain it. This goes back to before the accident, back to a time even before Kath ran off. I think I went cold on Stephen because at some subconscious level, I didn't trust him. Maybe it was the constant long hours at work, or the business trips that made me suspicious. Or maybe it was because he knew Kath and Lee before he met me, and they were both into extra-marital affairs, *swinging*, so maybe he was too and couldn't shake that lifestyle off, even after we were married.'

She abraded her head again, even more roughly.

'But really I'm getting everything mixed up, because I didn't even know the Meadows had an open-marriage until after Kath disappeared and Phil Richardson told me. Oh *Christ*, Olivia, I don't know what I'm talking about!'

When she looked up again, Joan saw with surprise that her sister's eyes had finally overflowed and she was quietly crying. She squeezed Olivia's hand tightly. 'Hey,' she said softly. 'Hey. You don't need to cry, that's my job.'

But it seemed that Olivia did have to cry, and Joan's tenderness only made her cry harder, her face twisting. 'What is it, Olivia?' Joan asked, sitting up. 'What's wrong?'

Olivia snatched a tissue from the box she had given Joan and held it over her whole face, as if to hide. Joan stared at her curiously.

'I want you to know something, Joan,' Olivia said. 'I want you to know how wonderful these last few months have been for me. It's been the best time of my life. Knowing how close I came to losing you for good made me realise how much I would miss you. How much I loved you. What a wonderful, generous person you are. When you were first sedated in the hospital, all I could think of was how many terrible things I'd done to you over the years - things I thought I'd never be able to make amends for, or even have the chance to try. That's when I made my decision to change. I couldn't carry on as I was. I wanted us to be real sisters. I wanted us to be friends.'

'But we are,' Joan told her. 'It's been wonderful for me, too. I'm sure that your friendship and love have helped me to recover just as much as Dr Stratton did. And you're here for me now, just when I need you most.'

Olivia was shaking her head.

'No, you don't understand. A part of what I promised myself was that from that moment on I'd be completely honest with you. And I haven't been, Joan, I haven't been honest, I've lied.'

Joan was more confused than ever. 'What have you lied about?'

'About Stephen.'

'Stephen?'

Behind her sodden tissue, Olivia took a hitching breath. 'I didn't know that he was having an affair right now. But I knew that he'd had them before. I knew that he'd had a lot. I know... because I was one of them.'

15

Joan couldn't speak, move, or breathe. The room spun like a mad carousel around her, all the colours and shapes distorting and blending. The brandy she had drunk was like an acid eating into her chest and stomach, and nausea threatened to make her vomit. At some point she became aware that her fingers had relaxed and that Olivia had withdrawn her hand.

Without being conscious of it, Joan was wiping her palm on the throw that was still around her shoulders, as though her hand had been soiled by the contact.

'The way I used to be, I couldn't help myself,' Olivia said quietly. 'I realise that's no excuse, but you know it's true. I had to look like you, I had to have everything you did. But I swear to you, I never once thought of trying to steal Stephen until he made a pass at me. It had never occurred to me that I might be able to. He wasn't some boyfriend you were already getting tired of, he was your *husband*. But when he started flirting with me, I realised that this was my chance… to be you.'

Olivia exchanged her wadded tissue for a dry one from the box. This one she held over her nose and mouth as she spoke, but she still could not bring herself to look directly at Joan.

'We arranged to meet at a bar he knew,' she said. 'It turned out to be a hotel bar, a very expensive hotel, and he'd stayed there before. He was so sure of himself that he already had the room booked. We had a couple of drinks downstairs and then went up. He'd prepared it for us. For him, really. It was like a little seduction suite. There was a real fire, and he'd set up a picnic of wine and cheese and pate on the rug in front of it.'

Joan closed her eyes and fresh tears began to bleed through her lashes. Once again the snapshots flickered by, clearer and more lifelike than ever, and she realised that the actress who was playing her in the film of her life was her own sister.

'I was nervous, but he wasn't. He was so smooth, so experienced and confident. He knew exactly what he wanted, and he knew he was going to get it. He was in total control, told me what he wanted me to do, how to move, everything. It was like he had a checklist of things he liked to do, and the order in which he liked to do them. I felt like a car being assembled on a production line. But he wasn't assembling me, he was taking me apart to see how I worked.

'When it was over, I felt like a whore. Worse, because I didn't even do it for money, to make a living. All I had was the satisfaction of knowing that I'd got the better of you - and it didn't feel the way I had thought it would, the way it had always felt before. I felt so dirty and cheap. I wanted to go back in time and change what I had done, but of course I couldn't.' She shook her head miserably. 'When I left in the morning, I thought that was the end of it, that I'd got it out of my system. But I was sick, Joan. No matter how badly I felt, eventually I went back for more. And more, and more, and more…'

Joan's paralysis broke and she sat up and shrugged the throw off her shoulders. With her eyes narrowed to slits, still gummed up with tears, she said, 'I can't listen to this anymore.'

'But you have to,' Olivia insisted. 'You have to understand, you have to know. Joan, I accept that I'm not worthy of your love, but Stephen isn't either. You can't forgive him. I wasn't a mistake as far as he was concerned, I wasn't a drunken fumble at an office party. Our affair lasted for two months. The only reason it ended then was because you got knocked down. And even worse - it was the *reason* you got knocked down.'

Joan opened her eyes wide. She and Olivia finally made eye-contact, and a door into the hidden past suddenly opened in her mind. What she saw through this door was astounding.

'This is the second time we've had this conversation,' she said wonderingly.

Olivia dropped her eyes again and nodded. 'I don't know how you found out about us, but you did. You were so angry you came over here without even bothering to put on a coat, and it was freezing that day, absolutely freezing. You barged in and screamed and shouted at me for almost half an hour, telling me what a bitch I was for seducing your husband, calling me everything I deserved to be called. You wouldn't let me try to explain. And then you left.'

'I took back my coat,' Joan said, almost to herself. She could see herself snatching it from one of the pegs on the coat-rack beside the flat door, where her case stood now.

'Yes, the one I stole from you. I saw you from the window, pulling it on as you started to run. And the next time I saw you was in hospital the following morning.'

Olivia shook her head at the memory.

'Seeing you in that bed, hooked up to all those machines, your leg in plaster; oh, God, Joan - I can't tell you how I felt. I told Stephen then that it was over between us, and that he should tell you the truth, that

93

it was just as much his fault as mine. But he said that he'd already spoken to you, and it was obvious that you didn't remember anything about that day. He convinced me that we should let it stay that way, because he said he'd learned his lesson, and he was going to change. He said it would be better for you to never know, never remember. And at the time, fool that I was, I believed him. But he didn't change, he never meant to, it was just something he said to get him off the hook.'

Joan remembered Stephen at the hospital, emotional and passionate at her bedside as he called her his Princess, his Queen, his Brave Little Girl, and she felt the Dragon's gullet opening wide to swallow her whole. Unable to fight anymore, she let it take her. What did it matter anymore?

She stood up and walked out of the room. She heard Olivia's voice as she came after her, crying, and felt the feeble attempts to hold her back, shaking fingers clutching at Joan's hands, her dress, the sleeves of her cardigan. She pulled away, flung open the flat door, collected her case and shoulder bag, and started to descend the staircase. Her feet began to follow the pattern of her thoughts, moving faster and faster with no real idea of their direction. Halfway down the stairs, her case hit the newel post and was knocked from her hand, tumbling away down the staircase, breaking open as it hit the hallway parquet, spilling clothes and shoes over the papers and junk mail. She didn't bother to retrieve anything on her way out. Her momentum was the only thing that was keeping her on her feet.

When she closed the front door on the sound of her sister's uneven voice calling her name, she knew that her life was over.

16

Out on the streets it was a twilight world, and it was a world Joan couldn't seem to recognise. She didn't know if she had spent longer with Olivia than she'd realised, or if she had somehow lost several hours since leaving her sister's flat, for she had no idea at all of the time, nor of where she was.

All she could think was that she must have wandered a long way, because there were no familiar landmarks for her to lock on to. Everything looked strange and menacing. She felt like a tourist in a foreign city, an alien, claustrophobic maze where she didn't understand the language and couldn't read any of the signs that might have helped her. Her face was wet with tears, her eyes like open wounds, and every part of her ached.

And then she realised that she was terrified. She was suddenly hands-shaking, skin-crawling, piss-down-the-leg terrified.

It was more than the sensation of being utterly lost, more than the paranoid fear that the strange, looming buildings were slowly closing in on her like the jaws of a vice and would eventually crush her. The worst by far were the people she passed as she hurried along the crowded pavements at a frantic pace, the people who milled around her on business and pleasures she could not guess and feared to learn.

Their faces were just smudges, ugly misshapen blurs without feature or expression. But she knew that behind each and every one of these non-faces there was a judgemental mind at work, one that was aware of all that had happened to her. She felt their scornful attention like heat from some strange nocturnal sun, and when they spoke aloud in their gibberish language, her mind translated their sly comments into English.

Look at that stupid woman, they said. *She's such a fool*, they said. *Run*, they said. *Your life is over*. And they laughed at her, like gleeful demons.

Joan needed time and space to think, to recover, some haven where the expression of love was not a mask for treachery, and where kindness was a simple truth, not a hideous lie. She needed all the things that had been denied her, all the things that had been taken away and forbidden. But she knew that she would never find such a place. This was the Dragon's gullet. This was misery heaped on misery. It was hell. She had not survived the hit-and-run at all, and her struggle to recover had been a self-serving lie, a near-death delusion that had now run its course.

A sea of alien faces swept toward her. She felt the increased pressure of their telepathic enmity, and she turned and ran from it, weaving and dodging as many of them as she could, shouldering her way past those she could not. She heard their voices raised in surprised anger, and ran even faster as her panic overcame her exhaustion.

Then, suddenly, in the distance, she at last saw something that was familiar, that she knew only too well. It was a lighted sign, with letters and words she could actually read: London Underground, Kentish Town. Now she knew exactly where she was. A strange thought arose in her mind, that time had doubled back on itself, but she ignored the sensation of danger this thought gave her. The promise of immediate safety overrode every other consideration.

Joan jumped between two parked vehicles and dashed out into the road. Instantly she heard some colossal noise that sounded like a scream, and she imagined that she was making it, that everything had finally got loose from her. But a second later she recognised the sound for what it really was, for she had heard it before, both in reality and in her countless, endless nightmares.

It *was* screaming, but it was not human. It was the scream of rubber on tarmac, the noise made by a car as it braked hard.

Joan turned, and saw the full-beam headlights racing toward her, and froze.

This time I'll really die, she thought.

17

The phone began to ring, waking Olivia from a dead sleep. Her living room was in darkness, and it was only the streetlight coming in through the window that let her know where she was. For a moment her mind was a blank and she wondered what she was doing lying here in the dark, and then the recent past lunged at her like an enemy and she felt sick and exhausted all over again.

Olivia had cried herself to sleep on the sofa where Joan had sat earlier, and the throw she had pulled over herself was now half on the floor and half wound about her legs, as though she had thrashed her way through a bad dream. Probably she had done just that, though she had no recollection of dreaming. She was sweating and the skin around her eyes felt crusty with old tears.

She sat up stiffly, and saw from the digital display on the DVD that it was after nine o'clock at night. She had been conked out for a good few hours. But that had always been her way of dealing with pain; she escaped into sleep. Joan's reaction, her last resort, had always been to run away, both physically and mentally.

Oh my God, she thought. Joan!

The telephone on the table under the window continued to ring, and her first fully conscious thought, her hope, was that it was her sister calling in response to all the messages Olivia had left on her mobile. Joan could abuse her to her heart's content as far as Olivia was concerned, because that would at least mean she was safe. Safe, and fighting back against the shock. But then she had a terrible premonition, made worse by how possible it all seemed.

The person who was trying to reach her, who was prepared to let the phone ring and ring, was Stephen. He was calling from a hospital, where he was at Joan's bedside. Either she had been knocked down again, or she had actually thrown herself in front of a car. Or maybe a train. Maybe she had gone down to the tube station, waited until the litter on the platform was being lifted off the ground by a constant stream of rushing air, and then thrown herself on to the tracks.

We'd be responsible, Olivia thought. Me and Stephen. We drove her to it. She didn't jump, we pushed her.

She got up off the sofa, brushing back lank strands of hair from her sweaty forehead, and went across to the window. Her hand hesitated above the telephone. She didn't know if she had the strength to do this. She could imagine Stephen's voice hissing through the line and into her ear, a low whisper that carried the psychic scent of his breath, as he said, 'It's okay, we're in the clear - she's dead.'

Olivia shook her head to clear it. Maybe she was still half asleep, because that last thought came straight out of the nightmare she may have had. The phone rang on and on, shrill and insistent, and eventually she picked it up. She brought the receiver to her ear, but found herself unable to speak. In the background she could hear a television news programme, some local politician being hammered by questions that he evaded with suave, insolent ease.

'Hello? Hello, Olivia? Are you there? Hello?'

She heard the sound on the television being muted. The complete silence that followed made her think that this call was probably not being made from a hospital. There was always a lot of background noise in a hospital. She knew this from experience.

'Yes, Stephen,' she said, her voice scarcely more than a breath. 'I'm here. Where are you?'

'At home.'

Olivia closed her eyes in relief.

'Thank God you're there,' Stephen said. 'I thought… Well, I didn't know what I was thinking.'

'Do you ever?'

Stephen was silent, and she could almost hear the cogs slowly turning as he tried to think of a snappy comeback. At last, he simply said, 'I'm phoning to speak to Joan.'

'Yes,' Olivia replied. 'I know you are.'

'Has she calmed down yet?'

'I very much doubt it.'

There were a few more seconds of silence as he digested the tone of her voice. Then he made a sound that was half-sigh, half-groan. 'What a bloody mess this is. Can I speak to her?'

'No.'

'I need to speak to her, Olivia. We've got to sort this before it gets completely out of hand. Put her on, please. I know she wants to talk to me. Whatever she *says* she wants, I know that she wants to speak to me. She needs to.'

'I don't think so.'

Stephen sighed again, this time in pure exasperation. 'Olivia, I want to speak to Joan - right now! Please put her on.'

'I can't do that.'

'Yes, you can. Just do it.'

'Stephen, she's not here.'

'Oh come on, spare me the fairy tales. You just said yourself--'

'She was here for a while.'

'Yes, and she's *still* there, so put her on.'

'She's gone, Stephen. We talked. I talked. And then she left.'

This time the silence from the other end of the line was immense, and Olivia quietly broke out into fresh tears.

100

'You told her, didn't you?' Stephen asked in a hollow voice. 'You told her *again*? You stupid little bitch.'

'She had a right to know,' Olivia said. 'She had a right to the truth. Between the two of us we've screwed her up so much—'

'Oh for fuck's sake…' Stephen then began to swear, abusing, insulting and threatening her in a venomous tirade that lasted for several minutes, during the course of which Olivia finally realised that he was thoroughly drunk.

'You should be grateful to me,' she said when his immediate anger had been exhausted. 'Now you're free to do whatever you want, sleep with whoever you want.'

'That isn't what I want!' he shouted. 'That was never what I wanted! All I wanted was…'

'What? What did you want?'

Stephen's silence was now as eloquent as his abuse. He hadn't known what he wanted; now he did, and it was too late, it was gone. They were almost the lyrics to a song, Olivia thought, but couldn't remember the name of the woman who sang it. She heard a bottle rattle around the rim of a glass. She heard Stephen swallow deeply. She waited.

'I wanted to change,' he said eventually. 'Just like I told you in the hospital last year. I tried to change. But then Joan went from being slightly crazy to being completely crazy.'

'I think we both had something to do with that, didn't we? On some level, I think she already knew about us, and it was destroying her.'

Stephen went on as though she had not spoken. 'It was bad enough before, but after she had her little accident, she…'

'Don't call it that,' Olivia said sharply.

'What?'

'She always hated you calling it that. Her "little accident". She felt you were making a joke of it, and of her.'

'All I was doing was trying to play it down,' Stephen protested. 'I was trying to minimise its effect on her life.'

'You were trying to minimise the effect of it on your life, Stephen, and that's not the same thing, is it?'

She heard him pouring himself another shot of whatever he was drinking. By now he would be red-eyed, his vision as bleary as his voice was becoming, and soon he would either fall asleep or throw up. A bitter, vengeful part of Olivia hoped that he would do both and choke on his own vomit.

'You're getting off on this, aren't you?' Stephen said, his voice a drunken sneer. 'You're *loving* this. What is it, Olivia - revenge? All this time you've been pretending to be Joan's best friend, the new improved Olivia, bloody arselicking Sister of the Year! But you've just been waiting for the right moment, haven't you? Saving up your precious honesty for the time it would cause the most damage. Are you finally happy now?'

It was some time before Olivia replied, in part because she made an honest attempt to examine her own motivations for what she had done in the light of Stephen's accusation. She also wanted a moment to bring the worst of her emotions under control, the immediate urge to strike back, because she realised that it was fuelled not by Stephen's attack but by her own feelings of guilt. Antagonising Stephen wouldn't help Joan, and helping Joan was all she cared about right now.

'I understand why you'd want to believe that,' she told Stephen calmly. 'It's the sort of thing I would have been capable of in the past. But not now, not after everything that's happened. I really have changed.'

Stephen grunted contemptuously, and then muttered something derisive that Olivia didn't hear properly.

'And if I managed to change, Stephen, after all these years, it means that you can too. You don't have to go on repeating the same mistakes. If you can show Joan that you've changed, you can win her back.'

'How could I do that after today?' He was at his lowest now, drunk, miserable, and defeated. 'What chance would I have?'

'Maybe no chance at all,' Olivia admitted. 'But you'll never know if you don't try. If you really love her, you'll try.'

Stephen was quiet for a while, and Olivia could only hear his laboured breathing. She thought that he was crying, and she hoped it wasn't just the booze.

'How?' he sniffed. 'How do I start?'

'One step at a time. A lot of small, careful steps. We'll both take them. The first is just to find her.'

Stephen seemed to pull himself together a little. 'I'll call her on her mobile.'

'No point, I've already tried that. She must have switched it off. I left messages asking her to call back, but I don't hold out much hope.'

'Okay, I'll start phoning round the hotels,' he said. 'Ask if she's registered.'

'Check under her maiden name, too,' Olivia suggested.

'Right. Good idea. What are you going to do?'

'Me?' She sighed heavily. 'I'll phone around the hospitals. Just in case.'

She didn't have to explain what she meant. They both knew.

After she hung up, Olivia felt a little better. Not much, but some. Enough to do what she had to, anyway. She reached for the phone book.

18

It was full dark now, and the wide lay-by where the white van was parked was striped with the long shadows of trees that stood between it and the well-lighted major road to which it ran parallel and rejoined about two-hundred yards farther on. The shadows clung to the numerous other vehicles also parked in the lay-by, vans and lorries mostly, and formed deep pools that hid the enormous pot-holes in the cinder road surface.

At the lay-by's centre, backing on to more trees, was the hub of this automotive community - an ancient eight-berth caravan converted into a transport café. Lights blazed from the two visible windows and steam escaped through an aluminium vent that had been let into the roof. It looked like the set of an extremely low-budget science fiction film.

Joan, still wearing her seatbelt in the van's passenger seat, was too weary to move. She was also too tired to think clearly and whenever she tried a blanket of confusion fell over her. All she really wanted was to do was sleep. Once or twice she had found herself nodding, but she had grimly fought it off. Sleep would have to wait, until she could decide whether she was safe or not. At the moment the circumstances were a little too strange for her to make that decision.

The image of those approaching headlights came back to her, and the scream of the tyres. She thought that she had either fainted at that point or had been about to, because her vision had seemed to explode into black static and she had the sensation of falling. But then she had found herself clasped firmly by a pair of strongly muscled arms, and a man was speaking into her ear. His voice was both gruff and gentle at the same time, with a strong accent that seemed very familiar but which she couldn't immediately place. His breath smelled faintly, but not unpleasantly, of tobacco.

In any case, it wasn't any of the elements that made up this man's voice that brought her back from her near faint. It was what he said.

'Mrs Crosby?' he'd said. 'Is that *you*?'

She remembered being led toward the vehicle that had almost hit her and being helped into the passenger seat. She had heard the seatbelt clicking home and felt the strap being adjusted across her chest. The door was closed, pushed to rather than slammed. All of these actions seemed to be performed with a kind of shy tenderness that for some

105

reason reminded her of the intimacies of teenage crushes.

Perhaps she actually did faint then, or perhaps slept without realising. When she next opened her eyes she was being driven through the London streets.

'Mrs Crosby, are you all right?' the voice asked. 'Are you hurt?'

Joan had shaken her head, and was dismayed by the way the world appeared to tilt from angle to angle, as though her eyes were mounted on springs. The headlights of on-coming vehicles were blinding. She closed her eyes again.

'What were you doing in the road like that?'

She shrugged.

'Where were you going?'

Joan shrugged again.

'Bloody 'ell,' the voice said. Now it seemed both rueful and bemused in addition to its other qualities. 'Look at the cut of you!'

Joan had a sense of the owner of the voice leaning closer, studying her even as the van sped on.

'How long is it since you've eaten anything?' he wanted to know.

After some careful calculation, which seemed much more difficult than it should have been, Joan managed to say, 'Breakfast.'

The voice grunted in an almost satisfied way. 'No wonder you look like death warmed up. Right,' it said firmly, 'let's do something about that first.'

Now Joan focussed on the makeshift transport café her mysterious saviour had disappeared into some minutes ago. Exactly how many minutes ago, Joan couldn't have said. Through one of the windows she could see two men in dusty blue overalls mopping up the remains of fried meals with folded slices of bread. Pint pots of tea steamed between them. The other window must have been the kitchen area, for it was completely steamed over, and murky silhouettes moved back and forth behind it like shadow puppets.

She glanced over at the road she could see between the trees, which was still rush-hour busy, and she realised that it was probably the North Circular. She sometimes came this way to get to the IKEA store at Wembley. How many times had she passed this little lay-by and never seen it?

She heard a door slam and she looked back at the café.

A tall, slim male figure, black against the café's lights, was walking across to the van, carefully weaving its way between the invisible pot-holes. As the man passed through shards of light from the nearby road, she saw that he was carrying a small cardboard box in both hands, but she couldn't see well enough to make out the details of his face.

Joan grew more nervous as he approached the van, and she looked away as he opened the door and slid into his seat. A strong smell of bacon accompanied him.

'Sorry it took so long,' he said. 'Busy in there tonight.'

He began unloading the contents of the cardboard box on to the dashboard; two polystyrene cups with plastic lids, a couple of spoons, some packets of sugar, and two bulging white paper bags liberally spotted with grease. He tossed the empty box over his shoulder into the back of the van, which Joan had already seen was a jumble of tools, drop-cloths, ladders, paint cans, fillers and mastic guns. He was a tradesman of some description, it seemed, probably a decorator. She watched his large hands as he delicately began peeling the lids off the cups.

'I don't know if you take sugar, but you should probably have some anyway. Help you get your strength back.'

While he was occupied, Joan stole a quick glance at his face, and was surprised. The owner of this gruff, gentle, kind voice was no older than twenty-five at the most, ten years younger than Joan herself. He was very good looking in a natural sort of way, and had piercing blue eyes, full lips, and mousy blond hair long enough to cover his ears. He was wearing paint-spotted jeans and a denim jacket, under which was a clean white t-shirt. The accent was broad northern.

At the very back of her mind, Joan experienced a tiny flicker of recognition.

'I'd've taken you inside to eat,' he said, 'but it's a bit rough and ready in there, if you know what I mean. And anyway, you didn't look like you were ready to be seen in public.'

Joan nodded. He was right about that. No way was she ready.

'Now, believe it or not,' the young man said, reaching for one of the greasy paper bags from the dashboard, 'these are the best bacon butties in the whole of London - not that that's saying much, mind.' He caught Joan looking at him and smiled. 'Come on, lass, they're getting cold.'

108

Joan automatically took the second bag from the dashboard and opened it. Inside was a large soft bread roll that appeared to have about half a pound of meat stuffed inside it. Now that the bag was open, the odour was no longer merely the smell of bacon - it was the very atmosphere of the Planet Bacon. Feeling like a cartoon character, Joan realised that her mouth was actually watering. Her stomach gurgled aggressively.

'Aye, I know how you feel,' the man said, and bit into his sandwich.

Joan forced herself to wait a few more moments, even though her whole body was crying out to be fed. There was something she had to know first. 'I know this is going to sound stupid,' she said, 'but you *know* me, don't you?'

'Aye, 'cos I do.'

'Then this is going to sound even more stupid. Do *I* know *you*?'

The young man paused with a mouthful of bacon and gave her a comical look. 'You should do.' He nodded at her sandwich. 'Eat that up, it'll do you good. We can talk after.'

Joan took a small bite from a rasher that protruded from the cheap bread roll and began to chew. The bacon was mostly fat and gristle flash fried to a smoky crispness. It had been years since she had eaten anything this unhealthy. The taste was unearthly, divine.

'Good?' he asked.

Joan nodded.

'Well don't be shy then - get stuck in!'

Nothing more was said for the next few minutes, as both of them were too busy eating. Once she had started, Joan found it impossible to stop. She wasn't sure if the bacon sandwich was really as good as she thought it was, or whether it only tasted that way because she hadn't eaten since eight that morning. But in the end it didn't matter - soon she was popping the last piece of bread into her mouth and looking for something to wipe the grease from her fingers with. The young man pulled a box of tissues out of the back of the van and they each took one.

When he reached for his tea, he smiled at Joan again. 'Go on, have you worked it out yet - where you know me from?'

Joan shook her head. 'No, I'm sorry, I haven't.'

'Bloody 'ell, you must go around with your head in the clouds.' He laughed, not unpleasantly. 'I'm your odd-job man, lass. Been working in your area for best part of eighteen months now. Done lots of work in your street. Your old man had me replace all your guttering last November.'

'Ah…'

Now it began to make a kind of sense to Joan. November had been a bad time for her. Very bad. It had been the month between her two non-social meetings with DCI Richardson, a time when she hadn't been taking a lot in. Not a lot of reality, anyway. Her head must indeed have been in the clouds. That explained why she felt that she half-knew the young man without exactly remembering him.

'Me name's Yorkie,' he volunteered. 'Sort of a nickname I picked up from when I was in the army,

110

cos I was the only one in the regiment from Yorkshire. Don't you remember the sign on me van?' he asked. 'Yorkie - no job too odd? That was an attention-grabber, that was. Got a lot of work out of that.'

Joan was caught halfway between shaking and nodding her head. 'I don't know,' she said. 'Maybe.'

The young man twisted in his seat to face her more squarely. He looked puzzled, amused and concerned all at the same time. It was a very kindly expression, one that Joan immediately warmed to.

'Why did you bring me here?' she asked.

He smiled. 'Well, I couldn't just leave you where I found you, could I? You'd have been knocked down, for sure. Besides, I never saw a woman in greater need of a bacon sandwich in me whole bloody life.'

Joan laughed a little, which in itself felt like a bit of a miracle.

'Look, mebbe it's none of my business,' he said, 'but you've made me right curious now. What's happened to put you in this state?'

Joan let out a tired sigh. 'That's a very long story.'

'Aye well, sometimes that's best kind. Bend me ear if you like, I don't mind.'

Joan looked back at his face, and got lost for a moment in the steady calmness of his eyes. To all intents and purposes this man was a complete stranger to her, and she wondered if she could tell him about Stephen and Olivia. She wondered if she could tell him about the Dragon's gullet.

She didn't know. But as he continued to stare at her, she was suddenly aware that she wanted to talk to someone, perhaps needed to. Why shouldn't it be a stranger? Why shouldn't it be him?

'You don't have to, you know,' he said gently. 'Not if you don't want. I get the feeling you've had enough pressure for one day without me adding to it. You look like…'

'Like what?' she asked.

He hesitated for just a moment more, and then said, 'Like somebody's hurt you really bad.'

Joan sipped her tea, stronger and a great deal sweeter than she liked, but good all the same. All at once, after years of abstinence, she wished she had a cigarette. When she asked the young man if he had some, he wordlessly took a tobacco tin from his jacket pocket and made a couple of roll-ups, one for her and one for himself, finally lighting them with an old worn Zippo that had some kind of crest or coat of arms on it. Joan inhaled deeply and did not cough. He opened his window a couple of inches, tapped out ash, and then turned back to her expectantly.

She could feel his kindly attention pressing against the side of her face. It wasn't an intrusion. It was comforting, like a pillow. She could also feel the nicotine invading her body, travelling swiftly along long-abandoned tributaries in her nervous system, and she found herself relaxing even more.

'Have you ever…' she said. 'Have you ever been married?'

19

The phone rang, a harsh rasp in the dusty silence of her flat, and Olivia awoke with a neck-breaking start. Wide-eyed, she focussed on the shrieking phone less than a foot from her face, and realised that she had managed to fall asleep yet again, this time with her arms resting on the table and her head resting on the phone book like a firm pillow. A small comma of drool she had left on the cover gleamed in the light from her table lamp.

It seemed to be her night, she thought fuzzily, for being woken by the telephone. This time, however, falling asleep had been the last thing on her mind, and it had taken her entirely unawares. There had been no discernible signs of drowsiness that would have alerted her to the urgent need for strong coffee. No drooping eyelids, no periods of blank inattention. Just *wham*, you're asleep, as though she had passed out. Emotional exhaustion.

The DVD display told her it was now after eleven o'clock, about two hours since Stephen's call. She guessed that she had been asleep for no more than twenty minutes at most, but her bad dreams, which this time she *did* remember, had seemed to last for hours. Usually Olivia dreamed in bright, vivid colour, but tonight she had dreamed in a kaleidoscope of soft greys, great swathes of images that had both the fibrous texture of moth wings and the durability of tattoos.

While she slept she had seen Joan twice leaving her apartment in tears. The first time it had been winter, the second time summer. She had also seen Joan slumped in a filthy doorway like a homeless person, her cheeks sunken and her eyes dead, all her prettiness swallowed up by premature age and unbearable loss. She had seen Joan swallowing a multitude of pills in a shabby hotel room, and Joan lying unattended on a hospital gurney as her spirit rose from a catastrophically broken body and dark blood pooled around the gurney's rubber wheels.

Hovering close to the ceiling, the spirit had looked accusingly at Olivia, its breathless blue lips sending her a message she could not bring herself to read, but which she knew anyway.

You killed me.

Olivia shook her head, as though she could dislodge this stubborn image or deny the fate it seemed to foretell for her sister, but it didn't work. That would have been too easy. She knew that she didn't deserve such a simple absolution.

She picked up the phone and croaked a hello.

There was no immediate reply, only a soft, somehow masculine breathing on the open line.

'Hello?' she called again, more clearly this time. 'Stephen, is that you?'

'Olivia?' It *was* Stephen, but his voice sounded impossibly distant, as though it came from the end of a long, long tunnel. 'Olivia?'

Olivia took a deep breath and forced herself more fully awake. 'Stephen,' she said loudly, 'speak into the phone.'

'Uh?'

There was a crackle on the line, then the whispering sound of the receiver being dragged over fabric. Olivia could see Stephen making hard work of raising the phone from his shoulder, wondering how it had got away from him.

'Oh, yeah. That any better?'

Better? It was louder, certainly. Unfortunately, now that she was able to hear him properly, Olivia could tell that far from sobering up, Stephen had had even more to drink. Either that or it was only now catching up with him. He sounded drugged.

'Olivia?' he shouted into the phone.

She winced. 'Stephen - turn the volume down, for God's sake.'

'What volume? Oh, I get it.' He unleashed an idiotic drunken chortle that set Olivia's teeth on edge. 'It's me,' he said. 'Stephen.'

'Yes, I'd guessed that.'

'Yeah, it's me.' He drifted away for a moment or two before coming back, and Olivia could see him in the darkened living room, feet up on the coffee table, temporarily distracted by the images on the muted TV. 'Mmm?' he said. 'Okay. Listen, how did you do? Any luck at the hospitals?'

'No, fortunately not.'

Olivia quickly filled him in on what she had been doing since they had last spoken. She had progressed from phoning the local hospitals, the Whittington and the Royal Free, to phoning all the hospitals she could find in the London phone book, of which there were a surprising number. Some of them were private hospitals, some of them had no A&E department, and some of them catered solely for specific conditions, like tropical diseases, or asthma, or even mental disorders.

But whatever they were, Olivia had called every one, braving dismissive receptionists, overworked staff, and infuriatingly indistinct answer-phones. Not one of the people she had spoken to had heard of Joan Crosby, or knew of any woman of her description who may have been involved in an accident or suicide attempt within the last few hours.

'Good,' Stephen said when she had finished, now managing even to slur this one simple word. 'That's good.'

'And, as you asked me first,' Olivia said, 'I'm assuming that you didn't find her either?'

'No, I didn't. I didn't. I phoned about a million hotels, though,' he said thickly, and made a noise that sounded to Olivia like a smothered belch. 'Thirty of 'em, at least. I don't think she was there.'

Olivia closed her eyes and tried to control her impatience. 'Stephen, what do you mean, you think?'

'Well, it's hard to be sure. When I called I gave 'em alternative names, like you said - even Olivia and Elaine, just in case she was being cryptic - and I described what she looked like, and what she was wearing the last time I saw her.'

'Okay - so?'

'So some of the hotels - the better ones, that is - wouldn't even talk to me. "We can't divulge our customers' details",' he said in a pathetic mincing drawl, 'they were all like that. They advised me to contact the police.' His voice began to take on a tone of injustice. 'Some of 'em thought I was just some kind of drunken practical joker. One even had the nerve to hang up on me!'

I wonder why, Olivia thought, sighing.

116

'Well, what about contacting the police?' she said. 'You have friends there, don't you? They could help.'

Drunk or not, Stephen paused before answering. When he did, his voice was cautious and defensive, and fractionally more sober. 'Yeah, I suppose I could... but they won't be interested in a domestic situation like this. It's not like Joan's a missing person, or anything like that. She just walked out on me. Must happen a million times a day.'

'Just walked out on you?' Olivia echoed sharply. 'With her history - what do you mean just?'

'You know what I mean, Olivia.'

'I hope I do.'

She listened to his breathing for a while, trying to calm down a little. Despite her needling of him, Olivia thought that Stephen was right about the police's probable reaction to their reporting of Joan's absence - certainly after such a short space of time, anyway. And although she believed that he was still more interested in his own reputation than in finding Joan, she decided to let it go for now. The situation was bad enough as it was. Fighting between themselves would only make it worse.

'Okay,' she said briskly. 'The question now is, where do we go from here? Where do we look next?'

'I don't know. I can try phoning around her friends - our friends - I suppose... David and Alicia, maybe... or... you know... but I can't believe she'd...'

Stephen's voice slowly trailed off. At first Olivia thought it was because he was thinking over an idea that had come to him while he was speaking, but after

117

the silence had drawn out for more than a few seconds, she realised it was because he had run out of ideas altogether. The alcohol had finally accomplished its work. His imagination was a radar screen upon which there was no traffic, not a single blip.

'Stephen?'

'Yeah, I'm here,' he said.

'What were you saying?'

'Saying? Nothing. I don't know, I'm tired.'

'Stephen, we've got to--'

'Listen. Olivia. I've had it for tonight, I really have. I need to get some sleep. I'll start over again in the morning, okay? I'll sleep now. I'll phone all the hotels again tomorrow, and this time I'll make them talk to me…I'll call friends…whoever…whatever it takes…'

Olivia listened as Stephen continued to ramble in this haphazard fashion, steadily becoming less coherent as the telephone once again drifted away from his mouth. She heard him say that he loved Joan, wanted her, and needed her, but in the face of his extreme drunkenness and her own jaundiced view of his character, it sounded like so much lip service.

After a while, Olivia quietly hung up on him. At some point Stephen would discover that he was talking only to himself and then go to sleep. Or not.

'Okay,' Olivia said to herself quietly. 'We'll both try again in the morning.'

Unlike Stephen, however, she knew that she wouldn't be content with making phone calls. The results would be too uncertain. But eyeball to eyeball, she believed that even the strictest hotel manager would tell her what she wanted to know, and she would drag Stephen around every hotel in London, if that was what it took. She thought it was important that they not only found Joan, but that they found her together. Failure was not an option.

But at the same time she couldn't help thinking, what if they still hadn't found her by this time tomorrow?

Well, she thought. Maybe then it would be time to take the advice of the better class of hotel, and involve the police.

20

It was just before midnight by the time the man Joan knew only as Yorkie parked his van under a broken streetlight in a long, unremarkable Bounds Green residential street about a mile from the Piccadilly Line tube station. On either side of the road lights still showed through the curtains of many of the houses, both upstairs and down, but the road itself was deserted. Not even a solitary dog-walker was in evidence when they climbed out of the van. No cars passed by.

As she stood waiting for Yorkie to walk around the van, Joan noticed the slightly cleaner rectangle on the van's side-panel where, presumably, the sign the young man had seemed so proud of should have been.

'What happened to it?' she asked.

'Eh?'

'Your sign, No Job Too Odd?'

'Vandalised,' he said, so quietly that she almost didn't hear. 'Graffiti all over both of them. Swear words, filthy drawings, the lot.'

119

'Oh, that's terrible,' Joan replied, unconsciously lowering her voice to match his. 'Aren't some people awful.'

'Aye, well, they are,' he shrugged. 'Luckily they were just them magnetised things, but I haven't got around to replacing them yet.' Then he noticed that Joan was shivering. 'Come on, lass, let's get off the street. Here, give me that.'

Yorkie took Joan's shoulder bag and carried it for her while she walked beside him most of the way down the road, pulling on her cardigan against the night's chill.

After sixty or seventy paces, he apologised about them having to walk so far. 'The parking's bloody terrible round here,' he told her in the same near whisper. 'I can get never get a place on my own street, they're like gold-dust.'

'It's the same everywhere, I think.'

A few seconds later, he turned left off the pavement and led her through a dark, narrow, weed-choked alleyway between houses and into another identically anonymous street, and then almost immediately down a short flight of stone steps to the front door of a basement flat. As she descended the steps, Joan glanced back at the road in surprise.

'Actually, there are lots of parking spaces,' she said.

'Aye, bloody typical, isn't it? And if I'd wanted one, it wouldn't have been there, would it.'

He let them in and walked ahead of her down a dark musty hallway to a second door. After he had slipped his key into the lock, he looked back at Joan with what looked like another apologetic expression

120

on his face. What little light there was seemed to gather in his blue eyes, making them luminous.

'Now, I told you not to expect a palace, didn't I?'

'I'm just grateful to you for giving me a bed for the night,' Joan replied honestly. 'I'm almost asleep on my feet, and the idea of looking for a hotel at this time… all I can say is thank you.'

'No need for that,' he smiled. 'We're old friends, now. And you don't have to thank friends.'

Old friends, Joan thought tiredly.

Well, in a way, maybe that's what they were. After listening to her tale of woe for the last hour and a half, the young man probably knew more about her life than her own psychiatrist. He was certainly more up to date. She remembered his single comment when she had finally fallen silent, mopping up yet more tears with a handful of tissues from the box in the back of the van.

'Bloody 'ell, lass,' he'd said. 'There aren't enough hours in the day for you, are there? What kind of crap have you got planned for tomorrow?'

As far as Joan was concerned, there had been more than enough hours in *this* day. It had seemed unending. And as for tomorrow - well, try as she might, she could not imagine what tomorrow would be like. Nevertheless, the young man had managed to make her laugh yet again, which he seemed able to do with remarkable ease.

Now he turned the key and opened the door on to a much deeper darkness. 'Here we are - home sweet home,' he said. His voice was filled with gentle irony as he bowed her in.

Joan recoiled a little as an acrid odour billowed out of the dark and invaded her nostrils. 'What's that smell? Damp?'

'Nah, that'll be me chemicals.'

'What chemicals?'

He snapped on the light-switch just inside the doorway, flooding the room beyond with harsh light. 'Developer, fixer, toner, stuff like that.' He stepped into the flat and gestured for Joan to follow him. 'For when I develop and print me own photographs, like. Don't worry, you'll hardly notice it in a minute.'

Joan doubtfully stepped into the small, grim room beside him and took a quick, almost horrified inventory. She thought it was a good job he had warned her not to expect a palace, because it was about as far from being one as a flat could be.

The white glossed woodwork was uniformly yellowed. The floor was covered, almost wall to wall, with a threadbare green carpet. There was a single bed along one wall with a cheap nightstand at its head, from the edges of which long strips of off-white melamine were peeling. Along the wall to her immediate left were a matching wardrobe and a chest of drawers, although only matched to the extent that they were in a similar state of dilapidation. Beyond these was a doorway without an actual door, leading to a short corridor, which was where the awful carpet gave way to a length of curling, cracked linoleum.

In the diagonally opposite corner of the room to the flat door, adjacent to the small, high windows, was a small table with an antique-looking enlarger on top and a jumble of bathing trays, boxes of photographic paper, and slide boxes underneath. The peeling, no-colour wallpaper was covered with unframed black and white photographs, mostly of easily-recognised London scenes, and a recent National Portrait Gallery exhibition poster. Apart from these few decorative touches, the only things in the whole place that looked even vaguely new were the black-out curtains over the windows and the plain blue linen on the bed.

To avoid passing comment for as long as possible, Joan pointed at the photographs on the walls. 'So this is your hobby - photography?'

'Yeah. I've sold a few images to photo libraries and the like, but yeah, it's just a hobby, really.' He looked at her. 'Well, what do you think?'

'Of the flat? Well…'

He laughed out loud. 'No need to be polite, you know. I know it's a bloody dump. But it's dirt-cheap, and the landlord doesn't bother me.' He put her bag on the bed and then closed the door. 'Besides, this isn't me real home. It's just a place to stay while I'm making some readies in London. More money down here than up there.'

He beckoned her across the room. Above the chest of drawers was an age-spotted mirror hung from a screw by a length of rusting chain, and blue-tacked to the glass was a matt eight-by-ten photograph of what at first glance looked like a large shed or small barn, brick built to waist height, the rest of it shiplap timber, with an ancient bowed roof of hand-made tiles. Two small windows flanked a plain wooden door. It was a farm out-building of some kind, Joan guessed.

'This is me real home,' he said as she stopped beside him. 'The ancestral pile, you might say.'

It was the pride evident in his voice that made Joan lean forward to examine the photograph more closely, and she was surprised. The building was much less basic than she had first realised. The small windows were double-glazed, and she could make out curtains hanging behind them. There was some kind of decorative knocker on the door, and a thin plume of smoke hung above a neat terracotta chimney pot. It was also bigger than Joan had thought. She had been misled partly by the enormous size of the trees that were its backdrop and which completely dwarfed it. Oak trees, they looked like, at least a hundred years old.

Close up, the young man's home didn't look like an outbuilding at all; it looked like the kind of cottage that would make a Hampstead estate agent's mouth water in anticipation at the size of his commission. Joan could imagine wealthy stockbrokers commuting to it at the weekend. They would boast to their friends of their country retreat's rural charm, the chunk of peace and serenity they had bought. In which they had invested. It seemed like a different world from the glorified bedsit she was standing in.

'This is yours?' she asked.

'Aye, all mine. It's called Hunter's Lodge.'

'Where is it?'

'On the border of the North Yorkshire Moors, about twenty-odd miles south of Whitby. Nice bit of forest, backs on to the National Park.'

'It's really beautiful.'

'Aye, it is.' He reached out and drew the tips of his fingers over the photograph. 'I grew up there, just me and me uncle. Me family were farmers originally, you see, but over the years they had to sell off most of the land. This's all that's left now, the cottage and a couple of acres of land, but it's enough for me.'

Smiling, he touched the images of the tall trees with the same reverence he had shown the cottage. 'When you're there it's like being a part of the forest,' he said. 'A part of Nature, almost.'

Joan was able to study his face as he continued to stare at the photograph. It was as though he had forgotten she was there. She thought that he actually seemed to have been transported there, his blue eyes seeing far beyond the walls of the grubby north London basement flat. He was breathing deeply, as though inhaling the scents of his childhood. Joan imagined pine, apple blossom, wood-smoke, and freshly turned earth.

'That's the place I'm happiest,' he said. 'I can wake up in the morning and step out of me front door stark bollock naked if I want to, and it doesn't matter, because it's like I'm the only man on Earth. I'm telling you, you can't whack it.'

When he came out of his self-induced trance, he noticed Joan smiling at him, and he laughed at himself. 'Aye, I know I go on a bit when I get going.'

'No, it's nice. It's more than nice. I don't blame you for being enthusiastic.'

He touched the photograph again briefly. 'Having that waiting for me,' he said, 'is worth putting up with this.'

Joan looked around the flat, to which he had indicated dismissively, and she nodded. 'I can see that.'

They looked at each other for a long moment, and then Joan said, 'Look, can I ask you a question?'

'Aye, probably.'

'What's your real name? I can't call you Yorkie all the time. It feels... I don't know, funny, I suppose.'

'Me name's Mark,' he said immediately. 'Mark Bowman.'

'Mark,' she nodded. She held out her hand. 'And I'm Joan.'

He took her hand and gently shook it. 'I'm right pleased to meet you, Joan,' he said.

A little while later, Joan took her shoulder bag from the bed and excused herself to go to the bathroom, a tiny square cube with just about enough space for a toilet, a basin and a corner shower cubicle. All of the fittings were old and dismally aged, but they were also, she was pleased to note, exceptionally clean. The equally small kitchen she had passed on the way to the bathroom had seemed to be in much the same condition. She could hear Mark banging about in there now through the thin plasterboard partition wall, as he filled the kettle and found a couple of mugs. Like most of the other northerners Joan had known, Mark seemed to hold the same belief in the curative powers of strong tea that stereotypical Jewish mothers did in chicken soup.

And who knew, maybe they were right. Both offerings were acts of kindness, and at this moment, Joan wasn't above kindness.

She quickly washed her hands and face in lukewarm water and then examined herself in the cracked mirror tiles that Mark's landlord had seen fit to stick to the wall above the basin with uneven globs of filler. The discoloured reflection was a depressing sight. Her hair had lost its shape and become a lacquered helmet that clung tightly to her head. Her face was pale far beyond any illusion of delicacy, and her hazel eyes looked dark and huge, with purple blotches beneath them.

She sought for the word that would precisely describe this careworn look, and what came to her mind was 'refugee'. Yes, that was the one, no doubt about it. Her last taxi driver would have taken one look at her and slapped her in an internment camp immediately.

Joan sighed tiredly. She had make-up in her shoulder bag but decided against using it, because she was afraid that the effect would be more garish than improving. Better a refugee, she thought, than a clown. Only sleep would help her now. An awful lot of sleep.

By the time she had finished in the bathroom, she found that Mark had taken their mugs of tea through into the other room, placing them both on the dresser before the mirror, and was taking a small, mostly full bottle of blended whisky from one of the drawers beneath.

'You look a bit better,' he smiled as she came in. 'Still mostly knackered, like - but better.'

127

He unscrewed the cap from the bottle and tipped an inch of whisky into his tea, then looked at Joan as he held the bottle over what was obviously her mug. She hesitated fractionally, remembering the brandy she had already drunk at Olivia's, but then she nodded.

'What the hell,' she said.

A moment later, Joan was seated on the neat bed and Mark was sitting on the room's only other available perch, a battered wooden folding chair that creaked at his every movement. They sat there for the most part in silence, sipping their laced tea, and occasionally glancing at each other. At one point, Joan asked Mark why he had left the army, and he told her that as much as he had enjoyed the life, he was always convinced that there had to be something else out there for him. 'Photography?' she asked, and he shrugged.

'Who knows.'

At another point, he asked Joan about her career as an interior designer, and she told him a couple of choice anecdotes about her customers' weirder requirements and tastes. Mark laughed easily at her stories, and contributed a couple of his own, drawn from his experience as an odd job man. When he had finished the last of these tales, he smiled at her unfeigned laughter.

'Well, me uncle were always telling me there were nowt so queer as folk - but he'd never been to London, so he didn't know the half of it.'

Throughout all this, Joan was amazed that she didn't feel the slightest bit embarrassed or awkward at this unaccustomed intimacy. In an odd way it reminded her of being at university. For a term she had shared a flat with another girl, and sometimes in the evenings they would just sit around, drink wine and talk. Occasionally, they would smoke a joint or two, and then, mildly stoned, they would just sit, as she and Mark were now, engaged in a broken, intermittent conversation that seemed as though it would never end, largely because it never really seemed to have begun.

As Mark had earlier predicted, Joan could no longer detect the harsh smell of his photographic chemicals. She felt calm, and strangely at peace. She felt hollowed out.

Joan was staring at one of the photographs on the wall, a study of Big Ben obviously taken from Parliament Square, when the image abruptly doubled, and then trebled, before her eyes. Her jaw opened wide in an incredible yawn. Mark, who had been explaining to her why he still largely preferred the messy physical processes of film as opposed to the pristine immediacy of digital photography, halted mid-sentence.

'Close your mouth, lass, there's a bus coming,' he said, amused.

'Oh God, I'm sorry,' Joan replied.

'Nah, it's me that's sorry, keeping you up like this. Time for bed, I think.'

And for the first time it occurred to Joan that there was only one bed in the flat, and that she was sitting on it. On the way here, she had assumed that there would be a spare bedroom, or at least a separate living room, and hadn't given the matter another thought even after she had seen the interior of the basement flat. She had been so comfortable in Mark's company that she hadn't worried. But now, against her will, she began to.

Mark must have seen the expression of alarm that slowly overtook her face, because he smiled and shook his head. 'Don't get any funny ideas, lass,' he said quickly. 'You're safe as houses with me.'

He put his empty mug down on the floor, went down on his knees and pulled something out from under the bed to the left of Joan's legs. It was a tightly rolled khaki-coloured sleeping bag.

'All above board, you see,' he said. 'You'll have the bed and I'll be down on the dog shelf.'

'The *what*?'

'The dog shelf. The *floor*, lass, right down here - unless you want me to sleep on the bathroom or kitchen floor.'

'There isn't much space in there, is there?' Joan asked dubiously.

He shrugged easily. 'It won't be comfortable, no, but I can if you want me to. I don't mind.'

Joan shook her head decisively, and then immediately wished that she hadn't moved at all. Her head was spinning now, so great was her tiredness. 'No, of course not. I should sleep on the floor, though. It's your bed.'

Mark gave her a look full of wonder, slowly shaking his own head. 'What kind of men are you used to?' he asked disgustedly. 'Don't any of them know how to treat a lady?'

Joan couldn't think of an answer to that.

'You're in the bed, I'm on the floor,' he said firmly. 'No argument.'

130

'You're really sure?'

'A'cos I am. Hey, it might be grim up north, but we're not bloody barbarians.'

'Thank you.'

Mark nodded easily. He unrolled the sleeping bag, then reached back under the bed to pull out a spare pillow. 'I sometimes have mates to stay, so I'm prepared for visitors.' He stood up. 'Right, lass, do you need the bathroom again?'

Joan shook her head.

'Okay, then. I'll go in for a few minutes and give you time to get into bed and make yourself comfortable. Turn out the light and give me a yell when you're ready.'

He crossed the room and was about to step on to the linoleum, but then paused in the doorway and looked back at her. For a moment the good humour that seemed to define his character left his eyes.

'I'm not claiming to be an angel, Joan,' he said seriously. 'Men'll be bad as you let 'em be, but we're not all arseholes.'

'I know,' Joan said, touched.

Sleepier than ever, she watched him disappear through the doorway. She had to force herself to her feet and pull back the blue duvet on the bed, thinking about what Mark had said and wondering if he was right – that men would be as bad as you let them be. Had she allowed Stephen to get away with too much in their marriage? She thought maybe she had. But she knew Mark had been wrong in one other respect. He was an angel. He had been for her, anyway.

She smiled to herself suddenly; the dog shelf was the floor. Have to remember that.

From the bathroom she heard the sound of running water. The urge to simply pull off the clothes she had been wearing all day, underwear included, and climb into the clean bed was almost irresistible, but a last fragment of elementary caution stopped her. She took off her cardigan, but that was all. Quite apart from sending out misleading signals, she didn't want to wake up in the morning naked and have to go through that old embarrassed routine.

She crossed the room to turn out the light, and then returned, kicked off her sandals and climbed into bed. Even after she had lain back, she felt as though she was continuing to sink. The mattress seemed to absorb her body like water. With the duvet pulled up to her chin, she could see the outline of the doorway lit by the spill of light from the bathroom, where the warped door wouldn't quite close. She heard the taps stop running, and water spiralling its way down the drain, a mini-whirlpool. The toilet flushed noisily and the old tank took a long time to refill. These aqueous sounds added to her illusion of immersion.

'Okay?' Mark called.

'Okay,' she called back, and the bathroom light immediately went out.

She heard the padded creakings of Mark's light footsteps as he came down the short corridor and into the room, but she could not see him. Now she felt as though she were floating, rising up in the darkness, higher and higher, and soon her nose would touch the ceiling.

'D'you mind if I open the window,' she heard him say. 'I like a bit of fresh air when I sleep.'

'No, that's fine, I do too.'

132

To Joan's right a small gap in the black-out curtains suddenly appeared, and in the thin light that brightened the room while he was opening the window, she saw that Mark had stripped down to a pair of clinging white boxer shorts. Above the waistband, his torso looked hard and lean, not an ounce of extra flesh on it, and his long legs were ropy with hard-earned muscle. She realised that he looked like a soldier in the peak of physical condition, and she imagined him swarming over the apparatus of an obstacle course.

He closed the curtains again, leaving only an inch-wide beam of light through which he moved as he went over to his sleeping bag and climbed in, never once looking in her direction. It would have been quite natural for him to look, she thought. To glance, to see what could be seen. A naked shoulder. A strip of thigh. Natural for another man, anyway. Stephen, for instance. Instead, she was the one taking a sneaky peak.

Joan closed her eyes against fresh tears. After a moment, she tried to speak, but found her mouth gummed up with sleep.

'Eh?' Mark asked.

'I'm sorry,' Joan replied. 'Very sleepy now. I just wanted to say thank you again. I know you said not to. But I am so grateful.'

'No problem.' His voice came from below the level of her head, which increased the floating sensation still more. Her head was pulsing, her blood lapping around her brain like a tide. Then Mark said something else that she didn't hear, only catching what sounded like the echoes of his voice.

133

'What was that?' she asked, and she could almost feel him smiling at her tiredness.

'I said, have you any idea what you're going to do now?'

Joan groaned. 'Well, I've given it a lot of thought, obviously. Considered all the possibilities.'

'And?'

'And - I don't have a clue.'

Mark laughed softly, and Joan found herself joining in, even as she was being pulled down into sleep, beneath the dark waves. 'I honestly don't know yet,' she said around yet another gigantic yawn. 'I'm open to suggestions.'

Mark paused for a long time, and then said, 'Let me sleep on it and I'll see what I can come up with. All right?'

'Mmm.'

'Don't worry.'

'Mmm.'

'G'night, then.'

But Joan was already asleep and did not reply.

21

It was the sort of dream that Joan instinctively knew was a dream, even as it unfolded around her. It had to be a dream, because it was impossible that it could be real. At first she felt disconnected from her body, as though it were happening to someone else entirely. Some other woman. In fact, she would have called herself a spectator, if she had been able to see, but she could not.

The dream was set in a dark place where she was totally blind. It wasn't the recurring dream she had told Dr Bob about, the one where the darkness was filled with the sound of roaring water and a thin voice called for help. No, in this dream she thought that she was in her own bed back at the Hampstead house, and she had been woken from a deep sleep. Someone else was there with her, someone had come into her bedroom at the dead of night and climbed onto the bed.

She suddenly felt the mattress shift with this other person's weight, and realised that she was no longer a spectator.

It's Stephen, she thought. He's come home late from the office, or wherever he's really been. He's drunk. He's drunk and horny and he thinks the barriers are down.

She felt his fingers insinuate themselves between the skin of her shoulders and the duvet that covered them. She felt it being pulled slowly down over the length of her body, whispering over the sheer material of her nightdress, and the night air touching the exposed flesh of her arms and lower legs. Warm hands enfolded her feet and gently squeezed before skimming up over her ankles, calves and knees. Her nightdress was pushed up to her waist as the hands continued their journey along her thighs, then rose higher over her belly, her breasts.

'No, Stephen,' she heard herself mumble. 'I don't want…'

The warm hands settled around her throat, the thumbs tracing the line of her windpipe, applying a steady pressure.

'No,' she said. 'You can't just…anytime you want to…'

The thumbs slipped up over her chin and gently sealed her lips together as the rest of the fingers cradled her jaw-line.

'Shhhh,' she heard Stephen say. '*Shhhhhh…*'

Unable to protest or move, she could only lay there as he continued to touch her, smoothing her hair back from her forehead with one hand while the other carefully roved and explored. As much as she didn't want it to, she could feel her body reacting to the stimuli. In happier times, this kind of attention was something she had loved, and her body remembered. A strong, firm hand moulded her breasts and teased her nipples into swollen life, and then, only a moment later, confidently slipped down to part her thighs. She knew she was already wet.

Joan felt a gentle tugging between her legs as her panties were moved aside. Then a thick finger slid inside her, and in her sleep and in her dream she gasped.

The other hand stopped stroking her hair, and the next moment she felt her own hand being lifted from the mattress and guided. She felt her palm being pressed against a hard, hairless male chest, being moved slowly down over the shelf of muscle, then over the ribbed smoothness of a washboard stomach, and she finally realised that this was not Stephen's body. She was not dreaming of her husband.

Joan's mind became invaded by guilt and pleasure.

She felt her fingers being trailed through a soft brush of pubic hair that she now knew would be sandy-blonde in colour, then pressed hard against a tight scrotum, and finally wrapped around a stony-smooth erection that was excitingly unfamiliar. When the guiding hand left hers, Joan discovered that her fingers refused to let the erection go. It burned and pulsed against the palm of her hand, thrillingly responsive to her touch.

After a brief moment of indecision, she began to stroke her hand over it in sync with the rhythmic thrusts of the finger inside her.

Guilt, pleasure. One and the same.

Deep inside her head, at the core of her dream, a voice huskily whispered, 'Aye, lass, that's the way.'

22

It was a night for dreams.

Unconscious on his bed, still fully clothed, stinking of alcohol, sour and wretched and crushed, Stephen Crosby dreamed that his late father, no mean philanderer himself in his heyday by all accounts, was speaking to him on the subject of morality and the obligations of marriage; on duty, on loyalty, and on love. It was a commanding voice, severe and yet completely without emotion, which Stephen had not heard for almost ten years.

When he tried to object to the hypocritical unfairness of this lecture, his father stepped quickly forward from his sheath of darkness and clasped Stephen's face in hands that were made of ice and burned like fire. He screamed when his father touched him.

'Your mother had to die for me to learn the truth,' his father told him. 'Don't repeat my mistakes.'

And lying on her mattress, with her single cotton sheet sweat-soaked and puddled on the floor at the foot of her bed, Olivia dreamed that she and Joan were young again, two little sisters, aged six and eight, two adorable little girls, bonded like twins, who lived for each other and could never be separated, never set against one another. They were dreams of memory. False memory.

She dreamed of an eternity of golden summer days, each spent in a blissful, innocent communion they had only really known during those first unguarded years, and Olivia's entire being was suffused with a love she hadn't remembered until it was almost too late to bask in its glorious solemn heat once more.

Then she dreamed that Joan was taken from her, stolen away from this idyll in the comatose night, never to return. She dreamed of their parents, angry, shadowy giants, standing over her demanding to know what had happened, how Olivia could have allowed it to happen. She felt their disappointment in her. Their coldness. Their growing hatred.

She dreamed that the rest of her life was overshadowed by this guilt and this loss, and she saw her own lonely, comfortless death, saw the emptiness of her soul as her eyes rolled up into her head and her final words reverberated in an empty room.

I'm sorry, I'm sorry, I'm sorry…

But all too late, always too late. Now it was gone.

She dreamed that the walls were closing in around her like a coffin, and her parents' spirits turned away from her as they had turned away in life, and a little girl who was her lost sister ran away from

138

her down a bright tunnel of light to which she would forever be denied access, and she woke up shaking and sobbing as though her heart was being torn from her body.

And the long night passed.

23

The black-out curtains had been opened wide at some time before Joan awoke, and when she opened her eyes it was to scaldingly bright sunlight that had saturated the damp basement room, making it feel hot and airless despite the open window. When she rolled over on to her back, a plume of her own body odour billowed out from beneath the duvet, and she became acutely aware that she hadn't bathed in more than twenty-four hours. She hoped that Mark's shower worked better than it looked.

Her first real conscious action was to look down at the floor to see the young man who had last night saved her life, but Mark wasn't there and neither was his sleeping bag. She wondered what time it was, and how long he had been up. It seemed rude to have slept in. Her second action was to take careful stock of her own condition, which, after only a short period of time, she realised could have been a lot worse.

True, the dress she had slept in was plastered to her body with sour-smelling sweat, her bra was cutting into the underside of her left breast, her knickers were up her arse, and she generally felt as though she had been dragged through a hedge backwards... But *apart* from all that, she actually felt good. Perhaps more than good.

And at least I'm still *wearing* my clothes, she thought.

She didn't remember everything about her dream, but what she did remember was so intense that she would have not have been surprised if she had woken up naked in Mark's arms. After that first sensation of being outside her body, it had felt so real.

What she remembered best was the beginning, if it had been the beginning; the touching in the darkness. Of the rest of it, she recalled only white-out flashes, like lightning strikes, of Mark leaning over her, of his soft voice firmly commanding her, and of herself mindlessly obeying those commands. She had been like a doll, she realised, some kind of malleable, voice-activated sex toy.

The whole thing seemed so unlike any other dream she had ever experienced, and so unlike any other sexual act she had taken part in, that she wondered if it had not been more of a fantasy than a dream. A mad fantasy brought on by stress, fatigue, and probably by more alcohol than she should have consumed.

Joan's face flushed red as she suddenly wondered if she had made any noises in her sleep, sounds of passion she might have made and that Mark might have overheard.

Oh Christ, she thought, I hope I didn't call out his name. Is that why he isn't here? She was mortified to think that he might have heard everything, and couldn't stand the embarrassment of facing her this morning. She sat up and softly called Mark's name, but there was no reply either from the bathroom or kitchen. Shit!

She pushed back the duvet and sat up. She took a few moments to compose herself, because her legs felt weak and untrustworthy, and now that she was upright her head had started to hum uncomfortably loudly, blanking clear thought. She silently promised herself that it would be a while before alcohol passed her lips again.

Finally, driven by the desire to pee, she pushed herself up off the bed and began to cross the room to the doorway, the threadbare carpet hot under her bare feet as she took the tiny, uncertain steps of the walking wounded. Halfway across the room she saw the piece of paper propped up on the dresser beneath the mirror, just below the photograph of Mark's cottage, and saw that her name had been printed at the top.

A note.

She changed direction and reluctantly approached the dresser, already afraid that she knew what the note would say:

Joan, Sorry for leaving you asleep but I had to go to work. Hope last night helped a little bit. Let yourself out when you're ready. Hope things get better for you fast. Mark.

A goodbye. A brush-off, in fact, but a polite and tactful one. Perhaps it was the best she could hope for.

She picked up the note, written in blue biro on a piece of cheap lined paper torn from a spiral bound pad, and wiped moisture from her eyes, which had once more begun to leak. She blearily focussed on the words, and had to read through them twice, because her own version of what they said conflicted so strongly with what she actually saw that she was stunned.

Dear Joan, the note said. *Couldn't bear to wake you, you looked so peaceful. Have gone out to get us some breakfast and will be back very soon. Make yourself at home until I get back. Had a think about your troubles before I went to sleep and have a couple of ideas that might help. Love, Mark.*

Her tears ran faster down her cheeks, now more an expression of relief and gratitude than self-pity. No, she thought, not all men are arseholes, Mark. You're one of the exceptions to the rule.

In the bathroom she once again stared at herself in the uneven mirror tiles and groaned in dismay. Her dream - oddly pleasant though it may have been - had detracted from her rest, and the night had not been kind to her. There were deep, liverish hollows beneath her eyes, and the skin on her face seemed as creased as her dress. While she tried to massage the lines away with a basinful of cold water, she thought again about her dream, about what it really meant.

Had it been a subconscious expression of genuine desire, or an outlandish rebound reflex? Or had there been more than a measure of revenge mixed in there too - what's good for the goose, and all that? And really, did it matter? It wasn't as if she was planning on trying to turn the dream into reality. She hoped that she wasn't as foolish as that. And, looking candidly at her reflection, there was no way that Mark would want to respond, even if she did lose her senses and make a play for him.

He was a good-looking young man who would have no trouble attracting women both younger and prettier than she was. Today she looked all of her thirty-six years, and felt twenty years older than that.

For an instant, Kath Meadows appeared in sharp clarity in Joan's mind, the first time she had done so for many months. She was sitting in the window of their coffee shop in Hampstead, surrounded by a golden aura of sunlight, and she was laughing as she spoke of her numerous affairs with younger men, a long succession of Perfect Days:

'Older men are tired, and they like younger women because they come without baggage,' she was saying. 'Younger men have more energy, and they like older women precisely because they are complicated. They like the challenge of it. Also, it's the only legal way they can fuck their mothers and shaft their fathers. It's incredibly entertaining, actually, like sleeping with a Greek tragedy.'

Joan angrily willed Kath's image and voice away. She didn't believe she needed advice on any aspect of her life from such a fair-weather friend as Kath Meadows, and certainly not on her love life. Or lack thereof.

She turned on the shower and held her hand under the spray until she felt the water grow warm on her palm. She unbuttoned her dress, feeling light-headed and exhausted, and wondered why she was even thinking like this in the first place. It was ridiculous.

Joan had time for a long shower before Mark came back, standing in the rusty stall for more than ten minutes while the spray from the limescale-choked shower-head drummed unevenly against her scalp. By

143

the time the hot water had run out, her head had ceased to hum and she felt halfway human again. She quickly dried herself, and then reluctantly dressed in yesterday's dirty clothes. In the absence of a hair-drier she towel-dried and then applied a thin layer of foundation to her face, which at least hid the worst of her tiredness and made her feel a little better about herself.

Now she only felt about ten years older than she really was.

She had just made herself a cup of tea in the postage stamp kitchen when she heard Mark's measured knock and then his voice, muffled by the flat's door. 'Are you decent?'

Good question, Joan thought. After last night's dream, she wasn't sure anymore. 'Yes,' she called back. 'Come in.'

She leant around the kitchen doorway and saw Mark walk in carrying a bulging 7-11 carrier bag in one hand. He tucked his keys away in his trouser pocket and smiled at her. 'Morning,' he said. 'I was going to ask if you slept all right, but I can see you did.'

'Thank you. I think I was more unconscious than asleep, though. I don't even remember dropping off.'

'Must've needed it, then.'

'Tea?'

'Aye, go on. Then I'm making us breakfast.'

As Joan stepped back into the kitchen and switched on the kettle to re-boil, she could feel her heart doing funny things inside her chest; jumping, twitching, whatever it was you called it when you didn't know whether you were excited or about to

144

have a heart attack. She didn't understand this reaction. Whether it was out of sheer relief because Mark hadn't told her that she had seemed to sleep 'uneasily' or not, she didn't know. Maybe it was simply because he was back. She didn't know what to think of that idea, either.

After making his tea, Joan retreated to the doorway and watched Mark remove the groceries from the carrier bag and begin his preparation, opening cans, snipping open packets, and assembling his plates, pans and utensils. She quickly became aware that she was more than just watching him. She was studying him.

He was dressed much the same as he had been yesterday, in jeans and a white t-shirt, but unlike Joan's, Mark's clothes were fresh and clean. He looked good, and she liked the way he moved about the small kitchen as he worked, the brisk economy of his movements, the preciseness of them. It somehow fitted in with his military background, and corresponded to her image of him as a confident, self-reliant man.

Once or twice she caught herself looking at the way the faded denim of his trousers clung to his tight buttocks and the way the muscles in his arms bunched and relaxed, and she felt her stomach muscles contracting.

No point now in wondering how to interpret her dream, she thought, it was bloody obvious. Without even trying, Mark had found some button deep inside her and turned her on. She tried to, but could not, recall the last time that she had looked at Stephen in this way, with this kind of intensity. Even yesterday,

145

at the heart of her planned seduction, there had been an emotional core. It hadn't been the kind of… lust, she supposed… she was experiencing now.

She watched Mark crack six eggs into a bowl, whisk them, add milk and seasoning, and whisk them again before dumping the mixture into a saucepan on top of the melted butter. She watched him wrap the eye-level grill pan in foil, skin the mushrooms, prick the sausages with a fork. She noticed that he efficiently tidied up after himself as he went along, the eggshells and mushroom stalks disappearing into the bin, the surfaces quickly wiped down in preparation for the next task.

So different from Stephen, yet again. If Stephen ever tried to cook, the kitchen always looked like a landfill site afterwards.

Whenever Mark glanced across at her and smiled, Joan could feel herself blushing beneath her foundation. She found herself idly wondering if her attraction to him was at all reciprocated, but then scolded herself, and then scolded Kath's corrupting memory. Mark was ten years her junior, for God's sake, and she was a married woman with more problems than the Middle East. What on earth would he see in her?

Forget about it, Joan commanded herself firmly. At the moment, this young man was her only friend, and she had no wish to alienate him by doing something idiotic.

Finally, when Mark had everything cooking and bubbling to his satisfaction, he turned to face her. 'Did you read my note?' he asked. When she nodded, he said, 'Well, like I say, I've had a couple of ideas. I

146

don't know whether you want to hear them. Have you had any of your own?'

'Not really, although I suppose I will have to speak to Stephen at some point. I'm not in any rush to do that. I wouldn't know what to say at the moment. It's too soon for me to do anything other than scream and shout, and I don't want that.'

'I don't blame you.' He looked down at his feet shyly for a moment, and seemed even younger than he really was, like a teenager. 'Right, here goes,' he said. 'Joan, you know my cottage, the one in the photo I showed you?'

'Hunter's Lodge.'

'Aye. Well, every few months, when I've earned enough money, I go back for a few weeks. Get back in touch with meself, like. You know what I mean?'

Joan was nodding.

'I'm going there today,' he continued. 'Setting off this morning.'

'Really?' Joan said in surprise, and she immediately felt her new sense of security begin to slip a little. It was frightening to discover how fragile it really was.

'Aye, I am. So, here's me idea - I'll be gone for a week or two, maybe even longer…'

And Joan was suddenly quite sure that she knew what Mark's idea was, she felt that she knew exactly what he was going to say. He was going to ask her to go away with him. She knew it, and didn't know how she would respond. But her heart was pounding again.

'… so, I was thinking… why don't you move into this flat while I'm gone?'

Oh, Joan thought. A small, absurd part of her felt crushed - how could she have been so wrong? But the rest of her knew that it was probably for the best.

She looked away, out through the small kitchen window at the overgrown, ignored garden and the backs of the neighbouring houses, and tried not to let her irrational disappointment show. It was the feeling of disappointment which told her that her subconscious had known all along how she would respond. If it had been the right question, that is

She tried to tell herself that Mark hadn't really let her down. She had just been getting her hopes up far too high. Presuming far too much on their short acquaintance, and mostly - quite absolutely ludicrously, she now thought - on the basis of one wet bloody dream.

It was the situation that was really pushing her, she knew that. Not desire. All her impulses were urging her to run away from her problems, and foolishly she had been listening to them.

'What do you think?' Mark asked. 'I mean, the landlord'll never know, and wouldn't care if he did. But I'd like to know you've somewhere to go if you need it. I can let you have your own key. You can come and go as you please.'

'Thank you for the gesture, Mark,' Joan said. 'I'll have to think about it. I don't know exactly what I'm going to be doing. But thank you for the offer, anyway. It's much appreciated, I assure you.'

She thought she did this pretty well, but Mark obviously heard something off in her tone of voice.

'Hey,' he said, 'me going isn't anything to do with meeting you. I was going anyway, I've had it planned for the last week or so. Honest. That's why I didn't have any food in the place for breakfast.'

'No, that's all right, I understand, really,' she said. 'You've been very kind to me.'

'Aye, well…'

They were silent for a few moments. Joan felt awkward and uncomfortable, as though she had reacted both badly and unfairly, which of course she had. She watched Mark stir the cooking food again, find plates, butter bread, wondering how she might put things right. But before she could even try, he suddenly turned to her with decision.

'That was one of me ideas, anyway,' he said. 'This is me other idea, and between you and me it's the one I like best.'

He looked up and met her eyes.

'Why don't you come up north with me?'

Joan's breath caught in her throat. Say no, she told herself. Please say no. You've forced him into this, and right now you're so vulnerable that you'll end up making a complete fool of yourself.

'It's a beautiful place,' Mark said quickly, seeing the indecision in her eyes. 'You can see that for yourself in the photo, and the cottage inside makes this place look like a pigsty. There's a spare bedroom and everything, and you'd have the time and space to think - which, in my opinion, is just what you need. You need to step back for a while, and think about what you really want.'

Mark swiped at his suddenly sweaty forehead with his wrist and blew out a thin stream of air.

'Fuckin' 'ell,' he laughed shakily. 'I made hard work of that, didn't I?'

149

'Yes,' Joan said, laughing along with him.

'And here was I, thinking I was so smooth and sophisticated. I wanted to ask you to come with me all along, but I just didn't want you to think I was trying it on.'

'Don't worry, I didn't,' she said, and privately thought, if only you'd known what I *was* thinking…

Deep down, Joan knew that she couldn't go with Mark, as attractive as the prospect undoubtedly was. Her problems were too big to ignore. She was fully aware that running away was not the right thing to do. It was hardly ever the right thing to do. Downright childish, when she came to think about it, and most definitely not the reaction of an adult. And if time and space to think were all she wanted and needed, then she could have that here, in this flat, once Mark had gone.

If time and space were all she wanted.

She took a deep breath as she made her decision. She couldn't remember the last time she had felt as reckless as she did right now.

'Yes, I'll come,' she said, before either of them had time to change their minds. 'I'd love to.'

He met her eyes again. 'Really?'

'Yes.'

And then a thought struck her. She saw Stephen's overnight case bounding down a staircase ahead of her and breaking open on a scuffed parquet floor. 'Oh!'

'What is it?'

She held up her arms, looked down at her crumpled dress. 'Look at me,' she said. 'I haven't even got a change of clothes. And I'll need toiletries, things like that…'

'Don't you have any money?'

She glanced down the short corridor, toward her shoulder bag, which she had left at the foot of the bed.

'Well, yes, I have a little bit of cash, and there are my cards, I suppose. But… maybe I should hang on to what money I have. I might need it later. Besides, there are some other things I'll want, too. My jewellery, my address book - I forgot them when I left yesterday. Personal things, you know? I don't see why I should leave them behind.'

'Is that the only problem?' Mark asked after a second's pause.

'What do you mean?

'It's not… just an excuse, is it?' He smiled. 'Not changed your mind already?'

'No, Mark. No. I really want to go with you. In fact, you'd be surprised how much I want to go.'

His smile widened, dazzled her, set her stomach fluttering.

'So,' he said, 'what you want is to collect your stuff from your house, probably without bumping into your husband along the way?'

'Yes, that's exactly what I want.'

Mark pulled down the grill pan and turned the sausages and the bacon. He stirred the eggs and the tomatoes bubbling in their saucepans. He nodded to himself.

'I think we can do that,' he said.

24

The tube was standing room only, every seat and most of the straps occupied. Olivia was jammed in a press of Saturday morning shoppers and tourists, grimly hanging on to a chrome pole unpleasantly sticky from other people's hands, as the train shuddered its way out of Camden Town and into the roaring darkness of the tunnel. There were still two more stations to pass before it reached Hampstead, and Olivia silently cursed herself. She had meant to be up at the crack of dawn this morning, but after a disturbed night she had awoken shamefully late having slept through the alarm.

She had virtually walked through the shower on the way to her wardrobe, and while she had been fighting her still wet body into the first items she plucked from hangers and drawers, she had called Stephen to ask if there had been any developments overnight. But Stephen hadn't answered either the landline or his mobile. Repeated attempts only got her the same irritating result, and she had slammed down the receiver in disgust.

She already knew what had happened - big fat nothing.

Last night's noble aspirations had been smothered by an alcoholic pillow. She could imagine the phone ringing in the living room amidst the debris of Stephen's drunken binge, the abandoned bottles and glasses, the cardboard city of takeaway packaging, and the ashtray filled by the fat stubs of his poseur cigars, looking for all the world like a mound of dog turds.

Stephen himself, of course, just like a dog that had finished its business, would be nowhere near the mess he had created. He would have staggered upstairs and selfishly unplugged the phone in the bedroom and turned off his mobile before he passed out on the bed, still wearing his clothes, and would now be wrapped up in a duvet, comatose, sweating, and occasionally breaking wind. Olivia had imagined herself having to hammer on the door for an eternity before getting to brave the stench of the house, throwing up the windows, pushing him through the shower, pouring coffee down his throat, and force-feeding him aspirin before they could even get started on the hotels.

But while simultaneously tying her boots and slopping down some cereal, Olivia had another idea.

She remembered Joan telling her that Stephen sometimes went into his office for a few hours on a Saturday morning, and she had suddenly thought how like him that would have been. His wife was missing, in probably the most distressed state she had ever been, and he had gone into the office to shuffle papers. It wouldn't have surprised her any more than her first scenario. Nothing about Stephen, she had decided, would ever surprise her again.

She'd found the phonebook where she had thrown it the night before and flicked through the pages until she found the entry for Stephen's firm of solicitors and then dialled the number. While she listened to it ring, she thought about how she would react if Stephen did answer the phone with his usual arrogant brio and decided that she would probably

153

just scream as loud as she could and split his cheating head in two.

There was an off-chance, she had supposed, that he might have gone to work because his office was in a more central position for all the big hotels, and therefore a superior command centre for the effort to find Joan before she either harmed herself or came to harm. Maybe. She had acknowledged that this might make a little sense, but thought that she still might scream at him anyway. It wouldn't be productive, but the satisfaction, she imagined, would be immense.

After twenty or so rings, Olivia had been about to hang up when the phone was finally answered:

'Crosby, Arnoult, & Davies, good morning, how may I help?'

The voice was not Stephen's, but a young woman's with a pronounced but carefully controlled estuary accent. One of the company's part-time receptionists, no doubt, Olivia thought. Molly or Dolly, or Nicci or Vicki, or something.

'Hello, I'd like to speak to Stephen Crosby,' she said.

'I'm afraid he's not in the office at the moment,' the girl replied, clearly on autopilot. 'May I ask what your call is in regard to?'

'This is Stephen's sister-in-law, Olivia Weir.'

'Oh yes, good morning Mrs Weir, this is Charlene, how may I help you?'

Olivia didn't bother to correct the title the girl had appointed to her, only noted that there was yet another new receptionist at the firm. It didn't take a great deal of brainpower to figure out why they got through so many.

'Charlene, I'm looking for Stephen, is he really not there?'

'Oh no,' Charlene said, sounding disappointed. 'He usually comes in Saturday mornings, but not today.'

Count your blessings, Olivia thought. 'Has he phoned?'

'No, he hasn't.' Her voice dropped to a confidential level and her accent broadened. 'Apparently he called last night in a bit of a tizz, saying he wouldn't be in today, but that's all I know. Is anything wrong?'

Olivia ignored the question.

'Listen, if he either calls or comes in, can you get him to contact me right away. It's very important.'

'Yes, of course. I'll make a note. Is there anything else I can do?'

'Yes, if you want to keep your job, don't accept any dinner invitations.'

'I'm sorry?'

Olivia sighed. 'It doesn't matter. If you see him, get him to call me on my mobile.'

She had given Charlene her number before grabbing her handbag on the way to the door.

Now the train rumbled into Chalk Farm station and jerked to a halt. The doors slid open, a dozen people left the carriage, and approximately two billion more piled in, squashing Olivia into a corner by the opposite doors. The train began to move again.

Only one more station to go before Hampstead, Olivia thought to herself, but she acknowledged that with her luck the train would probably get stuck in the tunnel. Weary, for the moment, of attacking Stephen,

155

she began to pick on herself. Why the hell did she come by tube, why hadn't she called a mini-cab to pick her up from home? She would have been there in ten minutes.

The carriage suddenly lurched and the lights flickered as the train passed over points, and a dirty, well-used rucksack was pushed into Olivia's face.

'Do you fucking mind!' she glared at the young male student who craned his head around to apologise, and everybody in the carriage seemed to turn around to stare at her.

She emerged from the underground fifteen minutes later and immediately turned left along Hampstead High Street, which seemed no less busy than the tube had been. A little bit of sunshine seemed to act on Londoners like rain on worms, she thought, bringing the buggers out in droves. The pavements were packed with people who only wanted to saunter when she felt like running.

Olivia wove her way as best she could through the throng, but was still kept to a slower pace than she would have liked. She could have moved faster by escaping on to the road and walking in the gutter, but Joan's hit-and-run accident had cured her of that particular bad habit along with most of the rest.

Forced to keep pace with the herd, she found herself being given strange looks by the people she passed, especially by the women, and after a while she began to wonder why. Eventually, she realised that it was because she was looking everybody in the face, staring and seeking eye-contact in a way people in the capital rarely did.

She was looking for Joan, that's what it was. Hoping against hope that she would simply bump into her, be able to say, please, let's sit down and talk about this, and go on from there. But it wasn't going to happen. She knew that this anxiety was a part of the price she had to pay.

Then, as she passed the plate glass window of a café, Olivia abruptly stopped dead in her tracks. The establishment was called Café Bleu, which seemed familiar. Her memory juggled with the name, trying to find a cross-reference, and soon turned up the answer. This was the café where Joan had spent so much time with her friend Kath Meadows, and if she was anywhere in the area this was the one place where she might have fled to for sanctuary.

And as this thought ran through her mind, Olivia suddenly saw her sister in the café's window.

Joan was sitting alone at a table for two, sipping contentedly at a large cappuccino as though she hadn't a care in the world. Olivia took a tentative step toward the window and raised a hand. The woman glanced at her briefly, and then looked quickly away, and Olivia's hand fell. It wasn't Joan at all.

The woman had short auburn hair like Joan's, but the shade didn't exactly match her darker eyebrows and almost certainly had come out of a bottle. Not only that, but her face was entirely the wrong shape, as was her nose. In fact, Olivia had to admit that the woman looked nothing at all like Joan - except in one uncomfortable respect.

In that brief moment when their eyes had met, the woman's expression had seemed identical to the look of condemnation Joan's spirit had given her in one of last night's dreams.

When she finally arrived at Joan and Stephen's house some ten minutes later, Olivia was surprised, and pleased, to see that the curtains were all wide open, upstairs and downstairs. Thank God for that, she thought. Her initial burst of optimism quickly faded, however, when she realised that this wasn't conclusive proof that Stephen was up and around. He had probably been too drunk to think of closing them in the first place.

She stepped off the garden path for a few moments and trampled the flowerbeds in front of the living room window, balancing on her tiptoes as she tried to look into the house. From the little she could see all was exactly as she had predicted earlier. The room was in chaos, including an open Domino's box that still contained a third of a pizza the size of a bus wheel, and a bottle of Jameson's down to the last half inch. There was no sign of Stephen.

She stepped back to the path, up on to the doorstep, and knocked. After a few seconds without response, she knocked again, longer and harder. When there was still no reply, she bent down to the letterbox and used her fingers to wedge open the brass flap. Through the gap she was able to see down the hallway, through into the kitchen, and about halfway up the staircase climbing the right-hand wall.

The house both looked and sounded unoccupied, but she could still smell the mingled morning-after-the-night-before atmosphere of Stephen's cigars, booze, and the mozzarella on the leftover pizza.

Still peering through the letterbox and up the stairs, Olivia began to alternately hammer on the door and shout Stephen's name, but the only reply was the thin echoes of the noises she herself was making. Next she retrieved her mobile phone from her handbag and dialled the landline. She heard the various extensions ringing inside the house, living room and bedroom, but no one moved to pick them up.

After the phone had rung twenty or thirty times, she roughly jammed the phone back into her bag as though it was solely responsible for her frustrations. She felt like screaming, but only swore under her breath. When she eventually found Stephen, she was going to kill him.

Emotionally exhausted and thoroughly depressed, Olivia slumped down on the doorstep and laid her head on her knees. This was the worst possible start to a day that had never promised to be easy. After a while she found that she was gently rocking herself for comfort, but she was not comforted. Instead, her mind worked obsessively back and forth between the foolishness of her own past transgressions and how she might seek to punish Stephen for his past and current sins.

And then a voice broke into her thoughts.

25

'Young woman?'

Olivia looked up and saw a small elderly gentleman standing at the gate, staring at her in polite but obviously firm disapproval. His white hair was oiled and smoothly combed across what she guessed would be an otherwise bald head, and he was nattily turned out in cream chinos and a burgundy cardigan, under which he wore a crisp white shirt and a black tie. From his left hand dangled a Waitrose carrier bag and tucked under his right arm was a folded copy of The *Daily Telegraph*. He looked, she thought, like The *Daily Telegraph* made flesh.

'Young woman,' he said crisply, 'you are wasting your time. I saw Mr Crosby leave this morning and his car is still gone.'

Olivia stood up and began to walk down the path toward the old man, who was half a head shorter than her. 'What time was that?' she asked.

'I beg your pardon?'

'What time did he leave?'

The aging bantam, unaccountably affronted by this question, drew himself up to his full, diminutive height, and increased the ferocity of his frown. 'That is no concern of yours. You have no right to be here. I would suggest that you should leave now, before you cause any further embarrassment for others and trouble for yourself.'

Olivia froze on the path, and felt her cheeks burning.

Unbelievably, this stuffy old man seemed to know her - and even worse, he seemed to know what she had done. But how could that be? She couldn't imagine her sister, even as distressed as she had been, confiding in anyone, much less someone like him. But if it wasn't Joan, that only left Stephen, and why would he ever do such a thing? To confess? To garner some moral support? To lay all the blame on Olivia?

She stepped back a pace as the man came a little way into the garden.

'It's people like you,' he said coldly, 'who are ruining this country, destroying marriages, and breaking up families. Once upon a time, there was such a thing as honour, and moral integrity. You should be thoroughly ashamed of yourself.'

Olivia was so shocked that she couldn't speak.

'Now listen to me,' he said in a lower voice. 'I happen to know that Mrs Crosby has been very unwell recently, and that can put a strain on any relationship. The last thing she needs is a grubby little tart like you placing temptation in her husband's way. So my advice to you, young woman, is to hop it.'

He shook his head, as though pitying her.

'You're not even the first, you know. There was another girl around here yesterday, causing a scene.'

'I know,' Olivia managed to say.

'And you still came?' He shook his head again, this time in open disgust. 'Well, let me tell you something, Missy, we don't like scenes like that in this neighbourhood. I don't like seeing them outside my own front door, and I won't have it. Leave now, and I mean immediately, or I will be forced to call the police and have you removed. You are trespassing.'

He turned his back on her and began to walk away. Olivia could hear him rambling on to himself under his breath about the collapse of society.

'Wait a minute!' she called.

The old man stopped and reluctantly turned.

'Who are you?' Olivia asked.

'I am a concerned neighbour,' he replied tartly, inclining his head toward the house directly opposite

Joan's across the road. 'That is all the information you deserve.'

'Oh!' Olivia said. She had suddenly realised who she was speaking to. 'It's Mr Unwill, isn't it?'

All the creases on the old man's face smoothed out in surprise, and then immediately returned as he stared at her in suspicion, beneath which was a faint undercurrent of alarm.

'How do you know my name?'

'Joan and Stephen have mentioned you to me, that's all,' Olivia said, trying to smile. She gave him her name. 'I'm Joan's sister.'

Unwill came closer again, a curious expression on his face, as though he was looking at a painting he didn't understand. Then he snorted dismissively.

'Nonsense. Mrs Crosby's sister has red hair, looks just like her twin.'

'Yes, I did, but I changed it - my hair, I mean. Mr Unwill, I know what happened yesterday. That's why I'm here, to try and help.'

She smiled at Unwill for as long and as hard as she could, and eventually his expression softened slightly.

'Ah,' he said. 'I see,' he said. 'Hmmph. Well, you're still wasting your time, nobody's home. Mr Crosby left at around a quarter to ten, just before I went out for my morning constitutional. I haven't seen Mrs Crosby since she… departed… yesterday afternoon. That is all I have to say.'

Unwill gave her a curt nod, wished her a good morning, spun around on his heels, and marched across the road and disappeared through the gate to his garden.

After his front door had slammed behind him, Olivia sighed and looked at her watch. It was now ten-forty-five. If she'd had the good sense to come by taxi, she might just have caught Stephen before he went out and avoided all of this. In a sense, she only had herself to blame.

But she knew whom she would blame, just as soon as she found him.

Olivia was back on Hampstead High Street, looking for a taxi, when her mobile phone began to trill inside her handbag. She almost dropped the phone getting it out.

'Hello?'

'Olivia, it's Stephen. Where the hell are you?'

'Where am I?' Olivia asked angrily. 'You cheeky bastard!' She could hear traffic noise over the line. 'Where the hell are you?'

'In the car - just leaving your flat.'

'Shit. I've just left your house.'

'Okay, good. Stay there, I'm going to…' Stephen broke off his sentence to hurl a stream of abuse at another driver. '…I'm coming back to change my clothes.'

'Why?'

'Why? Because I look like a bloody tramp, that's why. I slept in my clothes last night, and then I rushed out this morning. I haven't washed or shaved, I haven't--'

'Stephen, what's happened?' Olivia broke in. She felt her stomach turning over, because she thought she already knew. He'd received an early morning call from a hospital casualty department. Or a police station. 'Have you found Joan?'

'No, I haven't. But something odd is definitely going on. This morning I was woken…'

Stephen's voice disappeared again, and Olivia stared at her phone in disbelief. Of all the times to lose the signal.

'Stephen?' she yelled. 'Stephen?'

'Yeah, I'm here, it's just… oh shit, listen, there's a police car right behind me, and if they see me on the phone…. Hang on, I'm going to have to hang up…Olivia, I'll see you at the house in about ten minutes - wait for me.'

The line went dead and she swore out loud, causing several pedestrians to stare at her as they passed by. She ignored them.

Olivia retraced her steps to Haversham Row lost in speculation about what was going on with Stephen. Up early after last night's skinful, rushing out without even pausing to change his clothes or wash his face? She didn't get it. At least during their short conversation, he'd had time to tell her that he hadn't found Joan, so Olivia didn't have to spend the next ten or so minutes in agony wondering about that.

But what could have happened that Stephen would describe as 'odd'?

She turned the corner into Haversham Row for the second time that morning, and immediately fixed on a head of short auburn hair bobbing across the road about two hundred yards in front of her. Olivia's footsteps first slowed and then stopped altogether.

No, it can't be, she thought.

And yet the hair's owner was clearly walking away from the general direction of Joan's house. It could have been mere coincidence, of course, but...

The figure reached the other side of the road and cleared the blind of a car, and suddenly Olivia was sure. The figure, the walk, everything. It was Joan. Dressed in jeans and white cotton polo shirt she was hurrying down the street pulling a large wheelie-case after her.

Olivia opened her mouth to call her name, but then Joan turned a corner and was out of sight, and almost certainly out of earshot too. Olivia took a few uncertain steps forward, and then began to run.

She passed Joan's garden and noticed that the gate was now open and not closed, as she had left it. She had to pause at the kerb for a few agonising moments, impatiently bouncing on the balls of her feet before she was able to dash across the road between moving cars, and then pelted along the pavement until she reached the corner her sister had disappeared around.

And there she once more ground to a halt, hardly able to believe her eyes.

A hundred yards farther along the road, Joan was handing her case to a well-built young man who was also wearing jeans and a white t-shirt. He lifted the heavy case easily and slipped it into the back of a dirty white van, then slammed it shut. Joan then leaned toward him, and Olivia could see her lips moving close to his ear.

Without quite knowing why, she slipped back out of sight, just as the young man turned and glanced back down the road. A moment later, when she peeked around the corner, she saw them both hurriedly climbing into the van and closing the doors. Another moment later, she heard the engine fire into life.

Olivia, her mouth open wide, watched the van quickly pull away, watched it until it had passed from sight. It wasn't just what she had seen that had shocked her so much - Joan in the company of another man - although that was without doubt a major surprise.

No, it wasn't that.

It was the fact that she had *recognised* him.

26

By the time Mark had got them back on the North End Road and was driving toward Golders Green, Joan felt as though she were on an emotional roller-coaster - up, down, up, down. Right now, she was so up that she was practically hysterical. Her face was flushed from almost being caught in the house by Olivia, and she had been gabbling on about how strange the experience had been; both scary and exciting at the same time, like playing hide and seek in the dark as a child.

Unable to stop herself talking, she had also explained what she had heard Gordon Unwill saying to Olivia before he had been told that she was Joan's sister, and how, hidden behind the bedroom curtains, she had felt like cheering the old man on.

Go on, give it to her! Straight between the eyes!

In a matter of seconds, M had gone from being a long-standing nuisance and figure of fun to being her personal champion, a *Daily Telegraph*-reading gladiator. Mentally she took back every unkind thought she had ever entertained about the upright Mr Unwill, every joke she had enjoyed at his expense. In her excitement, she had not noticed how thoughtful Mark had become.

When she next paused for breath, he asked, 'She didn't see you, did she?'

Knocked out of her stride by the question, Joan took a second or two to respond. 'Olivia? No, I'm sure she didn't.'

'What about the old gimmer?'

'No.'

'You're really sure?'

'Yes, I was very, very careful to stay out of sight the whole time. They didn't have a clue I was there.' She shook her head slightly. 'I was getting a bit worried toward the end, though, I'll admit. I thought Olivia would never leave. I had this awful idea she'd sit on the steps all day, or at least until Stephen came home, and then I would have been trapped.' Again, she shook her head at the thought of this nightmare scenario. 'I don't think I could have handled that, Mark. No way am I ready for that.'

'You're absolutely, positively sure she didn't see you? She wasn't waiting at the end of the road when you came out, or anything like that?'

'Yes, I'm sure. I watched her leave. I specifically waited until she'd been gone for five minutes before I even left the window. She was long gone by that time, probably half way home.'

'And the old nosy-parker?'

'No, he wasn't at his window - I checked before I came out through the front door.'

She looked at Mark quizzically. The way he wouldn't let this go didn't seem like him at all.

'Why are you so worried, anyway?' she asked. 'I mean, even if one of them *did* see me, what business would it be of theirs? Or anybody's, for that matter? It's still my house, I was only taking my own clothes, my own jewellery…'

'I just wanted to make sure we weren't seen together.'

She looked at him again, her feelings obscurely hurt. 'Why is that?'

Mark shrugged and seemed to regain some of his easy-going nonchalance, the same kind of devil-may-care attitude that Joan now believed had attracted her to him in just the same way that a very similar quality had attracted her to Kath Meadows.

'Better you shouldn't be seen with me, that's all. For one thing, you're coming away to think about what you want to do with your life, aren't you?'

Joan agreed that she was.

'Well, think about it - if you decided you wanted a divorce, the last thing you'd want is your husband being able to claim that you were the one having the affair, not him.'

This thought silenced Joan instantly. She had not travelled this far in her thinking up until now. Naturally, she had turned the word 'divorce' over in her mind more than once during the last few hours, considering it almost abstractly, like the concept of death, but the idea of an actual divorce made her feel panicky, as though she were standing on the edge of a cliff, feeling herself drawn to the drop. The pull of gravity.

'I hadn't thought of that,' she admitted, more to cover her own sense of dismay than to agree.

'Also,' Mark said, grinning a little now, 'I think your sister and your husband might both deserve a few days' worry, don't you? Not knowing where you are, thinking the worst - that'll shake em up a bit, eh? Serve them right, don't you think?'

This Joan could imagine, and she returned his rather wicked grin with one of her own. 'Aye,' she said, mimicking his heavy accent. 'I do.'

They were both silent for a while, Mark concentrating on getting the van through the Golders Green traffic, Joan just thinking at first, but then brooding, as her mind steadily darkened. Up, down, up, down.

'Unbelievable,' she said eventually.

'What's that?'

'Everything. My sister, telling me that she'd changed and that there was nothing between her and Stephen now, and then as soon as I'm gone, rushing around to see him, like a...'

'Like a bitch in heat?' Mark offered.

'Yes, something like that. And all that bullshit she came out with to Mr Unwill about coming around to help, I mean, Jesus, who does she think she's kidding…'

'It just keeps getting worse for you, doesn't it?' Mark sympathised, shaking his head.

'Mark, I can't tell you. It's like a bad dream I can't wake up from.'

He reached across to hold the hands Joan realised that she was wringing in her lap, and she gripped him back tightly as she struggled not to cry again.

169

'Listen to me, Joan,' he said firmly. 'It's easy for me to say this, I know, but you can't let it get to you. You can't. I've met her type before, and they're not worth getting worked up about. I'm sorry, she's your sister and all, but people like that don't have feelings like you and me. They're only out for themselves, for what they can get.'

He gave her hands a last squeeze and then let them go.

'Anyway, you're out of there now,' he added. 'Good riddance to bad rubbish.'

'You're right,' Joan nodded, sniffing back her tears. 'It's hard, but I know you're right. That's the way I'm trying to think about it, anyway.'

He smiled across at her, and she smiled back.

'Hey, that was a good idea of yours,' she added, trying to respond in kind to his cheeriness. 'Phoning ahead to see if Stephen was in, I mean.'

'Aye, not just a pretty face, me.'

'I was surprised he was still there, actually, I thought he'd have gone to work as usual,' she said. 'I didn't really believe that me leaving would even cause a ripple in his pond, to be honest. It must have been a bit of a shock for you when he answered.'

'Nah, I handled it. Piece of piss.'

'What did you say to him?'

'Oh, I just made up some rubbish, you know.'

'Like what?'

He just smiled at her, blue eyes twinkling mischievously. 'Trade secret, I'm afraid.'

'Tell me!'

'Believe me, you don't want to know.'

'Come on, tell me!' Joan insisted, lightly punching his shoulder.

'All right, I will.' Mark pinned her with another blue-eyed blast that made her feel transfixed like a butterfly on a display board, and then he told her how he had managed to get Stephen out of the house so quickly. It was a short story. Pithy, with a punchline.

Joan listened, and was initially shocked by his succinct explanation, all her breath taken away for one stunning instant. But then she was laugh-out-loud amused.

'Oh my God, you didn't!' She laughed again when Mark nodded confirmation. 'What on earth did he say?'

'Not much, but he didn't sound pleased.'

'I'll bet he didn't!'

Joan's amusement continued to buoy her up as the van passed through Temple Fortune, crossed the North Circular Road not far from the place where they had last night eaten bacon sandwiches - butties, Mark called them, she remembered - and eventually on to Ballards Lane. But then she thought back to the shambles of her living room earlier; bottles, glasses, pizza remnants. It was the sort of scene she was used to seeing in the morning after an Arsenal football victory over a hated rival, or if Stephen had been watching his favourite movies into the early hours.

But for some reason, to her the aftermath of Stephen's binge hadn't seemed to have the same atmosphere of celebration - or any kind of pleasure, for that matter. More like the tail-end of a wake. Maybe that was just her imagination at work. Or maybe it wasn't.

She began to wonder if her husband had been genuinely upset, after all.

'What did Stephen sound like when he answered the phone?' she asked hesitantly. 'Before you told him where I was supposed to be, I mean. Did he seem... I don't know, depressed?'

Mark smiled without much humour, as if he had known what she had been thinking about and hated to tell her the truth.

'I'm sorry to say this,' he said, 'but he sounded like he'd had a hell of a party last night and was thinking about starting another. When I told him you were safe and sound, that's when he got depressed.'

'Oh.' Joan's emotional roller-coaster reached a new low.

Almost as soon as they passed Tally Ho Corner and hit the North Finchley High Road, Mark abruptly indicated left and pulled the van over to the side of the road, but kept the engine running. Joan saw that he was frowning.

'What's wrong?' she asked. 'Is it the van?'

'No, I was just thinking about something.'

'About what?'

He looked at her apologetically. 'It's not a nice thought.'

'What?' she asked nervously, wondering if it could possibly be any worse than his last one.

He paused for a moment, seeming unsure of himself, but then he shrugged and said what was on his mind anyway, his voice gruff with embarrassment. 'All your bank accounts and stuff - are they shared?'

172

'Yes, they are. Why?'

'Then it might be wise for you to draw out as much cash as you can right away.'

Joan was mystified. 'Why?'

'Well, for a start, there's not many cash-points where we're going. But what it really is, I was thinking your husband might put a stop on your accounts. When he realises that you've really gone. He might cut you off, like.'

Despite everything that had already happened, Joan was somehow shocked by this suggestion. 'He wouldn't!'

'Wouldn't he?'

'No!'

'Okay, fair enough,' Mark said with another shrug, this one of the if-you-say-so variety. 'You know him best, I suppose,' he added, managing by his lighter tone to suggest that perhaps Joan didn't know her husband very well at all, or perhaps didn't understand men in general. Didn't understand how men reacted to rejection, even when they were the ones at fault in the first place.

Joan slumped back in her seat. Suddenly, she was much less convinced by her own denial than she had been only a second ago. Now that Mark had planted the seed of doubt, a part of Joan could see it the way he obviously did. Except her vision was just that little more detailed, because, yes, she really did know her husband.

She could imagine that steely, professional detachment of Stephen's coming into play, as the side of him that was a solicitor turned their estrangement into a genuine separation, and then into just another

173

case. He was capable of cutting her off financially, of course he was. As a husband it would have been called an act of revenge, she supposed. But as a solicitor it would be called, what - damage limitation?

'Oh God, Mark,' Joan said helplessly. 'Please tell me what to do, I don't know any more.'

In reply, Mark simply nodded out through the windscreen. The High Road before them was crowded on both sides with shops and businesses of every description. Without even trying, Joan could see three banks and two building societies from where they sat. One of the banks was hers, and she had accounts at both building societies.

'Better safe than sorry, that's what I think,' he said. 'A'cos, it's up to you, it's your money...'

Joan slowly leaned forward and raised her shoulder bag from the footwell as though lifting the heaviest weight imaginable.

'I might not be right,' Mark added.

He sounded apologetic, but she could tell that he thought he was right all the way down the line. And despite the depression the admission wrought in her, Joan thought he probably was, too.

She sighed, reaching for the door handle. 'I won't be long,' she said.

27

During her short walk back to Joan and Stephen's house, Olivia's mind had been awash with many different emotions regarding the last glimpse she'd had of her sister. These emotions included both bewilderment and relief, and also, she had to admit, a surprising amount of anger toward Joan.

There she had been, utterly consumed by guilt and worry - frantically making phone-calls, having nightmares, seeing things in shop windows, and running around like a foolish, headless chicken - and all the time Joan had been perfectly safe. In fact, never mind what she had been through last night and this morning, Olivia had been eaten up with self-hatred for the best part of a year because of her affair with Stephen.

And yet it now turned out that one possible reason Joan had not been getting on with Stephen in the first place was because she might have been having an affair herself.

But this was only an assumption on her part, Olivia reminded herself. She didn't know it for certain. Just because her sister had found a man to help her move out didn't mean that she was sleeping with him. On the other hand, that was just what it could mean. And judging from the type of man she had chosen to help her, it was quite possible that Joan had picked up one or two pointers from her friend Kath Meadows. Like how to seduce tradesmen, for instance.

She had only seen the young man with the white van once, but once was enough because he was quite memorably attractive. A boyish face, stunning eyes, and a great body. He had been doing some work on the house, the guttering, she thought. She remembered him being up a ladder, anyway, stripped to the waist, a deep tan turning the skin over his lithely muscled back into a stunning animal pelt. She remembered that she had even tried to catch his eye on her way in or out of the house, but he either hadn't noticed her or was having none of it. Possibly, Olivia now thought, because he had had something going with Joan, even back then.

But with the state Joan had been in all those months ago, she thought, was that likely? Was it even possible? In retrospect, Olivia didn't believe it was, and she found it depressing that she had tried, however unconsciously, to tar Joan with a brush from her own unenviable collection.

I thought you'd changed, she said to herself.

Olivia had been sitting on the front step for only four minutes by the time Stephen turned up. He must have lost the police car that had been behind him almost immediately and then broken an unimaginable number of speed limits to get back so fast, she realised, walloped over an awful lot of speed-bumps. But then he had always been a fast driver. Fast, reckless, and sometimes dangerous.

Against her will, Olivia remembered several late nights during their affair when he had driven out of the suburbs in search of an open stretch of country road where he could really put his foot down. Speed turned him on in a big way - in several big ways, in fact. She remembered sucking his rigid cock with her eyes closed, hearing the wind buffeting the racing car, feeling its suspension shuddering, and wondering if Stephen would lose control when he came and they would both die in a terrible inferno after the car left the road. The memory chilled her.

Stephen's BMW announced its entrance into Haversham Row with an ostentatious screech of its tyres. Olivia stood up to watch it accelerate out of the turn and then brake to park clumsily at the kerb, one wheel actually riding up on the pavement. The large engine silently died, and Stephen climbed out of his beloved car, actually slamming the door behind him. He was not acting like his normal self and he did not look like his normal self, either, well-groomed and self-satisfied. He looked rumpled and haggard, and supremely pissed-off.

'Somebody's playing silly buggers,' he almost shouted at Olivia as he marched past her up the garden path, unlocked the front door, and left it wide open behind him as he hurried into the house.

Before a puzzled Olivia followed him in, a twitch of movement in a high window from the house across the street caught her eye, and she saw that Mr Unwill had joined the party, watching the proceedings with a jaundiced eye. For a moment, she was tempted to stick her tongue out at the stuffed-shirt, but didn't. Instead she followed Stephen into the house, and firmly closed the door. M had seen about as much as he was going to see today. Unless he'd had the secret service bug the house, that is.

She walked through into the kitchen in time to see Stephen powering cold water into the kettle so that a fine spray dampened the sleeves of his creased shirt, turning the colour of the heavy cotton from sky blue to royal blue.

'Would you mind telling me what you're talking about?' she asked after he had switched the kettle on to boil.

'Just what I said - someone's been playing silly buggers with me, and I don't like it.'

177

Stephen brought down a china mug from the cupboard above the hissing kettle and spooned two spoons of instant coffee into it, followed by three of sugar. Every time the spoon met the china, Olivia expected the cup to chip. She could tell from the way Stephen was moving and the unnatural rigidity of his back that he was genuinely angry, but when he turned around to face her she saw that he was at least as confused, and it was this more than his anger that was making him aggressive.

'Some-one-has-been-play-ing-sill-y-bugg-ers,' he repeated loudly, breaking each word into distinct syllables as though she were both hard of hearing and stupid, and Olivia remembered just how much she had grown to despise him.

'I know what you said. I heard, I'm not deaf, but it doesn't explain what you mean.'

Stephen threw the teaspoon into the sink where it clattered metallically, then raised his hands to his face and groaned. 'Christ, I'm still drunk. Come on, you fucking thing!' he said - to the kettle, Olivia thought.

'Stephen?'

'Okay. Yes, all right.' He rubbed his face, which looked ten years older than the last time Olivia had seen it a few weeks ago. His eyes were so red he might have been rubbing salt into them.

For the first time she realised that there were specks of grey in his stubble and a few strands at his temples, and she wondered how long they had been there. It was tempting to believe that they had appeared overnight, through worry, but the likelihood was that they had been on the way for months. Time was finally running out for the boy Casanova, it

178

seemed. Was that why his women were getting younger? In another ten years' time would he be trying to seduce teenagers?

Somehow calmed by these small signs of his disintegration, Olivia quietly asked him to tell her, please, what had happened this morning. How had someone played him for a silly bugger?

Stephen looked up at the kitchen ceiling for a long time, as though marshalling his thoughts. In reality, though, Olivia thought, he was trying to get a grip on himself, so that he didn't look like such a fool.

'Okay,' he said eventually. 'I was in a bad state last night, as you know. But I woke up fairly early, considering what I put away, and was just about to start calling around the hotels again when the phone rang. I thought it might be Joan, so I leapt for it. But it wasn't Joan.'

The kettle finally boiled and switched itself off, and he turned around to pour water into his cup. He seemed a little more in control of himself now - or more thoughtful, at any rate. Olivia waited for him to offer her a drink, but wasn't surprised when he didn't. He was fully absorbed in himself.

'So who was it who phoned?' she prompted.

'I don't really know.' He found a fresh teaspoon in a drawer and slowly stirred his coffee. 'He said he was the manager of the food hall at Harrods.'

'Harrods?'

'Yes, he said that his security staff had arrested a shoplifter shortly after they opened this morning. She had no identification on her, but she claimed to be called Joan Crosby and gave them this number and

179

my name, saying she was my wife. He described her perfectly, including the dress she was wearing yesterday. He said she was in a very confused state, incoherent most of the time, and pitching panic attacks if anybody tried to touch her. She was paranoid, claiming that someone was out to get her, she was being followed, and something else about being chased by a monster car...'

Stephen sighed tiredly, closing his red eyes.

'He said that they usually prosecute all shoplifters, but because the lady was obviously unstable - actually, he said 'unwell' - they were prepared to overlook the matter this time. He asked if I would I like to go down and collect her.'

'Which, naturally, you did?'

'Of course I did. Like I told you on the phone, I went without changing clothes, getting washed, anything. Drove like a fucking madman to get there as soon as I could.'

'Like you ever drive like anything else,' Olivia muttered to herself. 'Let me guess - when you got there, you discovered that it wasn't Joan after all?'

Stephen looked up at her from his coffee cup with an expression on his face that she could not have named to save her life.

'It wasn't anyone,' he said. 'Joan wasn't there, and never had been. The whole thing was a pack of lies. The food hall manager turned out to be a woman, for a start, and she knew nothing about a shoplifter in her department this morning. She even called around the other departments and asked the security guards to check it out, to see if I'd misheard the details or something.'

'But you hadn't?'

'No. In fact, at the time I was called, the store wasn't even open. Harrods doesn't open until ten, apparently, and the call I got was closer to half past nine.' He shook his head. 'I don't understand it.'

But Olivia did.

Obviously, the bogus phone-call had been a simple ruse to get Stephen out of the house long enough for Joan to get in and pack some clothes to replace the ones she'd abandoned at Olivia's flat last night. What it also suggested was that Joan's little helper had a more intimate knowledge of her sister's life than someone she had accidentally bumped into last night after leaving Olivia's flat. The man who made the call, who drove Joan away from the house, was thoroughly familiar with her recent history. Mixing her metaphors, Olivia realised that he had known all the right buttons to press in order to yank Stephen's chain.

Perhaps there really had been an affair, after all.

'Where the hell is she?' Stephen asked forlornly. 'What the hell is going on?'

Now, Olivia thought. Now was the time to tell him what she had seen, and see what happened to his face when he finally understood. But Olivia suddenly knew that she wasn't going to do that - not yet. Maybe it was wicked, and looking at Stephen's new, older face and greying hair, she *felt* wicked. But she couldn't help herself. She had admitted to herself as well as to Joan that she wasn't entirely blameless for the affair, but at the same time she genuinely believed that Stephen had played on her jealousy to get her into bed.

181

The truth as she saw it was that he had ruthlessly manipulated her throughout the course of their affair, and to see him now manipulated himself, so confused and stripped of his usual arrogance, gave her a delicious feeling of revenge. It was the righteous punishment she felt that Stephen deserved. That she was enjoying this feeling did not make Olivia particularly proud of herself, but neither could she deny that it was real, and as much a part of her as any other.

Anyway, she knew that Joan was really safe, so what did it matter? Stephen would find out soon enough on his own that some of Joan's clothes were missing, probably the minute that he went upstairs to change. She thought of the small case tumbling down the stairs outside her flat and springing open, thought of how much Joan had managed to pack into it. How much more had she managed to pack into that wheeled monstrosity she'd been dragging down the street earlier? Even someone as self-absorbed as Stephen should spot that soon enough.

Meanwhile, she had the distinct pleasure of seeing him suffer in ignorance. Afterward, when she finally let him in on her secret, she would have the pleasure of seeing him suffer in an entirely different way. It was bliss.

Stephen took another sip of his scolding coffee, and looked for a moment as though all he wanted to do was fall asleep again. But then he saw Olivia staring at him with avid interest and he visibly bucked himself up.

'I suppose it's time to hit the phone again,' he said.

'I'll make a start, shall I?' Olivia said quickly. 'Why don't you go up and shower and change first. It'll help sober you up.'

He looked at her statically for a moment, as though suspecting that this offer was either a test or some kind of sarcastic reprimand, but then he decided that it had been a genuine offer, and he smiled. 'Yeah, okay, I will, thanks.'

She smiled back at him as he crossed the kitchen, carrying his mug with him.

'Oh, by the way,' he said as he passed through the door. 'The phone in here doesn't work, you'll have to use the one in the living room.'

'Will do.'

'Ignore the mess in there, I'll clean it up later.'

Too bloody right, you will, she thought. 'Okay,' she said sweetly.

Once Olivia had heard Stephen's leaden footsteps reach the top of the stairs, she stood up, walked across to the work-surface where the kettle lived, and unhurriedly made a cup of tea for herself. She had absolutely no intention of going anywhere near the phone. She knew that she didn't need to. Feeling in a peculiar state of grace, she sat down again at the table with her tea and patiently waited for the eruption.

It wasn't long coming.

She heard Stephen moving about in the master bedroom, which was directly above the kitchen, and then move on to the bathroom. She heard the taps start to run. A few seconds later, she heard the water stop running. She imagined that he had reached for some shampoo or shower-gel, and then noticed that a

183

lot of the toiletries seemed to be missing from the bathroom cabinet - specifically, Joan's toiletries.

After a long period of anticipatory silence, she heard Stephen running back through to the bedroom, and then wardrobe doors being violently thrown open. Then she heard an astonished yelp. Ah, she thought, he'd noticed the missing case.

'Olivia!'

As she heard the thunder of his bare feet descending the staircase, she wiped the grin from her face and composed herself, assuming a bland expression of calm enquiry and practising her reception of Stephen's bombshell.

Oh really? How strange! What do you think it could mean?

How long, she wondered, would she be able to maintain her pose of astonishment before she simply broke out in a gale of laughter?

She could hardly wait to find out.

28

Joan climbed back into the Escort van slightly more than twenty minutes after she had climbed out of it, her purse just over two thousand pounds richer, and she felt unbearably guilty. It was as though by withdrawing what was, after all, her money - the bulk of it having come from her still active business account at the second of the two building societies - she had cheated Stephen. Stolen from him, betrayed a sacred layer of trust that somehow existed above the levels he had already shattered.

She knew it was all bullshit - obviously it was bullshit, after everything he had done to her. But still, she felt bad about it.

Mark, on the other hand, had displayed not one fraction of the dismay she herself felt so intensely. When she told him how much cash she had managed to withdraw, he had grinned that by now familiar grin - an expression that was half wickedness, half glee, and all charm - and called her his poor little rich girl. Then he had patiently waited until she had tucked the purse away in her shoulder bag and tucked the shoulder bag in the foot-well behind her calves and refastened her seatbelt before he started the engine.

Then he waited yet a moment more, until he caught her eye and held it.

'That's the hard part over and done with,' he said, smiling. 'I promise, from now on it's all plain sailing. You and me, we're going to have an absolutely perfect day. Are you ready?'

Mark seemed completely unaware of the way Joan's face had momentarily frozen or the way her spine had straightened as a sudden chill ran along it. It was that damn phrase, of course, Kath's secret code, and the memories it could still conjure up for her. Perfect Day, indeed.

Nice sentiment, she almost wanted to say, but would you mind rephrasing it? Mark, of course, could have had no way of knowing what kind of connotation it had for Joan. He wasn't a mind reader.

She realised that he was still looking deeply into her eyes, trying to turn this into a special moment for her, a watershed in her new life - into a special moment for the two of them, perhaps - and Joan

185

decided that she would not let him down. It was time to finally forget about Kath, just as Kath had forgotten her. Forget about that foolish code, too.

Either that, or claim it for her own.

'Well, are you ready?' Mark repeated.

'Let's do it,' she said, only a slight croakiness to her voice to betray the way her throat had dried up on her.

Mark rewarded her with a smile worthy of a movie star, and then he pulled out into traffic once more.

'We're already doing it,' he said.

A short while later they had passed through Whetstone and were taking the long meandering lane that ran through Totteridge. Totteridge Village was where the really rich people lived, in mansion-like houses set far back from the road in acres of landscaped gardens bordered by high walls and wrought-iron gates, and so many trees that it was more country than town. Joan, lulled by the sudden outbreak of greenery and by the cooling breeze that came in through the open windows, wanted nothing more than to fall asleep, but she forced herself sit up and take an interest in their journey.

'I suppose we're heading for the M1?' she asked.

'Nah, that's too much like hard work for me,' Mark replied. 'I never use motorways unless there's no other option. I like the A roads and B roads. Less stressful and more interesting. You get to see things, not just the back of the car in front of you. For this trip I always take the A1. Most of the way it's just a double-carriageway, like one long country lane all the way home.'

'How long will it take?'

'About five or six hours, depending on the traffic.'

'That long?'

'Aye, well, we're not in a BMW now, you know. Can't go doing the ton in this old girl. Besides, there's no rush, is there? Getting there's half the fun.'

'I suppose so,' Joan agreed, struck once more by the multiple differences between Mark and her husband. Stephen tended to see any journey as a battle campaign, and other drivers as enemies. His BMW was a tank, and it never went fast enough for his liking.

He glanced across at her thoughtful expression. 'You're not regretting coming, are you?'

'No, not at all. In fact, I'm glad it's a long journey. It makes it seem as though I'm going even farther away than I really am.'

'You'll be far enough away,' Mark assured her. 'You'll be in a different world. My world.'

Joan put her hand on his on the steering wheel. 'I'm looking forward to it.'

'Me an' all,' he smiled.

Joan waited until they had negotiated the jam-packed Apex Corner roundabout and were on the A1 itself before asking Mark if he happened to have a map in the car.

'Eh?'

'You know, like a road atlas. I'd like to see where we're going.'

Joan didn't add that she desperately needed something to concentrate on, otherwise the motion of the car would carry her off into sleep before too much longer. She was feeling slightly nauseous again, and presumed that her tiredness was the main cause. And she was filled with dread that if she did fall asleep, last night's erotic dream would pay a return visit and she'd wake up all sticky and disoriented and embarrassed because of the noises she might have made or the words she may have spoken in her sleep - this time with Mark right beside her and wide awake.

Mark made a brief show of checking his mirrors and the speedometer on the dashboard before eventually answering. 'Aye, I've a map. There's no pictures or anything,' he said discouragingly. 'It's not a tourist guide.'

'No, I know, but I could see where the road goes, and all the places we're going to pass.'

'Aye, you could do that, alright,' Mark nodded to himself. 'Should be in the back of the glove compartment.'

Joan leaned forward open the glove compartment and began to root around, entirely missing the irritated glance Mark threw her way as soon as her eyes had left him. She had to pull out a handful of A-Z city guides to get to the map she wanted, which was indeed crushed to the back of the compartment, and was just about to throw the books back in when she noticed that one of them was a guide to the City of Leicester. A city that now seemed to exist merely to remind her of Kath Meadows and her callous elopement.

'You worked in Leicester?' Joan asked.

'Eh? Oh, aye, I did a couple of weeks on a building site last year, when I was short of money,' Mark said dismissively. He glanced sidelong at the book in Joan's hands. 'Bloody 'ell, you can tell I've only been there the once, can't you? Look at the state of the one for London.'

Joan did. The London A-Z was so battered that it had lost its cover and loose pages protruded like veined wings. It had seen a lot of action.

'I see what you mean,' she said.

'Why'd you ask, anyway - you got friends there?'

'No,' Joan said. 'Not really.'

She began to flick through the atlas until she came to page seventeen, where, in the lower half of the page, there was the wheel hub of the capital, its uneven circumference being the M25. Just below Elstree two spokes, the M1 and the A1, angled apart and then extended north in almost parallel lines. Joan's fingers traced them up the pages as they began to diverge, eventually disappearing into the margins.

Unaware that Mark was watching her out of the corner of his eye, she flicked through the book again, locating the roads once more on pages twenty-four/twenty-five, each following approximately the same course about a hand's span apart. Halfway up page twenty-four, the City of Leicester, along with the appropriate junction to reach it from the M1, had been circled with a thick black marker pen.

'What was it like?' Joan asked.

Mark considered for a moment. 'Muddy,' he said. 'Concrete foundations, half-built walls, lots of portacabins…'

189

'Not the building site, you fool!' Joan cried, surprised into laughter. 'Leicester!'

'I don't know,' Mark shrugged. 'Didn't see much of it, too busy working. Just like any other city, I suppose. Too bloody grey for my liking.'

Still smiling to herself, Joan looked back down at the map. 'Did it look like a good place to run away to with a lover?' she asked.

If he was startled by this question, Mark made a good show of hiding it. 'Not that I noticed,' he said dryly. 'Best place for that would be the seaside, wouldn't it?'

Joan nodded her agreement silently. Before Leicester, that had always been Kath's choice - at least, according to DCI Richardson it had. On the M1, the junction for Leicester was number 21. Scanning horizontally across the page, Joan saw that the closest they would come to it on the A1 was a place called Easton on the Hill, just north of Peterborough. When they passed through Easton on the Hill, she would have to remember to look out of her window, to the western horizon, and wish Kath a happy life.

You're welcome to it, she thought, far more bitterly than she had anticipated. You've had your Perfect Day, and now I'm going to have mine.

'If you like the seaside,' Mark added, 'my place is only half an hour's drive from it. Whitby's closest.'

'Yes, I remember you telling me.'

Joan flicked through the pages again, following the course of the A1 up past Sheffield, Doncaster, Pontefract and Leeds, where it and the M1 briefly grew close again, and then up into North Yorkshire. She saw lots of places she thought she had heard of, or just imagined that she had: Wetherby, Knaresborough, Ripon. Another A road, this time eastbound, would lead them to the southern edge of the large patch of green nothing identified as the North Yorkshire Moors National Park, incorporating the North Riding Forest Park.

On yet another road that ran northward through the Moors themselves, she spotted a place called Lockton Dale, which she remembered Mark saying was the closest village to his little cottage, Hunter's Lodge. If Joan let her fingers do the walking, the coast was only a few inches away. Not far at all.

Joan nodded again. She had never seen Whitby, just knew that there was a ruined abbey on a cliff and that the bay was where Count Dracula was supposed to have landed in England. Odd, the things that stick in your mind, she thought, the things it throws up when you're tired. Maybe she and Mark could drive over there sometime in the coming week, and have themselves another little Perfect Day. Stand and watch the sea crash against the sea-wall, feel the spray, inhale the ozone. Heal. It sounded good.

It was only then that she made a connection between Mark's last two sentences, and she glanced at him sharply. What had he said? That the seaside was the best place to go with a lover to, followed by the fact that his home wasn't far from the sea and that they could go there, if she liked. What did that mean? Joan wondered. Was there a real, intentional connection there, or was she making it up, out of vulnerability or need?

She wished that she could see his eyes properly. Like Dr Stratton, Mark seemed to convey a lot of

191

information through his expressive eyes, but this time he wasn't making it easy for her, staring rigidly ahead as he manoeuvred the van past a sequence of heavy goods lorries struggling up a long incline. This way, the only way she would know what he had really meant - if he had meant anything at all - was if she asked, and she wasn't about to do that.

By the time they had passed the lorries and swung back into the left hand lane of the double-carriageway, the moment seemed to have passed, and Joan settled back in her seat, slightly confused and, she could not deny this to herself, slightly excited. The combination was very familiar. It felt like she was dating again.

'Are you thirsty yet?' Mark asked a few minutes later.

'A little bit. Why, do you want to stop somewhere?' Joan had noticed that the A1 was amply served by succession of fast food restaurants.

'Nah, I don't stop once I get going. I never stop. But if you lean over the back of your seat, you'll find a flask of coffee.'

Joan turned around and found the thermos, an old, tartan-coloured one that had obviously been around for several decades and was rusty in several places. She almost asked why he didn't buy a new one, but then realised that it would probably be for the exact same reason Mark still liked to keep his hand in with the old-school method of developing and printing his work, even though he was equipped with all the bells and whistles of modern digital photography.

He did it out of sentiment. He had inherited the old enlarger and all the other paraphernalia from his uncle, the man who had raised him as his own and who had passed along the hobby of photography like the shape of his ears or the colour of his eyes. Using the old gear, respecting the traditions and the craft, was one of the ways Mark kept the beloved old man alive in his memory, and Joan liked him all the more for it.

Stephen wasn't a sentimental man. To the best of her knowledge, he hadn't even kept any of the love letters she had sent him before they married. Fool that she was, she had kept all his.

'Are you okay?' Mark asked.

'Yes, of course.' She unscrewed the cup and offered Mark the first drink, which he declined.

'I'm not that keen on coffee,' he said.

When she asked him why, in that case, he'd made coffee instead of tea, which they both could have drunk, Mark laughed out loud.

'I don't know, I must be going doolally.'

'Going *what*?' Joan smiled.

'*Doolally*. You know, puddled'.

'Puddled?'

'Nuts, crazy, off me trolley.'

'Oh, I see. Well, I sort of knew that, anyway - you must be at least a little bit crazy to hook up with me.'

She poured herself some of the coffee, which, although instant, was good and strong and very sweet, with honey this time, she believed. Mark must have made it while she was in the bathroom prior to leaving his flat, thinking of her and not of himself.

193

Maybe, she thought, that was a part of her question answered right there.

Joan eventually drank two cups of the coffee, imagining that it would keep her awake and give her enough energy to last the whole journey, but she was wrong. The coffee had quite the reverse effect, and within half an hour she found herself nodding off and without the strength to resist. She reluctantly confessed this to Mark, but he wasn't upset at all.

'No problem, lass,' he said. 'Grab yourself forty winks. I'll still be here when you wake up.'

Joan's eyes immediately closed of their own accord, as though Mark had given her a hypnotic suggestion, and her mind drifted loose from her body. She felt that she was very deeply asleep, but for a while she could still hear and feel everything happening around her, the motion of the van, the wind whistling past her window. She could even smell the smoke when Mark lit one of the roll-ups he had made in preparation for the journey. It was exactly the same way she had felt during last night's erotic dream, and it convinced her that she was, indeed, asleep.

But then, to her considerable alarm, she heard her voice, her real voice and not some inner personality, speak aloud.

'Do you like me, Mark?' she asked in a slow, dragging voice, all husky and, to her at least, toe-curlingly suggestive. She was appalled at herself, but was as unable to stop speaking as she was to open her eyes properly. 'Do you really like me, Mark. Do you like me?'

'I think you're beautiful, Joan,' Mark replied calmly. He sounded completely unsurprised by what she was saying, and how she was saying it. 'In fact, I think you're perfect. You're just the kind of woman I go for.'

Joan felt her lips form into a wide, uncontrollable smile.

'Now go to sleep.'

'I will.'

'Now.'

'Yes.'

29

When he had come rushing downstairs into the kitchen, Olivia had seen that Stephen was already stripped down to his boxer shorts in preparation for his shower, and that most of his lower face was smeared with shaving foam from the can he still held in his left hand. He had forgotten he was holding it, she thought.

His greasy hair was stuck up at the back, like a cock's-comb, and when she looked down at the other end of his body, she saw that his pale feet and ankles were deeply indented by the weave of the socks he had worn for more than twenty-four hours. The pattern terminated at an even deeper groove that encircled his legs at the mid-calve level and gave his feet an odd detachable look.

He seemed completely unaware of the amusing figure he cut, his unaccustomed lack of dignity. If he'd wised up a minute or so later than he had, Olivia supposed that he would have rushed down totally naked, which would have made her fondest fantasies of this moment come true.

Stephen, it was very clear, had a lot on his mind.

Olivia knew that this should have been her moment of triumph. She should have taken an atavistic pleasure that the signs he showed of aging above the neck had begun to extend to the rest of his body, like Dutch elm disease spreading throughout the whole tree.

Like his hair and his beard, the dark curls on Stephen's chest and belly were frosted with the first scatterings of grey, and he had obviously put on more than a few pounds since Olivia had last seen him without his clothes on. His made-to-measures hid a lot of entropy. He was only an inch or so away from a pot-belly now, and the well-defined muscle-tone she remembered admiring in his shoulders, upper-arms and chest had vanished, submerged beneath a shapeless secondary layer of superfluous flesh. He had embryonic man-boobs. In body, at least, Stephen Crosby was no longer the man who had once seduced her.

All of this should have filled her with bitter joy. It didn't.

She had imagined that she would see outrage, and was quite prepared - eager, in fact - to see it displayed to the max. She had calculated that she would see flashes of panic, and breast-beating remorse, and the crocodile-tears of maudlin self-pity. She had expected to hear confessions, and numberless curses, and eloquent entreaties for her sympathy - all of which she would have been able take with a very large pinch of low-sodium salt substitute and a carefully hidden smile.

What she hadn't reckoned on, what had never even occurred to her, was what she actually got at full blast the moment that she looked into Stephen's eyes. And that was misery. Pure, unadulterated misery, which she knew could not be faked, and could not be ever fail to be recognised once it had been seen.

Olivia had seen it at least twice before, on her sister's face and in her own mirror.

This had all happened sometime between twelve o'clock and twelve-thirty. It was now after six o'clock in the evening, and steadily getting closer to seven. The sun had made its way from the front of the house to the back, and the kitchen, where Olivia was seated at the table once more, was now as saturated with sunlight as the living room had been earlier in the day.

She had just finished washing, drying and putting away the cups, glasses, plates and ashtrays that had littered the wrecked living room like the relics of a bygone age. Before that, she had been sweeping up broken glass and picking up broken ornaments, tidying up around Stephen, who had fallen asleep on the sofa through a savage combination of emotional distress and the glut of alcohol still poisoning his system. After Olivia had finished in the living room, she had covered him with a duvet she had brought down from upstairs. She had done it gently.

'What the fuck,' she asked herself in the bright kitchen, 'am I going to do now?' She could think of no satisfactory answer.

Stephen had already been in tears the moment he appeared in the kitchen doorway, and Olivia had instantly known that this was not what she wanted. It was similar to how she had felt after sleeping with him for the first time. Instead of the fierce pleasure of conquest, of taking something away from her sister and making it her own, however briefly, she had felt something more like loss.

She had watched Stephen try and at first fail to speak, feeling her own heart stuttering along with his speech. No solicitor's eloquence now. She had watched him battle to splutter the words out, tears almost bursting out his eyes like some kind of conjuring trick.

Joan's clothes were gone, he'd managed to tell her. Lots of them. Her jewellery, gone. All her cosmetics, gone. She had gone, this time for good.

Olivia had been struck silent by this display of raw emotion, but gained some measure of comfort from the thought that at least it could not get any worse. Amazingly, a short while later, it did.

It was the moment when Stephen finally made the link between his wife removing her possessions from their home and the duplicitous phone call which had taken him to Knightsbridge that morning. That and the fact that the caller had been male.

He sprang to exactly the same conclusion that Olivia had, and the thought that Joan might be in love with and was actively involved with another man took his legs from under him. He had sunk to his knees on the tile floor, lowered his forehead to the ground, and sobbed. The can of shaving foam rolled away over the tiles, finally coming to rest under the kitchen table by Olivia's feet.

After a moment or two, during which she had been too shocked to move, she had hesitantly left her chair and bent to comfort him. The instant her hand touched his bare shoulder, however, something else snapped in Stephen, and he jumped away and fled from the kitchen into the living room, catching his shoulder painfully on the doorframe as he passed through without seeming to notice.

For a while, Olivia could hear him stomping around in the other room in a rage, throwing things around, and shouting - at himself, it seemed, more than anything else. She winced at the small, tinkling explosions that followed, the heavier thuds as furniture was overturned, and the inarticulate bellowing of an animal in distress. During all this, she was too frightened to even move, for fear that his anger would be transferred to her.

Eventually the sounds of destruction had culminated in an almighty crash, and all that was left was a muffled crying. Was it time to tell him what she'd seen now, she had wondered.

No, of course it wasn't. She didn't dare.

On trembling legs, she had finally followed Stephen through to the living room, where she found him huddled up on the sofa, his face buried so deep in a cushion that he seemed to be trying to suffocate himself. Around him, the room looked as though a hurricane had blown through it.

The coffee table had been swept clear, a long, curved scratch now dominating the surface like a heraldic device, and the debris spread all over the carpet; stale pizza, broken glass and ash everywhere, as though a dustbin had been upended. Over in the corner, a bookcase had been toppled, the armchair had been overturned, and something heavy had imploded the screen of the TV. Scattered at its base and twinkling on top of the Blu-ray player, Olivia saw the remains of Stephen's whisky bottle. There were a series of dents in the otherwise smooth walls where other missiles had struck and smashed.

Olivia cautiously approached the sofa and sat down beside Stephen, feeling somewhat like an animal trainer about to put their head into a lion's mouth. But this time, when she laid a hand on his back, Stephen groped for her with the desperation of a drowning man and seized her around the waist with a strength that took her breath away. The muscles may have been well hidden, but they were still there.

After a slight hesitation, she held him in return, feeling the sick, sour heat coming off him in waves. Misery. She realised now that it even had a smell. Stephen's face was in her lap. She could feel her cotton trousers becoming saturated with a combination of the remaining shaving foam and an incredible quantity of tears, and his head, hard as a bowling ball, crushing against her ribs. She felt his body shaking uncontrollably. Instinctively she began to stroke his greying hair, murmuring words of comfort that had absolutely no meaning at all. Gradually, his shaking lessened and his breathing began to even out.

By that time she had leant over to embrace him more fully, and she suddenly became aware that her breasts were pressed against him. She was also aware that this was the closest they had been for over a year, and that like it or not the old chemistry, unbidden, unwanted, was still there. This discovery made her feel sick to her stomach, and all her old suspicions about Stephen, and about herself, returned.

For a while, holding her breath in anticipation and her own anger on red-alert, she waited for Stephen to react. Waited for the moment when their history of past intimacy and their current physical proximity dawned on him. Stephen, she realised, had always been an opportunist. She waited for him to nuzzle even closer into her, for his hands, with an accomplished ease born of experience and habit, to ferret their way through her clothes to her bare skin.

If that happened, she had resolved, she would leave. Immediately. She would walk out of the house and never return.

But after the tears eventually faded, Stephen didn't make a single move. Not until his grip around her waist abruptly eased, and it was only when she heard the first snore that she realised he had fallen asleep in her arms like an exhausted child. Olivia had been so relieved that she felt foolish.

In the kitchen, she stood up and stretched, still no closer to a clear answer. What should she do? She knew what she *wanted* to do, and that was to get out right now. Leave before Stephen woke up, leave before her newly-developed conscience and sense of responsibility forced her to tell him the truth. She did not want to be on the receiving end of the sort of anger she had witnessed earlier.

Weary and dispirited, she wandered back through into the living room, which after the pupil-shrinking brightness of the kitchen was dim and cave-like, to find that Stephen was still deeply asleep. He didn't seem to have moved so much as an inch since the moment she had eased herself out from under his weight and gone in search of a dustpan and brush. That had been something like five hours ago.

She hoped that sleep was helping Stephen to recuperate from his excesses, as it usually did for her, but she was far from convinced that this was the case. From the little she could see of his face, pale and twisted as though in a nightmare, he didn't appear to have found much peace.

'Stephen?' she whispered. 'Stephen?'

No reaction.

She gently tapped his shoulder and called his name again, but he did not respond.

She remembered thinking this morning that nothing about Stephen would ever surprise her again. Well, she had been wrong. Once more. Maybe she just didn't understand people.

Maybe she never would.

Olivia made her way around the scarred coffee table and eased herself down into the heavy armchair that she had managed to upright, wishing that she were anywhere but where she was, and knowing that she could not leave. Partly, she was afraid that if Stephen were to wake up alone in the same frame of mind he had fallen asleep in, he might do anything. She was worried that he might not restrict his destruction to furniture and *objet d'art*, and start in on himself, and she was haunted enough without having something like that on her conscience.

Mostly, though, she felt that she had to stay in order to redeem herself, if only in her own eyes. If nothing else, she owed Stephen the truth, and she would give him it no matter the cost to herself. This was just a part of the same life lesson she had begun learning the day that Joan had been knocked down.

It was called accepting the consequences of your actions.

30

Her sense of hearing came back first. The hoarse sound of the old engine, the air flowing by her window, even brief snatches of birdsong. Next came sensation, the warmth of sunlight bathing her face, a soft breeze from an open window caressing her hair, the mingled scents of the countryside all around her, as heavy as spilled perfume. She could feel her hands arranged just so in her lap, one on top of the other, as though formally posed for a photograph. She was in a perfect state of relaxation, her mind clear, her muscles fluid, her joints oiled. She was mellow.

'Back with us, are you?'

'Yes,' Joan said through lips that seemed to have been gummed together. 'I think so.'

'Here, have some of this, Joan.'

She opened her eyes, then immediately narrowed them against the strong, low sunlight. She felt a cool plastic bottle being pressed into her hands and she drank from it gratefully. The cold spring water seemed to line her throat with liquid velvet, and she sighed in appreciation.

203

'Better?'

'Yes, much.'

Joan hitched herself up in her seat and looked around. They were no longer on the A1, but on a narrow B road snaking through open countryside, fields of indeterminate crops on either side of the car as far as the eye could see. It looked pretty much the same as the countryside she was used to, but at the same time, it somehow felt completely different. Branches from the overgrown hedgerows clattered against the van's panels on Joan's side, and birds were startled into flight by their passage.

'Where are we?' Joan asked, looking down at her lap and then into the footwell. She could not see the map she had fallen asleep holding, but couldn't be bothered to pursue it. Everything around her was too beautiful.

'Nearly there,' Mark said. 'Not far to go now, just a few more miles.'

'God, I must have been asleep for hours.'

'Aye, you were. Must have needed it, then, I reckon.'

'I suppose so…'

Joan realised that she had missed her chance to say goodbye to Kath Meadows. At the time they had been on the same latitude as Leicester, she had probably been snoring her head off.

'Mark, I'm so sorry.'

He frowned. 'Why are you sorry?'

'I should have stayed awake to keep you company.'

'Don't fret yourself, I'm used to it. And anyway, you did keep me company.'

Joan was puzzled. 'How?'

'Oh, we had a nice long chat while you were asleep.'

Her heart sank. Oh Christ, she thought, what have I said? 'I talked while I was asleep?'

Mark laughed. 'No, you silly bugger! I talked, you listened.'

Joan was relieved. 'Anything good?'

'Not bad. You're a good listener, I'll say that for you. I just hope you don't tell anybody else what I told you, 'cos now you know all me dark secrets.'

'You can trust me,' Joan replied, warming up. Melodramatically, she added, 'I'll take them to my grave.'

'Aye, I reckon I know that.'

They smiled at each other.

Joan decided that it didn't matter about Kath. Perhaps sleeping through the tenuous psychic connection she had theorised had actually been the best message she could have sent her former friend. Total indifference. And if she were to change her mind, well, she could always do it on the journey back, couldn't she?

Just then, the van reached the top of a small rise, and Joan gasped in surprise. Away to the left, stretching as far as the eye could see, was a vast flat expanse of rugged moorland, all of it a rich, variegated purple. Against the cyclorama of a cobalt blue sky, unbroken by a single cloud, and in the wash of lowering golden sunlight, it was a hallucinatory landscape.

'My God!' Joan exclaimed.

'It's heather,' Mark said.

205

'I know, but...' Joan shook her head. 'Just look at it, it's incredible! I expected it to be bleak, not like this...'

'It's bleak in winter, all right,' Mark said. 'Right now, it's heaven. Do you see why I have to come back?'

Joan nodded, entranced. 'I can smell it.'

In the far distance she noticed a line of hikers with large back-packs trailing across the moorland. They looked like ants carrying leaves back to the nest. Knowing that they were too far away to see her, she waved anyway. Joan felt a kinship with them. She wanted to do what they were doing. To be in the heart of it all, not on the margins.

She glanced across at Mark when she heard the indicator clicking and felt the van began to slow for a turn. She looked through the windscreen and saw the entrance to the lane he intended to take, which would take them away from the moors, and she couldn't help protesting.

'Oh no, Mark,' she said with genuine dismay. 'Can't we stay up here a moment longer? It's so beautiful.'

'So's where we're going.'

'But--'

'Don't you worry, there'll be plenty of time for sight-seeing another day. Right now, I want to get us in and settled.'

He spun the van around the right-hand turn and barrelled down a long hill, the road bordered by high, untrimmed hedges. Joan turned around in her seat, watching the moors diminish through the rear window until finally the curvature of the road removed them from sight altogether. She sat back in her seat, feeling as though she had just been granted a vision.

'Beautiful,' she said again.

'Shape of things to come,' Mark replied.

As they descended the steep hill, trees began to spring up on either side of the hedges, all of them pine. Soon they were in amongst a dark forest of straight tall trunks so close together that they absorbed all light. Their strong scent easily overpowered the remaining traces of the heather.

Joan was surprised that there should be so many pine trees. It wasn't what she had expected from the area.

'This isn't the real forest,' Mark explained. 'Not my forest, anyway. It's the Forest Park. They started planting in the 1920s, so they could harvest the softwood. Sustainable, you see. Cut one down, plant another two.'

Joan thought that he sounded disapproving. 'But that's good, isn't it?'

'I suppose,' Mark shrugged. 'Me uncle hated it, though. Said it'd changed the landscape too much. Some of him rubbed off on me, I guess. I like the real forest. Broadleaf. Oak, Ash, Horse Chestnut, Birch. The old forest knows how to keep secrets.' He smiled to himself. 'That's where we're going, lass.'

Joan smiled at his smile. 'You seem to set a great store on keeping secrets,' she said.

'Aye. That's another thing I inherited from me uncle.'

Half an hour later, after a great many twists and turns and seemingly nonsensical changes of direction up and down a sequence of increasingly narrow lanes, Joan was thoroughly confused. Even if she'd had a detailed map of the area, she would still have been confused. Luckily, Mark seemed to know exactly where they were.

They had reached a long stretch of tarmac so old that it was brittle and crumbling away at the edges. It was scarcely more than a car's width across, and lined on both sides by vast trees whose branches overhung the road and interlocked overhead like the teeth on a zipper. As Mark had promised, the pine trees had now vanished entirely, replaced mostly by the kind of towering oaks she had seen in the photograph stuck on the mirror in his flat. The only sunlight that made it through the dense summer canopy was reduced to brilliant individual beams, which shifted second by second as the tree branches and leaves moved in the breeze. It was like passing through a living, breathing tunnel, which had unaccountably been equipped with a mirror-ball.

'Do you like it up here, then?' Mark asked.

Joan nodded immediately. 'It's lovely. So wild and untamed.'

'Just like me,' Mark said, and Joan swatted at his arm, but did not disagree.

They were the only car on the road and had not seen another vehicle for more than ten minutes, and that had been a farm truck they had quickly passed in a blizzard of windblown hay and left for dead. Nevertheless, Mark checked his mirrors carefully before stopping the van. Joan looked at him enquiringly, and he inclined his head to the trees to his right.

Almost completely concealed between two-metre-wide tree trunks was the entrance to another narrow lane, this one with long dry grass growing up along the centre. A thick, padlocked chain hung between the two trees, attached to rusted iron cleats hammered into the bark. Joan couldn't see more than a few metres beyond the entrance because of over-grown bushes and an abundance of bracken. It looked impassable.

'Up there?'

'Aye.'

Mark pulled his keys out of the ignition and quickly rooted through the ring until he found the padlock key.

'I told you it was private, didn't I?'

31

After pulling the car off the main road and quickly replacing the chain and padlock behind them, Mark jumped back into his seat and began to ease the van along at about five miles an hour, and occasionally, frustratingly, at even slower speeds. Joan at first suspected that he was teasing her a little, knowing how eager she was to see the cottage, but as they moved deeper into the woodland, she soon realised that it would have been impossible for him to drive even slightly faster on this kind of road with any degree of safety.

In fact, considering the nature of the surface they were travelling over, the word 'road' seemed generous, if not grandiose. It really was a dirt track, little more than the deep ruts carved by several generations of tractor tyres, the mud baked hard by summer heat. In winter, or even after a substantial rainfall, it would probably only be passable in a tractor. Either that or a tank. Anything else, she imagined, would simply stick or sink.

The track followed a gentle, snakelike route, tracing a line of least resistance through the ancient broadleaf forest, avoiding the large trees and carefully circling large outcroppings of rough, slate-coloured rock. The trees and the undergrowth growing either side leant inwards over the van, pressing in like a claustrophobic's bad dream, but Joan was only entranced.

There was something magical about this glut of greenery which appealed to the child that still lived in her. The scale and the intensity and variations of shade, shape and texture touched her with a kind of wonder, in just the same way that extreme weather displays always did. Like lightning storms, tornados, and ferociously lashing seas, the forest seemed almost profound, the possessor of a powerful, mystical wisdom.

It was the child inside that also made the association between her present surroundings and the fairy tales she had been familiar with throughout her early life. In particular, she thought of Hansel and Gretel, leaving their trail of breadcrumbs winding through the forest so that they would be able to find their way home again.

Joan was not at all surprised to have made this connection. She was aware that this trip was something on the order of a fairy tale itself, a fantasy not unlike dipping into a book. It was a moment of repose, a chapter of distraction to ease her heart and mind, granting her a temporary absence from her life. It was a time-out. A pit-stop. A rest-cure.

She didn't believe that there was anything wrong with that.

'Get ready,' Mark said. 'Any second now.'

Joan leant forward in her seat, her nose almost touching the windscreen as she tried to peer through the undergrowth to catch a first-hand look at Mark's 'ancestral pile'. She clutched at the dashboard for support as the van suddenly lurched beneath them as the wheels found a deeper rut, and a newly sprouted branch, still green and juicy with sap, raked across the windscreen in front of her eyes, making her blink. When her eyes opened again, they were there.

Hunter's Lodge.

The cottage stood at the far side of what was simply a large clearing in the forest, backing on to the enormous oak trees she remembered from Mark's photograph. But his black and white photography, good as it was, could not compare with the reality, which was even better.

The picturesque cottage was built on a low deck, reached by two broad steps made from railway sleepers, either side of which were overgrown flowerbeds dominated by heavy-headed red roses. The tile roof was bowed, covered by a thick carpet of moss, and the trees above it seemed even larger now, dressed in their summer clothes, sheltering the fairytale house like benevolent giants. Like parents, perhaps, because the cottage seemed so much a part of the forest that it might have grown from it.

211

'No marzipan, no gingerbread,' Joan said to herself, smiling, and then shook her head at the enquiring glance Mark sent her way. 'It doesn't matter. Little private joke.'

'You like it?'

Joan shook her head. 'I'm beyond liking. You can only love something that beautiful.'

Mark, who had stopped the van so that Joan could take it all in, now set it trundling forward again, drawing up before the steps on a large patch of hard-packed earth. He pulled on the handbrake and killed the engine, pulled the keys from the ignition, and heaved a contented sigh.

'Home,' he said.

They got out of the van together and Mark walked around the back to open the boot. Joan began to make her way to help him, but instead he waved her off. He tossed the keys to her with a smile.

'Open up, I'll bring the bags.'

Joan found the right key easily enough on the large bunch. It was the only mortise key there. As she turned the heavy lock, she heard the click echo back at her as though from a large, empty space.

The very moment that she pushed open the door, something happened to her, some kind of brainstorm that rapidly expanded to every nerve throughout her entire body. A voice in her head whispered, *this is wrong*. She stepped in through the doorway, and this time the voice screamed.

She could feel the heat of the lowering sun warm on her back and in her hair, but the front of her body was completely chilled. The hairs on her arms were standing up, as were her nipples. At the same time, her face was covered with a greasy film of perspiration. If she had been fifteen or twenty years older she would have been thinking menopause. What she was really thinking was panic attack.

What is it, she asked herself. What is this?

There was nothing to be seen in the cottage that could explain her strange reaction, although it was far from what she had expected. She had imagined something comfortable but basic - dark and earthy rural chic, perhaps minus the chic. But her imagination had led her astray. Mark had obviously utilised the money he made in London and his wide array of odd-job talents to their utmost.

The front door opened directly on to a room the entire size of the original cottage, serving as living room, dining room and kitchen, all laid with seamless wooden flooring. The kitchen was Scandinavian post-modern, complete with a beech breakfast bar and large butcher's block. The twin sofas flanking an open fireplace in the living room area were of walnut leather, the standing lamps were chrome with frosted glass shades. The ceiling had been lowered and inset with chrome-edged downlights. All the walls were smoothly plastered, distempered, and completely covered with small framed photographs of woodland scenes, all, presumably, taken by Mark.

At the back of the room were two plain pine doors, each ajar by a few inches, and Joan could see that the perfect flooring extended without a break into these rooms, too. Through the left hand doorway, she saw the gleaming white of an immaculate new bathroom suite. Through the right, she saw the corner post of a wood-framed bed covered by a down

213

comforter and the edge of a large sheepskin rug spread out over the floor.

Joan felt that she should have been amazed at what Mark had achieved. He had obviously extended the cottage back into the woods to include a further two rooms, had plumbed in a bathroom, fitted a kitchen, installed additional windows, and generally decorated and furnished in a way that should have confounded her.

But although she took everything in, none of it touched her. It didn't seem real.

She had the impression that what she was seeing was only a thin outer layer, a mask, which hid something foul beneath. Despite the brightness, the cottage seemed damp and dank and cold. The skeleton of the house, and the ground it was built on, seemed to project a nameless atmosphere that was making her pulses race. She felt echoes here, like the one that had greeted the turning lock, deep echoes that made her dizzy with fright. Terror. Pain. Anguish.

Betrayal.

And Joan suddenly wondered what the hell she was doing here, stranded in the middle of nowhere with a young man who was a virtual stranger - who had been a complete stranger to her before yesterday. She wondered why Mark's abrupt, unexpected appearance and his immediate involvement in her life had not prompted the kind of paranoia that had been her lot for the past year. It didn't seem credible.

Even as late as yesterday morning, she'd had a minor panic attack when her own doctor, who she both knew and had come to trust, had given her a simple hug in his familiar office. Yet here she was with this stranger, having contemplated much more than a simple hug; having fantasised about him sexually, in fact, and trusted him more than she felt she could trust anybody else in the world at this moment in time.

How had this come to be?

Then Mark stepped by her and walked into the cottage, carrying her wheelie case and his own bag, a long khaki kitbag that would have been at home slung over an infantryman's back, which he set down by one of the sofas. He rubbed his hands together briskly as he glanced around.

'Bloody hell, it's taters in here, innit?'

Joan double-blinked. At the sound of his voice, the wave of terrified doubt that had threatened for a moment to drown her receded with a speed that took her breath away. All the ugly, phantom echoes were instantly banished, their strength drained. She found herself actually smiling.

'Taters?' she asked, eyebrows raised.

'Aye, I'm practising me cockney wide-boy act. Apples and pears, all that gubbins.'

'I see. Has it fooled anyone yet?'

'No so's you'd notice. Well?'

Joan looked around the cottage again, shaking her head, this time in pleasure. 'It's so different to what I'd expected.'

'Better or worse?'

'Oh, better, of course. Much better.'

Mark smiled. 'Good. Have a look around if you want. I'm going to make a fire, get rid of this bloody damp. It's always like this when I've been away for a while.'

'A fire would be nice.'

'After that, I'll make us a--'

'A nice cup of tea?'

'Smart arse,' Mark scowled at her. 'Aye, and something to eat, an' all. I don't know about you, but I'm bloody starving.'

While Mark went about his tasks with the brisk efficiency she now expected of him, Joan took him at his word and explored the cottage.

As a trained interior designer, with a wide experience of tradesmen both good and bad, she immediately recognised that the work which had been carried out to transform the cottage had been finished to a professionally high standard. She was impressed by Mark's vision as much as his handiwork. He had managed to open the whole cottage out so that it seemed much larger on the inside than it appeared from the outside. Each area of the living-room/dining-room/kitchen flowed into the other, and yet each retained its own specific identity. He had an eye for composition that she guessed probably came from his photographic talent.

She also liked the fact that he hadn't gone the whole hog when it came to modernisation. There was no television, and not even a music system. More unusually, there seemed to be no telephone. Mark obviously wasn't a gadget man like Stephen, who always had to have the latest mobile phone, entertainment format and computer platform, and everything deemed even fractionally out of date had to be dumped immediately, as though it carried the risk of infection. Mark seemed to respect the past, and as if to prove the point there were a few items dotted around the cottage that were obviously remnants from his uncle's time.

The table and chairs in the dining room, for instance, were very old, made from solid, hand-turned oak, and Mark had simply refurbished and refinished them. A welsh dresser set against the wall facing the dining room area had received similar attention. Placed at strategic places around the room there were three brass oil-lamps, their wicks neatly trimmed and ready to light. Joan could imagine the warm, buttery light they would give forth. Even the lowered ceiling had been constructed so that the lower halves of the original beams could still be seen, thus retaining much of the cottage's original character.

Next she concentrated on Mark's photographs and saw that there was theme to them, a theme beyond the fact that each and every one depicted aspects of the forest that surrounded the cottage. The theme appeared to be the change of the seasons. On the wall to the right of the front door, winter was melting into spring. As the kitchen became the dining room, summer was beginning to bloom. On the wall above the fireplace, ripe summer gracefully gave way to rusty autumn, the photographs arranged in such a way that the fire Mark had lit seemed to be driving the change. Back at the front door, winter again held thrall.

A sharp pinging noise made Joan turn from the photographs. A microwave had been concealed inside one of the cupboards, and she watched Mark remove a large Tupperware bowl from it.

217

'Just defrosting some homemade soup,' he explained. 'I've always got something in the freezer for these visits.'

'Sounds wonderful.'

Joan watched him dump the soup into a saucepan and light the gas under it. On the work-surface she saw another 7-11 carrier bag packed with additional groceries that Mark had brought in from the van. He must have bought them at the same time as he was getting breakfast. She saw fresh, crusty bread, and a couple of bottles of white wine.

'I love your photographs,' she said. 'You're so talented.'

Mark shrugged modestly. 'I only take the pictures,' he said. 'Nature's the real artist. Growth, decay, change. Before, during, after. Everything in Nature is beautiful if you look at it right.'

Then he looked at her for so long that she blushed.

Joan had found a fallen tree just inside the treeline at the side of the cottage and had sat on it to smoke one of Mark's roll-ups and watch the sunset. The sun, huge and distorted, orange-red, was slipping down behind the tree canopy in steady increments that she could almost see. Its light blazed through the high, fluttering leaves so brightly, Joan almost expected to see them burst into flame, and to hear distant crackling as the branches were consumed. What she actually heard was birdsong, which she was unable to identify but was sure that Mark would have. Mark knew everything.

He was back in the cottage at the moment, having sent her out while he washed and tidied away the crockery of their simple meal. Joan was full now of his nourishing soup -vegetable and some kind of meat, probably pork, she imagined - and she felt more relaxed than she had for a very long time. The only thing about her that was not relaxed were the muscles in her stomach, which had a familiar tautness to them that was not in the least unpleasant.

Water had been running in the cottage for some time, and when she heard it being cut off, Joan dropped the butt of her roll-up to the floor and carefully crushed it into the mulch under her foot. Then she turned to watch the cottage door, waiting for Mark to come.

The electric lights inside were snapped off, but through the windows she saw that the pale walls were glowing steadily, not flickering with firelight, and she guessed that Mark had lit the oil-lamps, too. The scene is set, she thought. She smiled at him when he appeared in the doorway, a glass of white wine in each hand.

In the gathering dusk, she watched him take extreme care of the placement of his feet as he came down the sleeper steps from the deck. She watched him walk across to her tree trunk, at his answering smile, at the planes of his face, which caught the light, captured and held it. He was illuminated, rose-golden, beyond handsome. Beautiful. She couldn't take her eyes off him.

Mark sat down beside her and wordlessly handed her one of the glasses. He held his up, as though to toast the sunset, and she in turn raised hers, and when

219

their glasses chinked together, the sunset made their white wine into a rosé. They drank, their eyes never breaking contact.

'All those photographs on your walls,' Joan said. 'But there's only one in your bedroom.'

'Aye, that's right,' Mark said with a knowing smile.

The photograph hung on the plain wall above the bed, just a small square black and white print of a young girl a few years into her teens. She had been posed in the forest, of course, in profile to the camera, and she seemed unaware that her picture was being taken, all her concentration fixed on the pages of a book she was reading.

'She's very pretty. Who is she?'

'She was me first,' Mark replied simply.

'Your first photograph, or your first lover?'

'Me first everything.'

Joan digested this. 'Is she still around?'

'Sort of. But I haven't seen her for a very long time. I keep her photo because--'

'You don't have to tell me that,' Joan said. She remembered her first, too, but her memento was mental rather than physical. An unforgettable memory of divided sensation - of sweet pain, of sadness, and fierce joy. 'I understand.'

'I keep it because it reminds me of how good life can be,' Mark said. 'If you let Nature take its course. If you let yourself be what you are. If you set yourself free from man-made rules and laws.'

Joan nodded. 'You lied to me, you know,' she said.

Mark raised his eyebrows.

'You told me the cottage had a guest bedroom, but it doesn't. There's only one bedroom. Only one bed.'

'Oh aye,' Mark grinned. 'I lied about that.'

They took another drink.

'It's a pretty big bed, though,' Joan said thoughtfully.

'Made it meself.'

'Probably big enough for two people to sleep without ever touching.'

'If that's what you want, aye.'

Surprised by her own calmness and certainty, Joan slowly leaned across until her face was only inches from Mark's. She paused for the slightest moment, her eyes flicking over his face, and then she placed her lips on his. They stayed like that for a long time, not moving, simply enjoying the pressure, and then, as though at a prearranged signal, the kiss suddenly deepened. Joan opened her mouth to him, and his tongue found hers. She felt the delicious heat of him, tasted the spice of tobacco, and the flower nectar of wine. Then she eased away.

'I don't want,' she whispered.

Mark gently nodded, his head barely moving.

'You go along inside now,' he said. 'I've run a bath for you.'

Joan walked through the lamp-lit cottage and into the bathroom as though in a trance, leaving Mark to finish his wine outside. A single fat church candle burned on the window ledge, and its light played creamily over the surface of bubbles in the deep bath. Rose petals from the flowerbed outside had been cast across them, as though in honour of an ancient queen. She felt as though her skin had somehow evaporated over the few moments that had passed since their kiss, and now her whole body was a sheath of bare nerve-endings. Her clothes irritated this new-found sensitivity, and she pulled them off with languorous care, leaving them where they fell.

She lowered herself through the bubbles into the heat of the bathwater and instantly felt her body surrender even more to pure physical sensation. Mark had added something else to the water, she realised, some kind of scented oil that transformed her submerged flesh into silk. When they touched, her thighs slid across each other without friction, and as she slowly bathed, every part of herself she touched came fully alive.

And again, Joan was reminded of the story of Hansel and Gretel. Once trapped in the enchanted cottage, the old witch had prepared them for cooking by keeping them locked in a cage and feeding them up. Mark, on the other hand, had taken it to another level, and appeared to be marinating her too. She smiled to herself. The idea of being eaten by him was not without its attractions.

An unknown amount of time later, Mark came to stand in the doorway. He had still held his wine glass, but had stripped to the waist and was barefoot, and Joan let her eyes roam freely over the lithe strength of his shoulders, chest and stomach. Even through his jeans, she could see that he was aroused, and it gave her immense pleasure that she was the cause.

He stepped forward to stand above the bath, and looked her over from head to foot. By now most of the bubbles had dissipated, and she knew that nothing was hidden from him. So she didn't try to hide anything. Blood rushed madly through her head, and she displayed herself to him, guiding his eyes, squeezing her breasts, her painfully swollen nipples, pushing her fingers down over her belly and into her reddish pubic hair.

At last, Mark lowered himself and sat on the edge of the bath. He drained his glass, set it aside, and then leant over to kiss her, and when their lips met, Joan drank the wine from his mouth, a symbolic exchange of fluids that excited her even more.

They kissed again, hungrily, passionately, ever deeper. Under the water, she felt his hand touch her ankle, felt it slide slowly, maddeningly slowly, up between her slick legs, caressing them, parting them, until at last it reached the molten core of her.

Her eyes were closed as his fingers entered her, and she reached out blindly until her wet hand closed on the front of his jeans. Her fingers frantically plucked and pried at buttons until his erection was free. She squeezed him tightly and felt him groan into her mouth.

Joan broke their kiss and gasped for air, her head thrown back in complete abandon, and her thoughts fragmented like the images in a kaleidoscope.

This is what I want now, she thought. This. Him.

Aye means yes, butties are sandwiches. Doolally means puddled, and puddled means crazy, and the dog shelf is the floor.

I don't care about Stephen, she thought.

I don't care about Olivia.

I don't care about tomorrow.

This is what I need now.

And finally - this is just like my dream.

32

Hot. She was so bloody hot.

Her face was burning, her whole body was running with sweat, and on top of that her limbs seemed to be paralysed, or in some way restrained. They just wouldn't move at all. She tried to open her eyes, but a bright, lancing pain immediately forced them closed again. She became aware that her lower back was aching terribly, and her bottom was absolutely numb. Her feet were uncomfortable snarls of pins and needles. For a few horribly blank moments she had absolutely no idea where she was or why she felt the way she did. But then yesterday's events started to flood back on the incoming tide of consciousness, and she knew.

Olivia's first word as she awoke to the new day was a weak, dry-throated, 'Shit.'

This time she managed to keep her eyes open, although she had to slit them against the bright sunlight flooding in through the living room window. It seemed that she had fallen asleep in the armchair as she watched over Stephen. She had slept all night in the chair and her whole body had seized up as though she were in her late seventies, not her early thirties. She felt like absolute crap.

Still only half awake, she glanced across at the sofa and saw that Stephen was no longer there. Neither was the duvet she had covered him with. Probably he had awoken sometime in the small hours and staggered off to bed, dragging the duvet after him, like a middle-aged Linus from the Peanuts comic strip.

Then she looked down at herself and realised that she had been wrong. Wherever he was, in bed or not, Stephen had not taken the duvet with him, but had covered her with it just as she had covered him earlier. It was no wonder that she was sweating and had been unable to move. The 15 Tog duvet covered her up to the neck and had been tucked around her and down the side of the seat cushion. She was like a bug in a cocoon.

Groaning, Olivia shrugged her way free of the duvet, pitching it on to the floor. Then she flopped back into the armchair, stretching and yawning, shivering slightly as the morning air chilled the sweat on her skin. When she opened her eyes again, Stephen was standing in the doorway.

He was dressed in fresh, clean clothes, and had obviously bathed and shaved. She could smell his deodorant and aftershave from where she sat. Stephen seemed much more himself this morning. The only giveaway that things were not as normal was that the whites of his eyes were still massively bloodshot, and that although he was looking at Olivia, he seemed shy of making direct eye contact.

'Stephen.'

'Good morning.'

'Morning,' she said, stifling another yawn. 'What time is it?'

'It's seven o'clock.'

Olivia, who felt as though she had slept for days, said, 'God, is that all?'

Stephen nodded. 'I've been awake since before five. Couldn't sleep any more. I've been trying to think about what to do.' He shook his head. 'But I didn't come up with much. The only thing I thought we could try was getting in touch with her doctor at some point. Stratton. I have his number somewhere. She might have called him.'

'Good idea,' Olivia nodded.

He began to edge back through the door. 'You stay there. I'll make you some breakfast.'

Olivia opened her mouth again to tell him that she couldn't eat anything, but by that time he was gone, and she closed it again. She heard him pottering around in the kitchen, filling the kettle, rattling something, rustling something else. Soon she began to smell toasting bread.

She closed her eyes, making the world disappear for a blessed moment. Stephen was calm now, and seemed almost resigned to losing Joan. But once she told him what she had seen yesterday, as she knew she had to, who knew what it would do to him. What would he do? That was the question. Would he go on another smashing spree, or would he turn it his rage upon her?

It didn't matter, she decided. She had to tell him, even though the prospect made her nervous, even frightened.

But then, she thought, there were ways and there were ways of breaking bad news. Perhaps she could give him the story in bite-sized morsels. Truth by cumulative effect, rather than by a kill-or-cure dosage that would very likely send him out of his mind. Take it slowly, she told herself, build up to it…

You know, Stephen, it's strange, but I thought *I saw Joan on my way here yesterday. Well, I saw a woman who had a* look *of her - from behind, anyway. I'm not* convinced *it was her, even now, but… well, I sort of followed her, you know, just in case, and…*

Yes, perhaps that was the way to do it. It was the only way Olivia could think of, anyway.

Stephen put his head around the door. 'I'm sorry, I've forgotten if you take sugar or--'

'I saw Joan yesterday,' Olivia said.

It just burst out of her mouth without preamble or ornamentation. She just blabbed it out without meaning to. She could have bitten her own tongue off.

'What?' Stephen stepped through the doorway, frowning. 'What did you say?'

Sitting in the armchair, almost pushing herself back into it, Olivia suddenly became aware of how much bigger Stephen was than her.

Slowly, she cautioned herself, you have to take this very, very slowly.

But once again, her mouth instantly betrayed her. She started to speak and could not stop. She described how she'd spotted the woman crossing the road from the house dragging a wheelie-case, how she had realised that it was Joan, how she had tried to chase her, how she had seen Joan getting into the white van with another man. At the end of it she was breathless.

During the recounting, Stephen had come all the way into the room, but instead of standing over her menacingly, as Olivia had imagined he would, he had slumped down on to the sofa facing her. When she reached the part about the young man, he had dropped his gaze to his hands. Unconsciously or not, he was turning his wedding ring around and around on his finger, perhaps to see if it still fit.

He nodded into the silence, and quietly asked Olivia why she hadn't told him this yesterday. Once again, only the truth passed her lips.

'Because I'm a terrible person,' she said miserably. 'I'm mean-spirited, and vindictive. I'm evil.'

To her great surprise, Stephen actually laughed. 'No, you're not.' He shook his head in disbelief. 'A white van man, my God. We may as well be talking about Kath Meadows.'

'That's what I thought,' Olivia said. 'That's the first thought that came into my head.'

Stephen was still in a state of bemused shock. 'I wonder how long it's been going on.'

'We don't know for certain that anything's going on. We're just guessing.'

Stephen shrugged. He clearly didn't believe that.

'They may just be friends, and he's helping her out,' Olivia persisted. 'I mean, they probably had enough time to get acquainted when he was working here, didn't they?'

Now Stephen looked up. 'What do you mean, working here? Where here? At this house?'

Olivia explained who she thought the man was. Stephen was flabbergasted.

'The northern guy, did the guttering?' He sat back on the sofa, searching his memory, hands to his head. 'Yorkie,' he said finally, snapping his fingers. 'No job too odd.'

'That's it. I remember the sign on his van, but it wasn't there yesterday.'

Stephen put his hands over his face to smother another burst of irrational and slightly hysterical laughter. 'No job too odd. Well, you can't say he doesn't give you fair warning.'

Olivia watched him until his laughter faded and his hands dropped back into his lap. There were tears in his eyes again, but they were exhausted tears, with hardly the strength to fight their way over the lids.

'Good looking bastard, wasn't he,' he said, mostly to himself. 'Young, too. Younger than me.'

Olivia leant forward. 'Stephen, I know this is going to sound ridiculous at the moment, but maybe it still isn't too late.'

'Too late for what?'

'To find her, to bring her back.'

He shook his head. 'No. No use.'

'You don't know that.'

Stephen shook his head again. Lost cause.

'Look, don't you have this guy's address or telephone number? An invoice, a receipt…?'

Another head shake. 'No, he wanted to be paid cash-in-hand. I paid cash-in-hand.'

You bloody would have, Olivia thought. Avenue closed.

But then Stephen looked up, and Olivia saw the first stirrings of life there, a brightness in his eyes that could have been hope.

'What?' she asked.

'I think I know somebody who will have his address,' he said.

33

The forest was carpeted with a low ground mist that seemed to cling to the foliage and the trunks of the trees, but did not dare to invade the clearing before the cottage, so still and silent that it appeared totally unoccupied, as though trespass were forbidden. The long shadows of branches thrown by a golden rising sun stretched out like tentative fingers across the clearing and the patch of hard-packed earth, almost but not quite reaching the sleepers that led up to the deck. Forbidden. The only sounds were an occasional burst of birdsong and the faint drone, in the unidentifiable distance, of some unknown agricultural machinery.

But then there came a new sound, and new movement, as the cottage door was slowly opened.

Joan came tiptoeing out on to the small deck, squinting at the sunlight. She was dressed only in the white t-shirt that Mark had worn the day before, and she was carrying a heavy tumbler filled with the orange juice she had found in the fridge. She took a few deep breaths of fresh air, of the scent of the forest, enjoying the novelty of the complete absence of carbon monoxide. Then she sat down on the edge of the deck, her legs dangling down, heels resting on the lower of the two sleepers.

She sipped her juice, studied the trees, and watched the mist begin to dissipate as the sun gained in strength. And she thought.

What an incredible night it had been. Mark had surprised her. More than that, she had surprised herself.

She looked down at her legs, reaching down to run her hand gently over the inner surface of her thighs, where, although the discolouration could not yet be seen, she was convinced she had extensive bruising. She had a brief, but startlingly clear memory-flash of Mark's pelvis slamming against her repeatedly, and she expelled a long, shaky stream of air. She knew that once the bruises came through, her legs would look like hell, and she would have to wear long trousers for quite a while, weeks perhaps, which in this kind of weather would be a pain.

Not that she had minded at the time. Far from it. In fact, she had been holding on to Mark's tight buttocks with a death grip that may have left him with bruises of his own, as she urged him to plunge into her, to drive deeper and harder, though he had hardly needed encouragement, being quite rough enough already. Rougher than she was used to, certainly, and by a good distance.

Joan also thought she detected signs of a small bondage fetish in his love-making. There had been times last night when he had held both of her wrists above her head in an almost painful grip as he laboured over her body, and another time when she had been on all fours and he had suddenly yanked her arms behind her back, pressing her face into the pillows and making it difficult for her to breathe. In the moments before he came, he had slapped her buttocks six or seven times in rapid succession, each slap a little harder than the last. If it had been their second or third night together, instead of only their first, she suspected that he might have wanted to bind her wrists, and to take something else to her backside instead of just the flat of his hand. His belt, maybe.

She wondered how she would feel about it if and when Mark did ask for something a little more kinky, and decided that she had no way of knowing as yet. But she realised that if she left it until the last moment to make the decision, she would go along with anything he wanted. She felt that she could refuse him nothing. It was entirely ridiculous, but it was a little like being enslaved.

At the time, she had found Mark's increasingly aggressive technique to be a real turn on, because it was something entirely outside of her experience. Her sexual tastes to date had been strictly vanilla, but with Mark she was different. The rougher he had become, the more she had seemed to like it, and she had been carried away with a passion more fiery than any she had ever known. Those slaps had excited Joan almost to the point of her own orgasm. There had been no discomfort, only pleasure.

But that was last night. Now she felt tender just sitting on the wooden deck, and she realised that the joints of her shoulders were actually aching from the strain they had been subjected to. What's more, the embryonic bruises on her inner thighs were not the only marks her lover had left on her body. In the bathroom mirror she had seen superficial but visible scratches across her stomach, across her shoulders and down her back. There was a clear bite-mark on her right buttock, every tooth visible, and her neck and breasts were covered with angry suck-marks that reminded her of the one she had seen on Stephen's girlfriend as she had struggled to get into her sports car on Haversham Row. That memory brought home the reality of what she had done by sleeping with Mark.

I've committed adultery, she thought suddenly. I'm no better than Stephen is. What she found most surprising was that right now, she felt not the slightest twinge of guilt about it.

Until Mark, Joan had never thought about being with another man beside her husband. She had not even, so far as she could remember, fantasised about old boyfriends, or pop singers, or film stars. Not as a married woman, at any rate. For at least five years, Stephen had been the single erotic symbol in her life. Now, in the afterglow of the wildest night of sex she had ever had, she could not help making comparisons.

She viewed them as athletes, essentially.

Stephen had always been a long distance runner, a marathon man who lasted forever, never climaxing himself until he had seen her through two or even three extremely good orgasms. In contrast, Mark was a sprinter, with the ability of fast recovery, and although he had climaxed more times than Joan last night, her orgasms had been shattering, leaving her breathless and all but unconscious. Then, only moments later, he had been ready to go again. And again, and again. He had been absolutely insatiable.

Joan took some pride from the fact that she had apparently exhausted him just as much as he had exhausted her. She had no idea what time they had eventually fallen asleep, or what time it had been when a full bladder had finally awoken her, but Mark had been sound asleep when she had left his bed and snuck off to the bathroom. Away with the fairies, her mother used to say of anyone in a deep sleep.

Unbidden, a memory surfaced in her mind of another Sunday morning, long ago, a Sunday when she had been a little girl, and she had slept in, and had been allowed to do so. Olivia hadn't shouted her awake, her parents hadn't disturbed her. Perhaps she had been ill the night before, she couldn't now recall, only that they had left her to sleep while they went to church. She had awoken so slowly that she hardly knew she was awake. The house was silent, as was the street outside, the world caught in limbo. The sunlight was so strong it blazed through the curtains. The room, the air, was golden, and a million flecks of dust slowly moved and revolved through it, highlighted in the diffused sunbeams, and Joan remembered thinking that she had finally made it; she was so deeply asleep that she was with the fairies.

At that moment, a cold finger trailed across the back of Joan's sun-warmed neck and she started violently, spilling half of the juice left in her glass over the front of the t-shirt and into her lap. She yelped at the sudden shocking chill on her skin, and behind her, Mark chuckled.

'Sorry about that, lass, didn't mean to startle you.'

'Yes you did, you rotten bugger!' Joan plucked at the wet fabric and held it slightly away from her belly with her thumb and forefinger, and then twisted around to scowl at him.

Mark, wearing just his white hipsters, smiled down at her, the soul of boyish innocence. 'Honest,' he said.

'Yeah, I'll bet.'

Mark laughed again, stole the glass from Joan's hand and downed the remaining contents in a single swallow. 'What are you doing out here, anyway?' he asked. 'Not thinking of running away, are you?'

'No. I'm just testing out your theory.'

'What theory's that, then?'

'That in the morning you can step out of Hunter's Lodge and feel that you're the only person on earth.'

'And is it true?'

Joan nodded definitely. 'Yes. It's wonderful.'

Mark looked down along the length of her legs, and at his t-shirt where it still clung to her body, translucently orange, making Joan's nipples rise.

'You know, I seem to remember saying that you had to do it stark naked - to get the full effect, like. But you're not naked, are you?'

Joan looked pointedly at his underwear. 'Neither are you.'

Mark raised his eyebrows at the challenge. 'Oh, I see, like that, is it?'

'Yes, it's exactly like that.'

'Right, then!' Mark set the glass carefully to one side on the deck, and then hooked his thumbs into the waistband of his pants and whipped them off. He swirled them around his head and gave an ululating Indian war whoop as he tossed them aside, and then straddle-jumped over Joan's head. Although she ducked, she still felt a light impact on her scalp that could only have been Mark's dangling penis.

He landed on the dirt below the sleepers, pirouetted and bowed to her, raising his arms for her acclaim. Joan gave it, laughing and dutifully applauding. 'Want some more, lass?'

'Yes, please.'

To her considerable amusement, Mark began to make drum-beat sounds with his mouth. He began to swing his hips from side to side in time to the beat, his penis foolishly swinging to and fro. Joan clamped her hands over her mouth to stem her laughter. But when Mark also began to sing, she couldn't hold it back any longer. It was an old song, but one she recognised, about a woman whose lover made her feel like a virgin again. Who made her feel like she was being made love to for the very first time.

He was shouting the lyrics now, and jigging and jumping around in the dirt, his penis slapping at his belly, his thighs and hips. Joan howled with laughter.

'Come on, lass!' he yelled. 'Come and get into the groove!'

Joan looked around the clearing, half expecting to see curious faces peering through the undergrowth, drawn by the noise. But as Mark had promised there was no one to hear, no one to see.

'Come on!'

Joan pushed herself up off the deck, peeled off her wet t-shirt and joined Mark singing and dancing naked in the dirt. A part of her felt completely ridiculous jumping around like this, her breasts and his penis flapping around all over the place, but the larger part of her was intoxicated with a sense of utter release. A temporary insanity, granted only to new lovers and true free-spirits. Stephen would never do anything like this. She would never do anything like this, she realised, not back in the real world, back in civilisation.

But here… here she felt that they could do anything here, and no one would ever know.

Soon enough, their mad dance calmed and the half-remembered lyrics dwindled away, first to a hummed melody, and then to nothing but tuneless breathing. They were drawn together as though magnetised, bodies pressed tight, skin sticky with juice, lubricated with sweat. Mark was no longer dangling, but fully erect. As they slow-danced, she could feel him like a branding iron held against her belly. There was only one part of her that still ached, and that was out of pure need.

'Let's go back to bed,' she whispered into his ear.

'Let's not,' Mark said.

He smiled at Joan's sudden confusion as she drew back her head, wondering if she had heard him correctly.

'Let's do it here.'

'Here?'

'Aye, right here, lass.'

Joan glanced over his shoulder and scanned the forest once more. They were completely alone, completely unobserved, she knew this without a doubt, and yet despite her earlier conviction that she would be able to do anything, this felt like a step too far. She kissed his smooth chest, bent to lap at his tiny nipples with her tongue.

'Let's go inside,' she breathed.

'No,' Mark said firmly. 'Here. Now.'

He put his hand on top of her head and gently pushed down.

'Now!'

Astonishingly, Joan's body seemed to go limp. She found herself holding on to his arms, his waist, his legs, as she slowly sank to her knees in the dirt before him.

His fingers curled themselves into her short hair and he roughly ground her face against his cock and balls, and she was abruptly surrounded by the stale scent of last night's lovemaking.

'Smell it,' he ordered, pulling even harder on her hair. 'Smell it!'

Joan inhaled deeply, and felt her head swim.

'That's you and me, lass. You and me.'

She strained against his grip and looked up into his eyes.

'Now!' he commanded, and Joan took him into her mouth without another word.

34

Stephen hurried across the deserted road, his head up like a dog on point, while Olivia, who at this stage just felt like a dog, followed a few uncertain paces behind him, finger combing her hair and trying to smooth out the creases in her blouse. Unlike Stephen, who was washed, groomed and dressed in nice clean clothes, she was ten minutes from a dead sleep, dressed in yesterday's hastily-chosen clothes, which she had slept in.

Although she hadn't had time to look in a mirror, she was quite certain that she looked like hell. She had begged for a bathroom break at least, just five minutes, but Stephen wouldn't have it.

Now, he kept saying. Now!

As he'd opened the front door, she had mentioned that it was probably a little too early on a Sunday morning to go calling, but Stephen had just shrugged.

'He'll be awake, trust me. The Secret Service never sleeps.'

As they reached the pavement and were about to step through the gate, Olivia caught his arm. 'Are you sure he'll know it?

'If anyone does, M will,' Stephen replied. 'The first time I saw this Yorkie, he was working for him. Old Unwill even recommended the little bastard to me.'

'But if he only worked cash-in-hand…'

'Don't be silly, *Unwill* won't have paid cash-in-hand. That's not the way he thinks. The nosy old fool will probably have asked for references, invoices in triplicate...'

As soon as they reached Gordon Unwill's front door, Stephen immediately pounded on it with the heel of his fist, the sound loud, harsh and booming in the still Sunday morning air.

'Jesus, Stephen!' Olivia protested. 'Why don't you knock a bit harder next time!'

Stephen obligingly hammered on the door again.

Olivia pulled his arm down. 'Just calm down, for Christ's sake! You won't get anywhere with him if you rant and rave. And,' she added as an afterthought, 'don't be taking the piss out of him all the time. We need his help.'

239

'Okay, okay, I'll calm down,' Stephen assured her.

They heard a key turning in the lock, and a second later the door opened on a short brass safety-chain. Gordon Unwill's pale face, still puffy from sleep, edged defensively into the four-inch opening.

He stared at each of them in turn, looking mystified by their appearance, which Olivia thought he had every right to. They had obviously woken him up, and, like Olivia, he had yet to see a mirror this morning. His usually carefully tended comb-over had dried out and lifted at one side during the night and now had the look of a stale pie-crust perched on top of his head. As he looked at them, his mouth worked as though framing their names, which made him look even older and disconcertingly infirm.

'Mr Unwill!' Stephen said with a heartiness so patently false that Olivia actually winced. 'Gordon! Good morning!'

'Good morning,' Unwill replied warily, his voice rusty. 'What, er… Is anything wrong?'

'No, nothing wrong at all. I was just wondering if you could help us out with a little problem.'

Unwill looked from Stephen to Olivia, and then back again, still clearly confused. 'Help you? In what way?'

'I need you to dig in your files for some information.'

'Files?'

'Your intelligence reports.'

'What?'

Olivia shook her head at Stephen. Unwill was obviously unaware of his spymaster reputation and

240

was becoming more uncertain with every oblique reference Stephen threw at him. Tactfully nudging him aside, she approached the gap in the door and smiled warmly at the old man.

'Good morning, Mr Unwill, I'm Joan's sister, Olivia. Do you remember me from yesterday?'

'Of course I do,' Unwill said. He looked her over, at the creases in her clothes particularly, in a way that suggested he remembered the meeting all too well.

'Listen, we're very sorry to disturb you so early, but we do have a small problem that we hope you can help us with.'

'I don't see how--'

'Mr Unwill, you're the only person we could turn to.'

Unwill thought about this for a moment, and then seemed to have an inspiration. 'Have you had a break in?' he asked.

'No, nothing like that, but we really could use your help.'

The light that had briefly flared in the old man's face instantly died, and confusion returned. If it wasn't a matter for the Neighbourhood Watch, what could it be? Olivia smiled at him for a long time, unwilling to answer his unspoken questions out here on the doorstep, and finally he dropped his eyes from hers.

'Well, I suppose you'd better come in for a moment.'

He swung the door to, unlatched the safety chain, and then opened the door wide while they stepped past him into the hall. When he closed the door again, they saw that he was still in his pyjamas, traditional stripes with the jacket buttoned up to the top and the pants with ironed-in creases so crisp they appeared to have been starched. Over these he wore a surprisingly tatty and effeminate dressing gown that had been patched many times over.

When he caught them looking at his dressing gown, he drew himself up to his full diminutive height, as though daring them to say a word about it. It was only when she saw him at attention that Olivia noticed how much he stooped when there was no one around to see him at ease.

'Perhaps you would like to tell me what this is about, Mr Crosby,' he asked, his voice now much more confident, almost all the way back to yesterday's authoritative persona. Olivia was sort of glad to see its return.

'Yorkie,' Stephen replied immediately. 'No job too odd.'

Unwill's eyes flickered for a moment. 'Oh yes?'

'I saw him doing some work on your house, and when I asked if he was any good, you recommended him to me.'

'Yes, I recall the occasion.'

'I had him over to do my guttering.'

'So I saw at the time.'

Unwill waited for Stephen to go on, but Stephen, typically, Olivia thought, had frozen. Despite all his bluster he could not bring himself to explain the embarrassing situation to a man he privately ridiculed and regarded as something of a joke.

Once again, Olivia stepped in, saying the first thing that came into her mind.

'He did some other work in the house, too,' she said. 'Some…ah, plumbing. It seemed okay at the time, but now there's been a leak, and we need to get in contact with him to put it right.'

Unwill stared at her for a long moment, and she was afraid that he didn't believe a word she'd said. She thought that she had lost the knack of lying. But then Unwill turned back to Stephen with the trace of a smile.

'You paid him cash, didn't you?' When Stephen nodded, Unwill shook his head. 'People never learn, do they. Come along with me.'

He crisply about turned, marched down the hall and went in through a door on the left hand side of the hallway. Olivia and Stephen followed him into a large sitting room that in both decoration and furnishings showed all the hallmarks of an older woman's touch. Unwill had been a widower, Olivia remembered Joan telling her, for over ten years, and yet the room, and probably the rest of the house she guessed, was completely unchanged. It was clean and tidy, but it seemed dusty and neglected all the same.

'I have a great many years' experience of dealing with tradesmen,' Unwill said to them over his shoulder. 'Even the best of them try the old cash-in-hand ploy. But when it comes to property, I believe that a hand-shake and a gentleman's agreement is not good enough. Fly-by-nighters, like this Yorkie fellow, are the worst of the lot in my estimation. He didn't even want to give me a telephone number, you know. But as I said to him, if this lot falls down two months from now, I want to know where I can get hold of you! He didn't like it, I can tell you.'

Olivia nodded understandingly.

'He got quite nasty, in fact, but I stuck to my guns. Said I'd only pay him by cheque, posted to his residence. I've done it before, and I dare say I'll do it again. Sometimes you have to be tough. You have to be able to say, give me what I want or you won't get paid at all.'

Unwill sat down at a bureau made of a dark wood and very carefully opened it. Olivia instantly realised why he was so careful. Inside, every inch of every shelf, nook and cranny, was filled with address books, notebooks and seemingly random stacks of loose papers. One hasty move and the whole lot would have fluttered out in a blizzard. It was the hard copy of the old man's memory.

While Unwill began to rifle through the papers, Stephen stole an amused glance at Olivia and rolled his eyes. Olivia ignored him.

'How did Yorkie take that threat?' she asked Unwill.

'Badly. Fortunately,' he added, 'most of the work had already been carried out by the time the subject of payment came up, and the amount in question was for quite a considerable sum. If it had been any less, I believe he would simply have walked away rather than give in.'

Stephen stepped forward, suddenly intent. 'You think he would have walked away from a lot of money rather than tell you his address?'

'I'm not so sure that it was his address he was really concerned about, actually.' Unwill frowned, and shifted his attention from one bundle of papers to another bundle on a lower shelf. 'I think it was his real name he wanted to hang on to.'

Stephen and Olivia glanced at each other.

'Why would he be afraid of you knowing his name?' Olivia asked.

'Oh, the usual reasons, I suppose.'

'And what are they?'

Unwill shrugged lightly. 'I assumed at the time that he was signing on. You know, drawing Unemployment Benefit and working on the sly. Ah, here it is!'

He turned around in his seat, triumphantly waved a scrap of paper at them, and then held it at arm's length, squinting slightly, to read aloud.

'Flat 1a, Ollerton Road, Bounds Green.'

'And his name?'

'And his name is…' Unwill screwed up his face a little more, peering myopically at the slip of paper. 'His name is… Martin Bickley.'

Unwill offered the piece of paper to Stephen, who took it and read the information on it for himself, including a mobile telephone number that had been crossed out.

'This number's no longer valid, I take it?' he asked.

'Cut off the moment my cheque had cleared.'

'What was he like, Mr Unwill?' Olivia asked.

'Charming,' the old man replied after a moment's thought. 'Very charming, at first. He had a very broad Yorkshire accent, was very bright and amusing, knew his job, could turn his hand to anything. An accomplished photographer, too, always had a camera on him. He showed me some of his photographs once; nothing very startling, but you could tell he had a good eye. A very capable lad, had been in the army for a time, I believe. That's why I ran up such a high bill with him, really. I kept finding more work for him to do. To tell you the truth, I liked having him around.'

He looked at Olivia candidly.

'This will sound very foolish, I know, but we never had children, my wife and I, and for a while it became a kind of... well, a fantasy, for want of a better word. You know, I imagined that he was my son, helping me out, and not a workman at all.'

'I don't think it's foolish,' Olivia told him, and received in return the first genuine smile the old man had ever given her, although it was tinged with an air of sadness.

'That would explain why you hired him,' Stephen said, nodding. 'I can't imagine a man like you generally employs dole-cheats who come knocking on his door.'

'Oh, but he didn't,' Unwill said. 'Come knocking, I mean. I would have sent him packing, if he had. Like you, I saw him working on somebody else's house and asked the owner if his work was up to standard. The glowing testimonial I received in answer to my question was what convinced me to hire him. The fantasy came later.'

'I see. Do you happen to remember who recommended him?'

'Certainly,' Unwill said. 'It was the woman who left her husband a while ago, just down the road there. Husband's in imports or exports, or something like that. Meadows, that's the name, Lee Meadows. I believe his wife's name was Katherine.'

A few seconds later, Unwill showed them back to the front door. He was quiet now, subdued, and seemed lost in thought, nodding silently as they offered their thanks for his assistance. As they stepped over the threshold, Stephen remembered that he still had the slip of paper in his hand, and tried to pass it back to Unwill.

'No, that's all right,' the old man said hastily, 'you can keep it.'

'It's okay, I think I can remember the details until I get home,' Stephen said.

Unwill looked down at the scrap of paper in Stephen's hand, but made no move to take it. He shook his head. 'Keep it,' he said, with a note of finality.

'But won't you need it, just in case?' Olivia asked, nodding at Unwill's house.

Unwill shook his head again. 'I don't think so. I… I don't think I want to see that young man again.'

Olivia came back to the doorway, and gently laid a hand on the old man's arm. 'Why?'

Unwill shrugged. 'Perhaps I'm just being an old fool,' he said. 'It's nothing.'

Olivia squeezed his arm gently. 'Please, tell us.'

For a moment, Unwill was silent, and then he sighed. 'Because I had formed this - *attachment*, shall we say? - one of the reasons I wanted to keep his name and address was so that I could be sure of seeing him again. Perhaps to get to know him a little better. To be honest, in this instance, it was this desire

247

which drove my insistence more than the usual safeguards in case his work turned out to be faulty.'

He patted Olivia's hand on his arm, and seemed genuinely grateful for the support she was offering.

'At first, I made light of my request, tried to turn it into a sort of joke, you understand, and certainly not as though I didn't trust him. But when he refused, I felt offended in some way. It was as though he wasn't the person I'd thought he was, as though he had tried to fool me. So, as I say, I got up on my high horse and insisted, and made it a condition of payment. The conversation descended into a real argument, and then....'

'What happened?' Olivia asked.

Again, Unwill hesitated. Finally, in a low voice, he said, 'His mask slipped. I saw his secret face.'

'Secret face?' Olivia glanced back at Stephen, who seemed just as puzzled as she was.

Unwill nodded. He had fallen back into a stoop, and looked up at Olivia with a little smile. 'Everyone has a secret face. Perhaps you have seen mine this morning, young lady. If so, you will know that I'm a lonely, unfulfilled, foolish old man.' The smile faded. 'But his face, Yorkie's face, was... I can only say monstrous. I could see his rage, his madness, and I could see that he was barely able to control it.'

'What happened then?' Olivia asked, chilled, her voice barely a whisper.

'Oh, nothing terrible,' Unwill shrugged. 'Eventually he gave in and gave me his details. He couldn't afford to lose the money, especially as it wasn't just a matter of his time; he'd supplied most of the materials, too.'

He nodded toward the slip of paper that Stephen held.

'But my handwriting was shaky, as you can plainly see. It was fortunate that the confrontation was carried out right here, on the doorstep. Mrs Dewhurst next door was working in her garden, very properly pretending not to listen, and I was very grateful for her presence. If not for her, I suspect that something really would have happened.'

'He frightened you?'

'Yes.' Unwill hung his head and his stoop became even more accentuated. 'Yes, he did. Badly. I kept his address out of habit, but I already knew that once I'd sent him his cheque, it was over. There wasn't going to be a friendship, or any kind of relationship. I never wanted to have contact with him ever again. Certainly, I never again wanted to be alone with him.'

He looked at Stephen. 'I watched him very carefully all the time he was working on your house, Mr Crosby, waiting for him to be finished. On the day he left, I heaved a sigh of relief...and then I had all the locks on my house changed.'

Unwill became so silent and introspective that Olivia and Stephen began to quietly withdraw, leaving him to his thoughts. But then, as they were halfway down the garden path, he spoke once more.

'I tried to forget all about it. Write it off as a bad experience. But it must have been playing on my mind ever since, because every so often, I imagine that he's still around. I imagine that I see his van parked on the corner, or driving through the neighbourhood. As though he's stalking me, looking for revenge. Isn't that silly?'

Olivia stared at him. 'Do you think he could be?'

Unwill shook himself, forced his spine erect. 'No. No, of course not. It's just foolish imagination, that's all.'

They turned again to leave.

'Mr Crosby.'

Stephen looked back. 'Yes?'

'May I ask, how much did you pay him for the work he did on your house?'

'I don't remember exactly. Three, four hundred pounds, something like that. Why?'

'Take my advice,' Unwill said softly. 'Do as I did, and write it off. Just write it off.'

Back in the house, Olivia and Stephen sat in the kitchen, just staring at each other across with width of the table, each unwilling to break the silence as they mulled over the information that Gordon Unwill had given them. It was much stranger than they had expected.

'What are you thinking?' Stephen finally asked.

'I'm thinking that Joan may be even more useless at reading people than I am.'

Stephen stared down at the centre of the table, and then he raised a fist and struck it with all his might. 'What the hell is she up to, hooking up with a creep like that?'

Olivia shook her head. 'I don't know.'

Stephen struck the table again. 'What's the connection? What attraction could there possibly be between them?'

Olivia didn't feel that now was the right time to state the obvious attraction between men and women.

'Maybe it's because they met when she was feeling vulnerable,' she suggested instead. 'And when she was feeling vulnerable again, she remembered him, and just… turned to him.'

Stephen stared at her, chewing his lips, thinking it through. 'I don't buy that,' he said at last. 'It just doesn't feel right. There's something else going on here.'

'What?'

'How the fuck should I know.' He stood up. 'Come on.'

'Where are we going?'

'You *know* where.'

35

Olivia was sitting alone in Stephen's BMW, and she was uncomfortable, hot, hungry and thirsty. The car was parked directly across the road from the address that Unwill had passed on to them, which was a shabby Edwardian mid-terrace house indiscriminately carved up into separate residences by an unfussy, profit-hungry landlord. Yorkie, aka Martin Bickley, lived at 1a, the basement flat.

When they had first arrived, Olivia and Stephen had simply sat in silence, watching the flat's gloomy stairwell in the hope that either Bickley or Joan herself would suddenly appear. That hadn't happened, and Stephen, glancing at his wristwatch and realising that almost a whole hour had passed, had decided to venture out of the car and investigate.

Olivia had watched him approach the stairwell, glance cagily down into the shadowed darkness, and then begin to descend the staircase in careful, crab-like steps, trying to look everywhere at once. She thought that he must have picked up the way he was moving from a lifetime's addiction to American crime movies. All he needed was a two-handed grip on a semi-automatic handgun to complete the image. At any other time, in almost any other situation, Olivia would have found this act amusing.

Stephen had returned only minutes later to inform her that there was no name on the bell-bush and that he was unable to see anything through the letterbox, it was too dark. Had he actually rung the bell, she'd asked. No way. If they were in there he had no intention of giving either of them a warning. He was going to go around to the back of the houses and try to find a way into the gardens. If he could find a window…

If he could find a window, what?

He'd shrugged and moved off again, this time trying to look like an innocent pedestrian. It was a slightly more convincing performance than his cop routine, but only slightly. Since then, she'd been alone with her thoughts, which were not especially good company. Gordon Unwill's story had given her the heebie-jeebies, and she felt a strong but unfocussed sense of unease with regard to Joan's safety.

Olivia looked at the clock on the dash and discovered that Stephen had now been gone for approximately thirty-five minutes, and despite herself she began to feel a little nervous for him. She didn't know why she should feel that way, but she did. She twisted around in the BMW's leather upholstery and craned her neck to look up and down the street, still keeping to her own assigned role as look-out.

The idea was that if Joan or Bickley either came out of the flat or tried to get in, or if the white Escort van showed up, Olivia was to sound the BMW's horn. That was Stephen's cue to come racing back to the car. But so far there had been no sign of either of their quarries, and Olivia found that she was now looking for Stephen more than she was for them.

'Come on,' Olivia said to the absent Stephen. 'What the hell are you doing back there?'

She slumped back in her seat and closed her eyes. The leather seat swallowed her. Almost immediately, in her mind's eye, she saw images of Martin Bickley and Joan; they weren't in the gloomy-looking basement flat, they were far away, in some remote and beautiful spot, having what looked like a wonderful romantic time together. Or maybe it was a lovely platonic time, she wasn't really that sure anymore.

Then, without any warning, Joan inadvertently either said or did something that should have been innocuous, but which infuriated Bickley beyond all normal comprehension.

Just as Unwill had described, his mask slipped. The handsome face fell away, and Joan saw his secret face, and she screamed.

Olivia jumped awake as Stephen climbed into the car and slammed the door behind him. 'Jesus!' she yelled.

'What's wrong with you?' he asked.

253

'You scared me.'

'Were you just asleep?' he asked in astonishment. 'You were, weren't you? Some look-out you turned out to be.'

Olivia sighed heavily, unable to believe herself that she'd actually dozed off there for a while. The dashboard clock had moved on another five minutes. Then she looked at Stephen properly, and stared.

'What happened to you?' she asked.

'I had some difficulty getting into the back garden.'

'I guess you did.'

Stephen actually looked as though he'd been in a fight. Various parts of his clothes were marked with dirt and grass stains, he'd lost a couple of buttons from his shirt, and the knee of his left trouser leg had a three-inch tear in it. Three knuckles on his right hand had been torn open and were oozing blood. Olivia watched as he found his handkerchief and wrapped it around his hand.

'What did you see?' she asked.

'Not them, that's for sure. But I managed to get all the way up to the windows.' He shrugged. 'As far as I could see it's just another grubby little flat. Nobody home.'

'Great,' Olivia sighed. 'Let's face it, Stephen, for all we know he could have moved on by now. It's been months since he gave Unwill his address. If he was that secretive, he probably moved. He changed his phone quick enough, once he got his money.'

Stephen was nodding. But he was also smiling.

'That's what I thought at first,' he said. 'But then I noticed the curtains.'

'The curtains?'

'They're thick and black, completely opaque - like in a photographic studio - and hidden behind them in the corner of the main room is an old enlarger. Then there are the walls. They're covered with photographs – and I do mean covered.'

'Photographs of what?'

'London, from what I could see. Landmarks, scenery. Remember Unwill telling us Bickley was a photographer?'

Olivia frowned. 'A lot of people are interested in photography.'

'That's true. But I was thinking, Bickley's from the north, isn't he? In a sense he's a visitor here. And all the photographs in there are exactly the kind of shots a tourist would take.' He nodded to himself. 'This is his place all right. I know it.'

Olivia shrugged. 'Okay, so say he still lives here. What's your big plan - just wait until he comes home?'

'Why not?'

'It could be hours.'

'I've got nothing better to do. What about you?'

'It could be days,' Olivia said. 'I mean, what if they went away somewhere, like a trip?'

Stephen considered this idea broodingly, and then looked across at the head of the stairwell.

'Shall I tell you what I really want to do?' he asked. 'I want to break into that flat. The lock on the front door isn't strong, I could kick that open, no problem. I'm sure it's the same for the inner door.'

Olivia was shocked. 'You can't do that!'

'Can't I? Why not?'

'It would be illegal.'

Stephen laughed sourly. 'And your point is…?'

'Don't be an idiot, Stephen,' Olivia said. 'You getting locked up for breaking and entering wouldn't help us one bit. Now come on, think! There must be something else we can do!'

They both thought about alternative strategies for a while, but Olivia noticed that Stephen's eyes kept slipping back to the stairwell, so he obviously wasn't thinking too hard. She shook her head in dismay. Men were pathetic at finding their way around problems. They had to meet it full on, gung ho, Rambo-style. On the other hand, she thought, was she any better? Sure, she was the one who'd called Dr Stratton's office earlier and left a message on his answer-phone asking him to call back, but even that had been Stephen's idea. What was her smart contribution?

'Wait a minute,' she said suddenly. 'What about Lee Meadows?'

'What about him?'

'We could call him and ask what he remembers about this guy. He may have something new to tell us.'

Stephen pulled a pained face. 'I don't know about that, Olivia. To tell the truth, I'd be very reluctant to talk to him about this.'

'Why?'

'For one reason, Lee's not doing so well these days. I don't see that much of him anymore, but I know that losing Kath has hit him harder than he's letting on. Whenever I have seen him he puts on a brave front, but he's lost an awful amount of weight, and he's completely run down. You can see it in his

256

face, he's pale, drawn... He's ill all the time, always sniffling with a cold. There's something about him now, a darkness… like he's living in a cold shadow.'

Stephen shook his head regretfully. 'I've heard a few rumours about his business, too - that it's about to go down the toilet because he's not devoting enough time to it. He's close to the edge. Close to losing everything. I don't want to push him over by taking this to him. It could remind him too much of the way Kath left.'

Olivia was touched by Stephen's concern for his friend, but privately thought that if he had shown a similar amount of empathy and consideration for his own wife then none of this may have happened in the first place. She decided, though, not to share this opinion with Stephen; because, she thought, people who live in glass houses shouldn't you-know-what.

'Okay, so not Lee,' she agreed. 'I don't suppose that he would exactly consider Joan to be his best friend, anyway, not after the things she said to the police about him.'

Stephen turned on her angrily.

'Now that's something I really hate, and it's just typical of you, Olivia! Judging somebody by your own dog-eat-dog standards! For your information, Lee still regards Joan as a good friend. A very good friend. If you really want to know, he actually appreciated her concerns. He was pleased that she took them to the police. Do you know why?'

Olivia, completely taken aback by Stephen's outburst, just shook her head.

'Because it showed that someone apart from him cared that his wife was gone. Because he understood

257

that sense of loss. He knew that however ridiculous her suspicions were, they were simply an expression of her love. And because of that, he knew that he wasn't alone.'

Stephen sat back, breathing hard. Olivia began to frame an apology, but he waved her away.

'Do you know what Lee did, out of the kindness of his heart?' he asked. 'When I was looking around for a good psychiatrist for Joan, Lee put a word in for me with his own guy, Stratton. Stratton's a top man in his field, used to work with the police and everything. How do you think I was able to get her in with someone like that at such short notice? After everything Joan said about Lee, he was still trying to help her. What do you think about that?'

'I didn't realise,' Olivia said, humbly.

'Yeah, well, you don't know everything, do you.'

Stephen was still mad at her, but was slowly reining it in.

'Lee's been seeing Stratton himself off and on ever since Kath buggered off,' he said, more quietly. 'Depression. Suicidal tendencies… Do you understand now why I don't want to push him?'

Olivia nodded and the conversation died. She watched Stephen covertly out of the corner of her eye. He was pretending that she wasn't there. She took a deep breath. 'Okay,' she said. 'I have another suggestion.'

Stephen just looked at her.

'What about your friend in the police force, the one who Joan went to see - what was his name, Richardson?'

'For God's sake, why can't you leave my friends alone?' Stephen hissed. 'Aren't things bad enough without everyone knowing about it?'

'Aren't things bad enough without worrying what anybody else thinks of you?' Olivia countered.

Stephen sighed in exasperation. 'In any case, what has Phil got to do with it? He only really saw Joan when she was at her most deluded, what on earth do you imagine he would be able to tell us?'

Olivia faced him squarely. 'Well, he's a policeman isn't he?'

'Yes.'

'A detective?'

'Yes, he's a DCI, so what?'

'So, he may be able to pull a few strings and tell us if Binkley's got another address somewhere.'

Stephen blinked.

'He should also be able to tell us if he has a criminal record or not.'

Stephen double-blinked.

'What do you think?' Olivia asked.

36

There was no doubt at all now in Joan's mind that this had turned out to be one of the strangest twenty-four hours of her entire life. Bearing in mind her recent history, this was really saying something.

First of all, she had run away with a man she hardly knew, and she had spent the night with him, enthusiastically committing adultery; this morning she had fellated him outdoors, in broad daylight, and had then submitted to a range of sexual activities which before today she would probably have regarded as both demeaning and slightly perverse.

She still had no idea why she had allowed any of it to happen.

After they had finished in the clearing before the cottage - or, more accurately, after Mark had finished - he had lifted her into his arms like a child. He had asked her to let herself go completely limp, as though she were unconscious. Actually, he had not asked her, he had told her to do it. Now, he'd said. And she had immediately complied with his wishes.

He had carried her up the steps into the cottage and then into the bedroom, once again ordering her to stay limp. He was going to drop her on the bed, he said, and she must not move afterwards, but let her body come to rest naturally.

'Why?' she had asked.

'Because I want you to,' he replied, and that had been that.

He had dropped her on the mattress, where she bounced and flopped, ending up on her side across the bed, her arms and legs tangled together.

'Perfect,' Mark said. 'Stay just like that. Don't move a muscle.'

Joan obeyed. She didn't move, but she listened, and she heard what sounded like a door being opened. Without moving her head, she was able to see the edge of the sheepskin rug on the floor somehow rise up above the foot of the bed and then rest against it, stiff as a board. Then she realised that the rug was actually attached to a section of the floor that Mark had lifted. It was a trap door.

'What are you doing?' she asked.

Mark smiled across at her. 'When I built the extension, I dug meself a cellar at the same time. I use it as me darkroom now. Got a computer and printer hooked up. Sometimes use it as a small studio, an' all.'

'Can I see it?'

'Later,' Mark promised, beginning to descend the steps. 'I'll take you down later, show you around. You'll love it.' Just before his head disappeared from her line of sight, he said firmly, 'Don't move.'

Seconds later he was on his way back up. He asked her to close her eyes, which she immediately did. She heard the trap door closing, and Mark moving quietly around the bed. He was up to something, and she felt her body begin to tingle in anticipation. How did he do this to her?

Then she heard a sharp click, and the insectile whirring of a camera on autowind, and she abruptly sat up, shocked. 'Mark!'

He quickly took three more photographs of her appalled face, blurred by her movement. By the last shot, her face would have been obscured by her outstretched hand.

'Stop!' she said.

Two more shots. 'Why?'

Why? She thought it was obvious why.

'I don't want you taking photographs of me like this!'

'Why not? You're a beautiful woman, Joan.'

'But it's embarrassing.'

'You're not embarrassed when I look at you, are you?'

'That's different.'

261

'Why?' he smiled. 'Only difference I can see is now I'm looking through a camera lens. Nobody else is going to see the photographs, Joan, I promise you that. I even develop them meself, remember.'

'But why do you want them?'

'I'm a photographer,' he said simply. 'It's what I do. And it's fun.'

Seeing that Joan remained unconvinced, he handed the camera across to her. 'Here, then,' he said. 'You have a go at it. Tell me if I'm not right.'

Joan looked from Mark to the camera dubiously.

'Go on,' he urged. 'Do it now.'

Joan slowly lifted the camera to her eye, framing Mark's naked torso. He turned to his side and proudly displayed his manhood, which was already beginning to show signs of life again. Behind the camera, Joan couldn't resist smiling. From this angle the arc of his jerkily rising penis was comically outlined against the bright square of the living room window far behind him. She quickly took the snap, and then astonished herself by laughing.

'See?' He took the camera back. 'Come on, lass, do me a pose. You'll enjoy it.'

'Oh Mark, I don't know--'

'*You'll enjoy it.*'

After a moment's consideration, Joan snatched up the bed's single thin cotton sheet, and used it to coyly cover the front of her body. She gave him a similarly coy look, staring into the lens from under her lashes, imitating the pose she had seen a thousand times in magazines and newspapers. Mark took the shot. She could see him smiling behind the camera.

'Lovely. Now turn to the side a bit. I want a bit of arse in this 'un.'

Joan turned until Mark was satisfied. At the last moment, just before he took the photograph, she cheekily stuck out her tongue at the camera.

Mark lowered the camera and beamed at her. 'Let me get you a drink,' he said. 'It'll loosen you up.'

By the time the bottle of wine he'd brought from the kitchen was finished, they had used up the last three rolls of film between them, and Mark had switched over to his digital back-up. Joan had used most of one of those rolls on her own, getting a real thrill out of giving Mark commands and watching him carry them out. Her ideas were humorous at first, but steadily became more sensual. Explicit. Pornographic. It became a kind of foreplay, and Joan no longer felt awkward or inhibited. She had become noticeably less so with every mouthful of wine, allowing herself to be photographed in every conceivable position, from every possible angle. In long-shot, in close-up. Holding herself, caressing herself. Even penetrating herself. She had completely abandoned herself to Mark's control.

I'm enslaved, she thought.

And then he said, 'Let's spice things up a bit.'

She turned to watch as he reached under the bed and brought out a black leather bag.

'What's in there?' she'd asked, her limbs heavy, her voice lazy, her enquiry no more than a formality. She already knew what his answer would be.

'Toys,' Mark replied.

263

Joan opened her heavy eyes, still conscious of the diminishing waves of her last orgasm slowly fading from her body, like ripples radiating across the surface of a pond. Mark knelt between her slack thighs with his face turned to the ceiling, his eyes closed, and his naked body glistening with sweat.

Joan swallowed dryly, and asked if he would untie her.

Mark looked down at her, blessed her with that grin of his, the one that made her want to tell him to start all over again. But she didn't in this instance, she was too sore. Her arms and legs had been tied to the corner posts of Mark's home-made bed, which, with the benefit of hindsight, she could see had been constructed with just this kind of activity in mind.

She really didn't know how long she had been in this position, she had zoned out at some point, but it must have been for quite a while. She could see the way the rough loops of rope Mark had used to secure her had cut into her wrists and ankles, and the pins and needles were becoming increasingly intense and uncomfortable. Other parts of her hurt, too, but at the moment she didn't want to think about them.

Once again, she asked Mark to untie her, and this time he didn't smile.

'Why should I?' he said. 'Why shouldn't I just leave you as you are?'

Joan licked her dry lips uncertainly. 'Because I wouldn't much fun like this, would I?'

Mark shrugged. 'It'd be fun for me.'

She stared at him, beginning to be a little afraid. She had never seen his blue eyes look so cold.

'But I--'

Mark laughed, and suddenly his eyes were once again as warm as the summer sky she could see through the bedroom window. He began to untie her, slowly and carefully, and he kissed the tender skin on each limb as he released it.

When he had finished, he lay down on the bed and embraced her tightly, and although Joan wanted nothing more than to go to the bathroom and scoop handfuls of cold water into her mouth, she found that she couldn't move.

'Did I scare you?' Mark breathed into her ear.

Joan nodded. 'A little.'

'That's nothing to what's coming next,' he whispered. 'You won't believe it.'

'What?' she asked, squirming around to face him. 'What did you say?'

'Nothing,' he smiled at her. 'I didn't say a word.'

Joan, confused and tired, half-drunk, frowned doubtfully. 'I thought you said something about--'

Mark shook his head. 'You must be hearing things. You're worn out, aren't you? That's what it is. Baby's all tired.'

He began to stroke her hair and forehead, gently lulling her. Joan closed her eyes.

'Go to sleep, Joan,' he said softly. 'You're going to need it.'

'Why?'

Joan experienced the by now familiar feeling of slipping down a deep, dark hole, both awake and asleep at the same time.

'Why?' she asked again. Her voice seemed to echo in her own head.

'I've got plans for you, lass. Big plans. Now go to sleep. Sleep, and when you wake up, everything'll be different.'

'Different?'

'Better. No more pretence.'

Mark spoke more after that, but Joan couldn't seem to catch on to the words. They slipped by as the darkness swallowed her, although for a while, before all thought ceased, she wondered about this place Mark was able to transport her to so easily. This no-place, this hollow capsule of blackness. It reminded her of something.

Something…

It was the *gullet*, she realised at last in amazement. She had been anaesthetised against the pain, somehow, numbed, but it was still the Dragon's gullet.

How on earth, she wondered, did I end up back here?

37

Sitting alone at a small table in a corner, Stephen contemplated his half-finished glass of orange juice with disgust and dismay. He'd had to sit here sipping the foul stuff while Olivia threw several gin and tonics down her throat in quick succession, chasing the dubious-looking cheese baguette she'd consumed in a half-dozen mammoth bites. During the time they had been here, the pub, close to Bounds Green tube station, had steadily begun to fill up. There were too many people here now for Stephen's taste, all of them too loud, all radiating that Sunday lunchtime smugness, downing alcohol and stuffing their faces with shepherd's pie and lasagne, and steaming coils of Cumberland sausage that reminded Stephen of fresh offal.

He knew that his dislike of these people was irrational, based primarily on envy. He couldn't drink because he was driving, and he couldn't have eaten to save his life because he was too wound up. But still, he found himself resenting other people's gusto, their happiness. Although he knew that it couldn't be the case, not one of them looked as though they had a problem in the world.

To cap it all, the jukebox was right beside them, and some idiot had pumped in coin after coin and selected a Madonna retrospective from the play-list. The repetitive percussions kicked at his eardrums, aggravating his hangover, the singer's voice like a dull blade twisting into his brain.

Like a virgin, indeed.

He glanced at his wristwatch irritably. It was nearly one o'clock now, and he wondered how Phil Richardson was getting on. He had phoned the DCI at home from his mobile, giving him Martin Bickley's name and address and asking for him to be checked out. The cover story had been that Stephen was thinking of employing Bickley to do some work around the house, and as neither Stephen nor Joan was going to be around the whole time, they wanted to know whether it would be safe to give the workman a key.

Richardson, who hadn't sounded too pleased to be disturbed at home, had asked him if it was a joke, and Stephen had been at pains to make sure he understood that it was not. Eventually the policeman

267

had agreed to get back to him. That had been very nearly two hours ago, and Stephen was thinking of calling back. The day was quickly slipping away from them. They had left another message on Dr Stratton's answer-phone, too, but as yet there had been no response.

'Stephen?'

He looked up to see that Olivia had returned from the ladies' room and was standing at the bar.

'Another orange juice?'

'All right.' No, fuck it, he thought. Hair of the dog, that's what I need. 'No. Make it a double scotch.'

'You're driving,' Olivia snapped back.

Stephen sensed an unwelcome attention from the other pub patrons at this exchange. Sly glances from men who were amused by a woman ordering him around, telling him what he could or could not drink. Women watching to see how he reacted. Others just looking at the grass stains on his trousers and the missing buttons on his shirt, and smirking.

He leaned back in his seat, trying not to look as sulky as he felt, and watched Olivia place her order with the barman. He watched her find her purse and begin to fish out coins. Then heard his mobile's ring-tone.

Suddenly he forgot all about Olivia, drinks, drinkers, food and music, and pulled his mobile from his pocket.

'Is that you, Phil?'

'It's me,' Richardson said.

'Thank God, I was beginning to think you'd forgotten me.'

'Yeah, sorry I was so long getting back to you; there were a few phone calls involved to get the information you wanted, and I had to make notes.'

Stephen paused before replying. It was the implication of the word, 'notes'. It suggested that there was too much information on Martin Bickley to simply commit to memory. Something had changed in Richardson's voice, too. The last time they had spoken, he had sounded like any other aggrieved, put-upon friend. Now he sounded worryingly business-like, professional, like a policeman.

'Let me just check something with you,' Richardson said. 'Is that description you gave me accurate? Because there are three Martin Bickley's on our database. Two of them are a fair bit older than you guessed, though, and--'

'Yes, it's accurate,' Stephen said quietly. 'What have you got for me?'

He heard Richardson grunt to himself. 'Put it this way,' the policeman said. 'If you take my advice, you'll start looking around for a new odd job man. Bickley's got a history.'

Olivia had left the drinks at the bar as soon as she had heard Stephen's phone ring, and she now sat down beside him, watching with concern as his face darkened.

'He's a criminal?' Stephen asked.

'Yeah, sometimes,' Richardson said. 'Mostly, he's a nutter.'

Stephen met Olivia's eyes.

'Go on,' he said.

Martin Bickley was born on April 6th twenty-four years ago, Richardson told Stephen, in a small, half-derelict cottage known as Hunter's Lodge. The cottage and the acre or two of land it stood on was all that remained of a larger property once called Old Farm, situated near the small North Yorkshire village of Lockton Dale. Bickley's parents both died before his seventh birthday, and he was subsequently raised by his uncle, who himself had a minor history of mental instability and a police record, mostly credited to drunken violence and misbehaviour. Apparently, Bickley had been taken into care a few times as a boy, because of allegations of physical abuse, but somehow he always ended up back with the uncle. Largely, it seemed, because that's where he told the social services he wanted to be.

As he grew, he and his uncle formed a self-contained unit from which all outsiders were excluded, almost becoming outcasts within their own small community. He attended the local school without distinction, did not respond to positive encouragement from his teachers, and formed no significant friendships. When the uncle required adult company, he travelled to York to frequent the pubs and the prostitutes there, leaving Bickley the younger alone to fend for himself. Sometimes the boy was to be seen hanging around the village, clearly starving, but unwilling to ask for help.

Then, when Bickley was thirteen, both he and his uncle became suspects in the disappearance of a local girl.

Alison Sissons, the daughter of a Lockton Dale publican, was a dreamy girl, a loner, well known for wandering on her own through the woods around Hunter's Lodge, exploring and reading books, drawing, or writing in her voluminous diary. Martin Bickley was said to be infatuated with her, always following her around the village at a distance, always close to her at school, but never daring to approach. One day Alison went out into the forest with a picnic and a new book, and she never came back.

Nothing was ever proved, Richardson stressed, no trace of her was ever found or anyone arrested in connection to her disappearance. But to the present day the girl's father still insisted that Bickley knew what had happened to his daughter. He believed that Bickley had lured her to Hunter's Lodge, where the old man had raped and murdered her, and then Bickley had helped him dispose of the body somewhere in the forest.

Between the ages of thirteen and seventeen, Bickley had acquired a history of petty larceny, mostly shoplifting, and mostly for food. But then he committed a series of burglaries which landed him in a young offenders' institute for six months. While he was in there his uncle died of a heart attack on one of his periodic jaunts to York. The old man had collapsed in the street after leaving a well-known brothel, where he had only moments before beaten up a prostitute after refusing to pay for her services

After his release from the institute, Bickley immediately joined the army, but after two months basic training at Aldershot, he was thrown out. As was usual, the army was not forthcoming with precise details, but the official line was 'conduct unbecoming', which made Richardson suspect the

271

worst. Bickley returned to Hunter's Lodge and disappeared from the police radar screen for a while, but it was believed that during this time he apprenticed himself to a number of tradesmen around the local towns. No one in his own village would have given him the time of day, much less a job.

When he was twenty-two, Bickley had a restraining order placed on him by another local girl who didn't appreciate his attentions. Janice Evans. He had taken to following her around, spying on her - stalking her, in other words. As was usual in these cases, the restraining order didn't adequately rectify the situation, and the girl eventually moved away to London, ostensibly to study, but mainly just to get away from him.

After a month or two, having somehow found out her location, Bickley followed her and took to living in an old van parked outside her flat, continuing to make a nuisance of himself. But by this time Janice had found a boyfriend, who warned him off in no uncertain terms. Blows were apparently exchanged.

Bickley seemed to get the message and eased off. He found a room in a nearby hostel and started doing odd jobs around the area. He seemed to straighten himself out, the girl said later. If he passed them in the street, he'd just wave, and that'd be it. Cautiously friendly, was the way Janice had described their acquaintanceship. What she couldn't know was that his mental state was deteriorating further, and he had taken to using a number of aliases.

One night, a few months later, long after everything seemed to have cooled down, the boyfriend was knocked down in a hit-and-run accident, leaving him in a coma. The next day, Janice had been sitting by his hospital bed, and Bickley had walked in with a bunch of flowers. He had been full of sympathy for her. He felt terrible about her boyfriend, and told her he would help her any way he could. Janice, two hundred miles from home and knowing hardly anyone in London except the boyfriend, responded to Mr Bickley, a familiar face, who now appeared completely sane and normal.

As the days passed, she began to lean on him for support, and they started to get close. Bickley began referring to her as his special friend, and she had later admitted that there had been several intimacies between them during this time.

But then, nine days later, the boyfriend had come out of his coma and started talking to the police, immediately naming Bickley as the man who had knocked him down. That old van was unmistakable, having been parked outside his house for so long, and what had happened was no accident. Bickley was arrested, sectioned, and sent down for psychiatric evaluation. Over three months he'd had a dozen appointments with a court-appointed psychiatrist, who then declared him safe for release into the community. He had been released on parole, gone back to Yorkshire, and kept his head down ever since.

As far as anyone was aware, he should still have been in Yorkshire. The police had no record of the Bounds Green address Stephen had given Richardson.

Stephen listened to this story with increasing horror, aware but unable to respond to Olivia's impatient, silent questioning. He thought his face must have reflected every word of what he was hearing, because her face was bloodless, her eyes wide and frightened.

'Well,' Richardson said into the silence that followed his comments. 'What do you think about that?'

Stephen could think of no adequate reply.

'Now, Stephen,' Richardson went on, sounding more than ever like an interrogating policeman. 'Why don't you tell me what's really going on here? Because I don't believe what you told me earlier. Why are you so interested in this man?'

For a moment, Stephen deliberated over telling Richardson the truth, but what was the truth? His wife, finally aware of the full depth of his infidelity, had left him and was in the company of another man. The man had a strange, not to say disturbing past, but was that the point? Joan had gone with him willingly enough, and it seemed that their relationship, whatever it was, may have existed for some time. The blame lay with Stephen himself for giving her a very good reason for taking off. And ironically, he had brought Bickley into Joan's life in the first place, by hiring him to work on the house.

Was he going to tell Richardson all that, losing the man's respect in the process?

'Stephen?'

'Phil, thanks, but just let me think about this for a while and I'll get back to you.'

He disconnected before Richardson could ask any more questions. Then he turned his phone off. He looked up at Olivia, his jaw locked stubbornly.

38

Phil Richardson, sitting in his office, stared at the phone receiver in his hand with surprise and a mounting anger. Had Stephen really just hung up on him? He immediately stabbed at the redial button. In his professional life he tended to see a lot of arrogance from solicitors, but he was damned if he was going to put up with it in his private life - especially from an old friend, someone for whom he'd just done a big, big favour.

After a few moments an automated reply told him that the person he was trying to reach was unavailable, which he knew meant that Stephen had turned his phone off purposely to avoid him. This made him so angry that he declined the opportunity to leave a message. It had taken a long time, but he'd learned over the years that the knee-jerk reactions forged in the first flush of anger usually turned out to be bad mistakes, and he knew that leaving a voicemail while in the grip of such a mood would be downright foolish.

The message he wanted to get to Stephen above all others was that he had to be extremely discreet about the way he used the information Richardson had just given him. It had been obtained by methods not officially sanctioned by current Met' policies, and, in the case of the information concerning Martin Bickley's juvenile record, it had been obtained completely unlawfully. Richardson wouldn't have gone so far out on a limb for Stephen under normal circumstances, or for almost anyone else he knew for that matter, but his own curiosity had been piqued by the subject of the enquiry, and he hadn't been able to resist calling in a favour or two in order to satisfy it.

He carefully replaced the phone receiver in its cradle on the desk and glanced at the clock on his office wall. Christ, he thought, groaning - how time flies.

It only seemed minutes since he'd told his less than pleased wife that he had to pop into the office for a while, but actually it had been hours. This afternoon he was supposed to be taking Louise and their young son, Ben, over to the fun fair that had been set up in Battersea Park, and if he didn't get his skates on soon Louise would be chewing his balls off the moment he walked in the door. Not that he'd particularly blame her if she did. He'd been working a lot of overtime recently, weekends included, and there was no doubt that their small family unit had suffered as a result. Louise was as patient and understanding as any police wife he had ever known, but there were limits to everything, and he calculated that Louise had just about reached hers.

Richardson found his car keys, jingled them in his hand, but didn't move from his seat.

He suddenly found himself wondering why he'd decided that doing this favour for Stephen had seemed like a better idea than placating his over-stressed, fed-up wife. After all, it wasn't like they were close friends anymore, and certainly nowhere near as close as they had been three or four years ago. At the time Richardson and his wife had first become acquainted with Stephen's set, they had still been in their late twenties, childless, and reasonably adventurous, and it had been fun for a while, running around with the affluent, free-spirited crowd which had also included Lee and Kath Meadows. But then real life had come along for the family Richardson, promotions and a new baby along with it, and they'd gradually, perhaps even gratefully, bowed out and moved on.

But Richardson didn't think the fact that he rather pitied Stephen for still being stuck in that rather empty way of life several years on had anything to do with his willingness to help out on his first real day off for weeks. Putting his innate curiosity aside for the moment, he thought it was probably more to do with Stephen's wife, Joan. He still remembered those two uncomfortable meetings he'd had with her somewhere in the midst of her breakdown, and particularly the second occasion, at the height of her paranoia, where he had actually ratted her out to her husband - a decision, incidentally, he still felt guilty about.

So maybe that was it. He didn't feel sorry for Stephen, he felt sorry for Joan, who'd had such an amazing run of truly terrible bad luck.

He recalled that after she had been injured in the hit-and-run accident, Louise had made a point of trying to re-establish their friendship, but hadn't been able to make a connection with the psychologically-damaged Joan. She might even have persisted, she told Richardson, but every time she went to the house she got the impression that Stephen was thinking about ways to make a pass at her. It was also difficult because she didn't like to take Ben along with her, and always had to find a sitter.

When Richardson had asked her why she wouldn't take Ben along on the visits, Louise explained that she didn't want to rub Joan's nose in the fact of her motherhood. Then she told him about a conversation she and Joan had shared soon after they had started seeing each other socially.

Joan, more than a couple of glasses of wine past her limit, had privately confessed that she wanted children, was in fact desperate for them, but she knew that Stephen would never agree. It wasn't that he was incapable of fathering a child, it was that he genuinely didn't want one. It had been the only pre-nuptial condition he had insisted upon, and he never once wavered in his resolve to stand by it. Joan had been young and besotted when she had agreed to this condition - willingly enough, she admitted - but had no idea of the depth of longing that would later come to torment her.

'If you ask me, half of what's wrong with that girl is her husband,' Louise had told him at the time.

And now, apart from pure bad luck, Richardson began to wonder exactly what the other half might be... and what, if anything, Stephen's interest in this Bickley character might have to do with it. Then his mobile, stuffed away in his back pocket, began to vibrate as it announced the arrival of a text from his wife, and at last he guiltily jumped up from his desk.

'I'm coming, I'm coming,' he murmured contritely.

Even her ringtone sounded pissed off.

39

Once again, the BMW was parked opposite the steps that led down to Martin Bickley's basement flat. While they kept watch for signs of life, Stephen had filled Olivia in on everything Richardson had told him, and she felt giddy, almost nauseous, as her mind scurried over this alarming new information. She thought back to their conversation that morning with Gordon Unwill, and the old man's embarrassed admission of imaginary sightings of Martin Bickley's van in and around Haversham Row.

Suddenly, it all made sense.

'Unwill didn't *imagine* seeing Bickley's van around the neighbourhood,' she said, thinking aloud. 'He really did see it. But Bickley wasn't watching him at all - it was Joan he was after. Following Joan, just like he followed those poor young girls before.'

Stephen nodded slightly in response, but never once took his eyes from Bickley's steps. There was a contained violence about him now, a long slow burn Olivia found strangely reassuring. She could feel the waves of energy radiating out from his body.

'Joan was right all along,' she went on. 'She wasn't being paranoid at all - she really *was* being stalked. She tried to tell us, and we didn't believe her. None of us did. Can you imagine how she must have felt?'

When Stephen did not reply, she turned on him.

'For Christ's sake, Stephen, say something!'

He looked at her, his eyes flat and dark.

'I'm going in there now,' he said. 'Don't try to stop me.'

'I'm not going to,' Olivia replied, shaking her head. 'I'm coming with you.'

One sharp kick did it, and the flat door sprang open just as the entrance door had a moment before, the lock's screws twisting out of the rotten wooden doorframes like old teeth. Stephen and Olivia paused on the threshold of the grubby little rooms beyond. Olivia held her breath, expecting alarms to be raised, loud voices calling for the police. There was nothing.

'What on earth is that smell?' she asked, fanning a hand in front of her face.

'I don't know,' Stephen said, sounding almost eerily calm.

He stepped into the room, took in the single bed, the shoddy, mildewed furniture, and the mess of materials and chemicals under the enlarger, which explained the smell. Then he quickly walked through the rest of the flat, checking out the bathroom and kitchen. Olivia heard him pulling open cupboards and drawers before he reappeared only moments later.

'Nothing?' she asked.

Stephen shook his head. 'But she's definitely been here.'

'How can you tell?'

He shrugged. 'I can feel her. Can't you?'

'Maybe.' Olivia wondered if she could, or was just imagining it.

Stephen jerked his head at the wardrobe and chest of drawers. 'Come on, get busy.'

Without another word, he went across and knelt on the threadbare carpet in front of the enlarger and began pulling out the dozens of photographic paper boxes stacked underneath. Olivia just watched him for a few moments, her arms wrapped around herself. She looked at the photographs on the walls, finding them impersonal and anonymous. Unfeeling, uncaring. Then she came to the photograph blue-tacked to the mirror. This was of a different quality altogether.

'Stephen, look. Is this where he lives up north, do you think? Is this Hunter's Lodge?'

'Could be.' He had scattered prints from the boxes all over the floor and was feverishly sifting through them with his fingertips. 'There's more of it in here, from all different angles. He must like the place.'

'Hunter's Lodge,' Olivia said, and shivered. 'Is that how he thinks of himself, a hunter?'

Stephen, busy opening more boxes and pulling out the contents, did not reply. Olivia turned away and opened the wardrobe. Inside she found an old khaki parka, the sort of thing you could buy in army-surplus stores, several pairs of jeans, a selection of plain white t-shirts, and a couple of khaki jumpers with leather elbow-patches. A pair of weathered black Doc Marten boots, eighteen lace-holes high, sat at the bottom. Bickley was heavily into the military-look, it seemed, despite being drummed out of the army after only a matter of months. Propped up behind the boots were the magnetised signs from his van, which advertised that no job was too odd for Yorkie. They were clean and undamaged. Why had he taken them off?

Olivia thought she knew. It was to make his van as anonymous as possible.

281

In the chest of drawers, she picked her way through more t-shirts, jumpers, dark tracksuits, bundles of underwear and balled socks. She found nothing of Joan's, but she discovered a half-filled empty whisky bottle and a rent book made out to the name Mark Bowman, which she assumed to be yet another alias. She also discovered a small brown prescription bottle with a few pills rattling away at the bottom, which she lifted out of the top drawer.

She opened the child-proof lid and glanced inside. The pills were purplish, and the bottom of the bottle was filled with their chalky residue, as though the pills were very old or at some point in the past some had been crushed. She replaced the lid and slowly turned the bottle around to examine the label.

'Jesus Christ!' Stephen said behind her. 'Jesus Christ, look at this!'

Suddenly numb from her head to her toes, Olivia turned around and saw that Stephen had covered most of the threadbare carpet with jumbled layers of photographs. Mostly they were similar to those which covered the walls of the flat, but a few were of the same cottage in the photo stuck to the mirror and the trees surrounding it. The photographs Stephen held in his hands, shuffling them like a pack of outsize cards, were city shots similar to those on the walls, although their subjects did not appear to be the usual tourist sites.

Preoccupied though she was, Olivia still recognised them as places she knew well. Hampstead High Street, Kentish Town. Shops she had frequented, streets she had walked. Everything familiar.

'This is it,' Stephen said. 'This is proof that he was stalking her.'

Joan was in every photograph. Although the majority of the shots had been taken from long distance, she was at the centre of everything, with her long dark woollen coat swirling around her, the matching hat covering most of her short auburn hair. Walking away, turning away, never photographed clearly, face on, for then she might have seen her stalker.

Despite Stephen's grim excitement, Olivia barely glanced at the photographs. The prescription bottle creaked as she unconsciously tightened her fingers around it.

'Stephen,' she said.

'This is incredible, he must have been following her around for weeks. Look, photographs, photographs, photographs… he's absolutely obsessed with her.'

'Stephen!'

He looked up. 'What?'

'I found these pills in the drawer.'

He glanced at the small bottle in her fist. 'So?'

'They're called Flunitrazepam.'

Stephen shrugged.

'I read an article about them in Cosmopolitan not long ago. They're what's called a hypnotic. They're used to treat insomnia.'

'So what?' he asked impatiently. 'What has insomnia got to do with anything? Look at these!'

He thrust the photographs at her.

The closest, clearest shot he had found pictured Joan from behind, looking into a travel agent's window. Her head was half-turned to the side as she studied the prices of the holidays to Morocco, the Algarve, and Turkey, and the line of her jaw and cheekbone were in sharp focus. If Bickley had been standing a foot or so to his left when he'd taken it, he would have caught the reflection of Joan's face in the window.

There was something wrong with this photograph, but Olivia couldn't immediately tell what, and at that moment she hadn't the patience to work it out. The pill bottle in her hand seemed to be burning her flesh.

'Stephen,' she said. 'There's reason why I read that article, and why I remembered it. Flunitrazepam is marketed under the trade-name of Rohypnol. Does that name sound at all familiar?'

Stephen waved his hands at her in frustration. 'No, and I don't see what--'

'Rohypnol is a date-rape drug.'

She watched her words impact on him.

'Part of the article was an interview with a woman who'd had her drink spiked with it on a blind date. She said one minute she was fine, having a good time, but the next she felt as though she'd fallen down a deep, dark hole, and she had a dream. A terrible dream, she said. A sexual nightmare. She'd had no will of her own, no inhibitions. She did whatever this man, who she'd only met that night, wanted her to do. She did things she'd never normally think about. They didn't use condoms, and she let him come inside her.

'When she woke up in bed with him the following morning, he told her that she'd agreed to come home with him, but had then passed out before they could do much more than get undressed. And she thought that's all it had been, a weird dream. She said that she'd been grateful to him, because he hadn't taken advantage of her. Then, a couple of months later, she wound up pregnant, even though, as far as she knew, she hadn't had sex.'

Stephen had slowly risen to his feet, and Olivia saw that his hands were crushing the photographs. His face was dark with rage.

'If Bickley somehow slipped one of these to Joan, in a drink, or…'

'I'll kill him,' Stephen muttered thickly. 'If he did that to her, I'll kill him.'

'It may be even worse than you think,' she said, her voice trembling.

'Worse?' Stephen shouted. 'How in God's name could it be worse?'

Olivia glanced down at the bottle's label, wishing that she had been mistaken. 'These aren't Bickley's pills.'

She held out the bottle, so that Stephen could see for himself.

'They were prescribed for Kath Meadows.'

They hit the A1 less than twenty minutes later with the village of Lockton Dale plugged into the SatNav, barrelling along the dual-carriageway at almost a hundred miles an hour on the longer, straighter stretches. Olivia was holding on to the edges of her seat as Stephen constantly changed lanes to swerve around those vehicles that were going too slow for him, which was all of them. She still wasn't sure that they were doing the right thing, heading for Bickley's address in Yorkshire, but Stephen was absolutely convinced that this was where they would find Joan. While he had made his way through the London traffic, she had used her mobile to call Directory Inquiries, but there was no record of a number for Hunter's Lodge. No number for Martin Bickley or Mark Bowman, or any of the other aliases Richardson had given Stephen either, and Joan's mobile was still unreachable.

'He's like a fucking plague,' Stephen said. 'Stealing women away from their husbands - first Lee's and now mine.'

He'd been saying much the same thing for a while now. He was completely hooked on the sexual predator angle. But Olivia was looking through it, past it, to something else.

'But just think about this for a minute, Stephen,' she said. 'If he's finished with Kath, where is she now? Why didn't she come back to her husband, like she did before?'

'I don't know and I don't care. Probably she was too ashamed to come back. And who says he's finished with her, anyway? Maybe he's got her stashed in that cottage of his, drugged up to the eyeballs. If he thinks he's going to add Joan to his harem, he's got another thing coming.'

In Olivia's lap, under the Atlas of Great Britain Stephen had taken from the boot of his car and tossed at her, was a brown A4 envelope containing the photographs Bickley had covertly taken of Joan, a few shots of the cottage, the rent book, and the pill bottle. When he was bagging them in the flat, Stephen had referred to these items as 'evidence', although as he was still refusing to call the police, he obviously wasn't thinking of them in legal terms. Olivia suspected that his evidence was meant for Joan's eyes alone, to convince her that her new boyfriend, if that's what he was, was not what he seemed.

Olivia glanced out of the windscreen and was immediately blinded by the flash of a speed-camera. It was the second time the BMW had been flashed, and if they continued at the same speed, it wouldn't be the last.

'You're going to get banned,' she warned Stephen.

'You think I care?'

Strong words for a man so in love with his vehicle.

'How far is it now?' he asked, unable to glance at the SatNav as he swung around another vast lorry.

'Still the best past of two hundred miles,' she said. 'Just calm down, or you're going to get us both killed.'

Olivia pulled the photographs out of the envelope and began to leaf through them again, smoothing out the creases still further. She still didn't know what was wrong with the single close-up, Joan's back, the line of her face, but she knew there was something. It was preying on her mind. She worked her way through the rest, picking up that same 'something's-not-quite-right' feeling from each of them, before finally returned to the close-up. Her eyes wandered over Joan's back, the angle of her head and the direction in which she seemed to be looking.

287

Directly in the imaginary eyeline was a hand-printed card stuck to the travel agent's window, a bargain-buster offer, fourteen nights in Bali, flights only, at a ridiculously cheap price. And suddenly, Olivia knew exactly what was wrong.

Her hand went to her mouth. A series of realisations, each worse than the last, stormed through her mind. It was a chain reaction of explosions that ended at a terrible climax.

'Stephen,' she managed to say.

'What now?' he asked irritably.

'Drive faster.'

He risked a quick glance at her, saw her sudden pallor. 'What is it?'

'I've felt all along there was something odd about these photographs,' she said.

'Of course there's something odd about them,' he said aggressively. 'They're the product of a sick mind.'

'That isn't what I meant,' Olivia said, shaking her head. 'This isn't Joan.'

'What are you talking about?'

'Stephen, they're photographs of me.'

'What?'

'Back when I was trying to be Joan. After I'd stolen her coat. I remember standing in front of this window now. I remember the offers.' She flicked through the photographs again, searching for something more concrete. 'See, this one. Look carefully at the face, it's me.'

Stephen couldn't really look, and the detail was tiny. 'I don't understand.'

Olivia took a deep breath. 'That girl Bickley followed to London. How did he get close to her?'

Stephen cast his mind back to the telephone conversation with John Richardson. 'He tried to kill her boyfriend. Then he offered her comfort, wormed his way in like that.'

'Yes. What about Kath Meadows?'

'She didn't need any encouragement to leap into bed with anyone. She was up for everything.'

'But how do you think he got so close to her that she'd run away with him?'

'He drugged her, didn't he?' He frowned. 'Isn't that what you said?'

'No, I said they were her pills, prescribed for her. She was probably suffering from short term insomnia… after her brother was killed.'

Stephen turned his head slowly and looked at her for so long that he almost drove the car into the central divider as he recalled how Kath's brother had died. The black toad of the family. The tragic accident that had seemed in retrospect like a prophetic warning after Joan's "little accident". Olivia could see the three magic words in Stephen's eyes.

Hit-and-run.

'That's right,' she said. 'First that girl's boyfriend, then Kath Meadows' brother.'

She lifted up the photographs.

'I was next, Stephen. He was following me, watching my movements too, not just Joan. He'd photographed me in this hat and coat. He knew what to look for. He waited for his chance and he took it. This is what he does, this is how he softens his women up, how he makes them emotionally vulnerable....'

Stephen shook his head, confused. 'But you weren't knocked down, Joan was.'

'Yes,' Olivia nodded. 'That's the point - he made a mistake. She came to confront me over our affair, and she took her coat and hat when she left. Bickley saw her on the crossing and assumed that she was me. At the last moment, he realised that it was Joan, and he tried to stop.'

Olivia's arms dropped into her lap, the photographs falling in a mess into the footwell. She had lost all strength, realising that if everything had gone to plan she would already have been dead.

'And then he waited all through her entire recovery to get close to her again?' Stephen asked. 'Why?'

'I don't know. Because he'd chosen her. In his mind, Joan belonged to him. Just like Kath before her. Like the girl he followed to London. He was hunting her.'

'This is insane,' Stephen said, but didn't sound like he was convincing anyone, least of all himself.

'I wonder where that girl is now - did she go missing, and nobody put the pieces together? I wonder where Kath really is.'

'Where do you think they are?'

Olivia hesitated.

'I think they're both dead,' she said finally, her voice faint.

40

Joan emerged from the Dragon's gullet amazingly whole. Amazingly intact and unharmed. She simply opened her eyes, one moment asleep, the next wide awake. There was no grogginess, no period of uncertainty. She knew exactly where she was, and, for the first time since the series of revelations that had reshaped her world, she knew exactly what she had to do. The fuzziness that had engulfed her seemed to have gone. The Dragon had lost its teeth.

Mark was nice, Mark was sweet - in a kinky, slightly domineering sort of way, it had to be admitted - and he was as fit as a butcher's dog. But Mark was not her future, and her future had to be decided and quickly, before she allowed herself to drift. This trip, and her affair, had been a pleasant interlude, but it seemed that it had done its job.

Now that her mind was working clearly again, she was able to swiftly formulate, with no effort at all, a brief itinerary for herself: a) Get back to London; b) Either find a flat of her own or make Stephen move out of their home; c) In peace and solitude, take stock of her feelings for her husband and her sister; d) Make her decisions and live with them.

She understood that this had to be done immediately. A to D, right away, and she'd worry about the rest of the alphabet later.

Joan was convinced that Mark would understand her reasons for cutting short their trip. Maybe he'd be a little upset, but she was sure that she could talk him around. It didn't necessarily mean that it would be the end of their friendship - the intimate side of it, that is. Not unless she decided that her marriage could be

291

patched up. Meanwhile, they could still meet, spend time together, and enjoy each other's company. But there would be limits. That was suddenly as clear to Joan as anything else.

There would be no more bondage, or pornographic photographs, or sex toys, or submissive role-playing, for a start. The alcohol, or maybe the sheer novelty of making love to another man, had allowed her to indulge Mark against her normal impulses, but now she simply felt cheapened by the whole experience. She had no wish to repeat it. If Mark could live with that, all well and good. If he couldn't... well, she would always be grateful for what he had done for her, but it would have to be goodbye.

Naked on the bed, Joan focussed on her hand which lay curled up on the mattress in front of her face, her short fingernails absently worrying at a loose cotton thread, and she suddenly frowned. Her hand really was on the mattress - the sheet she had slept on had been removed. Where had it gone?

She sat up, feeling the pull of her aching joints, and stared silently at the bed, which had been totally stripped while she slept. Then she looked around the rest of the bedroom, sensing that something else had changed without being able to see exactly what. The sun was still shining, but it had a subtly different quality to it that made her believe it was now late afternoon, perhaps even edging toward early evening. A wind had risen, and through the window she could see the trees waving from side to side. Hours had passed while she slept, it seemed. Mark had left her to recover from his passions while he occupied his time another way.

She looked down at the bare mattress again, then across at the heavy armchair in the corner where their clothes had been dumped. It was empty. Mark had done the laundry? What a man.

'Mark?'

Joan's voice seemed to reverberate in the bedroom. The bedroom door, ajar just a few inches, for some reason reminded her of house-hunting, of doors in unoccupied homes, of doors left to their own inscrutable devices. She shivered and called Mark's name again, and once more there was no reply. Except for a voice whispering in her head.

When you wake up, everything'll be different.

Mark had said that, she recalled, just before she had fallen asleep in his arms. She hadn't understood it then and she didn't understand it now. But somehow, it was true. She felt different. This room felt different.

No more pretence.

Joan eased herself off the bed, hissing when the soles of her feet touched the wooden floor, absorbing the underlying chill dankness of the ground beneath. Obviously the fire had gone out, and this was a place that badly needed a fire. She felt a sudden surge of panic, similar to the one she had experienced on setting foot in the cottage for the first time. The hairs on her arms stood up, as though in response to an electrical charge.

She stepped toward the door, felt her feet brush the edge of the sheepskin rug, and looked down at it.

Built meself a cellar.

Was Mark in his cellar darkroom now? Was he using his computer to make prints of the pornographic digital photographs he'd taken of her earlier? She knelt down and rapped on the hollow floor with her knuckles.

'Mark? Are you down there?'

When there was no response, she grabbed a handful of the sheepskin and tried to raise the trapdoor as Mark had earlier, but it wouldn't move. The rug was bonded to the floor, and the floor felt completely solid, with no sign of a lock or catch. She wondered if she had dreamed that part about the trapdoor. God knows, the rest of it now felt like a dream.

Why had she let him do those things to her?

Joan stood up again, wrapping her arms about herself. Maybe it was just the floor transmitting its chill through the rest of her body, but she really did feel cold. The sunlight outside wasn't touching the room at all. She went over to the wardrobe where she had hung the rest of her clothes, intending to drape herself in an oversized sweater, and maybe some thick socks to warm her feet. A fresh pair of knickers wouldn't go amiss, either.

She swung open the double doors and stared in bemusement. The wardrobe was completely empty. Both her clothes and Mark's were gone. Even her wheelie case, stashed in the bottom with her shoes, had gone.

Good God, she thought, he can't have washed everything.

She turned next to the chest of drawers beside the wardrobe, and discovered that this too was empty. Oh come on, she thought, this is too much.

Still hugging herself, she shuffled over to the door and peeked through the gap. 'Mark?'

The rest of the cottage echoed just like the bedroom had before it. It had changed, too. It smelled damp. Unlived in.

Joan nudged open the door with her knee and tiptoed out over the cold floor. She called Mark's name a few more times, before finally accepting that she was alone. Gone into the village, she thought. To buy food. To do the washing at a laundrette. She didn't really believe any of this, but she didn't understand what else it could mean. Unless it was some kind of game Mark was playing with her.

Got big plans for you, lass.

It was only a few moments later that Joan realised what Mark's game was. It came to her after she had used the bathroom and reached for a towel that wasn't there. There were no towels in the small airing cupboard, nor under the basin, and the shower curtain that last night had been neatly tucked away behind a tie-back had been removed from its chrome rail. It was the missing shower curtain that clinched it for her.

Mark had removed from the cottage anything she could used to cover her nudity. Her clothes, his clothes, the sheets from the bed, the towels, even the shower curtain, just in case she felt like wandering around looking like a Vivienne Westwood catwalk model. She rushed out of the bathroom into the main

295

body of the cottage, and found her suspicions confirmed.

It was one of the things she should have noticed immediately, perhaps, but had only registered subliminally. The window curtains had been removed. The rug that had filled the space between the two facing leather sofas was also gone. She turned around and around. It was true. Every trace of fabric had been spirited away.

Cursing, angrier than she could herself believe, Joan stalked to the front door and threw it open. Mark's van hadn't moved. He hadn't left her alone, that wasn't the game. He was out there now watching her from the safety of his beloved forest. Most likely, he was watching her through a camera lens, taking more photographs of her.

Because it was what he did. And it was fun.

'Mark!' she shouted. 'Stop it! I don't like this! I want it to stop, right now!'

The wind moving the branches of the trees seemed to swallow her voice. Under the forest's gaze she felt very small and powerless, and this enraged her.

She stomped her way over the small deck and down the steps, not bothering to try to hide either her nakedness or her anger.

'I mean it, Mark! I will not be treated like this!'

Suddenly she kicked out at the driver's door of the van with the ball of her foot, making a small fist-sized dent. It hurt like hell, but there was a savage pleasure to it, too, a kind of primal release that eased some of the pressure in her head. She kicked it twice more, buckling the panel more badly. Fragments of dry mud flew off like shrapnel.

'Do you understand me?' she yelled. 'I want my clothes back right now!'

She turned away from the car and hurried back into the cottage, slamming the door behind her. She stood for a few moments, her back to the door as she hyperventilated. A sheen of perspiration appeared across her chest. After another moment, she went across and sat down on one of the sofas, staring at the door. Any moment, she knew, Mark would appear there with a sheepish grin on his face and her wheelie case dragging behind him. She could already hear him trying to explain that it was all just a game, and he didn't think she'd take it so badly.

You have no idea, she'd tell him, how badly I've taken it.

Then he'd turn on the charm, she supposed. And maybe she'd allow herself to be charmed, perhaps that would be easier in the short term. Then, when she had her clothes back and they were friends again, she could tell him what she had decided. It would probably make the whole thing easier.

How she would handle him when he came occupied Joan for almost five minutes, but then she was just waiting. Waiting, and waiting. She was patient, but gradually it dawned on her that Mark wasn't going to do as she'd asked, and the rage welled up in her once more.

She jumped to her feet and began to pace around, desperately thinking what she could do. Should she simply go out into the woods and look for him? Even if she didn't find Mark, she might at least find where he had stashed her clothes. But then she reconsidered. She pictured herself wondering around naked in the forest, and she thought that this might be exactly what Mark wanted her to do. To add to his portfolio. She remembered the single photo in the bedroom, the young girl reading her book, pretending that the camera wasn't there, and she realised that the girl probably wasn't pretending at all. She hadn't known that she was being watched, let alone photographed.

My God, she thought, he's a bloody *voyeur*. She recalled him dropping her on the bed, asking her to act unconscious. And she had done it, hadn't she? The snap, snap, snap of his camera. Shit!

Seething now, she went back to the door and opened it again. She was almost crying as she shouted into the forest.

'This game is over, Mark! I'm not playing your stupid game! I want my clothes, I want my things, and then I want to go home!'

She slammed the door again, then sank down to the floor, unable to stop herself weeping.

41

A short time later, even before the tears had dried on her face, Joan had an idea. She had been thinking of Mark hiding in the woods, perhaps actually sitting on her wheelie case, mocking her. But then she wondered whether he would have bothered to carry everything, clothes, curtains, towels, everything, out of the cottage and into the woods, all for the sake of what amounted to an ill-conceived practical joke. Maybe he had gone for a simpler, easier solution: the cellar. Maybe he'd just lifted the trapdoor while she was asleep and dropped everything down there.

But the trapdoor is locked, she thought.

So unlock it, she answered herself.

I don't have a key.

So find one.

Although she agreed with this voice, which was, after all, her own, she shook her head. It was the right idea, but she wasn't going to waste time looking for a key, which in any case Mark had probably removed. She was just going to force the trapdoor open.

She stood up and went into the kitchen. Last night, fetching a knife to cut up the crusty bread they had eaten with the soup, she had seen a fine collection of heavy professional carving knives in the cutlery drawer. She could use the biggest of these to wedge the trapdoor open. Quite probably she would ruin Mark's flawless wooden flooring in the process, but that wasn't her problem. He would only have himself to blame.

'See how you like *my* bloody game,' she muttered to herself.

She hurried through into the kitchen and snatched open the cutlery drawer. Her mouth fell open. The drawer was empty. After a second or two, she ransacked every other drawer and cupboard, only to discover that they had all been emptied. She left the kitchen area and ran across to the old Welsh dresser, but found that this too had been cleared out.

She glanced out of the window, her eyes making patterns within the moving trees. Random, shifting patterns her mind tried to organise into the shape of a man. Somewhere out there, Mark was watching her right now. She was sure of it. She moved back from the window until her back was against the wall, and she realised that she was trembling, and not from the cold. This wasn't right. This was more than voyeurism. This was more than a practical joke, ill-conceived or otherwise.

By removing every utensil in the kitchen, Mark had not only taken away everything she could have used for a tool, he had also taken everything she could have used as a weapon in her defence.

This was *not* a game.

Joan closed her eyes, willing herself to concentrate, to find her way out of this mess. But the thing that kept coming back into her mind was the trapdoor. Somehow, she had to find a way of opening it, with her fingernails if need be.

'Joan!'

Her eyes snapped open.

'Jooaaanie!'

Mark's voice, mocking, sardonic, drove her through to the bedroom, where she immediately went down on her knees. She tried to peel the sheepskin rug away from the floor, but the edges wouldn't give so much as a millimetre. She tried digging into the thin line of translucent glue she found glistening under the fringes, but only succeeded in breaking off a short fingernail, tearing it into the quick. The glue was set like cement. She grabbed a handful of fleece near the rug's centre and yanked as hard as she could, but nothing moved. Bright drops of blood from her finger began to stain the white fleece. In frustration and pain, she raised her face to the ceiling and screamed.

A long peal of laughter from the forest brought her head down again, and that was when she saw it.

The black and white photograph of the young girl reading had been removed from the wall above the bed. It had been replaced with another photograph, this one in colour. She stood up and walked toward it. It was a home-printed picture, she had known that instantly. What it was a picture of took a little longer to register, maybe because she simply didn't want to admit to herself that she knew.

The photo had been taken in the dark, relying on the camera's inbuilt flash to light its subject. As a result, the picture had something of the look of those old-time sepia portraits where the sitter was surrounded by a vignette of darkness. But Joan could see quite enough. She could see more clearly than she wanted to.

It was a photograph of her, asleep in Mark's flat back in London. But she wasn't really asleep, she was drugged. The camera flash blazed in her half-open eyes, only the whites showing.

The blue duvet had been pulled down to the foot of the narrow single bed, and the dress she had been wearing as she slept had been worked up around her body until it was gathered under her arms and rolled up beneath her chin. Her bra had been pushed up above her breasts. Her knickers had been pulled down, and they were stretched elastically between her knees, which had been lifted and spread apart. The flash glared on a naked muscular male arm that reached into frame, the wide-angle lens turning it into an anaemic tentacle. The fingers at the end of the arm were fanned out over her crotch, holding her open for

301

the camera. In the top left hand corner of the photograph, handwritten in blue biro, was the number 8.

Joan remembered her unusually powerful erotic dream. The flashes like lightning strikes that had occasionally punctuated the surreal experience. They had been the intervals at which Mark had recorded his abuse of her. She remembered adjusting her underwear in the morning, assuming that they had become twisted and uncomfortable because she'd slept in them, never once suspecting that they had been awkwardly replaced.

She snatched the offending photograph off the wall, twisting it in her hands. When it tore in half, she crumpled it up into a ball and tried to crush it to nothing. She collapsed on to the bare mattress, drawing her knees up to her chest and closing her eyes.

Not real, she told herself desperately. It didn't happen that way. It had been a *dream*.

'Jooaaanie!'

Joan would probably have lain on the bed for a long time, motionless, like a rabbit caught in the headlights of an oncoming car, but Mark's voice startled her. *Woke* her. No, it had not been a dream. Just as *this* was not a dream. She couldn't allow herself to think of it that way. She jumped up from the bed, intending to run, run anywhere, but her legs felt so weak she had to pause for a moment.

'Joan,' Mark called, seeming much closer. 'Have you found the surprises I left for you?'

Joan tottered out of the bedroom and looked at the front door. No key in the lock to turn, what did she expect? Then she thought, surprises? Plural? She looked down at the crushed photograph in her hand. Number 8. Were there others on view now somewhere, 1 to 7? What would they show?

She quickly glanced around the cottage, but failed to see any of the framed forest photographs missing, replaced with new images of her being defiled. It was exactly the same nature collage she had admired yesterday. Trees, branches, leaves, sections of undergrowth, the forest changing through the seasons. For the first time she realised that the set of photographs in each season were practically identical. The same shots, detailing about seven different locations. A second after this realisation had struck her, she saw that something had changed.

In the Spring season, about seven paces from the bedroom door, she saw a woman posed against a tree in one of the photographs. It was easy to see why she hadn't spotted it earlier. It was a framed study, just like the rest, and the framing of the tree was identical to the photograph she must have seen yesterday. Only the introduction of the woman was different.

Was this one of the surprises?

Joan took a single step toward the photograph and stopped. Even from this distance, something about the figure called to her, conformed to some pattern filed away at the back of her mind. She took two more faltering steps, and then covered the remaining distance in a headlong rush.

This was the real surprise.

'No!' She could literally feel the blood rushing through her head, surging. 'No!' she screamed, and heard through it the sound of Mark's laughter.

Over the next few minutes, Joan discovered nine more photographs of Kath Meadows carefully arranged on the cottage walls, seamlessly fitted into the display like pieces of a jigsaw. The photograph she had found first appeared to be the first in the sequence, and showed Kath happily posing for the camera, dressed in jeans and a heavy cable-knit sweater as she leaned back against a budding tree. The second photograph, a few feet farther along the same wall, had caught Kath in the same place and time, only in this one her face was invisible behind the sweater she was in the process of taking off. She wore nothing under the sweater, and her light-skinned breasts seemed huge in the sunlight, the contrast making her engorged nipples look black. The third photograph showed her completely naked, her clothes piled on the ground beside her, as she posed uninhibitedly.

In each of these three studies, she was smiling widely. It was the happiest Joan thought she had ever seen her.

The fourth photograph showed Kath presenting her naked bottom to the camera while she touched her toes. The fifth, the last one taken in the forest, showed her lying on her side on the forest floor, her arms and legs tangled up. It reminded Joan of the pose Mark had asked her to assume for his first photograph of her on the bed. Only she didn't believe that Kath was faking her apparent unconsciousness. A dark liquid smear stained her right temple and cheek.

If Joan hadn't already been in shock by this time, the sixth photograph alone would have put her there.

If she hadn't been in shock, the seventh, eighth, ninth and tenth would have driven her out of her mind.

The last five photographs of the sequence had been taken in an interior. In the background she could see neat rows of grey breezeblocks, and assumed that it was Mark's cellar.

I use it as me darkroom, me studio sometimes.

These photographs catalogued Kath's torture and death, and Joan recoiled from their clinical savagery even as she was drawn to them. Kath had been gaffer-taped naked to a chair, identical to those in Mark's kitchen. She was crying, her right eye puffed up and a thin line of blood leaking from the corner, running down her cheek and neck. Her face told its own story. Pain, anguish, terror, and betrayal. Most of all, pain.

In the sixth photograph, several long needles had been inserted into Kath's nipples and areolae. The seventh was a close up of her hand, blurred by frantic movement, but it was still possible to see that the little finger had been clipped off above the knuckle. In the eighth, her body was streaked with blood from a shallow wound that had been made on her torso in the shape of a y-incision, like those used in an autopsy. It was a guideline for what was to come next. Photographs nine and ten were visions of hell, and Joan turned away from them, shuddering and sobbing.

She remembered the letter she had written to Kath, that angry, accusing, self-indulgent letter that had made her feel so much better about herself. She remembered spitefully wanting to send Kath a dismissive psychic message during the journey up here.

305

You've had your Perfect Day, now I'm having mine.

And all the while, her friend had been dead. Tormented and tortured to death by a madman. A madman who now held Joan captive. The photographs were a message, she understood, a signpost to the future.

Mark meant to do exactly the same thing to her.

42

They had been travelling in silence for some time now, each willing the miles to melt away a little faster as they finally began to approach their junction, each lost in their own guilty thoughts. Finally, Olivia had to find a tissue to wipe her eyes, and Stephen glanced across at her. He debated for a few seconds about whether he should speak, and then decided to.

'Are you alright?'

'Not really,' Olivia said. 'Just punishing myself, thinking what a kind and forgiving person Joan has been over the years. All the terrible things I did to her and she never once gave it back, not once. And if I ever needed her, she was always there for me. There was always a second chance with Joan. And a third, and a fourth, and a fifth…. a hundredth, even, if that's what was required. It takes real strength to do that, you know - to keep turning the other cheek.'

Olivia blew her nose noisily.

'And she's brave, too. I don't think even she realises how brave she really is. When Mum was dying, going just the same way as Dad, and I couldn't face it again, not any of it, Joan stayed. I ran away that time, and she stayed. I knew that she felt just the same as me, but she had the courage to stay with Mum, and nurse her, and see it through to the end.'

Stephen didn't reply, but she could see his jaw working as he struggled with another internal debate. She waited and eventually he spat it out, the admission that had been eating away at him.

'I know her secret,' he said. 'I've known for a long time, but I've never let on.'

'What secret?'

'That she wants a baby. She thought I didn't know, but all you had to do was watch the way she was around other people's kids, the way she got caught up in them, and it was so obvious. We agreed before we married that there'd be no children, did you know that?'

Olivia nodded.

'That was my decision, not hers. I suspected that she thought I'd eventually change my mind, but…' He shook his head. 'I never wanted to be tied down like that, and made to feel old. And I hated *my* father, and I couldn't bear the thought of turning into him. But he was a serial adulterer, so I guess I did anyway...'

Stephen trailed off for a few moments, and then abruptly smiled.

'Speaking of her bravery, do you remember the dog in the park?'

'Yes,' Olivia said, smiling herself.

They had been walking through Golders Hill Park one Sunday with a group of friends prior to finding some lunch, and Joan had suddenly broken away from the group, moving toward a young family having a picnic on the grass. The younger of the two

307

children, barely able to walk, was standing a few feet away from the spread blanket, and it was to this child that Joan was racing. She had seen a short but powerful dog, a Staffordshire Bull Terrier, in fact, pull its lead out of its owner's hand and come pelting across in the child's direction, barking and snarling ferociously.

Unfazed by the danger she might be placing herself in, Joan had planted herself between the child and the dog and stood firm.

'I never knew anybody could shout that loud,' Stephen said.

'Or scream so piercingly.'

'Or swear so badly.'

'And then she started *barking*,' Olivia said, beginning to laugh. 'She actually *howled*.'

'And that's when the dog stopped and ran away with his tail between his legs.'

They were both laughing now, and Olivia realised what they were doing. They were like a couple of mourners at a funeral who'd run through their list of regrets and were now digging out the good old stories one last time. That stopped her laughing immediately.

'She's not dead,' she said abruptly. 'She's not.'

43

Carefully hidden behind a clump of bracken just inside the treeline, the hunter patiently waited for his prey. He was dressed in camouflage combat fatigues and he had painted his face in wide stripes of black and green. Afterwards he had looked at himself in the mirror of the make-up compact he had kept as a trophy of one of his kills. As always, he wondered that his blue eyes did not destroy the illusion he had created, but only made it better. They made him look like a section of forest come to life.

Nature was cruel and savage because it had to be, and so was he.

A leather sheath strapped to his right thigh contained a large double-edged survival knife that had not been cleaned for three years, and its wide blade was ingrained with dried blood. Only the edges were a different colour, a smooth, gleaming silver, from obsessive whetting.

Despite the strengthening wind shaking its way through the forest he had heard his prey scream, he had heard it crying. And he had attentively gauged the length of the silence that followed, having learned through experience the thought processes his prey would be going through. The first shock would now be wearing off, wild panic only held at bay by illusionary hopes of escape. Once that hope was crushed, panic would rule, and the hunter would hunt.

A small click came from the cottage, and the hunter, moving only his eyes, looked up in time to see his prey's pale face appear in the doorway. Even from his distance, without the aid of the telescopic lens of the camera attached to a short tripod directly in front of him, he could see its raw, red eyes, saw them scanning the treeline, passing over his hiding place without pause.

The prey opened the door a little wider. It was now staring at the van. That was what they always did. It was the first, easiest choice. Then, moving with the awkward, vulnerable speed of the naked, huddling into itself, it crossed the deck and jumped down to the side of the vehicle. It glanced in through the window. He saw its eyes light up when it spotted the keys dangling from the ignition. The hunter smiled.

With one last quick glance around the clearing, the prey snatched at the handle, looking comically surprised as the handle slipped through its fingers. It tugged at the handle next, with increasing strength, as its mind tried to deny the truth. The hunter had left the keys in the ignition, but had locked the van with the duplicate now buttoned safely inside his tunic pocket. He laughed aloud as he saw hope die.

His prey's head swung around, eyes wide and staring, but it was still unable to locate him from his laughter. To help it, he stood up. He even waved. It looked at him for the space of a single second that seemed to last an eternity. Somewhere in that endless vacuum of time and space, the hunter pressed the button of the frame release and his camera recorded his prey's expression.

As though the tiny click of the shutter and soft wheeze of the autowind had been a starting pistol, his prey suddenly lurched around the van and began to sprint across the clearing toward the dirt-track that would eventually lead back to the main road.

The hunter laughed again, raising his face to the waving treetops, and the laughter became the howl of a wolf. In one smooth movement, he dropped the frame release and withdrew his knife from its sheath, and then set off in pursuit.

Joan pounded along the dirt track as fast as she could, screaming for help at the top of her lungs. Sense should have told her that screaming was useless because there was nobody to hear, and she would have been far better off conserving her breath for running. But sense had long since departed.

Iron-hard ridges of mud and loose stones bruised and cut her feet as she fled, and the pain only increased her panic. She couldn't hear Mark anywhere close behind her, but that meant nothing. Even if she hadn't been screaming, her ragged breath would have closed off her hearing just as effectively.

She was passing around the third or fourth corner on the looping dirt track before she finally understood what an incredibly stupid thing she was doing. Following a twisting path that led back and forth through the forest, when the distance she had to travel to the main road could probably be halved if she ran cross-country. She began to slow her pace, looking for a decent break in the undergrowth, and as she did so, she risked a quick glance over her shoulder.

In that one brief moment of inattention, her foot caught on some obstruction, a buried stone, a tree root, she never knew what it was, but it sent her flying through the air.

She hit ground with a teeth-jarring smash and rolled over the rough dirt track in a whirl of limbs, finally coming to rest on her back. There was no part of her body that was undamaged. Her knees and elbows were grazed and bleeding, her left cheekbone felt about twice its normal size, and her back from the base of her spine to her nape was one long bar of burning pain. She thought that a few of the toes on her right foot might be broken.

Above her, high above the trees, she saw an armada of wind-chased black clouds scudding across a sky that was steadily changing from blue to grey. The weather was changing. The fine spell had ended. It felt like a metaphor for her life.

Shuddering, Joan forced herself through the pain barrier. She forced herself to sit up. Then forced herself on to her knees, and then back on to her feet. Bent over with her torn, bleeding hands resting on her grubby thighs, she glanced back along the track, but couldn't see anything that seemed big enough to have tripped her. Probably she had got her own feet entangled. Then she looked the other way.

Mark stood on the track no more than twenty feet in front of her.

He was dressed up like a soldier in a bad Vietnam movie, his face painted in a frond-like pattern that looked more suitable for a jungle than a broadleaf forest. Joan only realised that she was crying again, sobbing in fact, when she tried to speak.

'Why are you doing this?' she asked.

In reply, Mark showed her his teeth and his knife, and Joan reeled around and ran off the track and into the forest.

A quarter of an hour later, although it may have been hours for all that Joan knew, she was at the end of her endurance. Her mind filled with the image of the knife and Mark's inhuman snarl of a smile, she had pelted through the forest with no regard for the injuries and pains she had acquired through her fall, and without a care for the catalogue of new injuries she was picking up along the way.

She had fallen several more times, once down a steep incline and into the chilly, stagnant water of a narrow, sluggish creek, where she had caught her head on a rock. The thorns of wild gooseberry and blackberry bushes had torn multiple stripes across her body from her hips on down, while collisions with low branches and the trunks of trees had bruised and torn at her shoulders and chest. Blood ran in a steady stream from her scalp, and her body was glistening with sweat, irritating her wounds and drawing swarms of midges and gnats.

And all the while, she had imagined she'd been able to hear the sound of Mark's pursuit of her. In an auditory illusion like an amplified sound effect, she had heard Mark's bootsteps following her through the forest, snapping fallen branches and crushing bracken and churning up leaf mould. Unlike the sound of her own flight, Mark's footsteps had the regular, unhurried pace of a ticking clock, never faltering, never stopping, never increasing in speed. Whichever way she turned, no matter how fast she ran, they were always there. Behind her, to her side, in front of her, dictating her changes of direction and frantic pace.

It had been a while since she had heard the footsteps now, though. She hadn't a clue how long ago it was they had disappeared from her imagination, or if they had faded away or simply stopped dead. Consequently, Joan had slowed to a trudging lope, belatedly trying to keep the noise she made to a minimum. Maybe she had lost him. Probably she hadn't. He had grown up in this forest, after all. He knew every square inch of it. He could be walking two paces behind her and she'd never know it.

Joan was shivering. She didn't know whether it was out of fear or whether it was physical. All the light seemed to be going out of the world, the spaces between the trees growing darker, the lighter greens turning grey, the darker greens turning black. She concentrated on her feet, keeping them moving. They were filthy, encrusted with dirt and mud, networked through with tiny rivulets of her own blood, as though it was the thin cooling skin on a lake of lava.

Watching them move back and forth was hypnotic.

A little while later, Joan realised that something was different, and she stopped, swaying on the spot, her eyes fixed on her feet. Something had changed. But what?

Then she saw that the ground underfoot was suddenly smooth, cool beneath the aching soles of her feet, and her hopes soared. But it was not the road, not blessed tarmac. It was hard-packed earth. It seemed to take every last fraction of her strength to raise her head. When she did, she realised that she was back at the cottage.

Back at Hunter's Lodge.

She stood just outside the treeline on the west side of the clearing, and what light remained in the sky fell directly on the front of the cottage, making it look like a stage set.

She had come full circle. Mark had herded her like a beast.

Joan felt torn in two. A part of her wanted to scream in frustration. A part of her thought it was

314

hilarious and wanted to laugh. In the end, though, she hadn't the strength for either excess. Instead she allowed her legs to let go of the tension that had fuelled them for so long, and sank to her knees in resignation.

She did not hear Mark approaching. But she saw his thin shadow on the earth in front of her as he came to stand at her side. She felt his hand twine into her grubby, matted hair. Out of the corner of her eye she saw the gleam of the knife in his other hand as her brought it around toward her face.

'You're so beautiful,' he said.

Then a bright white pain exploded at her temple, and the ground swung up at her.

44

Stephen stopped the car at a T-junction where the narrow country lane they had been travelling along for the past five minutes met another, identical country lane. He was conscious of Olivia's eyes on him as he looked at the rusted signpost directly opposite his car. Turning right would take them to somewhere called Thripple, and turning left would take them back to the village of Lockton Dale, through which they had already driven a quarter of an hour earlier. While they were in the village, Olivia had asked him to stop and ask for directions to Old Farm or Hunter's Lodge, but he had been confident he could find it without help, and had refused. Unfortunately, the SatNav didn't recognise either name, and even the older road atlas from the BMW's boot had proved itself useless.

Olivia was growing frantic.

'Well?' she asked impatiently.

'It's got to be somewhere around here. If we drive around enough, we're sure to find it.'

'That'll take too long, Stephen. Look, just go back to the village, and we'll ask for directions from there.'

Stephen pointed to the signpost. 'It's five miles back to Lockton Dale. It'll be a waste of time, we're probably on top of the bloody place right now.'

'If we'd stopped and asked like I said, we might have been at Hunter's Lodge already.'

'Maybe so, but we didn't, and there's no use crying over--'

'Stephen!'

'Listen, just give me ten more minutes, and if we haven't found it by then, we'll go back and ask, okay?'

'No, it's not okay!' She shocked Stephen by grabbing on to his shirt with both hands and shaking him so hard that another button popped off and the cotton seam ripped open at the sleeve's shoulder. 'Don't you understand? We may not have five minutes!'

'I understand,' he said. 'Trust me.'

Stephen dropped the BMW into gear and turned right, away from Lockton Dale.

Olivia was so angry, she almost screamed.

45

Two hundred miles away, DCI Phil Richardson had passed a pleasant few hours with his wife and son in Battersea Park. They had been on just about every ride at the fair, both large and small, and eaten every type of junk-food the fair could offer, after which Ben had spectacularly thrown up over the bear Richardson had won for him at the shooting gallery. They had headed home soon after that, satisfied, or at least convinced, that they'd had the best of the day. In the car the radio was warning of a change in the weather as a cold front moved down from the north, bringing with it heavy rain showers and gale force winds.

Ben had taken a nap during the drive back, and Louise had shared her thoughts on the redecoration of their master bedroom while Richardson had driven in silence, only pretending to listen.

Throughout the whole family expedition, the conversation he'd had with Stephen Crosby earlier had never really left Richardson's mind. It had niggled away at him long after he should have forgotten it, distracted by his wife and son, by the day. He'd even tested Louise's limited patience on several occasions by trying to contact Stephen on both his mobile phone and his landline, all without success. Willing calmness upon himself, he had left three restrained voice messages, none of which had been answered.

As soon as they had got home, he'd shut himself in his small study in the box-room and begun the first of several phone calls.

There was, Richardson firmly believed, a much-derided and somewhat mythical quality called Copper's Intuition, and he liked to believe that he had it. He believed that his intuition was trying to tell him something about Stephen. He picked through the notes he had scribbled down that morning, and that niggling feeling only intensified.

Something about Bickley. Something about Bickley and Stephen. About Bickley and the girl he'd stalked. Something about Bickley and…no, it just wouldn't come.

After twenty minutes of frustration, he'd finally identified himself to the uniformed officer who had answered the phone at the small station house in the north Yorkshire village of Lockton Dale. He was now waiting for the call-back once PC Woodall had verified his credentials and ID. While he waited, he tried not to think at all. Sometimes, if you didn't try to force it, he knew that the subconscious did all the brainwork on its own, and then sprang the conclusion on you like a winning poker hand. So far he'd had no luck with this method, either, but his sense of foreboding was growing heavier with every second, and so was the feeling that the answer was almost close enough to touch.

Ten minutes later, Woodall rang back and asked how he could be of assistance.

'Thanks for calling back so quickly,' Richardson said. 'Strange question - do you know a man named Martin Bickley?'

'Yes, sir,' Woodall replied, sounding surprised. 'Well known in these parts, is Mr Bickley.'

'I bet. You know where he lives?'

'Aye. Hunter's Lodge, up by Old Farm, as was.'

'Do you know if he's there now?'

'Couldn't say, sir, it's a bit off the beaten track. I know he works away a lot. He's a builder these days, I'm told.'

'Yeah, something like that.'

'Has he been up to something he shouldn't've down there?' Woodall asked, when Richardson didn't volunteer any more information.

'I'm not sure.'

'Been keeping his nose clean up here for the last few years, far as I'm aware.'

'I know. A friend asked me to run a check on him today, that's all. Wanted to know if he could be trusted.'

'What did you tell your friend?'

'I told him no.'

Woodall grunted. 'According to local gossip, that was probably the right answer.'

After another long pause, Richardson took a deep breath and came to a decision. 'Look, Constable Woodall, would you be able to do me a big favour?'

'If I can, sir.'

'I'm going to check out an address somebody gave me for Bickley down here in London. Is there any chance you could have someone drive out to this Hunter's Lodge place?'

'For what reason?'

'I don't know. Just to see if he's there, I suppose. What he's doing, who he's with. Could you do that?'

'Aye, I could do that, but not for a while. There's only me here at the moment. Might be an hour or so before I can leave the station.'

'That'd be fine. I don't think there's any urgency. In fact, it'll probably turn out to be a waste of your time, but…'

'But you want it done anyway?'

Richardson sighed. 'Yes, I do.'

46

Joan's eyes fluttered open and she saw the cottage's false ceiling hovering high above her. Her recovering vision wavered in and out for a few moments, making the ceiling undulate like the deck of a ship in a squall - an image that was matched by her sensation of nausea and the sounds of the by now gale force wind whipping around the cottage. She could hear the timbers creaking under the onslaught.

The right side of her head where she had been struck felt like it was on fire, but when she tried to place a hand against the pain, as though pressure would contain and sooth it, she quickly learned that she was unable to move her arm. In fact, she found that she couldn't move any of her limbs. She was back on Mark's bed, and once again, he had secured her arms and legs to the bedposts with short loops of rope. This time, however, there was no give in the ropes, none at all, and her muscles were stretched taut.

The game, the pretence, was over. This was the real thing.

Through the window, she saw that the forest was prematurely dark, blanketed under a mantle of heavy, fast-moving cumulus, and she could feel cool drafts of air moving over her naked skin, bringing her whole body out in a rash of goosebumps. But oddly, she found that it was her back, pressed against the mattress, which felt coldest of all. When she managed to turn her head, she saw why.

Before laying her down, Mark had first taken the precaution of covering the mattress with several thick layers of translucent polythene sheeting. Joan knew what this was for. It was to prevent the bed becoming stained with her blood.

For several moments, she was overtaken by total panic, and began to thrash her body around on the bed, desperately trying to get her arms free from the ropes, or the ropes free from the bedposts, anything. A rapid series of clicking noises accompanied her struggles, and eventually brought them to a halt. Breathing hard from her exertions, she forced herself to look up.

At the foot of the bed she could see that the trapdoor to the cellar had been raised, resting as before against the bed frame. She could see the key this time, jutting out of the sheepskin a few inches from the edge. Mark had hidden the lock beneath the matted curls of the fleece, so that no one but he would be able to find it. She could not see the hole in the floor beyond the trapdoor, but she could sense it, yawning blackly, waiting for her like an open mouth. She could smell its noxious breath.

It all made a bizarre kind of sense now, she thought.

At the heart of the forest was Hunter's Lodge. At the heart of Hunter's Lodge was a dark cellar. The cellar was the real Dragon's gullet, from which she knew she would never emerge. Everything until now had merely been a premonition. This was the fulfilment of the nightmare.

Joan's eyes slid away from the trapdoor and found the source of the clicking noise, which was, of course, Mark's camera. He sat comfortably on one of the kitchen chairs, which he had drawn up to the side of the bed like a hospital visitor. After she had focussed on him, he took one more shot of her battered face, and then lowered the camera to stare at her.

While she had been unconscious, he had washed his face, removing most of the camouflage paint except for a few smears that had blended into his hairline and lodged under his jaw. For a few seconds no expression at all showed itself on his face, certainly nothing to indicate that he was anything other than the gentle young man who had offered her his help less than forty-eight hours ago.

And yet despite that, Joan realised that there had been a change. Not in him, exactly, but perhaps in her perception of him. His features seemed a little coarser now. He was still good-looking, but the beauty that had shone out of him, making him extraordinary, had vanished. She didn't believe that she was fooling herself about this, either. He really did look different, and she wondered how that could be.

'Mark,' Joan said, her throat as dry as paper. 'Why?'

He raised his hands, shrugging in mock puzzlement. 'Who's this Mark person? I don't know any Mark. There's no Mark here.'

Joan shook her head. 'What are you talking about?'

'Me real name's Bickley - Mark Bowman doesn't exist,' he said. 'He's just a name, Joan. One of many. If you like, you can call me Martin.'

'Who are you?' Joan's neck was trembling with the effort of holding her head off the mattress. 'Why are you doing this to me?'

'I'm not - Nature is. I'm the hunter, you're my prey. It's that simple.'

Joan let her head fall back. Soundlessly, she began to cry.

The camera clicked again and again.

'Why?' she demanded. 'Tell me why!'

'There's no point getting angry,' he said calmly. 'It's just the way things are, that's all - Nature, like I said. The hunter and the hunted. It's a relationship as old as time.'

'But why me?'

'Aye well, that's a bit more complicated this time round, I'll admit. Wheels within wheels. But at the bottom of it, it's still the same reason. You attracted me, Joan. You caught me eye. I wanted you, for me collection.'

'Like you wanted Kath,' Joan said.

'That's right.'

'And then you… you… butchered her....'

Bickley shrugged, completely unconcerned with her interpretation of his actions. What Joan thought simply didn't matter.

'She was too easy, to be honest with you. Too tame to be real sport. But you, Joan, you were a challenge. It needed patience, skill, perseverance and cunning to bring you down. You know,' he said, 'I almost wish…'

Joan raised her head and looked at him. A shadow of something that appeared to be dissatisfaction - or perhaps even regret - passed over his face, and she seized on it.

'What do you wish?' she asked.

'Never mind.'

'What were you going to say?'

'Just that I wish I could keep you for a little bit longer,' he said with a shrug. 'I would have liked to.'

'Why can't you?' she asked desperately. Even now she couldn't help hoping against hope that he wouldn't go through with what he had planned for her. 'We could have fun together, Mark - *Martin* - you know we could. We could carry on as we were. It doesn't have to end now.'

He smiled at her sadly, shaking his head, and she realised that it was beyond sex for him now. Maybe it never was about sex, not as Joan understood it. All she really knew at this moment was that she had to get out of this, somehow. She had to find a way to play for time. Time for what, exactly, she wasn't sure. Just time.

Time...

'There were others, weren't there,' she managed to say. 'Before Kath?'

'Six. Your friend was seven. You're number eight.'

Joan remembered the photograph tacked to the wall above the head of the bed, the number eight scrawled above her half-naked image - probably scrawled with the same pen he had used to compose the friendly, supportive little note he had left for her to wake up to back in his seedy basement flat. Earlier she had imagined that the number referred to the number of photographs Bickley had taken of her abuse, but apparently it did not. Her stomach turned over. Seven women before her had passed through this same ordeal. Her mind wanted to shut down, but she knew that she couldn't allow it to happen.

'And that young girl was the first?' she asked. 'The one in the photograph?'

'Aye. Alison Simmons, her name was. Beautiful girl. I was in love with her for years.'

'But you still killed her.'

'Alison was what they call a happy accident,' he grinned, crossing his legs comfortably. 'You really want to hear this?'

Joan nodded.

'All right. I suppose we've got time.' He straightened his body posture, clearing his throat dramatically, like an orator. He was having a lot of fun.

'Like I said, she were me first love. We were both thirteen and we were at the same school. She used to obsess me. The way she looked, the way she moved, talked, everything. I used to love taking pictures of her. Everybody thought I used to bother her, but the truth was we had an understanding. A real relationship.'

His eyes twinkled out at Joan like a pair of sapphires.

'I met her in the forest that day, just where that picture was taken about a week earlier. That was our secret place, you see, the only place we ever met or talked. We were at the teenage kissing stage by then, and sometimes she'd let me put me hand under her jumper and feel her little titties. But that day I wanted more.'

He smiled broadly, as though at a fond memory.

'She wasn't having any of it, of course. She was a good girl, and I was a bad boy. She pushed me off, started to run away, didn't heed me when I called her

325

to come back. So I started chasing her through the forest, and I discovered something wonderful.'

Joan stared in dismay at the blazing light in his blue eyes, burning into her. They had the bright heat of fanaticism, of insanity. Why had she never seen it before?

'She was running and hiding, running and hiding among the trees, and I was getting more and more excited the longer it went on. I almost forgot why I was chasing her. The chase - the hunt - became an end in itself. Eventually, she fell, twisted her ankle, and I caught her. I pinned her down, and I had her, good an' hard.'

'You raped her.'

'Oh aye,' he admitted. 'If that's what you want to call it. She enjoyed it, too, you know. Moaning, she was, saying me name over and over. But after we'd finished she started crying, said she'd tell her dad what I did to her…' He shook his head. 'Couldn't let that happen, could I?'

'So you killed her?'

'Only strangled her, to shut her up.' He leaned forward. 'But, you see, that got me excited all over again - even more excited than I was when I was chasing her, and a whole lot more than when I fucked her. That taught me a good lesson, that did. It taught me what I was, what I could do. What I was born to do.'

Joan wanted to scream, but instead she forced herself to speak as calmly as she could under these circumstances. She needed to draw this conversation out as long as possible, because once it ended… Once it ended, there was nothing left.

'What did you do with her body?'

'Buried it quickly, there and then. Just a shallow grave, but I disguised it well, with leaves and branches and what-not, and she was never found during all the searches. Later on, when it was safe again, I moved her to better accommodation. Played with her a bit more, then buried her in our secret meeting place, so it'd be ours forever.'

He winked at her.

'Romantic soul, aren't I?'

Joan could conjure no reply to this.

'I still go and see her, sometimes. Just like I do all me girls. Even that slutty friend of yours. I get me spade and go visiting. They're still photogenic, an' all.'

He smiled at Joan's shocked face.

'It's like I told you, everything in Nature's beautiful, if you look at it the right way. Before, during, and after. I've got some fairly recent shots down there,' he said, nodding at the trapdoor. 'Would you like me to go get them, so you can see for yourself?'

For Joan this was another unanswerable question. If she said no the conversation was over. If she said yes, she would have to look at the rotting remains of her friend - and see exactly what was in store for her. Maybe that would be a blessing, because she was sure it would drive her completely insane, and then she might not realise what was happening.

She tried desperately to think of something to say, something to do, some strategy to turn his mind away from torture, from murder, but finally it was too much for her. Her self-control slipped, and she began

327

to shout and scream for help, struggling against her bonds once more.

'You've got a good set of lungs on you, I'll say that much,' Bickley laughed, thoroughly amused. He began to wave his hands in the air before him, as though conducting an orchestra. 'Go on, lass, *go on -* give it some!'

Joan didn't even see him move.

One moment he was sitting comfortably on the chair, laughing, enjoying her performance, the next he was leaning over her, his hunting knife at her throat.

'Shut up!' His voice was low, dangerous.

Joan felt his spittle spray her face. She felt the sharp blade against her throat, and could not decide whether it felt hot or cold, or whether it had already opened her skin. She stared into his eyes, realising that they may be the last thing she would ever see.

But then she saw that Bickley wasn't even looking at her now. He was looking toward the bedroom window, his head cocked to the side, listening intently. And then Joan heard it, too.

A car engine. Distant, muted by the forest and the gale, but noticeably drawing closer.

He looked back at her suddenly, and she felt like cheering at the alarm she saw in his eyes. It was the very first crack she had ever seen in his cocksure composure. She flinched as he pulled back from her, fully expecting to feel his knife slicing her throat open. But then she saw him slip the blade back into its sheath on his thigh, silver, mottled with maroon, without a speck of fresh blood on it.

Bickley jumped up on to the bed, placing his heavily booted feet inside the inverted V of her naked thighs. He reached up and pushed aside a section of the false ceiling with one hand and reached inside the cavity with the other. A second later he withdrew his hand. In it was an old double-barrelled shotgun, the long barrels discoloured to the shade of pewter, the dark wooden stock covered with old scars. He reached up into the cavity again, and this time brought down a ragged box of shells.

He dropped to his knees, making the bed sway, broke the shotgun and swiftly inserted two fat red cartridges. Outside the noise of the car's engine grew louder as it approached the cottage. Joan was straining against her bonds, trying to see something through the window, but it was on the opposite side of the house to the clearing. All she could see were the upper branches of oak trees whipping from side to side under a boiling mass of dark cloud.

The sharp click of the shotgun snapping back together brought her head back around. The muzzle was pointing directly at her face.

'Don't make a sound now, Joan,' Bickley warned. 'This's probably me guests arriving. But just in case it isn't, I want absolute silence out of you. Understand?'

Joan's mind whirled. Guests?

'Do you hear me? No noise!'

Staring into the black emptiness of the barrels, fighting back her terror, Joan nodded. But at the same time, she found herself speaking, in a way that contradicted her head's gesture of agreement.

'Why not?' she rasped. 'You're going to kill me anyway.'

'Aye,' he said with a curt nod. 'True enough.'

He used the shotgun muzzle to gently caress the side of her face that wasn't swollen, and then trailed it down over her naked body until it rested between her open legs.

'Aye, I won't lie to you about that. Not that you'd believe me if I did, not now. But there are ways of dying and ways of *dying*, aren't there, Joan? If you're good, I might make it quick.'

Outside they both heard the engine stop, and then, a moment later, the sound of car doors opening and closing. Bickley climbed smoothly off the bed and glided toward the bedroom door.

Joan was still trembling, wondering whether he would keep his promise. But then she realised that he had promised her nothing, and she remembered the photographs he had taken of Kath's torture. Whatever atrocity it was he had planned for her, she knew that it certainly wouldn't be quick.

Almost as if he had heard her thoughts, he turned back, the shotgun swinging with him.

'And if you don't care for yourself,' he said, 'spare a thought for our mysterious callers. If it isn't who I think it is, then it's probably just lost tourists looking for directions, and if you're quiet, I'll let 'em go. But if you make a noise, I'll have no option but to kill them, an' all. And I'll make you watch.'

Joan heard footsteps on the deck outside, and then a brief knock at the front door.

'You think about that,' he whispered. 'Would you really want the deaths of innocent people on your conscience?'

Then, turning his back on her, he slipped through the bedroom door and closed it behind him. His boots ambled across the floorboards toward the front door.

She heard him open the door.

She heard the murmur of low voices.

Joan opened her mouth to scream for help - but no sound came out of her dry throat, not a single squeak. She closed her eyes tight in despair. Much as the thought disgusted her, she realised that Bickley knew her too well. He was right. She wouldn't want innocent people to die on her behalf.

But she was innocent too, wasn't she? She had done nothing to deserve this.

And what if the people at the door weren't lost, she thought. What if they weren't Bickley's 'guests'? What if they were here actually looking for her? To get here, wouldn't they have had to remove the chain and padlock at the dirt-track's entrance? A lost tourist wouldn't do that, surely. What if it was the police? How would they know she was here, in such terrible peril, if she didn't speak?

She opened her mouth… and closed it again.

In her heart, Joan knew that it was not the police at the door. There was to be no last minute reprieve, and there was no such thing as a knight in shining armour. No one knew that she was at Hunter's Lodge. No one knew that she was Bickley's prisoner, or that she even knew him.

She now realised how very careful he had been not to be seen with her in public. On the night he'd picked her up, he'd left her in the van while he went to collect the bacon sandwiches and the tea, telling her that he didn't think she was ready to be seen in public. In the morning he'd left her in his flat while he went out to buy more food for breakfast. At the start of their journey up here, after he'd convinced her to withdraw as much money from her accounts as possible, he'd stayed in the van while she collected it. When the police eventually started looking for her, if they ever did, the CCTV footage from the bank and building societies would show only Joan going about her business.

There would surely be a few witnesses to Bickley picking her up in Kentish Town the night before, but what would they be able to say if they came forward? Just that they had seen a woman answering Joan's description getting into a white Escort van. How many similar vans were there in London, she wondered. Thousands, probably. And, of course, no one would remember the licence plate, because nobody would have been able to read it. All that dried mud, she finally realised, hadn't got there by accident.

The futility of her situation abruptly crashed in on her. Until this moment Joan had not yet fully abandoned herself to fate, but now she was forced to admit that the end was in sight. She would disappear from the world like so many others, and would only exist in the same way that Kath Meadows now did - in the computer records of the withdrawals Bickley made as he used her debit card. She had no doubt that he would get her pin numbers out of her before she died.

Joan was startled from her thoughts by an unexpectedly polite knock at the bedroom door. 'Mrs Crosby,' she heard Bickley say, 'you have a visitor.'

Oh my God, she thought. What now?

The door slowly opened and she watched Bickley, still carrying his shotgun, nudge a second man into the room in front of him. The stranger was dressed in an expensive dark blue suit with a black waistcoat, and was immaculately groomed from his greying coiffured hair to his manicured fingernails. Despite his obvious opulence, the man was painfully thin, and an air of darkness hung all around him like a cloud.

All of this, Joan took in at her first glance. At a second, astonished glance, she realised that she actually *knew* this man - or, at least, she had seen him before. Many times before. It was the man with the newspaper. The man in Dr Stratton's waiting room, the man who hid from the world behind a copy of The *Financial Times*.

Financial Times Man.

It took a visible effort, but he finally managed to tear his gaze from the sight of Joan's naked crotch, and then he met her eyes.

'Please,' she said urgently, 'help me! He killed my friend Kath, he's going to kill me – the man behind you is a killer!'

The man quickly glanced over his shoulder at the shotgun that was loosely aimed at him. Then he turned back.

'Well, I should certainly hope so,' he told Joan. 'That's what I'm paying him for.'

47

The landlord of The Coach House clocked the young couple the second they entered his mostly empty taproom, almost pushed in through the door by a gust of chilly wind. He reckoned that he would have noticed them even if the pub had been packed to the rafters, simply because they weren't locals, although it wasn't the fact that they were tourists which attracted his attention. It was the fact that they were obviously in the middle of a bitter argument, albeit one conducted in hushed tones. Both of them looked anxious. The woman was also volcanically angry, so furious she looked ready to vomit.

The crux of their disagreement was equally plain to him, perhaps because he had seen it so often before. As far as he was concerned there was a lot of bollocks talked about the differences between the sexes, but in his experience one cliché at least always seemed to hold true: men never admitted to being lost and they never asked for directions. Women, sensible creatures that they mostly were, weren't so foolish.

He finished wiping his hands on a towel and smiled warmly at the woman as she began to approach the bar. The man hung back in the shadows by the doorway, overruled and embarrassed.

'Afternoon, love,' he said. 'What can I do for you?'

'Thank you. We need directions, please.'

The landlord gave himself a mental pat on the back. 'Where're you heading for this nasty day? The coast, is it?'

'No, we're looking for Hunter's Lodge. It's a cottage near some place that used to be called Old Farm. Do you know it?'

Instead of instantly replying, the landlord first studied the careworn young woman, and then her even more bedraggled male companion. His face had lost its welcoming smile.

'What do you want to go out there for?' he asked flatly.

The woman, seemingly put at a loss for words by the directness of the question, glanced back toward her companion, who reluctantly stepped forward. His embarrassment at the situation made him both aggressive and confrontational.

'That's none of your business,' he snapped. 'Just tell us where it is and we'll be off.'

The landlord didn't blink an eye, just kept staring at the man, giving him the full weight of his disdain.

'Look,' the man said tightly, 'we're with the police, all right? If you don't help us, you'll be charged with obstruction of justice.'

Out of the corner of his eye, the landlord saw the woman wince, and he looked the man up and down. 'You're lying,' he said calmly. 'You're not the bloody police.'

In the corner by the dartboard, two old regulars nursing pints of bitter, the only patrons left in the taproom, looked up from their dominoes and glanced over at the strangers suspiciously.

'No, we're not the police,' the woman admitted immediately. 'I'm sorry, he only said that because he's so worried. We're both worried. We don't mean any harm. Please, can't you help us…?'

The landlord looked back at the woman, saw the unshed tears in her eyes and the way her hands were clasped so tightly together under her breasts. Something, he knew, was terribly wrong here.

48

'A little privacy if you please, Mr Bickley,' *Financial Times* Man said, his over-bright eyes now fixed on Joan's face. 'I believe it's high time this young lady and I had a little heart to heart.'

Standing directly behind him with the shotgun now held at slope-arms, Bickley slowly transferred his gaze from Joan's face to the man's narrow back, but otherwise remained completely still. After a few seconds, when he realised that Bickley was still in the doorway, *Financial Times* Man half-turned and dismissed him with a curt, 'Out!', and closed the door in the younger man's face.

He turned back to Joan, his grey eyes like shards of broken glass embedded in the putty of his face. 'Here we are, at last,' he said. 'I was beginning to be think this day would never come.'

Completely speechless, Joan watched as he strolled over to the bed and sat down beside her, delicately raising the knees of his suit trousers so as not to spoil their perfect line. He smiled down at her, his pale, gaunt face almost luminous in the half-light, and she noticed that the sharp edges of his nostrils were speckled with traces of a fine white powder.

The glitter of his strange cold eyes had a chemical base. She wondered if that was what Dr Stratton had been treating him for, some kind of drug-addiction.

Abruptly, the man leant down toward her, making her flinch. Then he said something that seemed to come from the very depths of her imagination. 'Would you like me to get you out of here?' he asked in a hoarse whisper.

Joan was stunned by the offer, but nodded numbly.

With a hasty glance back at the door, the man reached into his inside jacket pocket and withdrew something that looked like a thin black metal tube about four inches long. He depressed a small silver button with his thumb and a thin, wickedly sharp blade sprang free with a precise click, locking firmly into place. After checking the door again, he leant over Joan and slowly began to saw at the rope securing her right hand to the bedpost.

Hardly able to believe what was happening, she turned her head to watch the knife do its work. Hope began to rise up in her chest like a bubble of air rising through oil. The rope was beginning to fray, she could see the individual bonds parting - but slowly, so slowly.

Too slowly.

After being so rudely dismissed, she knew that Bickley might walk back into the room at any moment. The knife was clearly sharp enough to cut through the rope at one attempt, why was he being so slow, why wasn't he applying more pressure?

Then, with the rope only about a half of the way cut through, the knife slowed to a complete halt, and Joan made herself look away from it. She found *Financial Times* Man staring down at her as before, but this time his face was twisted into the most repellent expression of gloating she had ever seen in her life, and she realised that he'd only been playing with her.

'You bastard,' she managed to croak out.

He shook his head, chuckling to himself as he folded the flick-knife away and replaced it in his jacket pocket with a flourish. 'Sorry, Joan,' he said, sounding anything but sorry. 'Can't do it, I'm afraid. For a moment I forgot just how much lovely money I'm going to make out of this little enterprise.'

'Enterprise?' Joan shook her head, completely confused. 'What are you talking about, who are you?'

'Oh, I'm sorry, we've never been formally introduced, have we? Although, in actual fact, we have met before – and not just in good old Dr Bob's waiting room, either. It was only briefly, admittedly, at a party thrown by mutual friends.'

He smiled at Joan's blank expression.

'No, don't apologise, I wouldn't expect you to remember. It was about five years ago, at the home of Lee and Kath Meadows. A big house party, very crowded as I recall. Blink and you'd miss me, which you obviously did. The name's Parrish - Roger Parrish?'

Joan shook her head again. The name meant nothing to her. When she had first started to notice this man back in her doctor's waiting room, she remembered thinking that he seemed vaguely familiar, but it was only very vaguely, and she had absolutely no memory of ever meeting him before.

'Well, I'm not surprised - or offended, in case you were wondering,' he said affably. 'Fact is, I used to be a bit of a porker back then. A lot fatter in the face and rounder round the waist, as my mother used to say. I am a man of enormous and extreme appetites, you see. I used to eat and drink inordinately, and I was very unhealthy. But now I

338

have other habits. Hell on the septum and the wallet, but much, much easier on the waistline.'

Parrish looked away from Joan's face and began a leisurely exploration of her naked body, his spit-grey eyes avid and greedy as he studied her varied selection of scratches, cuts and bruises. Joan, struggling to make sense of it all, and largely failing, seized upon one of the few things her mind had managed to hold on to.

'You…you know the Meadows?'

'Oh yes, very well indeed. I'm a businessman - an entrepreneur, if you will. I've done a lot of profitable business with Lee's importing company over the years...and I've had more than a few goes on the old wife, too, just like everyone else Lee ever knew. Or *didn't* know, for that matter. Christ, did that woman love cock, or what?'

Parish grinned.

'Of course, that was in the old days, when they were both still active swingers and part of my social scene. I still sort of like Lee, even though he's lost his bottle. It's a shame, because he used to be a man. Now he's going down in flames, and all because of that silly, interfering cunt of a wife of his. You know, I'm so *glad* she's dead. I'm *glad* she died in fucking agony. She almost took me down as well.'

Joan began to cry, she couldn't help it, hearing Kath talked about like this, and Parrish patted and rubbed her naked thigh in faux commiseration, and then left his hand there. It felt burning hot and freezing cold at the same time, like the edge of Bickley's knife. A moment later he slid his hand up her body and began to caress her breasts, plucking absently and painfully at her nipples.

'You had Kath killed? You paid…' Joan couldn't remember Mark's real name. '…*him* to kill her?'

'Yes, I did.'

'Why?'

'It was a matter of survival, really, either her or me. The truth is that following our affair - although I have to say that's romanticising the relationship more than a little - we parted on very bad terms. So bad, in fact, that she got that tame policeman friend of theirs…what's his name?'

Joan saw the detective facing her over an interview room table. 'Richardson,' she said.

'That's it, Richardson. Well, she got him to warn me off. Following that she effectively banned Lee from seeing me socially. Now, to tell you the truth, I didn't care so much about that. My tastes were growing more refined than the boring swinging scene, anyway. But Lee and I had other links that couldn't be broken just like that.'

'What sort of links?'

'Well, some of the business we did together was what I like to call twilight. It wasn't really legal, but it wasn't strictly illegal either. Shady, I suppose you'd call it…'

Joan had her eyes closed tight as Parrish's hand left her breasts and slid down over her belly before settling between her legs, his fingers rooting around inside her as though he were scratching a stubborn itch. Quietly, she began to sob.

'…but another part of this business, the immeasurably more profitable part that Kath eventually discovered we were engaged in, was very illegal, and she wasn't at all pleased about it.'

Parrish sniffed loudly, as he had been doing monotonously throughout this hellish conversation. If Joan had been capable of picking up on such nuances at this moment, this might have led her to believe she knew exactly what his business was concerned with importing.

'Basically, she gave us an ultimatum - extricate ourselves from the kind of business we were doing, or she would go to the police and blow us both out of the water. I agreed to her terms, of course, but it was never really going to happen. I was in the middle of negotiating the biggest deal of my life at the time. If it went ahead as planned it was going to save Lee's company and make me relatively wealthy. But if it failed, my backers would probably have me killed. I suppose we could have carried on behind her back, but it would only have been a short-term measure at best. While she was still alive the threat of exposure would always be there. I couldn't have that hanging over me.'

Parrish withdrew his hand from Joan and began to wipe his fingers on a silk handkerchief plucked from his waistcoat pocket.

'Then Lee had nothing to do with it?' Joan asked, when she was able to speak again. 'He didn't know you'd…'

'Of course not. Believe it or not, he still dotes on the bitch. It's unbelievable. That was one of the main problems – getting rid of Kath in a way that Lee would believe and accept. The other difficulty was that I couldn't risk killing her myself, much as I

341

would have liked to. If something obvious had happened to her then I would definitely have been in the frame as far as the police were concerned, because of our history. Richardson would have made sure of it. They'd have been on my doorstep in a couple of days, if not sooner. And with forensic science being as advanced as it is these days, they'd have found something to link me to her if there was anything to find.'

Joan knew he was right about that. She remembered Richardson telling her about Kath's romantic elopements, and the nasty piece of work he'd sent packing for her. It was now obvious that he'd been talking about Parrish. Even now, years later, Richardson still remembered him.

'The upshot of all this was that I needed someone to do the dread deed for me, but I didn't have a clue how to find that person. I mean, what are you supposed to do - put a card in the newsagent's window?'

Parrish snorted laughter.

'Anyway, I happened to be discussing my problem with one of my closest friends, with whom I share a great many interests, and I got the surprise of my life. What do you know - it seems that I wasn't the only man in the world who wanted a woman killed! And what's more, this friend of mine already had a wonderful plan figured out, and he was just waiting for the right moment to set it in motion. The plan was intended for his bloodsucker of a wife, but with a few amendments, I immediately saw that it was perfect for my purposes, too. We agreed to try it out on Kath first, and it worked like clockwork.'

Joan screwed her face up in concentration, trying to fight back the tears and her terror, which was now very great. But then she opened her eyes wide and stared at Parrish. Horrible thoughts were coming to her, thick and fast. Terrible thoughts. Parrish continued to smile down at her, as though he could read her mind and was willing her to say it out loud.

'This friend of yours,' she said. 'This man who wanted to kill his wife…was it…' The name in her mouth tasted foul. '…was it Stephen?'

'Stephen? As in your husband Stephen? Well…'

After a heart-stopping moment, Parrish laughed out loud.

'Christ no, not Stephen. He was never a member of my circle, he just happened to be a friend of the Meadows'. I haven't even set eyes on him for years, but as far as I know he stopped being any fun the day he met you.' He leant forward, eyes glittering. 'Did you know he had a thing with Kath about a year or so before I did?'

He grinned at her surprise.

'Oh yes, things got very hot and heavy between them for a few months apparently. Not that this should surprise anyone. She told me he was a shagging machine, and she should have known, being such a total slut. But then, as I say, he met you and everything changed. He told Kath he was changing his life, that he was going to be faithful to you. From all that I've heard, I don't think he ever quite managed it - but he never stopped trying, I'll give the silly bastard that.'

Despite her situation, Joan felt an immense sense of relief to learn that her husband wasn't involved.

343

'What about me?' she asked. 'Why am I here, what did I ever do to you?'

'At the start I just wanted to shut you up, Joan, to stop you going to the police, spouting your crazy stories about Kath's disappearance, making waves. Not only were you disturbing the cops, you were putting Lee on edge, too, just as our business was coming to a critical stage. He wasn't swallowing the run-off-with-another-lover story quite as well as I'd hoped, and to be perfectly honest I would have been more than happy if you'd been killed outright by the hit-and-run. I just didn't see the point of dragging it out, especially as I couldn't be connected to you.'

He shrugged.

'But by then, of course, the delightful Mr Bickley had fixed his sights on you, and my poor friend had to put his wife's disposal on the back-burner again. But in the end, you know, the delay turned out to be a good thing.'

'Good?'

'Yes, because it gave me a chance to take step back and consider the commercial possibilities of the project. It was partly Mr Bickley's hobby that gave me the idea, I must admit, but one day I just thought, why not take it to the next level? It suddenly seemed very logical. After my current importing deal is completed, I don't think Lee will be up for any more - he's falling to pieces, to be frank - so I'm going to need another source of income. This looks like it could be it.'

Joan could only stare up at him in confusion.

'I should really be thanking you, Joan. Your sacrifice is going to finance my new lifestyle. In a

344

few months, I expect to be sitting on a foreign beach drinking cocktails with a hot-blooded young Latina standing by, ready to sit on my face at a moment's notice. I'll think of you fondly.'

'I don't understand,' Joan said weakly. 'What are you talking about? What commercial possibilities?'

'The *video*, of course. Do you have any idea of the kind of revenue a video of this could generate?'

'What video?' Joan suddenly screamed. 'What is *this*?'

'It's a fucking goldmine, that's what it is. There's never been anything like it - not on the open market, anyway. Imagine it, raw footage of a serial killer at work on his latest victim! What would you pay to see something like that?' He laughed again. 'Actually, I suppose you're the wrong person to ask that question, aren't you?'

Joan almost blacked out. What Parrish was proposing to do was beyond belief. They were going to record her being tortured and killed. They were going to sell copies of the recording.

There was a small knock at the door.

'Go away!' Parrish snapped over his shoulder. 'We're busy in here.'

'Roger,' a man's voice whispered. 'I've got to come in - we need to talk, urgently.'

'Oh, it's you. All right, come in.'

He turned back to her.

'Joan, at this moment, I'd like to take the opportunity to introduce you to the man who is not only the owner of the video equipment we'll be using today but also my co-producer in this exciting venture - don't want to hog the glory all to myself. Although,

345

of course, you don't really *need* an introduction, as you're already very well acquainted.'

Behind Parrish the door opened, and Dr Robert Stratton walked into the bedroom.

49

If she hadn't been lying prone, Joan might easily have fainted as she absorbed the shock of her own doctor's appearance in this unlikeliest of settings. But there again, she might not have. Ever since the moment Parrish had come into the bedroom, before he even had a name for her, while he was still *Financial Times* Man, a part of her had sensed that this incestuous nightmare would deepen.

Maybe, she thought, she'd even been expecting this exact development. Because the part of her that would not have been surprised to see Lee Meadows, or even her own husband walk through the door, was similarly unimpressed by Dr Stratton's entrance.

Dr Bob.

She was in shock, she knew. Her limbs had lost all feeling, and her sight and her hearing both became fogged for a few moments. When they came back she saw that Stratton had drawn Parrish off to the side of the bed and was speaking to him in a low voice.

'...you've got to understand, you can't just walk in here like and start ordering him about in his own home,' Stratton was saying. 'It simply can't be done.'

That voice, Joan thought, that same calm, omniscient voice. Voice of wisdom, voice of understanding. That lying voice.

'Roger, you underestimate this man at your peril. You know what he is and you know what he does. He is not a normal man - a normal man wouldn't have been any use to us. He's a psychotic, completely unstable under pressure. You can't treat him like the hired help, his ego won't stand for it.'

'He needs to know who's in charge.'

'As far as he's concerned, he does know who's in charge - he is.'

'Not any more. This is my party now.'

'Roger--'

'Okay, okay,' Parrish said dismissively. 'I get the message. I'll take it easy for a while, I promise. I'll handle the little prick with kid gloves. But don't forget, when push comes to shove, it'll be my way or the highway.'

'Lord preserve us from management-speak,' Stratton whispered. 'And for God's sake, don't start dictating to him about the video straight away. I suspect he'll be highly resistant to the idea. Don't forget, he sees himself as an artist. His creative process is set in stone. Mess with that and he'll blow. In fact, we might do better to forget about it all together. I was never that happy about it, anyway.'

'Bob, the video is absolutely non-negotiable. It's a deal-breaker. You know that. I need that money.'

Stratton sighed, and Parrish patted him on the shoulder, clearly humouring him.

'Don't worry about it, I'll handle it.' He inclined his head toward the bed. 'In the meantime, why don't you renew your acquaintanceship with Joan here, and I'll go smooth things over with our precious Mr Bickley.'

He patted Stratton on the shoulder once more and left the room, closing the door behind him. Joan, in a trance-like state, watched the doctor wander over to her side. She wanted nothing more than to be able to hurl a stream of abuse at him, but her throat was locked and her mind was jammed. He smiled down at her. The same smile he had given her the last time she had seen him in his office two days ago. A Judas smile.

I'll miss you, Joan, he'd said.

'A little unexpected, isn't it?' he asked gently. He nodded when she didn't reply. 'I know, I know, it's a shock. You feel hurt and betrayed, and even a little stupid, I daresay. But you have nothing to recriminate yourself for, Joan. You just got caught up in something by accident, and unfortunately you've paid the ultimate price.'

'How can you be a part of this,' Joan spat. 'You're supposed to be a doctor! You're supposed to help people!'

'You were asking too many questions,' he shrugged. 'If it's any consolation, I wanted to make it easy on you. I wanted to give you a hypnotic suggestion so that you took your own life painlessly - sleeping pills, probably. That would have been easiest, and I could simply have rewritten my session notes on your case to make it seem plausible. People would have believed it, I'm sure. But by then, of course, Martin had fixed on you completely, and it isn't easy to change the mind of a psychopath, let me tell you.'

He saw the question in her eyes.

'Oh yes, I *was* able to hypnotise you - quite easily, as it happens, you're a very good subject. That's when I started to plant all the suggestions to make you immediately trust Martin. I gather that in the past he's always relied upon his natural physical attributes, but the fact that you were still so paranoid about being stalked made it necessary go for the belt and braces approach. I had Martin come in a few times while you were hypnotised so that you could be taught to trust and obey his voice, to find him irresistible. And then, naturally, he had to have the trigger-word that would release you from all the hypnotic suggestions, so that you would react like a normal person when he wanted to hunt you.'

Footsteps and voices began to approach the bedroom door.

'Hunting is very important to Martin, as I'm sure you've learned.'

'You're a monster,' Joan told him.

The door opened and Parrish and Bickley came in. Bickley was carrying three small tumblers and Parrish a new bottle of whiskey. Bickley looked slightly sullen, Joan thought, as though whatever Parrish had said to apologise for his earlier brusqueness hadn't completely smoothed the waters.

Stratton was still looking at her.

'One of the first things you learn in my profession, Joan,' he said quietly, 'is that everyone is a monster. Understanding that is the key to self-knowledge. Self-knowledge is the key to freedom. And true freedom places you above the law, because laws are only a menu of other people's narrow morality.'

'You sound like him,' she hissed. 'You sound like Bickley.'

'I think it's more that he sounds like me, Joan - I was his doctor too, once upon a time.'

Parrish had broken the seal on the whiskey bottle and was pouring generous measures into the three tumblers. 'Come along now, Dr Bob,' he said. 'Come and toast this splendid venture with us.'

Stratton joined them and Joan watched the three men formally clink glasses over her body. She felt like a prize animal, being admired by a consortium of butchers.

'You won't get away with this,' she said, feeling both stupid and pathetic even as she spoke. 'Somewhere down the line, you'll get caught. They'll put you away for life, all of you.'

Parrish laughed openly, while Stratton shook his head with his little half-smile. Bickley merely stared at her, his blue eyes vacant and his pupils enlarged. His glass was forgotten in his hand. She saw that he was preparing to go to the place in his mind where he was able to completely be the monster he really was. He was going to take Joan along with him on this journey, this last Perfect Day, and he was going to come back alone.

Parrish drained his glass and smacked his lips. 'Well, shall we make a start?'

Bickley's eyes focussed again. 'Not yet,' he said. 'We have to get your car out of sight first, just in case anyone sees it. It's the kind of car that people around here would remember for a long time. There's another little clearing behind the cottage we can hide it in. You remembered to padlock the chain at the bottom of the track, didn't you?'

Parrish looked at Stratton and Stratton stared back.

'Didn't you?' Bickley asked again.

'No, I'm afraid we didn't,' Parrish said. 'We were anxious to get the car out of sight of the road before anyone saw us turning in.'

'Well, that needs to be locked first. I told you that. It's the summer. Anyone could wander up here otherwise.'

'Off you go then, my lad,' Parrish drawled. He pulled a set of keys from his trouser pocket and tossed them in Bickley's direction before turning his eyes back to the bed. 'Dr Stratton and I will stay here and try to amuse ourselves with Joan.'

But Bickley didn't move. The keys had hit his chest and fallen to the floor. His eyes were locked to Parrish's profile, and Joan saw that the hand holding his glass was shaking slightly. His knuckles were white.

'I'm not doing it,' he said quietly.

Parrish turned back, raising his eyebrows, and Bickley glared at him.

'You'll do it yourself. I'm not your slave.'

Parrish drew himself up. 'Now listen to me, my friend, I've paid very well for the privilege of being here today - or have you forgotten that?'

'Fuck your money. I'm in command here.'

Stratton quickly stepped between them, his arms raised like buffers. 'Calm down, both of you. Take it easy, Martin, nobody doubts your authority here. You're in command, we all accept that. Roger, back off. This kind of bickering is completely unproductive.' He sighed heavily. 'I'll go lock the chain, okay? Will that satisfy everyone?'

He passed his half-full glass to Parrish and began to move toward the door.

'Let's not lose sight of why we're really here, gentlemen. This is supposed to be fun.'

Fun, Joan thought as she watched Stratton leave. Fun.

When she looked back at Bickley and Parrish, she saw that they were still eyeballing each other, neither man willing to back down. The car keys lay on the floor between them.

'Your car,' Bickley said, clearly forcing himself to speak quietly. 'We need to hide it.'

'Fine,' Parrish sighed. 'I'll do that right now.'

Some of the tension between the two seemed to evaporate.

'But you're going to have to help me unload first,' Parrish added.

'Unload what?'

'The video equipment.'

'Video equip--?'

'I'm going to record everything,' Parrish said, rolling over him grandly, 'every slice and every scream. When I get home I'll run off a couple of hundred DVD copies and we'll see what happens. I started putting out feelers on the Internet last week, and I've already got a long list of interested parties with their tongues hanging out. It'll make a lot of money, and you're going to share in the profits.'

'No,' Bickley said. 'That's not what I do.'

'You're not doing it, my friend, I am.' He smiled at the younger man, projecting the kind of confidence and assurance that carried gullible people along in its wake. 'Anyway, how is it any different from your photographs? The pictures will move, that's all. And scream, of course,' he laughed. 'I promise you, there are collectors who will pay a small fortune to get their hands on a copy.'

'What I do is private,' Bickley firmly insisted. 'It's personal, it's mine. I don't sell me work.'

'Then what are you doing now?' Parrish asked reasonably. 'Why am I here? Why is Kath Meadows dead? Why are you still taking money from her account?' He smiled again, his arrogance perfectly visible. 'It's all a matter of perspective, Martin. Of course you sell your work, and why shouldn't you? You're an artist. I want you to know that I have nothing but the utmost respect for what you do, and I want your dedication to be rewarded. All I'm doing, acting as any responsible agent would, is taking your art to a broader market.'

'You're only supposed to be watching. That's what we agreed to, and nothing more.' Bickley's jaw was set, his eyes dangerously bright. 'This is the last time I'm going to tell you - no video.'

Parrish considered for a long moment, and then shrugged as though resigned.

'Well, if you feel that strongly about it…'

Without warning, he threw the remainder of Stratton's whisky into Bickley's face. All three glasses tumbled to the floor and shattered explosively. Parrish used both hands to shove Bickley in the chest as hard as he could. Bickley hurtled backward, his head struck the plasterboard wall hard enough to leave an impression, and he went down.

Joan forced her head and shoulders up from the mattress, straining to see what was happening. Bickley was struggling to get his feet underneath him, but suddenly he froze, the crown of his head pressed back against the wall. Joan saw that the blade of Parrish's flick-knife was biting at Bickley's throat.

'Don't make me do it,' Parrish said, leaning in close. 'And I will do it, if I have to, make no mistake. No one is indispensable, remember that. We've humoured you this long because it was convenient for us to do so. If we have to, we can take care of Joan ourselves. I'm equally sure we can find another way of disposing of Dr Bob's wife, too. There are lots of other maniacs in the world, Mr Bickley, and Dr Bob knows quite a few of them. It wouldn't be too difficult to bring one of them on board. So if you don't want your little world to collapse, I suggest you learn to compromise.'

He relaxed slightly, but kept the razor-sharp blade tight to Bickley's throat.

'Martin, there's no need for this unpleasantness between us, no need at all. Until now we've had a very good relationship, based on trust and mutual interests. I'd like that to continue, if possible. But too much is hanging on this video for me to simply drop it. You have to understand this. I need the video.'

Bickley stared into Parrish's eyes for the longest time. Then Joan saw the blue fire in them slowly cool. He looked down, unable to meet Parrish's eyes any longer.

'All right,' he said gruffly. 'You can do it. But everything else happens the way I want it to. You don't have any say in that.'

'Agreed,' Parrish said immediately. 'That's exactly what I want.'

After a moment, he stood up, carefully stepping back out of reach of Bickley's legs as he clambered to his feet. Joan saw that Bickley's throat was lined with a thin ribbon of blood where the blade had nicked him.

'No more arguments?' Parrish asked. 'Friends again?

Bickley nodded his head mutely.

'Excellent. Then be a good lad and get the equipment out of the car, would you? Put it in the living room and then hide the car around the back. We've got to get this show on the road.'

Bickley nodded again, brushing himself down. Humiliated, he could not bring himself to look up, not even at Joan. He collected the keys from the floor without another word. Parrish watched him until he left the bedroom and then folded the flick-knife away again. He pushed the door to and turned back to the bed with a triumphant smile.

'Negotiation has always been my strongest suit,' he said.

'You've just made a big mistake,' Joan replied. 'He's not going to let you get away with that.'

'Are you still hypnotised?' Parrish laughed. 'You still think he's a superman, don't you? Well, he isn't. Shall I tell you what he is? At heart he's just an abused little boy who fantasises about having complete power over other human beings. At the first sign of resistance, he crumbles, reverts to type. You should hear some of the stories he told Dr Bob. Talk about funny. Abuse? Christ, Bob and I had it worse

355

our first year at boarding school. No, Bickley's useful, but in the grand scheme of things he's nothing. He's just a pathetic freak with an interesting hobby.'

'What do you think you are?' Joan asked in disgust.

'I'm exactly what I want to be. I do exactly what I want to do, and nothing can stop me.' Parrish's mood had now darkened. 'You know, you ought to thank me, Joan. I've just secured your immortality. Long after you're dead and buried, your image will live on, passing from hand to hand for the highest prices. You'll be a legend, you'll be history.'

Once again his eyes were crawling all over her body, and he began to unbuckle his belt.

'You know, I've wanted to do this for the longest time,' he said, slowly moving around the bed. 'Ever since Stephen paraded you around at that party like you were his little princess. All the way through your 'treatment' at Dr Bob's. I thought I'd never have the chance, but here we are. Here we jolly well are. Kath would probably have called it Karma, wouldn't she?'

He climbed onto the bed and walked up the mattress on his knees. Joan struggled as hard as she could, but she could not pull away from him. She couldn't even close her legs as he shuffled up between her thighs.

'No, don't. Please don't!'

She may as well have been offering prayers to a wooden idol. Parrish pushed his trousers and pants down over his narrow hips and began to manipulate himself as he leaned over her.

'I won't bother with a condom, if you don't mind. No chance of you getting pregnant where you're going. Not where *I'm* going, either.' He smiled at her savagely. 'Unless I'm very much mistaken, I suspect this is going to hurt you.'

Every muscle in Joan's body contracted, her arms and legs straining against her bonds as she tried to curl up into a protective ball - and she felt the rope around her right wrist, which Parrish had cut into and partially loosened, give just a fraction more.

Parrish leaned over her, his breath the breath of a carrion-eater, his white face gleaming, beaded with perspiration as he tried to push himself into her. At that moment, a hand wrapped itself around Parrish's throat, the blunt fingers digging mercilessly into his windpipe as he was yanked upright.

Bickley's face appeared over his shoulder, and Parrish was pulled back against the other man's chest, his eyes wide with panic. Joan saw Bickley's arm begin to piston backwards and forwards behind Parrish's back. On each forward stroke, Parrish's whole body spasmed and bucked and the plastic beneath him began to be spattered with bright rivulets of fresh blood.

Parrish was staring directly into Joan's eyes as his body gave one last convulsive jump, and he coughed a fine spray of blood over her chest and belly. His hands fell away from his throat, where he had been trying to prise Bickley's fingers free. Joan saw the life leave his eyes, as if a candle flame, already guttering, had suddenly been blown out.

The body was still trembling when Bickley slipped his hand up from Parrish's windpipe and

357

raised the other man's chin. He brought his hunting knife around from Parrish's back and opened his throat from ear to ear. Hot blood erupted from the gaping wound, splashing on Joan's naked stomach like hot water flowing from a tap.

Unaware that she was screaming, Joan watched Parrish's body collapse in slow motion. It landed on top of her, the head striking her chin so that for a moment she saw stars. Bickley's face materialised through the constellations, only inches from her own. It was the face of a wild animal, driven by bloodlust, the joy of the kill.

'He was right,' Bickley said. 'No one is indispensable.'

50

DCI Richardson stood halfway down the short flight of stone steps that led to Martin Bickley's London basement flat. Even from this distance, even in the perpetual shadow of the small alcove, he could see that the lock was hanging askew. The door had been kicked open, and shattered.

Under his breath, he said, 'You fucking idiot, Stephen.'

He was about to take the next step down, when a bright voice suddenly rang out above his head, stopping him in his tracks.

'What are you up to then, sir – flat-hunting?'

Richardson turned about and saw a young female police constable curiously staring down at him from the pavement, her eyebrows raised in enquiry and her hand poised on her Motorola radio, and he realised how the situation might look to an impartial observer.

He could easily have been an opportunist thief, taking advantage of a broken lock. He took out his wallet and showed the officer his ID.

'Who are you?' he asked.

'WPC Jo Ward, sir, from Wood Green. Well, Wood Green for now, but next month I'm transferring over to Whetstone, and--'

'Okay, Jo,' Richardson cut in. 'Shut up and listen to me. I believe this flat is a crime scene, and you and I are going to enter it and take a look around, okay?'

'Yes sir.'

'Good. Follow me.'

In his haste to leave his own house, and with his wife's dissatisfaction ringing in his ears, he had forgotten to put his basic crime-scene kit back in the car boot. It had been removed for the duration of the family day out, and Richardson was kicking himself for forgetting to replace it. He might have risked another tongue-lashing and gone back, but then some idiot on a bike had shot out into the road in front of him, and he'd had to brake and swerve to avoid knocking them down. And in the moment of relief that followed the near miss, all the hazy suspicions floating around in his mind abruptly began to coalesce.

Bickley's disturbing police record, and his use of attempted vehicular homicide to get closer to the woman he had stalked to London. Stephen's wife, Joan, worrying about her friend Kath who had gone missing only weeks after her brother had been killed in a hit-and-run. Joan again, this time claiming that Kath had been abducted and murdered, and that now she was the one being stalked. Then she too had been involved in a hit-and-run, and now Stephen was asking about Bickley. It was almost a cycle.

He didn't fully understand all the connections yet, and nor did he entirely trust the fantastical direction in which his thoughts seemed to be heading, but he knew there were far too many coincidences here to ignore.

'Listen,' he said to the WPC as he reached the broken door. 'Try not to touch anything inside. I haven't got any...'

A pair of latex gloves suddenly appeared over his shoulder.

He turned to look at Ward as he pulled the gloves on, and he saw that she was already wearing her own. She couldn't have been much more than twenty-three or twenty-four, but she seemed very calm, much more composed than he might have been at the same age and under the same circumstances, and he decided that she might be one to look out for in the future.

'Thanks.'

He turned and entered the building. At the end of the dark corridor, he saw that the inner door had also been kicked open. Through the doorway he saw the narrow single bed and the wall covered in black and white prints. The only thing he could hear was the rush of plumbing from the flats above.

He moved quietly along the corridor and stepped inside the flat, his eyes immediately falling on the mess of photographs that had been left all over the threadbare carpet. In the gloom, their subject was at first invisible.

He glanced across at the second linoleum-floored corridor while WPC Ward moved in behind him.

'This is the police,' he announced. 'Anyone here?'

No reply, except for a slight echo.

'Martin Bickley? Stephen Crosby?'

Nothing. The place was empty.

He found the light-switch on the damp wall and snapped on the overhead. The unshaded bulb harshly illuminated the photographs on the floor, and he used the toe of his shoe to poke them apart, at first puzzled by their content.

London scenes. Carnaby Street, Covent Garden, Tower Bridge. Then a seemingly pointless series of shots featuring a pedestrian crossing. Then the exterior of a café with a large plate glass window. Then Hampstead High Street, thronged with shoppers, the central figure a woman in the distance walking away from the camera, a long dark coat billowing in the wind.

'Where's this place?' the WPC asked, and Richardson turned to her.

Ward was admiring a photograph of a picturesque cottage stuck to a mirror above the dresser. He took a step closer and peered. Was that Bickley's real home in Yorkshire, Hunter's Lodge? Where he'd been raised, where he'd been a suspect in the disappearance of a young girl? Richardson remembered the reports of the grieving father tirelessly searching the forest for her body, but without success, and his bitter accusations regarding Bickley and his uncle.

'I think that may be where...' he began, but then stopped, and slowly turned about again, his eyes scanning the photographs once more. Beads of sweat suddenly appeared on his forehead like magic. Stalkings. Hit-and-runs. Disappearances. Bodies hidden in the forest. Kath Meadows running off for one of her little adventures, but never coming back.

'Joan,' he said to himself.

'Joan who?' Ward asked.

'That's why Stephen's looking for Bickley. Joan's disappeared, and he thinks Bickley's taken her.'

Ten seconds later he was back on the street, striding back toward his car with his mobile clamped to his ear. He had already dialled the number of Lockton Dale station house from memory, and was listening to the phone there ring and ring. WPC Ward was following on his heels. She had been confused by his sudden anxiety and clearly had questions, but he didn't have time right now to explain.

'Woodall?' he barked the moment the phone was answered. 'DCI Richardson here.'

The constable sighed. 'Yes, sir, I've just this second been relieved from the desk. I'll be setting off in about five minutes.'

'Do it *now*,' Richardson said. He still had his doubts, he still thought he might be jumping at shadows, but he couldn't take the risk that he might be right. 'Do it right now, immediately. Blues and twos all the way to Hunter's Lodge. She might not be there, but if she is....'

'Blue and twos? Sir, *who* might not be there? What is it you think--'

'Don't ask bloody questions, man!' Richardson shouted down the phone. 'Just *go!*'

51

Joan had her eyes tightly closed, and was taking in only short, constricted breaths. She was finding it hard to breathe, not only because of Parrish's dead weight on top of her, but also because of Bickley's weight. After slitting Parrish's throat, he had immediately straddled both their bodies like a horse, and now he was doing something unspeakable to Parrish's body that was making the bed shake. Her eyes were closed because she didn't want to see what it was, but she could guess.

She could hear his knife at work, scraping against bone and occasionally digging at the head slipping around in the thick film of blood that coated her chest. She could hear Bickley panting as she had heard him pant in moments of passion.

'You ought to see this, Joan,' he said breathlessly. 'It's really something.'

She resisted the urge to look. Resisted the urge to think. She was trying to hold a single image at the forefront of her mind. That image was the loop of rope that tethered her right arm to the bedpost. She could still feel the tight bracelet of pressure that had imprinted itself around her wrist. But she could also feel where the rope was right now - bunched up just below her thumb and the heel of her hand. She was sweating heavily.

In her imagination, she could see herself slipping that hand free.

'Never done a man before,' Bickley said. 'Not up close like this. Never wanted to. But he didn't give me any choice, did he? Just kept pushing, pushing, pushing…'

Abruptly, the bed stopped moving. Bickley stopped panting, and she heard a voice. Stratton's voice. It was coming from outside, from a distance, but getting closer all the time. He was shouting Parrish's name, his voice filled with panic. Joan felt Bickley climb off the bed just as Stratton's feet hit the deck outside.

'Roger!' he yelled. 'Someone's coming!'

Joan heard Stratton's footsteps hammering over the living room's wooden floor and opened her eyes. She saw that Bickley had positioned himself to the side of the door, his knife poised to strike. His hands, face, and jacket were smeared with fresh blood.

'I was almost at the end of the track and a car pulled in! It's coming up! We've got to get out of here, now!'

Stratton slid to a halt just inside the bedroom doorway, and his pale and panicked face slackened as he saw Parrish's body draped over Joan's. Bickley had sawn both of Parrish's ears off and was halfway through scalping him.

'What?' Stratton said, faintly.

He turned to stare at Bickley, goggling at the blood, and Bickley thrust the hunting knife deep into his stomach. Stratton doubled over, his mouth a wide, silent 'o', and would have fallen if Bickley hadn't caught him and held him up. He walked the doctor slowly backwards, almost gently, then let him fall off the knife down through the trapdoor into the cellar. Joan heard the impact as his body hit the packed earth beneath.

She looked up at Bickley, who had stripped off his bloody camouflage jacket and was wiping his hands clean on its inner lining. He was working quickly, trying to tidy himself up. They could both clearly hear the sound of an approaching engine now.

Time, Joan thought. *Time.*

'Your face,' she said. When Bickley looked at her blankly, she said, 'There's blood all over your face.'

'Shit!'

Bickley ran out of the bedroom and hurried to close the front door. Then she saw him pass the doorway again on his way to the bathroom. Once she heard the water beginning to run, she glanced up at the rope around her right hand, and gave it an experimental tug. The rope slipped a little more over her sweaty skin, and she could see the fibres where Parrish had cut it parting, stretching.

This might actually be possible, she thought.

The water stopped running in the bathroom. She looked back at the doorway just as Bickley reappeared. His face was still wet. The blood was gone, even though a few traces of the face paint still remained, and he had done well enough to pass a casual inspection. He looked like a man who had been hard at work on his land, perhaps repairing a piece of machinery. The shallow wound on his throat could have been a scratch where he had caught himself accidentally with a tool. The film of water could have been sweat. The residue of the face paint could have been grease or oil. In his hands he held the shotgun.

They heard a car draw up in the clearing outside, and the ratcheting sound of a handbrake being applied. The engine stopped.

'The same rules as before,' Bickley whispered. 'Make a sound and whoever it is, they're dead. Men, women, or children. Understand?'

Joan nodded.

The second that he closed the door, Joan tried to make her hand as narrow as possible, took a deep breath, and then pulled with all her might. There was an instant of bright white pain as the rope bit into her skin and crushed all the bones in her hand. Ignoring it, she increased her efforts still more and her thumb threatened to dislocate. She clenched her teeth, compressing her lips tightly so not the slightest whimper would escape her, and pulled again. And then her hand simply popped free, landing on the plastic-covered mattress beside her, fizzing with pins and needles.

Before Joan had time to feel elated, her hand moved as though it were a separate entity, slipping down to squirm between Parrish's body and her own, searching for his inside jacket pocket.

52

Olivia and Stephen stepped up onto the cottage's small deck and paused in front of the door. Olivia took a breath, and then knocked. She glanced over her shoulder and saw Stephen staring back at the charcoal grey Porsche that he'd parked beside.

'For heaven's sake, Stephen,' Olivia said in an aggravated stage-whisper. 'This is no time to start salivating over a bloody car!'

'I'm not salivating,' Stephen replied without heat. He frowned at the car, and at the number plate.

'You know, I'm sure I've seen this car somewhere before.'

'Where?'

He shook his head. 'I'm not totally sure, but I think I've seen it parked outside Lee Meadows' warehouse a couple of times.'

'What?'

Olivia jumped when the cottage door abruptly opened. She took an involuntary step back as she saw herself being scrutinised through a five-inch gap. Bickley was stripped to the waist, dirty and perspiring. He also looked as though he was secretly amused, and not trying too hard to disguise the fact. She had not rehearsed this moment in her mind, and now found herself lost for words, able only to stare.

'Well, well, well,' Bickley muttered to himself. 'Faces from the past.'

Olivia shook herself. 'Mr Bickley?'

Bickley blinked at the use of his real name, but was otherwise unmoved. 'Aye, that's me.'

'My name's Olivia Weir. I'm Joan Crosby's sister.'

Bickley cocked his head.

'And this is Stephen, her husband.'

He glanced between them both, still amused. 'Aye, I recognise you both. Remember you visiting, Miss, when I was working on the house. How's the guttering holding up?'

Stephen stepped up beside Olivia. Down by his sides, his hands had curled into fists. 'Where's my wife?'

Bickley made a wry face, which Olivia could see might be completely charming in the right situation. This wasn't it.

'I would have thought you of all people ought to know, being her husband, an' all.'

'I think she's here,' Stephen said.

'I can't help what you think,' Bickley shrugged.

Stephen stepped aggressively close to the door, all but barging Olivia out of his way. 'Stop fucking around. We know she's here. We know *everything*.'

The amusement left Bickley's eyes, and they went cold. Olivia felt the chill immediately. She tugged at Stephen's sleeve in alarm, but he didn't respond.

'What d'you mean by that?'

'Take a wild guess, Mr Bickley – or should I say Mr *Bowman*, or Mr *Brown*, or Mr *Bowie*, or Mr *Bowers*?' Stephen said, dredging up some of the other aliases Richardson had told him the man had been known to use. 'We know absolutely everything about you.'

From deep within the cottage, they all heard a loud thud, as though someone had fallen over.

'That's her back there now, isn't it?' Stephen took another step forward, one hand pressing against the door. 'Let us in or we'll call the police.'

Bickley had glanced over his shoulder into the cottage, and now turned back to Stephen. 'Aye,' he said. 'It's her. And I reckon it's about time you were reunited, don't you?'

He swung the door open, and Olivia and Stephen found themselves staring into the barrels of Bickley's shotgun.

'Mind you, under the circumstances, I'm not sure how pleased she's going to be to see you.'

He backed away from the doorway, using the shotgun to beckon them in. Once they were in the centre of the living room area, he circled around behind them, kicked the door closed, and nodded toward the bedroom door.

'In there,' he said.

He herded them toward the door and told Stephen to open it. He smiled as the pair of them froze in the doorway, rooted to the spot. He heard Stephen's sharp exclamation of shock, saw Olivia's legs give and her hands grasping at the architrave for support. Bickley was calmly thinking about the logistics of the situation. First he'd force Olivia to tie Stephen up, immediately taking out the biggest threat, and then he reckoned he'd be able to tie her up afterwards without too much trouble. That would work. Then everything would be under control again.

'Say hello, everyone,' he said cheerfully.

He used the shotgun to nudge the both of them further into the bedroom, and only then saw that what Olivia and Stephen had reacted to was Roger Parrish's mutilated body, lying on the floor by the side of the bed where it had fallen.

The bed itself was empty, and the bedroom window was open.

He saw the ropes dangling from the bedposts, saw the way they had been cleanly sliced through, and he remembered the flick-knife Parrish carried and had threatened him with earlier.

Olivia turned to him, her face anaemia-pale. 'What have you done to her? Where is she? Where's Joan?'

Bickley looked at her speculatively.

'That's what you're going to help me find out,' he said.

53

Joan tripped over a hidden tree root and fell headlong to the forest floor, only narrowly missing impaling herself on Parrish's knife. This was not the first time she had fallen and it was a while before she could even muster the energy to raise her face from the cool mulch. When she did she realised that she was completely lost.

After leaping out of the window, she had run for the first cover she had seen and kept on going, running as fast as she was able. A minute or two later she had turned sharply to her left down a narrow trail, hoping that she was heading in the general direction of the road. But it seemed that the forest itself was against her. The trail she had been following ran out after less than fifty paces, and time and again she found her path blocked by clusters of trees and heavy patches of thorny undergrowth. The wind-blown trees seemed to be reaching out to hold her back, and strike her down. It was as though Bickley had possessed the forest.

Her one clear thought was to put as much distance between herself and Hunter's Lodge as possible, and as time went on she had come to believe that the direction didn't matter. But now, exhausted and traumatised, she realised that direction was everything. She remembered her first attempt at escape, when despite all her efforts she had wandered in a circle and ended up back at the cottage. She didn't want that to happen again. She would rather use Parrish's knife on herself.

Shakily, she rose to her hands and knees, and felt the first drops of rain speckle her naked back, shockingly cold. Away to her right she saw a dead tree that had clearly once been hit by lightning. It had been split in half and scorched along its entire trunk. The felled half of it lay in a brittle clump at the base, with mounds of fresh green bracken growing up from the ground beneath. A natural hiding place. It could give her time to rest and recover. Time to get her bearings.

She crawled over and squirmed her way into the heart of the undergrowth, and for the first time in a long while, she felt safe. Sheltered. She leaned back against the broad trunk and closed her eyes, completely exhausted. Almost instantly half asleep, she somehow found herself thrust back into the middle of the recurring dream she had told Stratton about two days ago – my God, she thought, can it really have been only two days?

In the dream she was in a world of blackness. Around her the sea roared like an animal, and from somewhere far away, she heard the sound of someone crying out for help.

She remembered giving Stratton the details, and then the psychiatrist agreeing with her that it seemed largely insignificant. But now she wondered. Had it been a prophetic dream? A warning from her deepest subconscious, as it tried to let her know the depth of betrayal that surrounded her? Had she really been hearing herself, her own lost voice, screaming from the depths of the Dragon's gullet?

But if that was the case, why was she having the same dream again now, when the time for warnings was over?

A heavier burst of rain showered down over her, falling unhindered by the dead and leafless branches above, and Joan opened her eyes to the dark, swaying forest, and she realised that she was not asleep and she was not dreaming. The sounds she could hear were quite real.

The roar of the sea was really the wind moving massively through the ancient forest, and it always had been. The voice screaming for help had never been her own.

It was her sister's.

54

Stephen Crosby lay curled up on the dirt clearing before Hunter's Lodge. Both of his hands were pressed to a wound in his belly, blood oozing out through his fingers and pooling on the ground beneath him, diffusing into the gathering rainwater and soaking into his clothes. He was still conscious, but only just.

'Don't do it,' he murmured to Olivia. 'Don't.'

But Olivia, shrieking her sister's name, didn't hear him. Bickley held her by the scruff of the neck, showing her to the forest like a trophy. He had stripped her from the neck down, her blouse hanging in tatters, her bra pulled down to encircle her waist like a garter belt. In his other hand he held his hunting knife, which he was using to prick Olivia's breasts as he urged her to shout louder. Her torso was streaked with blood turning translucent in the rain. The shotgun lay safely on the ground by Bickley's side, wedged under his boot.

No answer came from the forest.

He pulled Olivia closer to him, and whispered something into her ear that almost made her pass out. Then he raised the knife until the blade was flat against her ribcage under her right breast and slowly began to apply upward pressure as if he meant to slice it clean off, and Olivia screamed Joan's name again.

'I'm here,' Joan said.

She stepped out of the treeline about twenty feet to their left, Parrish's knife clutched in her dangling right hand and hidden from Bickley's sight by her mud-streaked thigh. She looked at her sister, at her husband, and then at Bickley.

'I knew you'd come back, Joan,' he grinned. 'I knew you couldn't leave your sister behind. Not you.'

When, Joan did not reply, Bickley hurled Olivia away from him where she tripped over Stephen's body and fell heavily to the ground. She lay there sobbing, her hands pressed to her breasts. Stephen was now either unconscious or dead, Joan couldn't tell which.

Bickley swiftly bent down and retrieved his shotgun. 'Come here, Joan.' When she didn't move, he levelled the shotgun at her one-handed, the stock wedged against his hip. He used the knife in the other hand to gesture her to come closer. 'I said, come here, Joan. Nice and slow.'

Joan took half a dozen steps forward and stopped again. She was shuddering with suppressed rage. An intense adrenaline surge had moved her toward Bickley more surely than the threat of the shotgun or his command, but she could see that he had spotted the flick-knife.

'Planning to use that on me, are you?'

Joan shook her head. 'Not against a gun,' she said. 'If it was a fair fight, yes, I'd use it. I'd kill you.'

'Fancy your chances, do you?'

'I'd cut your fucking heart out.'

He laughed at her.

'Why don't you try me,' Joan said. 'Give me a chance.'

Bickley laughed again. 'Why should I do that?'

Joan couldn't think of any reason that would speak to him.

'To be honest, Joan,' he said, 'I don't need the gun. I don't even need me knife. I could stop you with a single word. Stratton gave it me months ago. It'd put you back under me control instantly, and you'd do anything I said. I could make you help me finish off your husband. I could even make you kill your own sister. Make you hold her down while I fuck her, then have you help me torture her to death. How would you like that?'

Trembling, Joan took another step forward, raising the flick-knife in a challenge.

'Behind your back, Parrish called you a pathetic freak,' she said, 'and I think he was right. Scum though he was, he was right. You're not a hunter. You're a jackal. You're a hyena. I bet you didn't leave the army by choice. I bet they threw you out, because they saw you for what you really are. A pervert, and a coward.'

Bickley raised the shotgun again, and sighted along it at Joan's head. 'I think you've said enough now. Drop the knife and come to me.'

'I know how it all started, too. Your precious uncle abused you when you were a little boy, and when you--'

'Shut up,' Bickley said coldly. All his good humour had vanished. 'If you know what's good for you, you'll--'

'And when you grew up you tried to do the same to other people, but you had to tie them up to do it. Or drug them. Or hypnotise them. They had to be helpless. You weren't man enough for anything else.'

'Shut up!'

'No!' Joan shouted back, waving her knife wildly to and fro. 'Come on! If you want to shut me up, come and do it! Be a man, a real man, for just once in your gutless, pathetic, twisted life!'

After a second or two, she contemptuously dropped her arms to her sides and sneered at him.

'No, you can't, can you? You haven't got the balls.'

Bickley looked at the shotgun for a moment, and then he cocked his arm and tossed it, end over end, into the forest. His eyes were the blue flames of gas burners. He passed his hunting knife from hand to hand, then spread his arms out wide, inviting an attack.

'Okay, Joan, you asked for it,' he said. 'Let's see what you've got.'

Joan maintained her focus on his face. At the periphery of her vision, she could see that Olivia had crawled around Stephen and was slowly making her way up behind Bickley, her bloody, tear-streaked face a shapeless blur. Joan risked another step forward, careful to stay just out of striking range. All Olivia had to do was distract him for a second, grab his legs, kick his ankle, anything, and Joan would be able to leap forward and bury the flick-knife in his chest.

She knew that she could do it. She knew that she was capable, because she *wanted* to do it. She wanted to do it for Olivia and Stephen, and she wanted to do it for herself. For all his other victims. Most of all, she wanted to do it for her friend Kath.

'What are you waiting for?' Bickley asked. 'A printed invitation?'

Olivia was within reach of Bickley now, and Joan's eyes inadvertently flicked downward. When she looked back at Bickley, she saw that he was smiling.

'Oh, please!' he said, and kicked out backwards, his heavy boot catching Olivia square in the face.

When Joan heard her sister's nose break, she screamed a war-cry and charged forward with the flick-knife held out in front of her like a lance.

Without even moving his feet, Bickley easily evaded her desperate thrust. As he twisted his body and the flick-knife whispered by his chest, he grabbed Joan's arm and pulled her to him, used her own momentum to spin her around, savagely jamming her arm up behind her back. The flick-knife popped out of her hand like a slick bar of soap and was lost in the mud.

Bickley kicked her in the back of the thighs and Joan's legs collapsed and she fell. He reached down to grab a handful of her hair, which he used to haul her over on to her back, and then sat on her chest with his knees pinning her shoulders to the ground. She couldn't move. She didn't have the strength to raise her arms, to kick or to buck.

Bickley teased her by dangling his knife over her face by his forefinger and thumb, swinging it back and forth like a pendulum.

'You were saying?' he said.

He lowered the swinging knife until the tip snagged on her cheek, instantly drawing blood, and then allowed the heavy knife's weight to carry it deeper into her flesh. His other hand was spread across her forehead, preventing her from twisting her face away.

'I know you're a good looking woman, an' all, Joan,' he said, 'but have you ever considered a face lift? Don't worry about the cost. I'll do you a freebie, just like I did Parrish.'

'Bickley!' a man's voice shouted.

Joan thought at first that she had imagined the voice, but Bickley's head jerked away from her, and turned toward the forest. As the tip of the knife blade left her face, she turned her head, too. Her cheek came to rest in a shallow puddle of cold rainwater, and she saw a figure making its way through the trees and foliage and stepping out into the clearing.

'Drop the knife!' the man shouted. 'Get off her!'

He was in his late middle age. His clothes were sodden with rain, plastered to an ample body, and what little hair he had left was lacquered to his pink

377

scalp. In his hands he held Bickley's shotgun. Joan had never seen him before in her life.

Then she felt the muscles in Bickley's legs lock solid as he prepared to rise, and she opened her mouth to scream a warning.

Without the slightest hesitation, the stranger cocked both hammers, raised the shotgun to his shoulder, and pulled the triggers. Bickley was thrown off her as though by a giant's fist. The immense sound of the gunshot rolled around inside her head like something physical. Its aftermath sounded like static, and Joan wondered for a moment whether the blast had deafened her. Then she realised that the static was really the increasingly heavy rain striking the leaves of the trees. Seconds later, another sound began to make itself heard. It sounded suspiciously like a police siren.

Joan forced herself up on her elbows. The stranger had fallen to his knees, dropping the shotgun in the mud. He was staring past her, his face a twisted mask that could not decide upon its identity. He was laughing and sobbing at the same time.

She turned to follow his eyeline and saw Bickley's dead body lying six feet beyond her, his arms and legs twisted and tangled around in a way that reminded Joan of herself, posing on his bed about a thousand years ago. She could not see Bickley's face. His face and most of his head were gone.

As the siren came warbling closer and closer, Joan turned to look at the stranger again.

'Who are you?' she asked.

55

Five months later, at nine o'clock on a crisp January morning, Joan Crosby sat on the staircase in her Hampstead home. She was swaddled in an oversize black sweater and baggy grey jogging bottoms, waiting for the doorbell to ring, and she knew everything there was to know.

The man who had saved her that day was Roger Simmons, the publican Stephen and Olivia had asked for directions to Hunter's Lodge, and the father of Alison Simmons, Bickley's first ever victim - the girl in the photograph he'd hung above his bed at the cottage. The teenager's remains, along with those of a further eleven women, had eventually been located in the forest surrounding the cottage following careful examination of Bickley's exhaustive photograph collection. This was five more victims than Bickley had claimed for himself in his conversations with Joan, and there was forensic evidence that pointed to these extra bodies having been in situ since long before Bickley's time.

Suspicions for these murders had now fallen on the deceased uncle, and twenty-five-year-old Missing Person reports were being carefully sifted for clues.

Dr David Stratton, like Stephen and Olivia, had fully recovered from the injuries he had received at Bickley's hands, and was now on remand in a high security prison awaiting sentencing after a highly public trial. Stratton, perhaps in a misguided attempt to earn the court's leniency, had cooperated fully with the police investigation, revealing the secrets of his perverse partnership with Roger Parrish, as well as the location of his private patient records. These records were substantially different from those in the filing cabinets at his consulting rooms. Among them were files which catalogued, in coldly clinical detail, over fifteen years of systematic sexual abuse of the female patients in his practise, largely through the indiscriminate use of hypnosis.

There were also a large number of explicit images and videos that had been made with the help of his friend, entrepreneur Roger Parrish, including those made of Joan's hypnotherapy sessions. Following the outraged newspaper reports, more than a dozen women had come forward with accusations that they had hitherto been too afraid to voice or had believed to be delusions.

The tabloids loved Stratton to bits. He was their cash cow. They called him Dr Bob.

Also among Stratton's records were notes on a handful of court-appointed patients he had released with clean bills of health, having being quite aware of their dangerous pastimes. Most of them had been rapists and stalkers. The most dangerous by far had been Martin Bickley, who had boasted of having killed several women during the course of his 'treatment', and had even given Stratton several photographs to back up his claims, which had been found and placed into evidence along with the rest of his collection.

Stratton, at that time in the midst of a messy, acrimonious divorce, was impressed by Bickley and had already begun to form the nucleus of a plan to rid himself of his wife when Parrish, his lifelong friend, had come along and hijacked it to remove Kath Meadows.

But neither man had reckoned on Joan placing herself into the equation after Kath's murder, and the outspokenness of her suspicions had forced them to delay the murder of Stratton's wife. It had seemed to them like an instance of serendipity when Bickley had fixed on Joan as his next victim, and it had given Stratton time to superficially improve his relationship with his soon to be ex-wife, pretending to become her friend while remaking his life with a woman half his age. The make-over that Joan had noticed was only a cover up, intended to deflect suspicion in any subsequent investigation.

Lee Meadows was also under arrest, having been implicated by Stratton as an accessory to Roger Parrish's drug importation scheme. He had confessed to everything but the knowledge of Kath's murder and the plot to kill Joan, and the police - and Joan - believed him. Especially since Stratton had further revealed that Parrish had already discussed the probability of getting rid of Meadows next, to tidy up the last loose end.

Joan had spent most of the time since that day at Hunter's Lodge alone in her house. She had been to see the psychotherapist recommended by the police, but only once. Sitting there in a virtual facsimile of Stratton's green room, she had been faced with a woman younger than herself, who seemed to speak entirely in a tabloid agony-aunt psycho-babble that alternately bored and enraged her.

Looking at the woman's fresh, earnest face, Joan had not believed that she knew any more about life than Joan did, which was nothing. She hadn't a clue about what Joan had been through, or what she was still going through. Halfway through the initial session, Joan had excused herself and left. She had retreated to her house, and stayed there, in a tight, hopefully self-healing cocoon, and she tried to draw comfort from the realisation what that she had never been crazy.

It was like that old joke - it's not paranoia if they're really out to get you.

There had been a few surprises over the months, some more unexpected than others. DCI Phil Richardson, his wife and young son had become occasional visitors. Richardson never stopped apologising for his earlier lack of belief, and for not figuring out earlier what was happening with his fabled but sadly-misfiring Copper's Intuition. His wife, Louise, was more practical, a window on to the world and, possibly, a way back into it, offering friendship and sisterhood. Their little boy, Ben, seemed to fascinate her more than any other child she had ever met, and to a degree she did not entirely understand at first. Later, of course, it became obvious.

Another surprise visitor was Gordon Unwill, the neighbour formerly known as M. Unwill began visiting her soon after she arrived back in Hampstead, during that period when it seemed like the world's media was camping out on her doorstep and her phone rang and night and day with offers from newspapers, television, and even a film company who wanted to turn her experiences into a feature film. More often than not Unwill turned up at the back door, having sneaked in through a neighbouring garden, bringing with him small gifts of food and magazines, and sometimes just his own company. It had been Unwill who had accompanied her to Kath's funeral, as her remains were finally given a proper burial.

The rest of the time Joan had devoted to the complete redecoration of the house.

She had chosen her materials from a vast stack of brochures Unwill had collected for her, and she had arranged for their delivery herself, over the phone and the Internet. For the better part of two months she had worked twelve or fifteen hour days, painting walls and stripping woodwork and sanding floors, entirely remaking her home. She had emerged from this fugue of labour in complete mental and physical exhaustion and had slept almost continually for a week.

And then one day, this day, she had woken up and called both her sister and husband and invited them around to visit.

Over the months both Olivia and Stephen had spoken to her on the phone almost every day, both of them pleading to be allowed back into her life. Sometimes they pleaded on each other's behalf, one picking up where the other left off, like a tag-team. Stephen phoned most frequently, usually first thing in the morning and the last thing at night, from the hotel room that had become his home after his discharge from hospital. Their persistence was exhausting, but until now she had refused to meet with either one of them.

Sitting on the newly varnished staircase, staring at the freshly painted front door, Joan could not now imagine what had possessed her to make these calls. Olivia and Stephen would arrive believing that she

383

had come to a conclusion regarding their separate relationships, but as yet she had not finalised her feelings in her own mind.

The jury was still out.

They had come after her when they realised she was in danger, there was that. They had tracked Bickley down and interrupted him before he was able to do her serious harm, giving her the chance to escape. And she knew that when they in turn had been threatened by Bickley, she had gone back to try to save them. Her reaction had been instinctual. She did not know what theirs had been, genuine care or simple guilt.

Quite often, though, she thought about her recurring dream, which had not recurred since Bickley's death. Hearing Olivia screaming for her through the storm. Had it been meant to be all along? Was there a grand plan, and if so, was what was happening to her now a part of it? And she thought about Roger Parrish and Robert Stratton, and Lee Meadows, too, and knew that despite everything, there were worse husbands she might have had.

The truth was that she had no idea what she was going to do about Olivia and Stephen. To take one or both of them back, or neither of them. She supposed it all hinged on her first reaction when they arrived at her front door.

If she opened it, she would know.

If she turned away again, she would also know.

Lost in these and other thoughts, Joan only looked up as she heard footsteps approaching the door, two sets that hesitated outside, nervously shuffling. She waited, and finally the doorbell rang.

She rose awkwardly from the step, using the banister handrail to help get her to her feet, and stepped forward. She placed her hand against the door for a moment, and felt the tremor as either her sister or husband gently knocked, and she felt the second-hand contact transmit itself from the wood and sink into her flesh.

Two perfectly matched impulses tugged at her.

Open the door, urged one.

Turn away, said the other.

Joan took a deep breath, and then she opened the door.

Two sets of eyes immediately locked on to hers. Although they were smiling, Joan saw that Olivia and Stephen's expressions perfectly reflected the doubts she knew were evident on her own face. She knew that she needed help, but wasn't sure that she wanted their help. They wanted her forgiveness, but didn't know whether it would be given.

And then, in unison, their eyes dropped from her face, and the fixed smiles suddenly died, replaced by expressions of horror. They stared at her belly under the outsized sweater, five months swollen.

'I think I'm going to keep it,' Joan told them.

The End
of
PERFECT DAY

Now read the prologue to
PERFECT PEACE

It was around seven-thirty in the morning and the southerly wind was unseasonably powerful, driving heavy bands of rain inland to lash at the Sussex coastline like a flail. It was a miserable start to a summer's day, but Julia Meredith, in her current frame of mind, found it entirely satisfactory. In fact, she dearly wished the bad weather would persist, although apparently this was not to be.

As unlikely as it seemed right now, according to a weather report she'd heard on the radio late last night, the sun would be back at full strength before midday, and the dark rain-clouds packed away again like winter coats. The wind would drop and the temperature would soar, and that would bring the day-trippers, who she despised, back in force. At the moment, though, the beach where she stood was thankfully deserted, the choppy surf lapping harmlessly over her boots as she looked out to sea, her eyes narrowed against the rain as she watched an endless field of whitecaps racing in.

There was a kind of bitter satisfaction to the way the chill drilling rain soaked her hair, numbing her scalp and her forehead. It was the same strange pleasure she derived from the long cold showers she had begun to take both mornings and evenings, when she only allowed herself to clamber out of the bathtub once she was completely rubber-limbed and could no longer feel the pain when she pinched herself.

Julia would be sixty-three years old in just over a month's time, and last year her husband had left her for another woman. As a nice ironic touch, the other woman, a former friend, was actually a few years older than Julia. As another nice ironic touch, Julia still liked the other woman, and certainly she liked her a lot better than she had liked her husband by the time he eventually got around to leaving. She sincerely believed that if circumstances were ever to arrange themselves so, she could quite happily share a house with the other woman, even now. She was no longer sure she could say the same about her husband.

But life went on, didn't it? Or, at least, that's what they said.

She got to the beach most mornings these days. Every morning, if she was truthful. Her son, an office manager in Salisbury, believed she was taking long meditative walks, breathing in tons of healing ozone. He had spoken positively and kindly about exercising muscles and exorcising demons, and coming to terms, and moving on, and many other strategies for coping she thought he must have learned on various management training courses over the years. Her son believed her early morning trips to the beach were a healthy habit. Julia was not so sure.

Sometimes she found herself here long before the sun had fully risen, with hardly a single memory of waking and rising herself. She found herself shivering in the pre-dawn chill, and staring unblinkingly at a restless, molten sea which seemed like a mirror that had been held up to the way she felt inside. At these moments she felt the yearning pull of the riptide like an additional heartbeat in her chest, and she imagined that she could hear something in the deeper water, something relentless and eternal, calling out her name.

Whenever she thought these thoughts, experienced these emotions, she also felt herself to be foolish and pathetic. A cliché, a joke of a woman. But then she would look at the sea again, as she was looking at the sea now, and begin to wonder how it would feel; if she listened for that siren-like voice just a little harder, if she tired of the endless struggle and gave in, if she finally made it all real. She imagined the enormity of it, of taking that first step, and then walking into the cold water, and not stopping, never stopping, until everything stopped hurting, forever.

The sea. The British called this part of it The English Channel. The French, she believed, called it La Manche, The Sleeve. But Julia had gradually come to believe that the true name of the sea, of any sea or any part of any sea, was Freedom.

Freedom. Escape. Release. Peace.

Without warning a sound suddenly broke into the dark rhythm of Julia's thoughts. It was a barking dog, somewhere in the distance.

She looked to her left and saw that the animal, a large black Labrador, was surprisingly close by, only about two hundred yards away, but almost hidden behind a groyne, one of the long timber barriers built out into the sea to help prevent the coastline being eroded by the tides. She had seen the dog before in the mornings on a few occasions, but she had never before heard it bark like this. She could see the two children who routinely walked the dog, too. They were locals, she believed, not tourists, although she only knew them by sight; she had never spoken to them, nor they to her. They had never even waved to each other.

It had crossed her mind once or twice that the children must have thought of her, if they thought of her at all, as quite mad. An insane old woman, who only came to the beach to stare out at the sea. It was no wonder they had kept their distance, until now.

The youngest child, a boy who looked to be around five or six, stood about halfway between Julia and the groyne where the dog was still barking. The girl, perhaps three or four years older and very pretty, was racing along the beach towards Julia, almost stumbling as her small booted feet sank into the wet sand and shingle. Her long dark hair was plastered in coils to her head and neck and feathered across her cheeks, and her pale face seemed to be all eyes, huge and glassy and empty.

The girl reached Julia seconds later, but words were temporarily beyond her and she could not speak. Instead she grabbed a small handful of Julia's coat and pulled. She was surprisingly strong, and Julia only resisted for a moment before allowing herself to be led across the wet beach at an increasing pace. They passed the boy who was standing stock still with his thumb almost in his mouth and clearly beginning to be frightened. The girl recovered her voice and shakily told him to be a good boy and to stay where he was, to make her proud, not to move, not to follow her, and then she hurried on again.

'What is it?' Julia asked the girl, now that it seemed likely she would be able to answer. 'What's happ—'

But then she realised that she already knew what had happened. It was quite obvious, really; what else could have caused this kind of extreme reaction?

The children have found a body, she thought calmly.

Yes, a drowned body, washed up on the beach by the high tide, and then left in a shallow trough in the shingle like a dead crab as the sea receded once more. It was a scene she had imagined often enough before, but in those speculative, wondering daydreams it had always been her own body that was found. And not by innocent children, either, but by the people she wished to punish, but could not, and so punished herself as a form of revenge.

The young girl was clever and considerate, Julia thought with, for her, an unusual level of approval. Perhaps alerted by the dog, she had seen the body first, and then immediately taken the boy away so that he wouldn't have to see it at all. Saved him a few screaming blue nightmares, no doubt, and saved their mother and father a few sleepless nights as a consequence. The girl had also been responsible enough to realise that she needed help, adult help.

Which is when she must have noticed Julia at the water's edge.

In the zippered pocket of Julia's raincoat was the mobile phone her son had bought her over all her objections and prejudices after his father had walked out. You don't need to keep it turned on all the time, Ma, he'd told her patiently, nobody's trying to keep tabs on you. Just keep it charged and keep it on you, in case there's an emergency, in case you need help, or if you just need to hear a friendly voice sometime. Now, for the first time, Julia saw the intrusive technology as the boon it was always meant to be, and she was finally glad of its tiny compact weight in the pocket of her thin waterproof, nudging her bony hip.

Ahead of her, the young girl stopped moving so sharply that Julia almost walked into her back. Only a dozen more steps away the Labrador was still barking, his tail wagging in an unconscious contradiction of his apparent unease.

Whatever the dog was barking at was still hidden from sight by the groyne, the seawater-saturated timber all but black, which Julia now found herself very reluctant to look around. She suddenly had the feeling that if she looked she would see herself after all, her body stripped naked by the undertow, bleached pale and bloated by the saltwater, the character of her face erased for all time; the horrible reality of the stupid little fantasy she had been playing with now for a good many months.

'It's a body,' the girl abruptly confirmed in a voice that seemed extremely loud, making Julia jump. 'It's a man.'

At first this was almost a relief. It meant that Julia would not have to see her own identity projected upon a dead woman's body, like some strange prophecy fulfilled. But then, with the same kind of superstitious dread that made her avoid black cats in her path and walking under ladders, she began to fear it would be someone she knew. Perhaps even someone she loved, or used once to love.

Julia edged slowly forward. She didn't want to, but she made herself do it. The dog barked continually, like the pulse of a headache in her temples. Behind her she heard the girl take a few backward steps, perhaps checking on her little brother, the shingle shifting and crunching under her boots. She was making a low sound at the back of her throat that may have been a moan.

Then Julia's head finally cleared the top of the groyne, and she saw. She stared. She recoiled, turned away, fell to her knees. Her mouth filled with a sour, metallic-tasting saliva, and then she vomited onto the beach, a thin dark bitter liquid that was her morning coffee.

A little over an hour and a half later a fat man in an ugly brown suit, somehow even uglier for being soaked through with rainwater, wove his way through the collection of patrol cars and other police service vehicles assembled on the promenade and ducked under the blue and white barrier tape currently forbidding public access to the beach. He paused briefly to mutter a number of obscenities under his breath while he glowered up at the dark grey cloud cover that was at last beginning to fragment, revealing promising patches of the blazing blue sky above, but which nevertheless continued to spit down upon him in the meantime — maliciously, he felt. Then, slowly and carefully, he began to pick his way down over the slippery banks of gleaming shingle to the crime scene tent that had been erected over the body, close to the water's edge.

DI Abbot was fast approaching the wrong end of middle-age and generally contrived to look every single day of it, with short dishwater-coloured hair he obviously cut himself, badly, dark pouches under his eyes, and a broad face constantly raw with razor-burn. His appearance and weight might have made him a figure of amusement to anyone who didn't know him, but only a few short moments in his abrasive, sometimes abusive company was usually enough to correct most people of that mistaken notion. Above the dark pouches he had small, sharp grey eyes that missed very little and liked to pry. Although when it came to sharpness, his eyes were nothing in comparison to his tongue, which was not only sharp but famously poisonous, too.

The two young constables who had been stationed outside the white PVC tent sensibly drew themselves up a little straighter as he approached, a gesture Abbot only barely acknowledged with the slightest of nods. But then the boldest and most ambitious of the two made the error of trying to wish him a good morning, a greeting that came out sounding inappropriately cheery considering the situation, and Abbot, his hackles instantly rising, made an abrupt course correction that swiftly brought them face to face.

'A good morning, is it?' he asked. 'D'ye want to try telling me what you think's so fucking good about it, son?' Abbot had come south from his native Glasgow more than twenty years ago, but from the strength of his accent it may as well have been only twenty minutes. He didn't so much speak as growl. 'Are you enjoying yourself out here, is that what it is? Is this how you get your wee kicks of a morning? And may I inquire as to what kind of entertainment you'll be hoping for this afternoon — an RTA decapitation, perhaps, or maybe a family of four roasted alive in a house fire?'

The young constable's cheeks had quickly turned a solid brick-red colour while Abbot had been speaking, and he had to swallow deeply several times before he could stammer a faint, 'No sir,' in reply to all these impossible, unfair questions.

'Congratulations, laddie, *No sir* just happens to be the correct answer...' Abbot pinned him to the spot with his cold grey eyes for a few more long, agonising seconds before turning to the other constable. 'The pathologist here yet?'

'Already been and gone, sir, him and the Coroner's Officer. Said he'll call you later, but ideally he'd like the body moved ASAP, before the tide starts coming in again.'

Abbot nodded, unsurprised to have missed them. He'd been a fair time away from the crime scene, speaking to the children once their minder had been summoned, and then to Julia Meredith, who had been relatively lucid but also clueless and unhelpful, clearly numbed by shock and running on automatic. They had all been sent home now. Meredith would no doubt be required to attend the inquest when the time came, but he had already decided that the boy and the girl could be spared the ordeal. Abbot never put children in any kind of courtroom situation unless there was absolutely no way to avoid it.

He glanced across at the choppy grey waves, and saw that the tide had turned and was already beginning to drag at the shingle just bare feet from the crime scene tent. Gibbons, the Home Office pathologist, had been right, of course, feet of clay or not. The body needed to be moved. Abbot turned his attention back to the promenade, where the railings were lined with a couple of dozen civilian gawkers as well as a few photographers, all of them snapping away as though they were at a fashion shoot. Despite the distance, Abbot caught himself foolishly trying to memorise the faces, already speculating on the identities of the individuals present and the possible motives behind their interest.

Was it the usual morbid curiosity, he wondered, or could it be something else, something more?

Then he saw the stick thin figure of DS Mike Parlour duck under the promenade barrier tape and begin to crunch his way down through the shingle towards them, a number of sheets of A4 paper flapping around in his left hand, and he turned back to the uniforms.

He pointed at the second constable, the one whose mouth wasn't quite so large. 'You, get yourself back up to the promenade, pronto, notebook out and biro poised, brain fully engaged. I want the names, addresses, and telephone numbers of every last bastard member of our audience up there, press included, understand?'

'Sir.'

All three men looked up at the sound of a news helicopter moving in to hover high overhead. The vultures of the fourth estate were gathering in earnest now. Abbot quickly let himself into the tent, wishing, and not for the first time in his professional life, that he possessed both a surface-to-air missile and the authority to launch it. Inside the tent he found the last two members of the SOCO team meticulously packing away both their gear and the samples they had collected from the naked male body and the area immediately around and underneath it. He told them they could send the boys from the mortuary over to collect their takeaway as soon as they were ready, and they nodded their assent as they began to leave.

He waited until the SOCOs had gone and then went down on one already sodden knee beside the body and took a second look at it, a longer and closer look than the first time around, and found himself no less sickened or outraged.

It had been immediately apparent that this death had not been accidental. The injuries the body had received were many. They were huge and terrible, some running bone deep, and immersion in the sea had not only washed the body clean but also seemed to have entirely leeched it of all its natural fluids, bringing an awful, stark clarity to the wounds. Not one single solitary detail had been left either masked or mercifully diffused by a scrim of drying blood, and Abbot found himself reminded of a long-ago boyhood trip to Madame Tussaud's Wax Museum on a family holiday to Blackpool.

He remembered the gruesome spectacle of the bloodless anatomical models that had been on display in a series of glass cabinets, of internal organs laid bare, and coils of viscera, and foetuses in utero, and numerous other pallid horrors besides, and he remembered the cloying, nauseating stench of the old wax that in conjunction with the images had eventually driven him outside gasping for fresh air before he was forcibly parted from his guesthouse breakfast. There was no smell here this morning except the overwhelming briny smell of the sea, but the body with its unlikely, bloodless injuries looked exactly like a waxwork, false, and vaguely surreal in this setting.

But that was exactly the sheer bloody hell of it, Abbot thought, it wasn't false. He felt a familiar pressure of anger and a sense of injustice building up inside him as they always did, and God willing always would, no matter how many bodies he saw. The pitiful, ruined object before him was no skilful example of wax modelling, a vaguely macabre but otherwise harmless entertainment. Not so very long ago this had been a living, thinking, feeling human being. This had been somebody's beloved son. Somebody's friend or brother, husband or lover. Somebody's father, perhaps. Somebody's victim, certainly.

He heard DS Parlour blunder into the tent behind him.

'Well?' he asked, without turning.

'Turns out there are about fifteen male MisPers on our books right now, boss,' Parlour said, rustling his papers noisily. He was chewing noisily, too, either gum or one of the toffees or other sweets with which he habitually stocked his car and person.

Abbot was aware that all this frantic activity was just Parlour's way of distracting himself from the shocking sight of the body. He knew that it was his sergeant's own personal version of whistling past the graveyard, and that the sweetie in the man's mouth was pure bravado, but he still found it irritating in the extreme. It suddenly occurred to him that the young constable outside the tent may have been attempting much the same thing with his jarringly bright greeting, but he couldn't find it in himself to regret his outburst. There were other people far more deserving of his pity.

'Tell me about the most recent one first,' he said to Parlour.

'The most recent was reported just under a week ago, it looks like. Name is...let me see... Colin Forbes. *Restaurateur*, it says here, reported missing by his business partner on the twelfth of this month, and last seen on the evening of the eighth.'

'Restaurateur?' Abbot grunted. 'That might fit. Definitely looks like someone's had a go at him with the old meat cleaver, anyway...'

So, last seen on the eighth, and today was the eighteenth. Missing for a maximum of ten days in total. But Abbot didn't think the body looked like it had been in the water for much longer than a few hours. No longer than overnight, surely, and death itself must have occurred only shortly before, otherwise the evidence of decomposition would probably be that much more pronounced, with the body beginning to bloat, and the odour of rotting flesh far too strong to be overpowered by proximity to the sea.

Where could the man have been in the interim, he wondered, and what kind of trouble had he managed to get himself into to end up in this appalling condition?

Upon closer examination, Abbot was also doubtful that a meat cleaver could have been the principle murder weapon. The edges of the wounds would have been much neater with a cleaver, he believed, and the trauma simply less immense. Some of the deeper wounds he could see looked as though they had almost been ripped through the flesh by sheer bludgeoning force, and where the blade had actually met the bones beneath, the bones had in most instances shattered, not just chipped. A large blade, then, and not merely sharp, but heavy, too.

'Would we be lucky enough to have a photographic likeness of this missing restaurateur to hand?' Abbot asked, fully expecting the answer to be in the negative.

Parlour rustled once more and passed a photocopy over Abbot's shoulder.

'Wonders will never cease.'

Still kneeling beside the body, Abbot held out the sheet at arm's length and looked from one to the other. The man in the photo appeared to be much fuller of face than the dead man, and in addition sported a large flamboyant moustache, which the corpse did not. But the hair was very similar indeed; although much shorter than in the photo, it was greying and still slightly curly, even when soaking wet. Both the hairline itself and the position of the ears were good matches, too. Perhaps with a crash diet and a shave...

'What d'ye think?' he asked Parlour.

'Hard to say under these circumstances, boss, considering the state of the body, and all.'

'Gut feeling?'

Parlour considered the question at maddening length, still chewing away, his open mouth now distributing a scent Abbot was able to isolate and positively identify as chocolate éclair. 'Nah,' he said eventually, 'I'm pretty sure it's not him.' He began to shuffle through the other photocopies, looking for a more likely option.

Abbot, however, paused for a moment or two longer, staring intently, and then slowly shook his head. 'You're wrong, it *is* him,' he said quietly, and then more quietly still as he leaned over the body, 'Hello there, Mr Forbes. Whatever in the world has befallen you?'

But over the following days and weeks, Abbot would begin to despair of ever learning the answer to this question...

Other Works

Crime
The Queen of Hearts
Perfect Peace
The Hunted Man 1: Old Dog New Trick
The Hunted Man 2: Identity Crisis
The Crime Short Story Collection

Horror
(writing as Jim Mullaney)
Comeback – a novel
The 1st Horror Short Story Collection
The 2nd Horror Short Story Collection

Please visit me at:
storiesneverend1.wordpress.com
or my **Amazon Authors Page**
or contact me at:
crimemysterysuspense@gmail.com

Thanks for Reading

Printed in Poland
by Amazon Fulfillment
Poland Sp. z o.o., Wrocław